Hunting Fear

Also by Kay Hooper
in Large Print:

Stealing Shadows
Hiding in the Shadows
Out of the Shadows
Touching Evil
Whisper of Evil
Sense of Evil
Once a Thief
Always a Thief
On Wings of Magic
Eye of the Beholder
On Her Doorstep
Mask of Passion
The Matchmaker

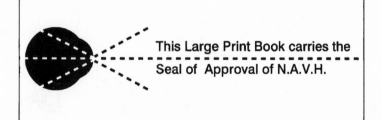

This Large Print Book carries the
Seal of Approval of N.A.V.H.

HUNTING FEAR

KAY HOOPER

Thorndike Press • Waterville, Maine

Published in 2004 by arrangement with Bantam Books, an imprint of the Bantam Dell Publishing Group, a division of Random House, Inc.

Thorndike Press® Large Print Americana.

The tree indicium is a trademark of Thorndike Press.

The text of this Large Print edition is unabridged. Other aspects of the book may vary from the original edition.

Set in 16 pt. Plantin by Minnie B. Raven.

Printed in the United States on permanent paper.

Library of Congress Cataloging-in-Publication Data

Hooper, Kay.
    Hunting fear / Kay Hooper.
        p. cm.
    ISBN 0-7862-6269-9 (lg. print : hc : alk. paper)
    1. Government investigators — Fiction.   2. Serial murders — Fiction.   3. North Carolina — Fiction.
4. Kidnapping — Fiction.   5. Psychics — Fiction.
6. Large type books.   I. Title.
PS3558.O587H86 2004
    813'.54—dc22   2004055340

To my brother-in-law,
Christopher Parks,
For being an all-around great guy

As the Founder/CEO of NAVH, the only national health agency solely devoted to those who, although not totally blind, have an eye disease which could lead to serious visual impairment, I am pleased to recognize Thorndike Press★ as one of the leading publishers in the large print field.

Founded in 1954 in San Francisco to prepare large print textbooks for partially seeing children, NAVH became the pioneer and standard setting agency in the preparation of large type.

Today, those publishers who meet our standards carry the prestigious "Seal of Approval" indicating high quality large print. We are delighted that Thorndike Press is one of the publishers whose titles meet these standards. We are also pleased to recognize the significant contribution Thorndike Press is making in this important and growing field.

Lorraine H. Marchi, L.H.D.
Founder/CEO
NAVH

★ Thorndike Press encompasses the following imprints: Thorndike, Wheeler, Walker and Large Print Press.

Prologue

Five years ago

Sssshhhh.

Half consciously, she made the sound out loud. "Sssshhhh." But it was a breath of sound. Less than that.

She had to be quiet.

He might hear.

He might get angry at her.

He might change his mind.

She kept herself very still and tried to make herself very small. *Don't draw his attention. Don't give him any reason to change his mind.*

She'd been lucky so far. Lucky or smart. Because he'd said so, he'd said she was a good girl and so he wouldn't hurt her. All she had to do was take the medicine and sleep for a while, and then be still and silent for a little bit when she woke up.

Count to five hundred when you wake up, he'd said. Count slowly. And when she was done —

"*— and when you're done, I'll be gone. You can move then. You can take off the blindfold.*

But not until then, you understand? If you move or make a sound before then, I'll know. And I'll have to hurt you."

It seemed to take forever to count to five hundred, but finally she got there. Hesitated. And counted to six hundred just to be safe. Because she was a good girl.

He'd had her lie down so that her hands were underneath her bottom, her own weight holding them flat and immobile. So he didn't have to tie them, he'd said. She could put her hands underneath her like a good girl or he could tie her up.

He had a gun.

She thought her hands were probably asleep by now, because she felt the medicine had made her sleep a long time. But she was still afraid to try moving, afraid he was somewhere nearby, watching.

"Are — are you there?" she whispered.

Nothing. Just the sound of her own breathing.

She shivered, not for the first time. It was chilly, a little damp. The air she breathed was stale. And in the tiniest corner of her mind, way back in the dark where a terrified little girl crouched, was an idea she didn't even want to think about.

No. Not that.

It wasn't that.

Cautiously, very slowly, she began working her right hand from underneath her. It had gone to sleep, the pins and needles sharp, the sensation as creepy as it always was. She kept her hand alongside her hip and flexed the fingers slowly as the blood returned to them. It made her want to cry or giggle. She worked her left hand free and flexed it as well.

Refusing to admit why she did it, she slid her hands to the tops of her thighs, then up her body, not reaching out, not reaching up naturally. She slid them up herself until she touched the blindfold covering her eyes.

She heard her breath catch in a little sob.

No. It wasn't that.

Because she was a good girl.

She pushed the cloth up her forehead, keeping her eyes closed. She drew a deep breath, trying not to think about how much more stale and thick the air seemed to be.

Finally, she opened her eyes.

Blackness. A dark so total it had weight, substance.

She blinked, turned her head back and forth, but saw nothing more. Just . . . black.

In the tiniest corner of her mind, that

little girl whimpered.

Slowly, fraction of an inch by fraction of an inch, she pushed her hands outward. Her arms were still bent at the elbows when her hands touched something solid. It felt like . . . wood. She pushed against it. Hard. Harder.

It didn't give at all.

She tried not to panic, but by the time her hands had explored the box in which she lay, the scream was crawling around in the back of her throat. And when the little girl crouching in the tiniest corner of her mind whispered the truth, the scream escaped.

He's buried you alive.

And nobody knows where you are.

"I'm telling you it's no goddamned use." Lieutenant Pete Edgerton had an unusually smooth and gentle voice for a violent-crimes detective, but it was harsh now. And filled with reluctant certainty. "She's gone."

"Show me a body."

"Luke —"

"Until you can show me a body, I am not giving up on that girl." Lucas Jordan's voice was quiet, as it always was, but the intensity lurked, as it always did. And when he turned and left the conference room, it was with the quick, springy step of a man in excellent physical shape who possessed enough energy for at least two other men.

Maybe three.

With a sigh, Edgerton turned to the other detectives scattered about the room and shrugged. "The family hired him, and they have the mayor's backing, so we don't have the authority to call him off."

"I doubt anybody *could* call him off," Judy Blake said, her tone half admiring and half wondering. "He won't stop looking until he finds Meredith Gilbert. Dead or alive."

Another detective, surveying the stack of files in front of him, shook his head wearily. "Well, whether he's as gifted as they say or not, he's independent and he can concentrate on one case at a time for as long as it takes. We don't have that luxury."

Edgerton nodded. "We've already spent more time than we can afford — and a hell of a lot more manpower — on a single missing-persons case with squat for leads and absolutely no evidence that she was abducted against her will."

"Her family's sure she was," Judy reminded him. "And Luke is sure."

"I know. I'm sure myself, or at least as sure as I can be with a gut feeling." Edgerton shrugged again. "But we've got cases backed up and I've got my orders. The Meredith Gilbert investigation is officially a cold-case file."

"Is that the federal conclusion as well?" Judy asked, brows lifting as she turned her gaze to a tall, dark man who leaned negligently against a filing cabinet in a position that enabled him to watch everyone in the room.

Special Agent Noah Bishop shook his head once. "The official federal conclusion is that there's been no federal crime. No evidence of kidnapping — or anything else that would involve the Bureau. And we weren't asked to officially participate in the investigation." His voice was cool, like his pale gray sentry eyes. He wore a half smile, but the vivid scar twisting down his left cheek made the expression more dangerous than pleasant.

"Then what are you doing here?" the same weary detective asked mildly.

"He's interested in Jordan," Theo Woods said. "That's it, isn't it, Bishop? You came to see the so-called psychic's little dog-and-pony show." The detective was hostile, and it showed, though it was difficult to tell which he despised more — supposed psychics or federal agents.

Matter-of-fact, the agent replied, "I came because there was the possibility of a kidnapping."

"And I guess it's just a coincidence that you've been watching Jordan like a hawk."

With a soft laugh that held no amusement, Bishop said, "There's no such thing as coincidence."

"Then you are interested in him."

"Yes."

"Because he claims to be psychic?"

"Because he is psychic."

"That's bullshit and you know it," Woods said. "If he really was psychic, we would have found that girl by now."

"It doesn't work that way."

"Oh, right, I forgot. Can't just flip a switch and get all the answers."

"No. Unfortunately, not even a genuine and gifted psychic can do that."

"And you'd know."

"Yes. I'd know."

Edgerton, aware both of the simmering frustration in the room and the resentment at least a few of his detectives felt toward the Bureau and its agents, intervened to say calmly, "It's a moot point, at least as far as we're concerned. Like I said, the Gilbert investigation is cold. We move on."

Judy kept her gaze on Bishop. "What about you? Do you move on as well? Go back to Quantico?"

"I," Bishop said, "do what I came here to do." He strolled from the room, as seemingly relaxed and unconcerned as Lucas Jordan had been wired and focused.

"I don't like that guy," Theo Woods announced unnecessarily. "Those eyes look right through you. Talk about a thousand-yard stare."

"Think he really is after Luke?" Judy asked the room at large.

Edgerton said, "Maybe. My sources tell me Bishop's putting together a special unit of investigators, but I can't find out what's special about it."

"Jesus, you don't think he's rounding up phony psychics?" Woods demanded incredulously.

"No," Edgerton replied with a last glance after the federal agent. "I don't think he's interested in anything phony."

Bishop assumed there was speculation behind him as he left the conference room, but beyond making a mental note to add Pete Edgerton to his growing list of cops likely to be receptive to his Special Crimes Unit in the future, he thought no more about it. He went in search of Lucas Jordan, finding him, as expected, in the small, windowless office that had been grudgingly allotted to him.

"I told you I wasn't interested," Lucas said as soon as Bishop appeared in the doorway.

Leaning against the jamb, Bishop watched as the other man packed up his copies of the myriad paperwork involved in a missing-persons investigation. "Do you enjoy going it solo that much?" he asked mildly. "Operating alone has its drawbacks. We can offer the sort of support and resources you're not likely to find anywhere else."

"Probably. But I hate bureaucracy and red tape," Lucas replied. "Both of which the FBI has in abundance."

"I told you, my unit is different."

"You still report to the Director, don't you?"

"Yes."

"Then it's not that different."

"I intend to make sure it is."

Lucas paused, looking at Bishop with a

slight frown, more curious than disbelieving. "Yeah? How do you plan to do that?"

"My agents won't have to deal with the Bureau politics; that'll be my job. I've spent years building my reputation, collecting and calling in favors, and twisting arms to make certain we'll have as much autonomy as possible in running our investigations."

Somewhat mockingly, Lucas said, "What, no rules?"

"You know better than that. But reasonable rules, if only to placate the powers that be and convince them we aren't running a sideshow act. We'll have to be cautious in the beginning, low-key, at least until we can point to a solid record of successful case resolutions."

"And you're so sure there will be successes?"

"I wouldn't be doing this otherwise."

"Yeah, well." Lucas closed his briefcase with a snap. "I wish you luck, Bishop, I really do. But I work best alone."

"How can you be so sure of that if you've never done it any other way?"

"I know myself."

"What about your ability?"

"What about it?"

Bishop smiled slightly. "How well do you know it? Do you understand what it is, how it works?"

"I understand it well enough to use it."

Deliberately, Bishop said, "Then why can't you find Meredith Gilbert?"

Lucas didn't rise to the bait, though his expression tightened just a bit. "It isn't that simple, and you know it."

"Maybe it should be that simple. Maybe all it really takes is the right sort of training and practice for a psychic to be able to control and use his or her abilities more effectively as investigative tools."

"And maybe you're full of shit."

"Prove me wrong."

"Listen, I don't have time for this. I have an abduction victim to find."

"Fair enough." Bishop barely hesitated before adding, "It's the fear."

"What?"

"It's the fear you pick up on, home in on. The specific electromagnetic-energy signature of fear. The victims' fear. That's what your brain is hardwired to sense, telepathically or empathically."

Lucas was silent.

"Which is it — their thoughts or their emotions?"

Grudgingly, Lucas said, "Both."

17

"So you feel their fear and know their thoughts."

"The fear is stronger. More certain. If I get them at all, the thoughts are just whispers. Words, phrases. Mental static."

"Like a radio station moving in and out of range."

"Yeah. Like that."

"But it's the fear that first connects you to them."

Lucas nodded.

"The stronger the fear, the more intense the connection."

"Generally. People handle their fear in different ways. Some of them bury it, or hold it so tightly reined none of it can get out. Those I have trouble sensing."

"Is it the fear of being . . . lost?"

Meeting the federal agent's steady gaze, Lucas shrugged finally and said, "The fear of being alone. Of being caught, trapped. Helpless. Doomed. The fear of dying."

"And when they stop feeling that?"

Lucas didn't respond.

"It's because they're dead."

"Sometimes."

"Be honest."

"All right. Usually. Usually I stop sensing them because there's no fear to sense. No thoughts. No life." Just saying it made Lucas angry, and he didn't try to hide that.

"The way it is now. With Meredith Gilbert."

"I will find her."

"Will you?"

"Yes."

"In time?"

The question hung there in the air between the two men for a long, still moment, and then Lucas picked up his briefcase and took the two steps necessary to get to the door.

Bishop stepped aside, silent.

Lucas walked past him but turned back before he reached the top of the stairs. Abruptly, he said, "I'm sorry. I can't find her for you."

"For me? Meredith Gilbert is —"

"Not her. Miranda. I can't find Miranda for you."

Bishop's expression didn't change, but the scar twisting down his left cheek whitened so that it was more visible. "I didn't ask," he said after a momentary pause.

"You didn't have to. I pick up on fear, remember?"

Bishop didn't say another word. He just stood there and looked after the other man until Lucas was gone.

"I almost didn't call you," Pete Edgerton said as Bishop joined him on the highway above the ravine. "To be honest, I'm surprised you're still around. It's been three weeks since we closed the investigation."

Without commenting on that, Bishop merely said, "Is he down there?"

"Yeah, with her. Not that there's a whole lot left." Edgerton eyed the federal agent. "I have no idea how he found her. Those special gifts of his, I guess."

"Cause of death?"

"That's for the ME to say. Like I said, there isn't a whole lot left. And what is left has been exposed to the elements and predators. I have no idea what killed her, or what she went through before she died."

"You're not even sure she was abducted, are you?"

Edgerton shook his head. "From the little we found down there, she could have been walking along the edge of the road here, slipped and fell, maybe hit her head or broke something, couldn't get back up. Lot of traffic here, but nobody stops; she could have been lying there all this time."

"You think the ME will be able to determine cause of death?"

"I'd be surprised. From bones, a few

shreds of skin, and some hair? We wouldn't have been able to I.D. her so fast — if at all — if it hadn't been for the fact that her backpack was still mostly intact and there was plenty of stuff inside with Meredith Gilbert's name on it. Plus that odd pewter bracelet of hers was found among the bones. The DNA tests will confirm it's her remains, I'm sure of that."

"So she wasn't robbed and her killer didn't take a trophy."

"If there was a killer, doesn't look like he took any of her belongings, no."

Bishop nodded, then headed toward the wide gap in the guardrail that should have been repaired long before.

"You'll mess up your nice suit," Edgerton warned.

Without responding to that, Bishop merely picked his way down the steep slope and deep into the ravine. He passed a few crime-scene investigators but didn't pause until he joined Lucas Jordan in a boulder-strewn area in the shade of a twisted little tree.

Lucas appeared quite different from the man Bishop had last seen. He was decidedly scruffy, unshaven, thinner, his casual clothing rumpled as though he had slept in it. If he had slept, that is. He stood, hands in the pockets of his denim jacket, and stared down at the rocky ground.

What held his fixed gaze were bits and pieces only experts would have recognized as being human. Bits of bone and scraps of clothing. A tuft of chocolate-brown hair.

"They've already taken her backpack," Lucas said. "Her parents will get it, I guess."

"Yes," Bishop said.

"You knew. From the moment you got here, you knew she was dead."

"Not from the moment I got here."

"But from the day."

"Yes."

Lucas turned his head, staring at Bishop incredulously. "And said nothing?"

"I knew she was dead. I didn't know where she was. The police would never have believed me. Her family would never have believed me."

"I might have."

"You didn't want to. You had to find her yourself. So I waited for you to do that."

"Knowing all the time she was dead."

Bishop nodded.

"Jesus, you're a ruthless bastard."

"Sometimes."

"Don't say it's because you have to be."

"All right. I won't."

Lucas grimaced and returned his haunted gaze to the ground and the scattered remains of Meredith Gilbert.

"It ends this way more often than not." His voice was beyond exhausted. "With a body or what's left of one. Because I wasn't fast enough. Wasn't good enough."

"She was dead an hour after he got his hands on her," Bishop said.

"This time, maybe." Lucas shrugged.

Judging that the time was right, Bishop said, "According to the laws of science, it's impossible to see the future, to know ahead of time what's going to happen next. Impossible to have that sort of edge as an investigator. I don't believe that. I believe that telepathy and empathy, telekinesis and precognition, clairvoyance and all the other so-called paranormal abilities can be tools to give us more than an edge. To make us, maybe, better. To make us faster."

After a moment, Lucas turned his head and met Bishop's steady gaze. "Okay. I'm listening."

Two days later, both looking and feeling considerably better after round-the-clock sleep and a couple of showers, Lucas pushed his plate away, picked up his coffee cup, and said, "You don't have to baby-sit me, you know. I'm not going to bolt on you. I said I'd give your new unit a try, and I will."

"I know that." Bishop sipped his own coffee, then shrugged. "I just figured we might as well get an early start back, since we're heading east. The jet's warmed up and waiting for us."

Brows lifting, Lucas said, "Jet? You rate a Bureau jet?"

Bishop smiled slightly. "It's a private jet."

"You rate a private jet?"

Replying seriously, Bishop said, "I'm trying to do more than build a unit with the FBI. I'm also working on building a civilian support structure, a network of people in and out of law enforcement who believe in what we're trying to accomplish. They'll help us in different ways, including fast and effective transportation."

"Hence the jet."

"Exactly. It's not overhead for the unit or the Bureau and isn't a burden on the taxpayers. Merely a generous contribution from a private citizen who wants to help."

"One of these days," Lucas said, "you're going to have to tell me how all this came about. I am, after all, another man who understands obsession."

"We'll have plenty of time to talk."

Lucas set his cup down, murmuring, "But I wonder if we will."

Bishop didn't reply to that, merely saying, "If you're packed and ready, why don't we go?"

"Before I change my mind?"

"Oh, I don't think you're going to do that. As you say, we both understand obsession."

"Uh-huh. I have a hunch the Bureau doesn't have a clue what they're really getting into."

"Time will tell."

"And if they close us down once they realize?"

"I won't let that happen."

"You know," Lucas said dryly, "I almost believe you."

"Good. Shall we?"

The two men left the small diner and within an hour were in Bishop's rented car on the road to the airport. Not a lot was said at first, and it wasn't until they were nearly there that Bishop finally asked what he had to.

In a very controlled voice, he asked, "Why can't you find her for me?"

Lucas replied immediately, obviously expecting the question. "Because she isn't lost. She's hiding."

"Hiding from me?" The question was clearly a difficult one.

"Only indirectly. You know who she's really hiding from."

"She's afraid. You can feel that."

"Distantly, through you. You two were linked at one time, I gather. Your fear for her is strongest. What I got from her was brief and faint. She's afraid, but she's strong. Very strong. In control."

"She's safe?"

"As safe as she can be." Luke glanced at him. "I can't predict the future. You know that too."

"Yes," Bishop said. "I know that. But somewhere out there is someone who can."

"Then I expect you'll find them," Luke said, returning his attention to the road ahead of them. "Just like you found me."

1

Present day
Thursday, September 20

"Sssshhhh. Be very quiet," he said.

It was almost impossible, but he managed not to groan or moan or make any other sound behind the duct tape covering his mouth. The blindfold kept him from seeing anything, but he had seen all he'd had to before the blindfold had been tied in place: his abductor had a very big gun and he clearly knew how to handle it.

His instincts were screaming at him to struggle, fight, run if he could.

He couldn't. The time for even attempting escape, if there had ever been one, was past. His wrists were duct-taped together, like his ankles. If he so much as tried to get up from the chair where he'd been placed, he would fall on his face or on his ass.

He was helpless. That was the worst of it. Not the fear of what might be done to him, but the realization that he couldn't do a goddamned thing to stop it.

He should have paid attention to the warning, he was sure of that much. Even if it *had* sounded like bullshit, he really should have paid attention.

"I'm not going to hurt you," his abductor said.

He unconsciously tipped his head a bit to one side, his agile mind noting the slight emphasis on the first word. *He* wasn't going to hurt him? What did that mean — that someone else would?

"Don't try to figure it out." The voice was amused now but still careless as it had been from the beginning.

Mitchell Callahan was no fool; he'd weighed far too many powerful men over the years to be deceived by a quiet voice and seemingly negligent manner. The more ostensibly indifferent a man seemed to be, the more likely he was to blow your balls off, metaphorically.

Or literally.

I can't even reason with the son of a bitch.

It was truly Callahan's idea of hell, being helpless and unable to talk his way out of it.

"I'm sure your wife will pay the ransom, and then you can go home."

Callahan wondered if the duct tape and blindfold hid his reflexive grimace. His wife? His wife, who was on the verge of filing for divorce because she had arrived at his office unexpectedly after hours to find him screwing his secretary on his desk?

Oh, yeah, she really wanted him back. She was undoubtedly just eager as hell to pay major bucks to save her husband's cheating ass.

"Don't worry; I asked for a reasonable ransom. Your wife can get her hands on it easily, I imagine."

Callahan couldn't stop the strangled sound that escaped him, then felt his face get hot with furious embarrassment when his captor laughed.

"Of course, she may not want to, when that private investigator she's hired discovers that your secretary is only the latest in a long line of women you've enjoyed. You really don't know how to keep your fly zipped, do you, Mitchell? And she's such a nice lady, your wife. She deserves better. You really should have been a good and respectful husband to her. It's not all about being a successful breadwinner, you know. And, after all, why does the world need another cookie-cutter subdivision ruining the view up here?"

Callahan felt a sudden chill. His captor

was talking too much. Why give his victim a chance to memorize the sound of his voice? Why betray so much knowledge of Callahan's life, his business?

Unless you know he'll never get the chance to tell anyone.

"Unsettling, isn't it?"

Callahan jumped, because the low voice was right next to his ear now. Soft, cool, menacing without even trying to be.

"To have some stranger dissect your life. To have all your power, all your certainty, taken away. To be absolutely helpless in the knowledge that someone else controls your fate."

Without meaning to, Callahan made another strangled sound.

"I do, you know. I do control your fate. At least up to a point. After that, it's in someone else's hands."

Callahan was more than a little surprised when the blindfold was suddenly removed and for a minute or two could only blink as his eyes adjusted to the light. Then he looked, saw.

And everything became much clearer.

Oh, Christ.

"The ransom was paid." Wyatt Metcalf, Clayton County Sheriff, sounded as angry as any cop tended to be when the bad guys won one. "The wife kept quiet out of fear, so we didn't hear anything about it until it was all over with and he hadn't come home as promised after she left the money."

"Who found the body?"

"Hiker. It's a busy area this time of year, with the leaves changing and all. We're surrounded by national forests and parkland, and we'll have tourists coming out of our ears for weeks. It'll be the same all along the Blue Ridge."

"So he knew the body would be found quickly."

"If he didn't, he's an idiot — or doesn't know the country around here at all." Metcalf eyed the tall federal agent, still trying to get his measure. Lucas Jordan was not, he thought, a man who would be quickly or easily assessed. He was obviously athletic, energetic, highly intelligent, both courteous and soft-spoken; every bit as obvious was the focused intensity in his striking blue eyes, something close to ferocity and just as unsettling.

A driven man, clearly.

But driven by what?

"We're holding the body as requested," Metcalf told him. "My crime-scene unit was trained by the state crime lab *and* took a few Bureau courses, so they know what they're doing; what little they found here is waiting for you and your partner back at the station."

"I assume there was nothing helpful."

It hadn't been a question, but Metcalf replied anyway. "If there had been, I wouldn't have needed to call in this Special Crimes Unit of yours."

Jordan glanced at him but returned his attention to the rocky ground all around them without comment.

Knowing he'd sounded as frustrated as he felt, Metcalf counted to ten silently before he spoke again. "Mitch Callahan wasn't a prince, but he didn't deserve what happened to him. I want to find the son of a bitch who murdered him."

"I understand, Sheriff."

Metcalf wondered if he did but didn't question the statement.

Jordan said almost absently, "This was the third kidnapping reported in the western part of this state this year. All three ransoms paid, all three victims died."

"The other two were in counties outside

my jurisdiction, so I only know the general facts. Aside from being fairly wealthy, the vics had nothing in common. The man was about fifty, white, a widower with one son; the woman was thirty-five, of Asian descent, married, no children. Cause of death for him was asphyxiation; for her it was drowning."

"And Mitchell Callahan was decapitated."

"Yeah. Weird as hell. The ME says it was very quick and exceptionally clean; no ax hacking at him, nothing like that. Maybe a machete or sword." Metcalf was frowning. "You're not saying they're related? Those other kidnappings were months ago, and I just figured —"

"That it was a coincidence?" A third person joined them, Jordan's partner, Special Agent Jaylene Avery. Her smile was a bit wry. "No such thing, if you ask our boss. And he's usually right."

"Anything?" Jordan asked her; she had been working her way around the mountainous clearing where Mitchell Callahan's body had been found.

"Nah. This near a rest and observation spot, a lot of people pass through and by. Far as I can tell, though, nobody paused for long."

Metcalf took due note of tone and expression as well as posture and body language between the two of them: Jordan was the senior partner, but Avery was entirely comfortable with him and confident in her own right. The sheriff had a hunch they'd been partners for quite a while.

As seemingly relaxed as Jordan was wired, Jaylene Avery was a lovely woman in her early thirties with black hair she wore rather severely pulled back, flawless coffee-with-cream skin, and intelligent brown eyes. A slight Southern drawl said she was probably closer to home here in North Carolina than she was while at Quantico.

Unlike Jordan, whose low, quiet voice was also a bit clipped and rapid, and pegged him as being from some point considerably north of his present location.

"What did you expect to find?" Metcalf asked Avery, not quite able to keep the tension out of his own voice.

She smiled again. "Just trying to get a feel for the place, Sheriff, not look for anything you and your people might have missed. Sometimes just stepping back and looking at the big picture can tell you a lot. For instance, from walking around here where the body was found, I can feel pretty secure in saying that our kidnapper is in excellent physical shape."

"To get the body out here, you mean."

"We know the vic wasn't killed here. Hiking paths crisscross the area, but they're for dedicated hikers, not Sunday sightseers: steep, rocky trails that are barely visible unless you know what to look for. Just getting here from any of the main trails is enough of a chore, but to carry something heavy and not exactly ergonomically balanced all that way? No marks from any kind of wheel or hoof, no drag marks. And he not only had the body of a larger-than-average man to transport out here, he had the head as well."

Metcalf had to admit he hadn't given the matter of transporting the body — and disembodied head — quite so much thought. "I see what you mean. He'd have to be a bull and damned lucky not to fall and break his own neck while he was at it."

She nodded. "Treacherous terrain. And since we know there was dew found under the body, he must have carried it up here either during the night or very early morning. So he could have been juggling a flashlight as well."

Jordan said, "Late or early, he brought the body here when there was the least chance of being seen. He was careful. He was damned careful."

"Maybe he was just lucky," Avery said to her partner.

Frowning, Jordan said, "I don't think so. The pattern is too clear, too set. All these people were taken at a point in their day when they were most likely to be alone; all were held forty-eight to seventy-two hours before they were killed; and all were killed, according to the medical evidence, *after* the ransom was paid. And in every case, the ransom call came in on a Thursday, giving the families time to get their hands on the money and ensuring that banks would have plenty of end-of-the-week pay-roll cash on hand. He's never asked too much, just the upper limit of what the relatives can manage. He planned every step, and he kept these people alive and in his control until he was certain the money was his."

"Cold-blooded," Metcalf noted.

Understanding exactly what the sheriff meant, Jordan nodded. "It takes an utterly calculating nature and a particular brand of ruthlessness to spend time with someone you know you may have to kill. A nameless, faceless victim is one thing, but if they become individuals with personalities, if you put a human face on that object, then destroying it becomes much, much more difficult."

It was the sheriff's turn to frown. "How do we know he spent time with them? I mean, he could have kept them locked in a room or a basement somewhere, tied up, gagged, a bag over their heads. I would have. What makes you believe he actually interacted with them?"

"Call it a hunch."

"Not good enough." Metcalf's frown deepened. "What did we miss?"

Jordan and Avery exchanged glances, and she said, "*You* didn't miss anything, Sheriff. There's just some information you weren't aware of. For the past eighteen months, we've been following a series of kidnappings in the East and Southeast."

"*Following* being the operative word, since we tend to get there too late to do anything to help the victims," Jordan said, half under his breath and with more than a little bitterness.

His partner sent him a brief look, then continued to the sheriff, "We believe they're connected. We believe this kidnapping and the other two in the area are part of that series; as Luke says, they certainly fit the pattern."

"A serial kidnapper? I've never heard of that."

It was Jordan who responded this time. "Because the vast majority of successful kidnappings for ransom are designed and engineered to be one-shot deals. Whether the victim lives or dies, the kidnapper gets his money, usually enough to live in some kind of style for the rest of his life, and vanishes to do just that. Even when they're successful, very few try a second time."

His partner added, "In this day and age, it's become increasingly difficult for any kidnapping for ransom to be successful, and because of the inherent complications it really isn't a common crime."

Thinking of possible complications, Metcalf said, "Electronic security, bodyguards, ordinary surveillance at banks and ATMs, now even on the streets — that sort of thing?"

Jordan nodded. "Exactly. Plus stiff penalties and the sheer logistics of abducting and holding a living person. Many victims end up being killed simply because it's too much trouble to keep them alive for the time necessary."

"That isn't what's happening with this serial kidnapper, assuming there is one?"

"No. He doesn't leave anything to

chance. Holding his victims securely as long as necessary is just another step in his plan, and one he takes obvious pride in successfully devising."

"Like interacting with them is another step?"

"We believe so."

"Why do you believe so?"

Again, Jordan and Avery exchanged glances, and he said, "Because we had one survivor. And according to her, he was very friendly, very chatty. He treated her like a person. Even though it's at least possible that he intended to kill her from the beginning."

Carrie Vaughn was not what anyone would have called an easy person to live with, and she was the first to admit it. She was strong-willed, opinionated, extremely self-confident, and very set in her ways after twenty years on her own. Any lover was expected to adapt to her rather than the other way around, and those who hadn't been able to accept that fact had been no more than a blip on her radar.

Which was probably why she was uninvolved more often than not.

But that was okay. Carrie liked being alone, for the most part. Her career as a software designer was both lucrative and creative, plus it allowed her to work out of her home and to travel when and where she wanted. She had a lovely home she took a great deal of pride in, a passion for jigsaw puzzles and old movies, and the capacity to enjoy herself even when no one else was around.

She was also extremely handy, so when the late September afternoon turned unexpectedly chilly and her heat pump refused to come on, Carrie got her toolbox from the garage and started around back to check it out.

"That's dangerous, you know."

Startled, Carrie swung around to find a strange woman standing in her driveway. She was, maybe, ten years younger than Carrie, medium height, slight build, and with the darkest hair and eyes Carrie had ever seen accompany such ultrafair skin. She wasn't exactly beautiful, but definitely arresting; there was something curiously exotic in her heavy-lidded eyes and sullen mouth.

The bulky sweater she wore was a size too big for her and her jeans were worn to the point of being threadbare, but her straight posture held a kind of simple pride and there was something both cool and confident in her voice.

"Who are you?" Carrie demanded. "And what's dangerous?"

"I'm Sam."

"Okay, Sam. What's dangerous?"

"Your carelessness. No fence, no dog, no security system — and your garage door has been up all afternoon. None of your neighbors is even close enough to hear if you should need help. You're very vulnerable here."

"I have a gun inside. Two in fact." Carrie frowned at her. "And I can take care of myself. Hey, have you been watching me? Just who are you?"

"Somebody who's worried that you're vulnerable here."

"And why the hell should you care?"

For the first time, Sam's dark gaze faltered, darting away for just an instant, and her mouth twisted a little before it firmed again. "Because I — I don't want you to end up like that man. Callahan. Mitchell Callahan."

Carrie felt absolutely no threat coming from this woman and wasn't in the least frightened of her, but something told her not to laugh or dismiss what she was hearing. "The real estate developer who was kidnapped?"

"And murdered, yes."

"Why should I end up like him?"

Sam shifted her weight slightly and thrust her hands into the front pockets of her jeans. "There's no reason you should if — if you're careful. I'm just saying you should be careful."

"Look," Carrie said, uncertain why she was even allowing the conversation to go on, "I'm no target for a kidnapper. I have a little in savings, sure, but —"

"It's not about money."

"Kidnappings usually are."

"Yes. But not this time."

"Why not this time? And how do you know that?" While the younger woman hesitated, Carrie studied her and had a sudden realization. "Wait a minute, I know you. Sort of. I've seen your picture. On a poster."

Sam's thin face tightened. "Possibly. Miss Vaughn —"

"You're with that carnival out at the fairgrounds. You're supposed to be some kind of fortune-teller." She heard her own voice rising in indignation and wasn't surprised. A *fortune-teller*, for Christ's sake! On that poster advertising the services of *Zarina, All-Knowing Seer and Mystic* she'd been wearing a turban.

A purple turban.

"Miss Vaughn, I know you don't want to take me seriously. Believe me, I've seen the reaction before. But if you'll just —"

"You have got to be kidding me. What, you read the tea leaves and they told you somebody was going to kidnap me? Give me a break."

Sam drew a breath and spoke rapidly. "Whoever he is, he was at the carnival. I didn't see him, but he was there. He dropped something, a handkerchief. I picked it up. Sometimes when I touch things, I can see — I saw you. Tied up, gagged, blindfolded. You were in a small, bare room. And you were afraid. Please, I'm just asking you to be careful, to take precautions. I know I'm a stranger, and I know you have no reason to believe me, but would it hurt to just humor me?"

"Okay," Carrie said. "I'll humor you. I'll be careful. Thanks for the warning, Sam. See you around."

"Miss Vaughn —"

"Bye." Carrie shifted her toolbox to the other hand and went back into the house, deciding to check the heat pump later. When she looked out a front window just a few minutes afterward, it was to see Sam trudging down the driveway toward the road.

Carrie watched, frowning, until she could no longer see the other woman.

Every ounce of her common sense told Carrie to shrug off the "warning" and go about her business normally. She was rather on the fence when it came to believing in psychic abilities but was definitely skeptical of carnival fortune-tellers and was not at all inclined to believe this one.

But.

It wouldn't hurt, she thought, to take a few sensible precautions. Lock her doors, be wary. Because Mitch Callahan had, after all, been kidnapped and murdered, and she would never have picked him to be a target for something like that.

So Carrie locked her doors and went on to other things, thinking about the warning for a good hour or two before it faded from her memory.

"I guess you guys see a lot of rooms like this one," Detective Lindsay Graham said to the two federal agents.

Lucas Jordan glanced around at the functional if uninspiring conference room of the Clayton County Sheriff's Department, exchanged glances with his partner, then said, "A few, yeah. They always seem to look the same; only the view outside the windows changes. If there is a view."

This room had no view, since it was central in the building, but it was well-lit and spacious and seemed to contain all the necessary furniture, equipment, and supplies.

"We haven't generated a whole lot of paperwork on the Callahan investigation so far," Detective Graham said, indicating the file folders on the big table. "And all of it after the fact, since Mrs. Callahan only called us in when the kidnapper got his ransom and her husband never showed. Statements from her, his coworkers, the hiker who found the body; the medical examiner's report; our forensics unit's report."

"Since you only got word he was missing on Saturday, and the body was found Sunday morning, I'd say you had accomplished quite a bit," Jaylene Avery said. "I'm Jay, by the way."

"Thanks, I'm Lindsay." She barely hesitated. "We don't have a clue who the kidnapper is, dammit. The boss says you guys believe it could be a serial deal?"

"Could be," Jordan told her.

"And you've been tracking him for a year and a half?"

"Don't rub it in, please," Jay requested humorously. "We've been one step behind him all the way, and Luke is taking it personally."

Eyeing the fair and decidedly good-looking Jordan, Lindsay took note of that very intense gaze and said, "Yeah, he looks the type to take it personally. Does he make lists? The sheriff makes lists, and I hate it."

"He swears he doesn't, but I don't believe him."

"I'm still in the room, ladies," Jordan said, sitting down at the conference table and selecting a file folder.

"He's also a workaholic," Jay confided, ignoring his comment. "In the four years I've been his partner, not one vacation. Not one."

"I went to Canada last year," Jordan objected mildly.

"That was a law-enforcement seminar, Luke. And you ended up spending nearly a week helping the RCMP locate a missing teenager."

"They asked for my help. I could hardly say no. And I came back rested, didn't I?"

"You came back with a broken arm."

"But rested."

Jay sighed. "An arguable point."

Lindsay shook her head. "Does anybody ever ask if you two are an old married couple?"

"Occasionally," Jay said. "But I always tell them I wouldn't have him on a platter. In addition to his very irritating perfectionism and workaholic nature, he's got one of those dark and stormy pasts that would frighten any sensible woman out of her wits."

Jordan lifted an eyebrow and was clearly about to speak when they all heard Sheriff Metcalf's voice approaching. He sounded a bit like a bear somebody was poking with a sharp and annoying stick.

"I don't know why the hell you've got the nerve to be surprised I'd want to talk to you again. You came to me last week, remember?"

"For all the good it did." The woman's voice wasn't exactly bitter, but it had an edge to it.

Lindsay happened to be looking at Lucas Jordan's face, and as the unseen woman spoke, she saw it change. He seemed almost to flinch, a momentary surprise and something much stronger tightening his features. And then he was utterly expressionless.

Interested, Lindsay turned her gaze to

the door in time to see Sheriff Metcalf come in, followed by a slender woman of medium height with extremely dark eyes and black hair in a short, no-fuss hairstyle.

She stopped in the doorway, her unreadable dark gaze going immediately to Jordan. As though, Lindsay thought, she was not only not surprised, as he had been, but had fully expected him to be there.

He, however, got in the first jab.

"I see the circus is in town," he drawled, leaning back in his chair as he looked across the room at her.

Perhaps oddly, she smiled, and her voice was dry when she said, "It's a carnival, as you well know. Hey, Luke. Long time no see."

"Samantha."

Metcalf was the one who was surprised. "You two know each other?"

"Once upon a time," she replied, her gaze still locked with Jordan's. "Obviously, he was . . . slumming . . . when we met."

Jordan was the first to look away, his mouth twisting slightly.

It was his partner who said casually, "Hey, Samantha."

"Jay."

"You been in town long?"

"Couple weeks. We're at the fairgrounds

for another two." Her dark gaze fixed on Lindsay, and she inclined her head politely. "Detective Graham."

Lindsay nodded but remained silent. She had been with the sheriff when Samantha Burke had shown up here at the station early last week, and her disbelief — like Metcalf's — had been just this side of hostile. She felt her face heating up now as she remembered that scorn.

Misplaced scorn, as it turned out.

Because the carnival "mystic" had tried to warn them, and they hadn't listened.

And Mitchell Callahan had died.

2

Metcalf was frowning as he looked from the federal agent to the carnival fortune-teller, and he didn't try to hide his unhappiness, uncertainty, and frustration with the situation.

She didn't let it show, but Samantha could sympathize.

To Jordan, his tone not quite questioning, Metcalf said, "She came to us last week and said a man was going to be kidnapped. Didn't know his name, but gave us a damned good physical description of Mitchell Callahan."

"Naturally," Samantha said, "they didn't believe me. Until his wife called in to report it late Saturday. Then they came straight back to me, of course. Filled with questions and suspicions."

The sheriff's frown deepened to a scowl as he stared at her. "And I would have had your ass behind bars if so many of your fellow carnies — who also *all* had alibis — hadn't sworn by all they supposedly hold dear that you'd been there and in full view virtually all day on Thursday when

Callahan disappeared."

"Miles away and with my car being worked on here in town by your own mechanic," Samantha reminded him. "I think somebody might have noticed if I'd ridden one of the ponies down Main Street, don't you think?"

"You're not the only one of that bunch with a car."

"Nobody else loaned me a car or found theirs missing," she reminded him coolly. "I was at the carnival every day until after midnight, from Tuesday afternoon after I left here until you guys showed up there on Saturday to . . . talk . . . to me."

Obviously trying to be fair and impartial — at least now — Lindsay said, "Golden isn't a regular stop for the carnival, and we couldn't find a single connection between any of them and anyone in town. Plus, none of them had been in the area long enough to know Callahan's habits well enough to pinpoint the best time to grab him, and there wasn't a sign of the ransom money anywhere near the carnival. There was absolutely no evidence to indicate that either she or any of the other carnies could have been involved."

"Except," Metcalf said, "that she knew before it happened there would be a kid-

51

napping. Something I still don't have a satisfactory explanation for."

"I'm psychic," Samantha said, without a trace of defiance or defensiveness in her matter-of-fact tone. She had long ago learned to make that particular declaration calmly and without fanfare. She had also learned to make it without the bells and flourishes necessary in advertising a carnival "act."

"Yeah, Zarina, all-knowing seer and mystic. I read the signs out there at the carnival and in town."

"The carnival owner decides how to promote my booth, and his hero is P. T. Barnum. There's not much I can do about the result."

"Get a new picture. The purple turban makes you look ridiculous."

"And made you instantly decide it was all bullshit. That I con people for a living."

"That's about the gist," Metcalf agreed.

"Are you always right, Sheriff?"

"About cons, usually."

Samantha shrugged. She came into the room and took a chair at the conference table across from Lucas but kept watching the sheriff. And kept her manner calm and relaxed, difficult as that was. "Usually isn't always. But trying to convince somebody with a closed mind is worse than talking to a post. So let's keep doing this the hard way. Want to go into one of your tiny little interview rooms and shine a light into my face, or shall we have the next interrogation here where we can all be comfortable?"

He grunted. "You look comfortable enough."

"There's more room in here. And I assumed you'd want your new federal friends to participate. I'm sure they have questions too."

Since Jordan and his partner had been singularly silent, Metcalf wasn't so sure. And he was tempted to order Samantha Burke into one of the interview rooms just to make it clear who had the upper hand here.

Except he was afraid it was her.

More angry because he knew it showed, he said, "I want to know how you knew about the kidnapping."

"I told you how. I'm psychic."

"So the tea leaves told you. Or is it a crystal ball?"

"Neither." Her voice was measured and calm, as it had been all along. "Last Monday night I was running the sharpshooting booth —"

"Nobody wanted their palms read, huh?"

Samantha ignored that, continuing as though he had not interrupted. "— and when I picked up one of the guns I had a vision."

"Was it in Technicolor?" Metcalf asked with wonderful politeness.

Lindsay, who had been watching the two federal agents unobtrusively, decided that both of them were uncomfortable, though she couldn't tell if it was with the questions, the answers, or the antagonistic attitude of the sheriff. Or merely the subject, for that matter.

"They always are," Samantha replied to the sheriff, her voice dry this time.

"And what did you *see* in this vision?"

"I saw a man, sitting in a chair, bound and gagged and blindfolded. In a room I couldn't see too clearly. But I saw him. His hair was that rare orange-red, like a carrot, and he was wearing a dark blue business suit and a tie with little cars all over it. I think they were Porsches."

Lindsay said, "Exactly what Callahan was wearing when he was abducted."

Metcalf kept his eyes on Samantha. "You knew he'd been kidnapped."

"It seemed fairly obvious. Either that, or

54

he was into some very kinky bondage games. Since he was fully dressed and didn't look at all happy, I thought kidnapping was probably the more likely explanation."

"And there was no one near him?"

"No one I saw."

Lucas finally spoke, asking quiet questions. "Did you hear anything? Smell anything?"

"No," she replied without looking at him. She wondered if he'd expected a different reaction from her when they met again. If they met again. Had he expected her to be frozen? To lash out at him?

Metcalf said, "You knew Callahan, didn't you? Maybe he got rooked at that carnival of yours and threatened to sue or something. Was that it?"

"I had never seen Mitchell Callahan — in the flesh, so to speak. As far as I know he never visited the carnival."

"Really wasn't his sort of thing," Lindsay murmured.

But Metcalf wasn't willing to let go. "He was trying to buy up the fairgrounds for development, everybody knew that. If he had, it would have put your carnival out of business."

"Hardly. We can fit in a parking lot,

Sheriff, and there are plenty of those in Golden."

"They'd cost you a hell of a lot more."

"And put us closer to the heavier traffic of town." She shrugged, trying not to show the impatience she felt. "Probably a financial wash at the end of the day."

Again, Lindsay spoke up, her tone neutral. "True enough, Sheriff. We've got at least two former shopping centers and one strip mall with acres of parking lot going to waste, and I'm sure any of the owners would have loved to make a few bucks hosting a carnival."

Metcalf sent her a quick look that just missed being a glare, then returned his attention to Samantha. "Trouble follows you carnies, I know that much. Things turn up missing, property gets destroyed, people get cheated with your so-called games of *chance*. And how many times have *you* taken money from people only to tell them what you knew they wanted to hear?"

"A few," she replied calmly, answering the last demand. But she couldn't resist adding, "Some people don't want to hear the truth, Sheriff. And others wouldn't recognize it if it bit them on the ass."

He drew a breath to launch a retort, but

she was going on, her voice still calm, still measured.

"Your views about carnies are a few decades out of date, but never mind that. Whatever you may believe, we run a clean show, from the games to the very well-maintained rides, and our safety record is spotless."

"I didn't question that."

"Not openly. That's because you checked us out the day we got here and started setting up."

"I was doing my job."

"Fine. All of us carry police I.D. cards with our fingerprints, like the one I showed you when I first came to you. Feel free to check out the prints belonging to everyone else in the show, the way you checked out mine. It may surprise you to discover that not one of us has a record, even for something as minor as an unpaid parking ticket. And we have good relationships with the police in every town along our normal seasonal route. This is our first time in Golden, so I suppose you can be forgiven a few doubts as to our honesty, but —"

Lucas interrupted to ask, "If Golden isn't part of your normal schedule, why are you here?"

Her eyes flicked toward him, but

Samantha didn't turn her head when she answered him.

"The next town on our usual schedule just hosted a circus a couple of weeks ago, and we've learned never to follow a big circus into a town. Golden was the best alternative in the general area, especially when we discovered we could rent the fairgrounds for the duration."

"Aren't we lucky," Metcalf muttered.

"Your town seems to be enjoying the rides and games."

He glared at her. "And I'm charged with protecting my town from people who would abuse their good nature. And take advantage of their gullibility."

"Prove we're doing that, and we'll leave. Peacefully. Happily."

"And send my best suspect on to another innocent town? I don't think so."

"You know goddamned well I didn't kidnap or kill Mitchell Callahan."

"You knew about it before it happened. In my book, that says you're involved."

Samantha drew a breath, for the first time showing visible restraint, and said, "Believe me, Sheriff, if I have to have them at all, I'd just as soon my visions were restricted to simple things like where somebody lost their grandmother's ring or

58

whether they'll meet their perfect mate. But I didn't get to choose. As much as I'd rather it were otherwise, sometimes I see crimes being committed. Before they're committed. And my bothersome conscience and inability to ignore what I see drives me to report the visions. To hostile and suspicious people like you."

"Don't expect me to apologize," Metcalf told her.

"Like you, I don't believe in impossible things."

Lindsay decided it was past time to intercede. "Okay, Ms. Burke —"

"Samantha. Or Sam." She shrugged.

"Samantha, then. I'm Lindsay." It wouldn't hurt, she thought, to try to establish a less combative relationship; it was just a pity Wyatt couldn't see that. "Tell us something we don't know about Mitch Callahan's kidnapping and murder. Something that might help us catch the person responsible."

"I wish I could."

The sheriff said, "But your *visions* don't work that way. Damned convenient."

"Not at all convenient," she retorted.

"Then how am I supposed to believe —"

Lindsay got up and headed for the door. "Sheriff, can I talk to you outside for a minute, please? Excuse us, everyone."

There really wasn't much Metcalf could do but follow her, scowling, from the room.

Jaylene said, "Well, that was fun."

Samantha turned her head and stared at Lucas. "Thank you *so* much for your support," she said.

Lindsay didn't exactly drag her boss into his office, but she got him there quickly and shut the door behind them. "What the hell's wrong with you?" she demanded.

"Hey, watch the tone," he snapped right back. "We're in the office, not at your place or mine, and I damned well outrank you."

"Then fire my ass if you want to, but stop acting like an idiot," she told him. "Wyatt, she's not involved. You know that, and I know that. We wasted a hell of a lot of time yesterday trying to break her alibi, and we couldn't do it."

"That doesn't mean —"

"What? That she isn't involved?" Lindsay counted off facts on her fingers. "She didn't know Mitch Callahan. She's been in Golden barely two weeks. She has absolutely no criminal record. There is no trace *anywhere* around Samantha Burke or that carnival of the ransom money. Absolutely no forensic evidence ties her to the place where Callahan was grabbed or to his body and where it was dumped. And lastly, in case you hadn't noticed, she's not exactly a bodybuilder, and Callahan was a martial-arts expert twice her size. We didn't find a sign of a gun or other weapon in her possession, remember?"

"She did not see the future," he said grimly.

"I don't know what she saw. But I do know she didn't kidnap or murder Mitch Callahan."

"You can't *know* that, Lindsay."

"Yeah, Wyatt, I can know that. Fifteen years as a police officer tells me that. And nearly twenty years as a cop would be telling you the same goddamned thing if you'd just get past this rampant hatred of anybody you perceive as a con artist and look at the *facts*."

The sheriff stared at her.

Lindsay calmed down, but her voice was still flat and certain when she went on. "It'd be easier and a lot less painful to blame something like this on an outsider, and she's certainly that. She's an easy target, Wyatt. But, just for the sake of argument, what if you're wrong? What if she had nothing to do with it?"

"She's a viable suspect."

"No, she isn't. Maybe she was Saturday or yesterday, but we know now she couldn't have done it. She flat-out couldn't have. Yet you still had her brought in to answer more questions. And how many reporters are lounging around keeping an eye on the comings and goings here at the station? How many saw her brought in?"

His jaw tightened even more. "A few."

"Uh-huh. And just what do you think the anxious and worried people of Golden are going to do when they read in the papers that an avowed fortune-teller from a little carnival just passing through town is under suspicion for the kidnapping and murder of a local man?"

Metcalf was beginning to look unhappy, and not just because Lindsay was telling him how he should be doing his job. He was unhappy because she had to tell him. "Shit."

Quiet now, Lindsay said, "She doesn't deserve what might happen to her because of this. All she did was try to warn us. We didn't believe her, and I doubt we could have stopped the kidnapping even if we had. But either way, she doesn't deserve to have a target painted on her back."

He struggled with himself for a moment,

then said, "It's not possible to see the future."

"A hundred years ago, it wasn't possible to land on the moon. Things change."

"You're comparing apples and oranges. Landing on the moon was science. Physics, engineering. Touching something and seeing into the future is . . ."

"Today's new-age voodoo, yeah, maybe. And maybe tomorrow's science." Lindsay sighed. "Look, I'm not saying I believe she did what she says she did. I'm just saying that there's a hell of a lot more going on in this world than we understand — today. More than science understands *today*. And in the meantime, all our police science and procedure says that lady didn't have anything to do with the kidnapping, and common decency as well as due process says we let her off the hook unless and until that changes."

"Christ, I hate it when you're right."

She cocked an eyebrow at him. "And I love it when you admit that. The thing is, you have to go back into that conference room with two FBI agents and one maybe-psychic and try to salvage the situation."

"There's nothing to salvage. I might have gone overboard, but —"

"Have I ever told you how pigheaded you are?"

"Yes. Look, I am not going to apologize to her."

Lindsay shrugged. "So don't. Just move on. Maybe she'll be the gracious one."

"You're pushing it," he warned her.

Lindsay turned toward the door, saying dryly, "Just trying to make sure you get re-elected. I like sleeping with the boss."

"What did you expect me to do?" Lucas demanded of Samantha, his voice a bit tight.

"Oh, I don't know. Vouch for me? Confirm that I am, in fact, a genuine psychic, all tested and validated and everything? Maybe say that even the FBI has legitimized psychics, so the good sheriff might want to table his hostility and pay attention."

It was Jaylene who murmured, "We had pretty much decided not to go into detail about the unit or our abilities."

"Right. And of course that decision had nothing to do with me showing up."

"No, it didn't," Lucas said.

"Bullshit. There can't be any taint of carnivals or roadside fortune-tellers to sully your precious unit's *serious* reputation; you don't have to remind me of that."

"Even you have to admit Metcalf would have taken you a lot more seriously if he hadn't seen a picture of you in that wild gypsy outfit."

"I wasn't born independently wealthy, Luke; I have to make a living. Please excuse me for using the only skill I have in the only way available to me. At the time, I really didn't have a whole lot of options."

"And I don't have a lot now, dammit. We're investigating a series of fatal kidnappings, Samantha, and we do *not* have time to educate every cop we have to work with in the reality of psychic abilities. Sometimes the best we can do is get in, do our jobs, and move on with as little discussion as possible."

"You're good at that, as I recall. Moving on without discussion."

Whatever Lucas might have replied to that cutting comment was lost — at least for the moment — as the sheriff and his detective returned to the room.

"Any progress?" Lindsay asked cheerfully.

Jaylene murmured, "Not so you'd notice."

Lindsay lifted an eyebrow at her, but

said to Samantha, "If there's nothing else you can tell us, we won't keep you any longer."

"Yes, you will." Samantha sat up straighter in her chair and looked at the sheriff. "You'll put me in your jail or under house arrest with a couple of watchdogs — or I'll sit out in your damned lobby where everyone can see me."

"Why?" he asked warily.

"Because there's going to be another kidnapping. And considering the way people are beginning to look at me around here, I'd really rather not continue to be a suspect in anybody's mind."

Lucas was on his feet immediately. "Another? Christ, why didn't you say something before now?"

"Because she's not in danger yet," Samantha replied.

"How do you know that?"

"The vision. I saw her tied to a chair in what looked like a small, windowless room, and on a desk nearby was a newspaper with this coming Thursday's date. I think he'll send a photo of her with the newspaper, to prove she's alive when he demands the ransom. I think he'll expect to be doubted, especially after Callahan was found dead."

"So you know he'll have her on Thursday," Lucas said. "What's to stop him from grabbing her tonight or tomorrow?"

"He never does, does he? Grabs them late on Wednesday or early Thursday, and always makes the ransom demand on Thursday to give the family just enough time to get the money."

"That's the pattern," Lucas said grimly. "Want to tell me how you know about it?"

"Wait a minute," Metcalf interrupted. "Do you know who she is? What she looks like?"

"This time I made damned sure I found out who she is."

"How?" Lucas asked.

"In the vision, she was wearing a shirt with the logo of a local softball team on it. Turns out she's the assistant coach. Carrie Vaughn. She lives out on Highway 221. I tried to warn her a couple of hours ago, but I got the feeling she didn't believe she could be in any danger."

"Get somebody out there," Metcalf said to Lindsay. "I'd rather be embarrassed than sorry later."

Lindsay nodded and hurried from the conference room.

Lucas said, "Answer the question, Samantha. How did you know what the kidnapper's pattern has been?"

"Lucky guess?"

"Not funny."

Samantha's smile twisted. "Oh, you're wrong about that. It is funny. In fact, this whole thing is a cosmic joke. You just haven't heard the punch line yet."

"How did you know about the pattern?"

She looked at him for a long moment, expressionless, then said, "We're staying at that little motel near the fairgrounds. If you'll go there —"

"I thought you people stayed in those campers and RVs," Metcalf interrupted.

"Usually we do. Sometimes we like hot showers in bathrooms large enough to turn around in. Some of us are at the motel. Okay?"

The sheriff shrugged. "Just wondered."

"We've paid in advance, if you were wondering that."

"It had crossed my mind."

"Yeah, I figured it might have."

Lucas said, "Will you two please stay on the subject and stop sniping at each other? Sam, what's in your motel room?"

She didn't let herself react to the shortened version of her name. "Check the top drawer of the nightstand, and you'll find a handkerchief in a plastic bag. He dropped

it at the carnival, probably yesterday.
When I picked it up late yesterday afternoon, I had the vision."

"And?"

"I told you what I saw."

"What else?"

"Flashes of the others. The other victims.
Ten, twelve of them. Men and women, different ages, nothing in common. Except
him. I knew what he was doing, what he's
been doing all these months. His pattern.
And I knew why."

"Why?"

"Sure you want to know, Luke?"

"Of course I want to know."

Samantha shrugged. "Okay. I saw a
chessboard. Not a lot of pieces; it was an
endgame. Two players. I saw their hands
moving the chessmen. And then I saw the
face of one of the players."

"Who was it?"

"It was you, Luke. Get it? Get the joke?
You're here because he wants you to be
here. It's not about the money. It was never
about the money. He's playing a game.
He's matching his skills and his wits
against you. You, personally. And he won't
stop until the game has a winner."

Metcalf said something profane under
his breath and then, louder, said, "If you

expect us to believe any of this —"

"I don't expect *you* to believe a thing, Sheriff," she said without taking her eyes off Lucas.

"Why me?" Lucas demanded. "Why would he fix on me?"

"Because you're the best. The past few years, you've really made a name for yourself in solving kidnappings and abductions. And since those crimes tend to be high-profile, you've gotten a lot of press, other media. You've been very visible. I guess he's been watching."

"No," Lucas said. "I just don't buy it."

"Maybe you just don't want to buy it." She seemed to hesitate, then said slowly, "Why do you think he kills them?"

"He didn't kill them all," Lucas said immediately.

"He didn't kill the first one," Samantha agreed. "Let her go once he had the money like a nice little kidnapper, even though she's convinced he'd planned to kill her. If he had planned to, he must have changed his mind. But I guess he found something lacking in the way that ended, huh? Because he's been killing them ever since."

Lucas was silent.

"So what was it, Luke? Why did he start killing them? They never see him. They couldn't identify him, so they aren't a threat. He gets his money, or has almost every time. So why does he kill them? Come on, Luke, you're a natural profiler. What possible reason could he have for slaughtering these people once their ransom is paid?"

Despite his own antagonism, Metcalf found himself watching the federal agent and waiting for his answer.

Lucas sat back down in his chair without looking away from Samantha, and after a moment said slowly, "According to the official profile, he's not willing to take the risk that they might be able to identify him."

"What about the unofficial profile? You must have your own ideas. Don't tell me you and Bishop actually saw eye to eye on this one?"

"It makes sense, Sam."

"Sure it does. It makes perfect psychological sense. And I don't have a degree in psychology, so maybe I'm the last person you should listen to. It just seems to me that broken minds don't work the way they're supposed to. That's why they're broken."

Jaylene said, "Broken minds. Good description."

"He wouldn't be kidnapping and killing people if he didn't have a few screws loose."

"We can only hope."

Lucas said, "The point is that the profile fits what little we know about the kidnapper. It makes sense that he kills them to avoid the risk of identification."

"But if he knows he's going to kill them, why bother to keep them blindfolded?"

"We have no proof that he does."

"I'm telling you. He does. Right up until the moment they find out they're going to die, he keeps them blindfolded."

"And we're supposed to believe you?" Metcalf demanded.

"As I said, Sheriff, I don't expect you to believe me. But Luke knows I'm telling the truth."

Eyeing the federal agent, Metcalf said, "You two obviously have a history of some kind. *Do* you believe her?"

The silence dragged on much longer than was comfortable before Lucas finally replied.

"Yes. I believe we can trust what she knows. What she sees."

Samantha, hearing the qualifiers, smiled wryly. But all she said was, "So why keep them blindfolded if he knows he's going to kill them anyway? Why kill them? What could he possibly gain by killing them?"

"You tell me."

"Points, I guess. In the game. Maybe . . . if he gets his money, he also gets points. If you don't get to the victims before he gets his money, he wins points. You rescue a live victim, and you get points. Which means he's ahead on points."

"Goddammit," Metcalf muttered.

She glanced at him. "Sorry to sound flippant, Sheriff. See, the thing is, all I really know is that he's playing a game and Luke is his opponent. Everything else is guesswork."

"This is insane," Metcalf said.

"Oh, I agree. He's probably insane too, the kidnapper. That broken mind we were discussing. Broken and brilliant."

"Why brilliant?" Lucas asked.

It was Jaylene who replied to that. "Because you're very good at what you do. Because the odds are always stacked against a successful kidnapping, and this guy has been successful way too many times. Because it isn't about the money."

Samantha nodded. "He's invented a very special game just for the two of you to play. And don't think he doesn't know his opponent. The first few kidnappings may well

73

have been test runs, just to lure you in and watch what you did."

"I can't believe you're buying any of this," Metcalf said to Lucas.

"You don't know all the background, Sheriff," Lucas responded, frowning. "The cases going back eighteen months. This . . . theory . . . fits."

"It's not a theory, Luke," Samantha said flatly. "It's a fact. This is all a game to him."

"Games have rules."

"Yes. Which means you have to figure out what his rules are before you have a hope in hell of saving the next victim's life, catching him — and winning the game."

3

Tuesday, September 25

"I don't need watchdogs," Carrie Vaughn said with a considerable amount of force. "I can take care of myself, and I don't like people hovering around me."

"They aren't hovering, Miss Vaughn. I've got a patrol car parked across the highway on that old dirt road; you can barely see them when you look out a window." Sheriff Metcalf kept his voice as patient as possible. "They're just keeping an eye on things, is all."

"Because some gypsy fortune-teller says I'm in danger? Jesus, Sheriff."

"I have to act on information received, Miss Vaughn, especially when we've already had one kidnapping that ended in murder."

"Information from a fortune-teller?" She didn't try to hide her disgust. "I hope you aren't planning on running again at the next election."

The rest of the conversation was brief, and Metcalf hung up the phone a minute or two later, scowling. He turned to face Lucas, who was on the other side of the conference table, and said, "Tell me again why we're listening to her."

Lucas didn't have to ask which "her" the sheriff was referring to. "She's genuine, Wyatt."

"You're saying you believe she can see the future before it happens."

"Yes."

"Because she proved it to you in the past."

Lucas nodded.

"I've never in my life met a gullible cop. You sure you're a fed?"

"Last time I looked." Lucas sighed. "I know it's difficult to accept, especially given her role in a carnival."

"You can say that again. I think the lack of credibility sort of accompanies the purple turban."

"She warned you about Callahan."

"A fluke. A coincidence. The one lucky guess in a thousand tries."

"And if she's right about Carrie Vaughn?"

"The second lucky guess." Metcalf grimaced when Lucas lifted an eyebrow at him. "Okay, so a second lucky guess that specific would be pushing it. But you are not going to convince me that she can see the future."

Lucas had heard that particular note in someone else's voice often enough to recognize it: for Wyatt Metcalf, believing that it was possible to see the future before it occurred was a direct challenge to some deep and long-held belief. It would require drastic evidence to convince him, and he would be angry rather than happy if that evidence presented itself.

So all Lucas said was, "Then treat her information the same way you'd treat any anonymous tip; take precautions and check it out."

"In this case, watch Carrie Vaughn and wait."

"I'd say so. Unless and until we have another lead or information more useful than this lot." He gestured toward the files, reports, and photos spread out on the conference table.

"Nothing positive from Quantico?"

"Not so far. Your people are thorough and well-trained, just as you said; they didn't miss anything. Which means we're not left with much in the way of evidence."

"What about that handkerchief Zarina says she got her vision from?"

Lucas cleared his throat. "At Quantico

being tested. We should have the results by tomorrow."

Metcalf eyed him. "Something on your mind?"

"I wouldn't keep calling her Zarina if I were you."

"What, she's going to put a gypsy curse on me?"

"She isn't a gypsy."

Metcalf waited, brows raised.

Lucas really didn't want to get into this with the sheriff, and that reluctance was in his tone when he said, "Look, she doesn't deserve scorn or ridicule. You don't believe she's a genuine psychic, that's fine. But don't treat her like a joke."

"I can't get past the turban," Metcalf admitted.

"Try."

"I seem to remember you making a crack about the circus being in town."

"I'm allowed," Lucas said wryly, even as he wondered if Samantha would agree with that.

"Oh?"

"I don't think I'll show you my scars, if it's all the same to you."

"Ah, so there is a history."

"You didn't need a crystal ball to figure that out," Lucas muttered, frowning down at the postmortem report on Mitchell Callahan.

"No, it was fairly obvious. And very surprising. I don't see you as the type to visit carnivals."

"No."

"Then she was involved in one of your cases before this?" Metcalf didn't try to disguise his curiosity.

"Something like that."

"I gather it ended badly."

"No, the case ended successfully; we got the guy."

"It was just the relationship that tanked, huh?"

Lucas was saved from replying when Lindsay spoke from the open doorway.

"Jesus, Wyatt, you're worse than a woman."

"I was investigating," he told her.

"You were being nosy." She came into the room, shaking her head. "Luke, Jaylene's on her way in. She says she didn't get anything new from Mitch Callahan's wife."

"Well, we didn't really expect to," he said. "But the base had to be covered."

"So this is what you guys have been doing for a year and a half?" she asked, curious herself now. "Zipping around the country on that private jet of yours as soon as the kidnapping reports come in? Double-checking everything, combing through reports, talking to family and coworkers of the abductees?"

"When we get a case after the fact, yes." He knew the frustration was in his voice but didn't try to hide it; after more than twenty-four hours in Golden and working with Wyatt and Lindsay, they knew much more about the serial kidnappings and Lucas felt more comfortable with what they knew.

He had not, however, told them the whole story of the SCU or his own and Jaylene's abilities, an omission that bothered him less on his and Jay's account than on Samantha's.

A sobering realization.

"What about when you get the case right away — after the abduction but before the ransom is paid or a body found?" Lindsay was asking, still curious.

"It's only happened twice, and both times we were a step behind him all the way." He hesitated, then added, "In fact, I got the distinct feeling we were being led by the nose."

"Which," Lindsay said, "lends weight to Sam's theory that this guy is playing some kind of game with you, and has been for some time."

It was Metcalf who said, "You two seem to be getting awfully chummy."

"You mean just because I don't treat her like a leper the way the rest of you do? That I might sit down and have a cup of coffee and a conversation with her?"

"I don't know what you mean."

"The hell you don't." Lindsay shook her head. "She volunteers to stay here at the station, under your and everybody else's eye for the duration, and you're still acting like she stole your dog."

"Dammit, Lindsay, I'm getting a lot of questions and you know it. I can't hold her here legally, and explaining that she's here voluntarily just opens up a whole new can of worms."

"I don't see why it should," Lindsay responded. "She has a cot in one of the interview rooms and she's paying for her own food, so it's not like the taxpayers have an extra burden. The press certainly understands what she's trying to do."

"Oh, yeah," the sheriff said sardonically, "they had their headlines for today, all right. *Gypsy Seeks to Prove Innocence by Remaining in Police Custody*. The problem is, the more astute among the media have figured out that the only way she can prove herself innocent doing this is if we have another kidnapping while she's in custody."

"Tomorrow's headline," Lucas murmured.

Metcalf nodded. "Judging by the questions I've been getting. Naturally, they're wondering how we could expect another kidnapping. As Luke and Jaylene pointed out yesterday, most kidnappers don't try it twice, and very few even stick around after a successful delivery of the ransom."

With a grimace, Lindsay said, "I hadn't thought about that. But of course they would wonder, wouldn't they?"

"And they aren't the only ones," the sheriff told her. "The mayor called, as well as two members of the town council, demanding to know why I believe someone else could be kidnapped and whether I know who it will be."

"I'm guessing you didn't tell them."

"Of course I didn't tell them. There's no way I'm going to admit to anyone that the ravings of a lunatic carnival fortune-teller are dictating any part of this investigation."

Lucas stopped himself from wincing at Metcalf's vehemence, but it was another reminder that Bishop had been right to take the course he had while forming the unit. As unbelievable as psychic abilities often seemed, people were far more inclined to at least accept the possibility when the ones who claimed to have them worked in "serious" jobs and relied on scientific explanations — even if the science was speculative — to describe and define their abilities.

And having a federal badge didn't hurt.

"Wyatt, she's not a lunatic and she hasn't been raving," Lindsay objected. "Besides, with all the psychic stuff you see on TV and in the movies these days, people are a lot more open to the idea than you might think. Most people, anyway."

"If you're talking about that guy on TV who claims to read minds, all I can say is that you're a lot more gullible than I ever would have imagined, Lindsay."

"He's very convincing."

"He's a con artist. It's called a cold reading, and whatever skill it takes I can promise you isn't paranormal."

"You can't be sure of that," she said.

"Want to bet?"

The argument might have continued indefinitely if one of the young deputies hadn't knocked on the doorjamb just then, peering into the conference room with a very anxious look on his face. "Sheriff? If it's okay, I need to run home for a few minutes. I know I've already had my lunch break, but —"

"What's up, Glen?"

"It's just . . . I need to make sure Susie and the baby are okay. I called, but didn't get an answer."

"Maybe she has the baby outside," Lindsay offered. "It's a nice day."

"Yeah, maybe. But I'd like to be sure." He smiled nervously. "Maybe it's just being a new dad, but —"

"Go ahead, take off," Metcalf told him. "You'll worry 'til you know for sure."

"Thanks, Sheriff."

When the deputy had gone, Lucas didn't give the other two a chance to resume their argument. At least in his presence. "Since we agreed to split the duty as much as possible, why don't you two go on to lunch? I'll wait for Jaylene to get back, and we'll go later."

"Suits me," Metcalf said.

Lindsay agreed with a nod, and the two left.

It was probably five minutes later that Lucas swore under his breath when he realized he'd read the same paragraph three times and still didn't know what was in it. Instead of trying again, he leaned back in his chair and drummed his fingers on the table, arguing silently with himself.

Finally, however, he admitted defeat just as silently and got up. He left the conference room and made his way to the lower level of the sheriff's department, which housed the jail cells and interview rooms.

The deputy on duty down there nodded as he passed, then returned to the magazine in his hands. The only occupant of the cells was one very unhappy young man brought in on a destruction-of-property charge, and he was too busy feeling sorry for himself to cause any trouble, so the deputy's only responsibility was to keep an eye on the cells and on the closed door of Room 3.

Where Samantha Burke was currently staying.

The door wasn't locked. Lucas hesitated, then knocked once and went in.

The small room was normally spartan, with a table and chairs, a security camera high in one corner, and a small TV high in the opposite one; the addition of a cot and the duffel bag holding Samantha's things reduced the floor space considerably and did nothing to make her temporary accommodations even appear to be comfortable.

She was sitting at the table, a soft drink

and a Styrofoam box containing a partially eaten salad before her.

"Still eating like a rabbit, I see," he said, mostly for something to say.

"Old habits." She sipped the drink, eyeing him, then said dryly, "And I doubt interest in my lunch is what brought you down here. What've I done now, Luke?"

"That deputy, Champion. He brought you your lunch, didn't he?"

"Yeah. So?"

"Did he drop something? Did you touch his hand?"

Coolly, she said, "I don't know what you're talking about."

"I'm talking about him leaving here one breath away from panic to rush home and check on his wife and kid."

"New dads worry, I'm told." Her voice was still cool. "And he's such a proud one. Showed me a picture. Pretty wife, cute kid. He's right to be proud of them."

"So that was it. You touched the picture. And?"

She leaned back with a sigh. "And I told him he needed to go home and unplug their clothes dryer until he can get someone to check it. Because it could cause a fire."

"When?"

"Today." Samantha smiled wryly. "His wife dries clothes in the afternoon, when the energy demand is lower. Plus the baby likes the sound, it helps her to go to sleep. But drying clothes today wouldn't be a good idea. So I told him that. And even though he didn't want to believe me, I expect he went home to unplug that dryer. Just in case."

He'd been watching her for a while now, so he had her routine down pat. He knew when he would take her, and how. By now, that part of things was almost second nature, so that he could perform on auto-pilot.

That wasn't the fun part, not anymore.

This was the fun part, and he was enjoying himself even more knowing that at last all the necessary players were in place and paying attention.

He'd begun to think they would never catch on.

But now . . . now they were finally starting to understand, and all the long months of planning and careful, calculated actions had put all the pieces on the game board.

Really, it was all falling into place so beautifully that it made him wonder if there actually was a God.

He hummed to himself as he checked the seals, making certain there would be no leaks. Going over it meticulously, because he refused to make mistakes.

It wouldn't be a true test of which one of them was smarter if he made any mistakes.

So he checked every inch, every detail, going over and over the plan until he was absolutely positive there was nothing left out, nothing forgotten, nothing wrong.

He polished the glass and metal until there was no hint of a fingerprint or even a smear, vacuumed the space for the third time, compulsively took apart all the connections so he could wipe down each component individually.

They would find only the signs he wanted them to find.

When he was done this time, he stood back and studied the room, playing out in his head how it would be. She was tough, so he didn't think she'd be all that scared at first. Which was good for his purposes.

Once he'd figured out it was the fear that drew Jordan, he had chosen his lures even more carefully. He liked the tough ones, the ones that didn't scare easily. Because that made it all the sweeter when they realized what was going to happen to them and how helpless they were to stop it.

This one, he thought, would be one of the best. When she finally broke, her terror would be extreme. He didn't know if Jordan could feel it or smell it, but either way it would hit him like a punch to the gut.

To be this close.

To have an innocent taken from beneath his very nose.

To begin to really understand the game.

"Jesus, Sam."

"What? What was I supposed to do, Luke? Ignore what I saw? Let that lady and her baby die?"

"Of course not."

"Well, then. I gave him the calmest, most low-key warning I could come up with, spur-of-the-moment. I'm sure you could have done better in disguising the psychic origins of the information, what with all your training and experience in these things, but —"

"Will you *stop* with that shit? I didn't make the rules, Sam. I wasn't the one who decided that anything that smacked of carnivals or sideshows could never be part of what we are. But you know what? For the record, I agree with Bishop on that one. I have had to deal with too many hard-nosed, skeptical cops like Wyatt Metcalf not to have learned that we have to look serious and act serious if we have even a hope of being accepted for what we are and *believed*. So we can do our jobs."

"Oh, I'm sure you're right. You usually are, after all." She closed the take-out box and pushed the salad away. "Lost my appetite. Can't imagine why."

Lucas was sorely tempted to turn around and walk out but fought the impulse. Instead, he pulled the other chair out and sat down across from her.

"Please," she said, "join me."

"Thanks, I will." He kept his voice even. "Do you think we can talk like two rational people for a minute?"

"Maybe a minute. Though I wouldn't bet on it."

"Jesus, Sam."

"You already said that."

What he said then was something he hadn't wanted or intended to say. "I never meant to hurt you."

Samantha laughed.

Lucas supposed he deserved that, but it didn't make it any easier to take. "I didn't. I know you don't believe that, but it's the truth."

"As a matter of fact, I do believe it. So what?"

He wasn't a man who was easily knocked off his balance, but he had to admit, at least silently, that Samantha always managed to do just that. "So can we stop fighting?"

"I don't know. Can we?"

"Christ, you're a stubborn woman."

"That's not even conversation."

"Do I have to remind you again that I'm in the middle of a serial kidnapping and murder investigation?"

"*We're* in the middle. I'm here too, Luke."

"You being here is just —" He stopped, then slowly finished, "a fluke."

Samantha didn't say a word.

"Happenstance. A coincidence."

She picked up her drink and sipped.

Lucas was aware of a second impulse to get up and walk out of the room, and he very nearly obeyed that one. Instead, he drew a deep breath, let it out slowly, and said, "The carnival isn't in Golden because the next town on the schedule just hosted a circus. The carnival is in Golden because you wanted it to be here."

"I didn't *want* to be here, Luke, believe me. In fact, I would have gone a long way to avoid being here just now. But we both know some of the things I see simply can't be changed. And unfortunately for us both, this is one of them. It's the real punch line of the cosmic joke. In that vision where I saw you playing chess with the kidnapper, I also saw myself standing behind you. You can't win the game without me."

Lindsay stretched languidly and yawned. "God. Do we have to go back to the station?"

Metcalf eyed smooth flesh still clinging to its golden summer tan and reached over to touch her. "Somebody might wonder if we never come back from lunch," he noted absently.

"Ummm. What lunch? I've lost ten pounds with these *lunches* of ours."

"We can stop for a quick burger on the way back."

"You always say that, but when it comes down to it neither one of us is hungry."

"So we lose a few pounds and go back to work relaxed and de-stressed; I'd call that a good lunch break."

Lindsay started to reach for him but saw over his shoulder the clock on the nightstand and groaned. "We've been gone almost an hour now."

"I'm the sheriff. I can be late."

"But —"

"And so can you."

They were very late in returning to the station, and when absolutely nobody commented, Lindsay wondered for the first time if their "secret" affair was as secret as she'd believed.

People were very studiously not commenting.

They found both Lucas and his partner in the conference room. He was pacing with the wired energy of a caged cat; Jaylene was sitting on the end of the conference table, watching him meditatively.

"Sorry," Lindsay said as they came in.

Lucas paused and looked at her. "Why?"

"Lunch. We're late getting back."

"Oh. That." He resumed pacing. "I'm not hungry."

Gesturing to two Styrofoam containers behind her on the table, Jaylene said, "I brought him something, but he's been a little . . . preoccupied."

"Has something happened?" Metcalf asked.

"No," Lucas said. He glanced at Jaylene, then added, "Nothing's changed."

Metcalf looked at Lindsay. "Was that a

qualified statement? It sounded qualified to me."

"Don't ask," Lucas told him. "You won't like the answer, believe me."

"It's Samantha," Jaylene said. "She believes she's meant to be here, to be involved in the investigation. To help Luke win the game."

"Shit," Metcalf said.

Lindsay asked, "Help him how?"

"If she even knows, she isn't saying."

"I don't think she knows," Lucas said. "Just that she's somehow involved."

"That's what I've been saying," the sheriff reminded them.

Lucas stopped pacing and took a chair. "Involved in the investigation. On our side."

"Your side," Jaylene murmured.

"Is there a difference?" he demanded.

"Maybe so."

He gestured slightly as though pushing the comment away, then said, "Whether Sam's involved doesn't change the fact that we've got nothing to go on. No evidence, nothing to I.D. him or even point us in his direction. If this bastard follows his usual pattern, he's already in another state and planning his next abduction."

Lindsay said, "But Sam says his next abduction is here in Golden." She frowned. "If we assume for a minute that she's right, why would he change his M.O. now? I mean, why plan two kidnappings in the same area? Isn't that asking for trouble?"

"Maybe it's asking for Luke," Jaylene offered. "Maybe part of the game was to eventually get us in position before the fact. It would be the first time."

"And really the only way he could do it," Lucas said slowly. "We're here investigating his last abduction, so if he wanted us on the scene before his next one, he'd pretty much have to plan it here, while we were here."

Jaylene looked at the clutter of files and photographs on the table. "So . . . if he got us here before the fact, and it's part of his game, then it's at least possible that he has left us a . . . clue, for want of a better word. Something that offers Luke at least a fighting chance against him. Otherwise, the game's winner is predetermined. And there's no contest."

Metcalf scowled. "I hate to admit that Zarina had a point, but that comment about broken minds makes a certain amount of sense. I mean, can we reasonably expect this guy to play by any kind of rules?"

"He'll play by his rules," Lucas said slowly. "He has to. Being careful and meticulous has been a point of honor for him, so this will be too. The game has rules. And he will abide by those rules. The trick for us . . . is figuring out what they are."

Jaylene said, "Which goes back to my point. He can't reasonably expect you to play his game unless and until the rules are clear. So at some point they have to be. Maybe at this point. And since he didn't send us a printed list, they have to be here." She gestured to the paperwork spread out on the table. "Somewhere."

Metcalf said, "You can't be serious? It's the proverbial needle in a haystack."

"Not much of a haystack," Lucas reminded him. "Even after eighteen months, we have very little in the way of evidence. We have cause of death; we have crime-scene reports but only from locations where the bodies were found, never where the vics were killed; we have the statement from the single surviving victim, which tells us only that he spoke to her, sounded intelligent and, in her words, 'scary as hell'; we have statements from friends, family members, and coworkers of the vics; we have some minor trace evidence, hair and fibers that may or may not be connected to the kidnapper; we have ransom notes printed on a very common brand of ink-jet printer — and that's about it."

"Lotta paper," Lindsay said. "But not a very helpful haystack."

"Yeah, but it has to be," Jaylene pointed out. "Doesn't it? He's here, we're here. After following him around for a year and a half, we've apparently reached the next stage of the game."

"If Zarina's right about that," Metcalf reminded them.

"Her name," Lucas said, "is Samantha."

"That's not what the posters say."

"Wyatt," Lindsay murmured.

"Well, it isn't. She goes by Zarina, right?"

"Only when she's working," Lucas said. "Wyatt, please. The problem with assuming about Sam's prediction — either way — is that we have to wait. We won't know if the kidnapper is still in this area unless and until he abducts another victim. Now, we can assume he's already gone and wait for a kidnapping report somewhere in the East, or we can assume he's still here and about to snatch his next vic — and wait for that to happen."

"Our part of the game plan sucks," Metcalf noted.

"Or," Lucas continued, "we can expect him to grab someone by tomorrow evening or Thursday morning — Carrie Vaughn, if Sam's right — and we can spend that time looking for his goddamned game rules and watching the potential target very, very closely."

"We already know one of his rules," Lindsay said. "When he takes the victims. Sometime between noon on Wednesday and noon on Thursday. Right?"

Jaylene nodded. "Right. Every single victim was snatched during that twenty-four-hour period."

"Rule number one," Lucas said. He reached out to draw a file folder close. "Let's start looking for rule number two."

Wednesday, September 26

Metcalf came into the conference room, saying briefly, "Carrie Vaughn has a detective in her living room as well as a patrol car in her driveway. She's safe. She's not happy, but she's safe."

Lucas glanced at his watch. "Just before noon. If he's still in Golden and has another kidnapping planned so soon, he'll move by noon tomorrow."

"If we got that rule right," Lindsay said.

"Yeah. If."

Metcalf said, "Just for the record, I locked Zarina in her room."

Lucas frowned slightly but didn't look up as he said, "A sensible precaution, from your point of view."

"I thought so. And she didn't seem too upset about it."

"Probably because you didn't call her Zarina to her face."

Shrugging, Metcalf sat down at the table. "I'm still surprised all her carnie friends haven't shown up here."

"She probably told them what she meant to do and asked them to stay away. They're a tight group; they'd handle it however she asked them to."

"You almost sound like you respect them."

"I do. Most of them have been on their own since they were kids but still managed to carve out a fair living for themselves without breaking a law or hurting others. That puts them in the Decent Human Being column of my book."

Lindsay noted that her hardheaded lover wasn't pleased to hear that information; it put human faces on his easy targets and made it more difficult for him to lump them together under a neat label. It also made him aware of what he was trying to do, and that naturally irritated him.

She couldn't help smiling wryly, but all she said was, "I guess we're all eating lunch in today. What does everybody want, and I'll go get it."

For the remainder of that day, they were all in and out of the room, going over the paperwork again and again, discussing the previous kidnappings and murders. And getting nowhere.

Even what had seemed a promising clue — the handkerchief Samantha had picked up at the carnival — proved to be fairly useless according to the report from Quantico. Mass-produced and sold in any retail store one might name, the handkerchief held a few grains of dirt, undoubtedly acquired when it was dropped onto the ground, but no sign of any human secretions whatsoever.

The lab technician allowed that there was a faint spot containing an oily residue, as yet unidentified, but it would require more time to determine what it might be.

"Ten to one," Metcalf said, "it'll turn out to be popcorn oil. And they've got — what? — at least two booths selling the stuff?"

"Four on a busy night," Lucas said with a sigh.

"Dead end," Jaylene murmured.

There was no good reason for them to remain at the station that night and every reason for them to rest while they could, so they called it a day well before midnight and went to their respective homes or hotel rooms.

Thursday morning proved to be busy, with numerous calls pulling both Metcalf and Lindsay out of the station for a considerable period of time, so Lucas and Jaylene found themselves alone in the conference room more often than not.

"Is it just me," he said around ten-thirty, "or is time crawling by?"

"It's definitely dragging." She glanced up to watch him prowling restlessly back and forth in front of the bulletin boards where they had pinned information and a timeline for the kidnappings and murders. "At the same time, we're running out of it. If he's going to act this week . . ."

"I know, I know." He hesitated, then said, "You talked to Sam this morning."

"Yeah."

"And she didn't have anything else to add?"

"No. But she's as restless and jumpy as you are."

Lucas frowned, and returned to his chair at the conference table. "I just hate knowing I'd rather he went ahead and did whatever he's going to do so we might have something new to work with. I don't want another victim, and yet —"

"And yet another victim will tell us we're on the right track. More or less."

"Yeah, goddammit."

Metcalf came into the room and sat down with a sigh. "Did everybody go nuts all of a sudden? It's Thursday, for Christ's sake, and you'd think it was Saturday night. Fender benders, B&Es, domestic disputes — and some asshole just tried to rob one of our three banks."

"Unsuccessfully, I gather," Lucas said.

"Yeah, but not much credit to my people. Guy had a flare gun. A *flare* gun. I was ready to shoot him just on general principle. And because he fucked up my morning."

Jaylene chuckled, and said, "Quite a lot of action for a small town. Maybe it's the newspaper stories getting people all riled up."

"Yeah, let's blame them." Metcalf sighed. "So have you two made any progress?"

"No," Lucas replied shortly.

"He's a little cranky," Jaylene explained.

"Aren't we all." Metcalf looked up with a scowl as one of his deputies came in and handed him an envelope. "What the hell's this?"

"Dunno, Sheriff. Stuart told me to give it to you." Stuart King was the deputy on the front desk today.

Lucas looked across the table as the deputy left and Metcalf opened the letter. He saw a quiver disturb the sheriff's long fingers. Saw his face go dead white.

"Jesus," Metcalf whispered.

"Wyatt?" When he got no response, Lucas left his chair and went around the table to the sheriff. He saw the printed letter addressed to Metcalf. Saw a photograph. He actually looked at the photograph, conscious of a deep shock.

"Jesus," Metcalf repeated. "The bastard's got Lindsay."

103

4

Lucas dropped the bagged photograph on the table in front of Samantha, and said evenly, "Please tell me you have something to say about this."

Samantha picked it up, frowning, and lost what little natural color her skin could boast. "I don't understand. Lindsay? He took Lindsay?"

"Obviously. Now tell me why you told us to watch Carrie Vaughn."

"She's the one I saw. Not this, not Lindsay."

"Is everything else in the photo the same?"

"Lindsay. I don't understand why —"

Lucas brought his hand down hard on the table, making her jump and finally look up at him. "Think, Sam. Is everything else the same?"

Clearly shaken, Samantha returned her gaze to the photo and studied it. "Same room. Same chair, same newspaper. Even the blindfold looks the same. The only difference between this and what I saw is Lindsay." She dropped the bagged photo and half consciously pushed it away.

Lucas sat down across from her. "The photo has been printed; it's clean, of course. Open the bag. Touch it."

"I would have gotten something even through the bag."

"Maybe not. Open it, Sam."

She hesitated, then pulled the bag back and opened it. She took out the photo, handling it gingerly at first. And her frown told him even before she shook her head and said, "Nothing."

"You're sure?"

"Positive." She returned the photo to the bag. "He took her this morning? It can't have been too long ago; she was in and out, I saw her."

"Wyatt received the note less than an hour ago. Twenty minutes ago, her car was found parked at the side of a small café where she often gets coffee." His voice was still even, unemotional, as it had been from the moment he'd entered the room. "No one inside saw her arrive, and she didn't go in. So far, we haven't found anyone in the area who saw her."

"The sheriff got the ransom demand?"

Lucas nodded.

"How much?"

"Exactly what he's got in savings. Twenty grand."

"*Exactly* that?"

Again, Lucas nodded. "The kidnapper has never been so precise before, just in the ballpark of what the family or significant other could afford. This time it's almost to the penny. And I doubt it's a coincidence."

"No. No, I don't think it is. He's being bolder, isn't he? Like he's thumbing his nose at you."

"At someone." Lucas shook his head. "He took a cop this time, which is either very, very stupid or very brazen. And I don't think he's stupid."

"When is the ransom to be delivered?"

"Tomorrow afternoon at five."

Frowning, Samantha said, "But if he knows Metcalf has the right amount in savings, he must know the sheriff could get his hands on it today. Why give you more than twenty-four hours to try and find Lindsay?"

"Just for that reason, I think. To give us time to search. To see how good we are. Maybe he's even out there watching, observing our methods."

Samantha studied him across the table. "What else do you think? What do you feel?"

"I don't feel anything."

"You know Lindsay, you've been around her for days. You don't feel anything from her?"

Lucas shook his head.

Refusing to leave it, Samantha said, "Because she's unconscious, maybe."

"Maybe."

She didn't have to touch him to know what lay behind the calm tone and expressionless face, but all she said was, "If Metcalf got the ransom note, do you think it's because he's Lindsay's boss — or her lover?"

Lucas was clearly unsurprised by her knowledge of that relationship. "The latter. He knew their secret, and he wanted us to know he knew. He's making it personal."

"Where's Metcalf now?"

"On his way out to the carnival."

Samantha came up out of her chair. "He's what? Jesus, Luke —"

"Calm down. Jay's with him; she'll see to it that nothing gets out of hand."

"He can't possibly believe anyone at the carnival had anything to do with this."

"The carnival is fairly close to the café where Lindsay's car was found. Someone could have seen something. He's justified in wanting to talk to people out there."

"Talk? You know damned well he wants

to do more than talk."

"I know he wanted to come in here and throw that picture in your face about ten minutes ago. Sit down, Sam."

She did, but said bitterly, "Oh, it's my fault again, is it? Because my prediction was only half right?"

"He's not entirely rational at the moment. And don't expect him to be anytime soon. You're an easy target, we both know that, and he badly wants to get his hands on whoever's responsible for this."

"It is not me." Her voice was flat.

"I know that. On some level, Wyatt knows it. Even the media outside knows it. Which is another complication, since they also knew you were in here to prove your innocence."

She sighed. "And what I've really proven is that I knew or strongly suspected there'd be another kidnapping."

"Business should be brisk at your booth tonight, assuming you mean to open up for readings."

Samantha leaned back in her chair, staring at him. "Yeah, genuine psychics are rare beasts. Isn't it dandy — and useful — publicity that I'll be validated in the media now."

"I didn't say —"

"You didn't have to."

Lucas drew a breath and let it out slowly. "People will be curious, that's all I meant."

"Yeah, right."

"Stop being so goddamned touchy and help me find Lindsay Graham before this bastard kills her."

"Are you asking?"

Getting to his feet, he said roughly, "Yes, I'm asking. Because I don't have a clue, Samantha. Is that what you want to hear? I don't even have a place to start. And I have no time for regrets, or explanations, or this little dance you and I always seem to do. I'm out of time because Lindsay is out of time; if we don't find her by tomorrow night, in all probability she'll be dead. So if you don't want to help me, at least try to help *her*."

"The sheriff," Samantha said, "is not going to like it."

"I'll deal with Wyatt."

She gazed up at him for a long moment, then shrugged. "Okay," she said, getting up. "Let's go."

Lindsay wasn't sure how much time had passed, but she was fuzzily aware that it had. Try as she might, the last thing she could remember was eating breakfast that

109

morning with Wyatt; everything after that was a blank.

She wasn't worried about it. In fact, she wasn't worried about anything, and had the suspicion that it was because she'd been drugged. This groping-through-the-fog sensation was one she recalled experiencing years before while being heavily dosed with Valium before a minor medical procedure.

Okay, so she was drugged; she knew that much.

She was lying on a hard, chilly surface, on her belly. She also seemed to have something dark loosely covering her head, a hood or something like that. And her wrists were taped together behind her.

An experimental twitch — all she could really manage — told her that her ankles were not bound, but she couldn't seem to make her muscles work well enough to roll over or try to free her hands. She wasn't even sure she could feel her hands.

Bound, hooded, drugged.

Oh, Christ, I've been kidnapped.

Her strongest emotion just then was sheer incredulity. Kidnapped? Her? Jeez, if he wanted ransom money, then he was sure as hell out of luck. She had part of her last paycheck in the bank, but beyond that —

Wait. Sam had said it wasn't about money. That it was all just a game, a broken, brilliant game — No. A man with a broken, brilliant *mind* wanted to play a game. A twisted game. With Lucas Jordan. To see who was smarter, faster. To see who was better. Like a chess game, Sam had said.

Which made Lindsay a pawn.

And she didn't have to grope through the fog for long to remember what had happened to virtually all the other pawns.

Dead.

"Oh, shit," she heard herself whisper.

She half expected someone — him — to reply to that, but even with her brain fogged she had a strong certainty that she was alone here. Wherever here was. Alone, bound, drugged.

Even through the muffling, quieting effects of the drugs, Lindsay began to feel the first faint twinges of anxiety and fear.

They went out the back way to avoid the media camped out front and encountered Deputy Glen Champion before they could leave the building.

He hesitated for an instant, looking at Samantha, then blurted, "Thank you. The dryer was — I had it checked out. The electrician said it was a fire waiting to happen. So thank you."

"My pleasure. Take care of that baby."

"I will." He sort of bobbed his head. "Thanks again."

Gazing after the deputy, Lucas said, "Well, you made a friend there. See something in the baby's future?"

"Yeah. She's going to be a teacher." Samantha led the way out of the building.

Lucas didn't say anything until they were in his rental car and safely out of the parking lot without drawing the attention of the media. Then, thoughtfully, he said, "Aside from Bishop and Miranda, you're the only seer I know of who can see that far ahead. The baby becomes a teacher in — what? — twenty-five years?"

"About that."

"And you saw her as a teacher."

"A good teacher. A special teacher. And her sort of teacher will be needed more than ever then." Samantha shrugged. "The bright moments of seeing something good I can help bring about are generally outnumbered by the dark moments I see tragedy or evil that I can't do a damned thing to change."

"Which is why you warned Champion."

"I warned him because it was the right

thing to do. Just like warning Carrie Vaughn when I thought she was going to be a victim, and Mitchell —"

Lucas shot her a quick look, then fixed his eyes on the road again. "You warned Callahan? You said you'd never seen him in the flesh."

"I said I *hadn't* seen him . . . before I had the vision about him."

"Splitting hairs," Lucas muttered.

"I can be very literal-minded, re-member? And, anyway, I didn't see him, I just talked to him." When Lucas didn't respond, Samantha said, "It was obvious Metcalf didn't take me seriously when I went to talk to him about a possible kidnapping, so I called Callahan and warned him to be careful. I doubt he took me seriously either, and it obviously made absolutely no difference, but I had to try."

Lucas shook his head slightly but didn't comment on that. Instead, he asked, "And what did you see that brought you and the carnival to Golden?"

"What makes you so sure Leo would change the carnival's normal route just because I asked him to?"

"Leo would go out and rob a bank if you asked him to. Setting up shop in a small but prosperous town when you asked

113

wouldn't have given him a moment's hesitation."

Samantha was silent.

"So? What did you see? You didn't know about the series of kidnappings before you got here, right?" He wasn't very surprised when she answered the last question rather than the first one.

"Not really. We'd heard rumors when we passed through the state last spring heading north that there'd been a couple of kidnappings. Unusual enough in this area that it was noticed and talked about. Heard a few more rumors over the summer as we traveled through Virginia, Maryland, New York, and Pennsylvania, but since we were never in the actual towns where people went missing, we never heard more than rumors."

"What did you see, Sam? What brought you here?" For several long minutes, she remained so silent that he thought she wasn't going to answer him. Then, finally, she did.

"I had a dream."

He frowned. "Your visions don't present themselves as dreams."

"They never had before."

"Then how can you be sure this dream was different?"

"Because you're here," she said flatly.

He was pulling the car into the parking lot of the café where Lindsay's car had been found, and didn't say anything until he had drawn off to the side and stopped near the yellow crime-scene tape surrounding the sheriff's department cruiser.

"You came to Golden because you knew I'd be here?"

Samantha got out of the car, waited until he did as well, then said coolly, "Don't flatter yourself. Your being here was just part of the package. An indication to me that my dream was a vision. I'm here because I have to be here. And that's all you get, Luke."

"Why?"

"Because, as Bishop was so fond of saying, some things have to happen just the way they happen. If you're meant to know more, you'll have a vision of your own. Otherwise . . . you'll find out when you get there."

He stood gazing at her, trying to decide if she was just being stubborn or honestly felt that by telling him about her vision she would negatively affect whatever she had seen. She was good at hiding her thoughts and feelings when she wanted to; he had never been able to read her, perhaps because he'd never known her to be afraid.

Of anything.

"Shall we?" she suggested, gesturing toward the cruiser.

The two deputies standing watch informed Lucas that the Crime Scene Unit had come and gone, apparently finding no forensic traces they felt would be helpful in either locating Lindsay or identifying her kidnapper.

"He's not going to make it easy for us," Samantha said. "He's not the type to give you points just for showing up."

The two of them ducked beneath the tape and approached the car.

Lucas said, "If you're right about this game —"

"I am. And you know I am. It feels right, doesn't it?"

Without replying to that, Lucas said, "What Jaylene said makes sense. He can't expect me to play his game until the rules are made clear."

"Not if he means to play fair, no."

"I think he'll play fair — even if by his own warped ideas of fair play. At least as long as he feels confident of coming out on top. But if I start . . . getting ahead on points, then I'd say his rule book will probably go right out the window."

"You're the profiler," Samantha said.

He eyed her. "You disagree?"

"I just think it would be a huge mistake to assume or infer anything about this one, at least until you know a lot more. He's different from anybody you've ever come up against." She hesitated, then added, "And I think that's part of the game, you know. To keep you guessing. To challenge your assumptions."

"What *aren't* you telling me?" Lucas demanded.

She looked to make sure the deputies were out of earshot, then said, "You were facing each other across a chessboard, Luke. Both masters. Both equal in ability. Don't you see what that means? As well as you understand the criminal mind, he understands yours. He's a profiler too."

Sheriff Metcalf eyed the dark-eyed, swarthy owner/manager of the Carnival After Dark and tried to keep a rein on his temper. "You're telling me not one of you saw anything at all?"

Leo Tedesco smiled apologetically. "I'm sorry, Sheriff, but we're a nighttime carnival, you must understand that. My people are generally up very late — and sleep very late. The maintenance crew was up early caring for the animals, of course, but they're housed on the back side of the fairground, far from the road. I can assure you that none of us saw your Detective Graham at any time this morning."

"You're speaking for them all? I don't think so. I want to talk to everybody."

Tedesco sent Jaylene a rather rueful look, having obviously decided that she possessed the cooler head of the two. "Agent Avery, Sheriff, I hope you both know we'll be more than happy to cooperate; I'm only trying to save you wasted time and energy. I understand time is a factor, and —"

"And just how do you understand that?" Metcalf demanded.

"Please, Sheriff, do you really believe anyone in Golden is talking about anything else? Plus we've had the media out here more than once, and from their questions and speculations it's obvious you're dealing with a serial kidnapper who's a bit anal about his timetable. He always demands the ransom be delivered by five o'clock on Friday afternoon. Which in this instance would be tomorrow afternoon. Correct?"

Metcalf glared at him.

Jaylene said mildly, "That's common knowledge, is it?"

Tedesco nodded. "A reporter I know from one of the Asheville newspapers followed a hunch and has already uncovered a few more kidnappings here in the East with the same . . . elements, let us say. And he was too excited to keep the discovery to himself. I'm guessing the six o'clock news today will be filled with lots of information you probably don't want to get out."

"Thanks for the warning," she said.

"Don't mention it." He smiled widely, displaying a gold tooth. "Honestly, Sheriff, Agent Avery, I'll do anything in my power to help. Especially now that Sam has to be off your suspect list."

"Who says she is?"

Tedesco looked at the sheriff, brows lifting. "Isn't she? She was in your own jail, Sheriff, when your detective was taken. And has dozens of witnesses to place her here when the first gentleman was kidnapped, aside from the fact that you've found absolutely no evidence linking her to the crime. Aside from her very obvious lack of motive and physical strength. Surely even you must admit she's a most unlikely suspect as a kidnapper."

Since it didn't look as though Metcalf was willing to admit any such thing, Jaylene said, "Mr. Tedesco, could you excuse us for a moment?"

Promptly, he nodded and turned away, saying, "I'll be in the office caravan, Agent. Sheriff."

Staring after him, the sheriff muttered, "Caravan. It's an RV that cost every penny of a hundred and fifty grand."

"And his home," Jaylene pointed out quietly. "Wyatt, we've checked out these people. You've checked them out. Police in about eight states have checked them out. They're decent, law-abiding citizens who run clean games and shows, treat their animals well, and educate their children. They've caused absolutely no trouble and have even been going to church in Golden since they've been here. Half your town would make better suspects than these people."

"Goddammit."

"You know it's the truth. And what Tedesco said was also the truth. We'll only waste time we don't have in concentrating our efforts here. Leave a few of your deputies to take statements if you feel you have to, but we need to move on. We won't find Lindsay here."

"And you're *absolutely* certain of that?" he demanded.

She held his gaze steadily. "Absolutely."

Metcalf looked away finally, his shoulders slumping. "Then we've got shit for leads, you know that too."

"We've got a little more than twenty-four hours to find something before the ransom is due. I'm telling you, we won't find anything here."

"Then where?" The desperation in his voice was clear, and he made no effort to hide or disguise it. "I don't know where to look, Jaylene. I don't know what to do."

"I'll tell you what you might have to do," she said, still quiet. "You might have to look past a few of your beliefs and limits and accept the undeniable fact that ordinary police work may not be able to help us here."

Grim, he said, "You're talking about Zarina."

"I'm talking about Samantha Burke."

"Same difference," he snorted.

Jaylene shook her head. "No, there is a difference, and that's what you've got to get into your head. Zarina is a carnival seer and mystic, who takes money to tell fortunes. It's how she makes her living, and it's mostly theater, drama. Give the customers what they expect. Offer them a show. She sits in a booth draped in exotic silks and satins and wears a ridiculous turban while she peers at palms and into her crystal ball. That's Zarina. But Samantha Burke is a genuine, gifted psychic."

"I don't believe in that shit."

"I'm not asking you to believe, Wyatt. I'm just asking you to accept the fact — the *fact* — that there are things beyond your and my understanding, things science will undoubtedly be able to explain one day. Accept the fact that Samantha Burke may well be one of those things. And accept the fact that she will be able to help us. If you let her try."

After a moment, he said, "You sound very sure of that."

"I am," she said. "Absolutely positive."

"Because she helped you and Luke before? Helped resolve another investigation?"

"Yes. And because I know Sam. She'll do everything in her power to help us."

"You, maybe. I doubt she'll be too eager to help me."

"She likes Lindsay. And besides that, she has a strong sense of responsibility. She'll help."

"How?"

"Let's go see," Jaylene said.

"You mean he's a natural profiler," Lucas said.

"I doubt he has a degree in psychology so, yeah, probably self-taught. God knows there are plenty of books on the subject now, never mind the Internet. Maybe he got interested in the art and science of profiling — beginning when you entered the picture."

"You're giving me too much credit for this."

"Or blame?" she murmured, then shook her head. "You didn't create this monster. If he wasn't playing this game with you, he'd be playing some other game in which people died. It's his thing. Killing. Playing with people's lives. But I'm willing to bet that if you ever get the chance to interview him, he'll tell you that he decided to play this particular game when he saw you on TV or read about you in the newspapers and realized that you were so good at finding people — and he was so good at losing them."

"Christ," Lucas said.

Samantha shrugged, then turned her head to study the cruiser Lindsay had driven. "It's just a theory, mind you. An uneducated shot in the dark."

"It was never about education," he said.

"I know. It was about a purple turban." Her mouth twisted a little, but she kept her gaze on the car. "It was about . . . credibility."

"We walk a fine line, Sam. Without credibility, we wouldn't be allowed to do this work. And it's important work. It's necessary work."

"I also know that."

"Then stop blaming Bishop for making the decision he had to make."

"I don't blame Bishop. I never blamed him." She took a step closer to the car, adding almost absently, "I blame you."

"What? Sam —"

"You took the easy way out, Luke. You let Bishop clean up the mess you left behind. And you moved on, telling yourself it was all for the best."

"That isn't true."

"No?" She turned her head and looked at him. "My mistake."

"Sam —"

"Never mind, Luke. It hardly matters now, does it?" She returned her attention to the police cruiser. "This is the car Lindsay usually drove, right?"

Lucas wanted to refuse the change of subject, but the ticking clock in his head as well as the proximity of the deputies guarding the car told him this wasn't the time or the place. So he merely said,

"Yeah, it was her assigned car."

Samantha circled the car warily, hoping her reluctance didn't show but very afraid Luke saw it. Chances were, she wouldn't get anything when she touched the car, sat in it; most of the time she went through life touching things without feeling anything except the physical sensation of them, just like any normal person.

Most of the time.

But emotionally charged situations, she had learned, tended to increase the frequency and intensity of her visions. Luke would say that the strong emotions altered the electromagnetic fields around them, bringing those fields and her own brain into sync — and opening the door for the visions.

She wasn't much interested in the science, established or speculative, behind her abilities. She never had been. Understanding how and why they worked didn't change the fact of them. All she knew for certain was that the visions that had so affected and shaped her life were real and painful, always a burden she couldn't escape, and sometimes terrifying.

She wondered if Luke even realized that.

"We have no leads, Sam," he said, watching her. "No evidence. No hint of who this bastard is or where he might be holding Lindsay. We need something. Anything. Just a place to start."

Stalling, she said, "You still don't feel anything?"

"No. Either I can't connect with her or else she's drugged or unconscious."

"Or already dead."

His jaw tightened. "Unless he's changed his M.O., she isn't dead. He always waits for the ransom to be delivered."

"So far."

"Yeah. So far. No matter what, unless I can get closer to her I may not feel anything even if she does."

"You mean closer physically?"

"Distance seems to make a difference. So do other things. How well I know them or can get to know them. Some idea of how they react to stress and trauma. Even a direction, an area. I need something to focus on, Sam."

"And if I can't give you that?"

"I don't believe traditional police work will get us close to Lindsay by tomorrow afternoon."

"But no pressure?"

For the first time, he smiled, crooked though it was. "Sorry. I never was much good at sugarcoating the truth."

"Yeah. I remember."

Lucas decided not to comment on that. "Please. See if you can get anything from the car."

Mentally bracing herself, for all the good it wouldn't do, Samantha reached out for the driver's side door handle. She felt something the instant she touched it, a familiar sort of inner quiver that was impossible to describe, but didn't pause; she opened the door and slid behind the wheel.

Samantha had been told more than once that her visions were unnerving for onlookers. Not because they saw what she saw, of course, but because they saw *her*.

Apparently, it was quite a show.

All she saw, however, was the black curtain that swept over her, always the first sign. Blackness, thick as tar. Then the abrupt, muffling silence. She felt the wheel beneath her hands as she gripped it, then even the sense of touch was gone.

The chilling sensation that enveloped her was one Samantha had often thought of as limbo. She was suspended, weightless and even formless, in some void that felt emptier than anything most people could imagine.

Even she could never remember just how

horribly empty it felt until she was in it.

And the only way out when a vision pulled her in this deep was to wait, grimly, for the glimpse into another life, another time, another place. Wait while her brain tuned in the right frequency and the sounds and images began playing before her mind's eye like some strange movie.

Flickering images at first. Echoing sounds and voices. Everything distorted until it, finally, snapped into place.

. . . *understand.*

. . . *you understand.*

. . . *personal, you understand.*

"It's nothing personal, you understand."

Lindsay was still a bit groggy from the drugs, but she knew a lie when she heard one. "It's very personal," she murmured, instinctively stalling for time even as she tried to hear something in that cool, conversational voice that might help her to understand her captor.

A chink in his armor, that's all she asked for. A chink she could work on, widen. A vulnerability she could exploit.

"Not at all. At least, not where you're concerned."

"I'm a pawn," she said, regretting it the instant the words were out of her mouth.

"A pawn?" He sounded interested. "A chess game. I wonder who put that image into your head. Lucas?"

Lindsay was silent. She was in a chair now, her wrists still bound and the bag over her head keeping her in darkness. Her captor was somewhere behind her.

"So he's at least figured out it's a game, has he?"

"You know it's only a matter of time before you're caught." She kept her voice steady, concentrated hard to damp down the terror crawling deep inside her, so she could think clearly enough not to give away any knowledge that might help her captor. "Especially now. Kidnappers who stick around too long paint themselves in neon."

"Oh, I imagine I'm safe enough for the time being." His tone became relaxed, almost chatty. "I have no connection to Golden, you see. No connection to any of you."

"So we're just random victims, huh?"

"Definitely not. No, you were chosen with care, all of you. Each of my guests has been an important element of the game."

"I'm sure that was a great comfort to them."

He laughed. Actually laughed in amusement.

And it didn't give Lindsay even a tinge of hope.

"It's good that you have a sense of humor," he told her. "Humor is a great help in getting through life."

"And through death?"

"You'll find out before I will," he said cheerfully.

5

Santa Fe, New Mexico

"A place this beautiful," Special Agent Tony Harte said, "should not have a murderess living here."

"You won't get an argument," Bishop said.

"How sure are we that she *is* living here?"

"Reasonably. The police chief is getting the warrant now."

"So we'll be closing up shop?"

"If we're right about her. And if there are no problems in arresting her."

"Should I pack?"

"Did you even unpack?"

"Some of us aren't as good at living out of a suitcase as you are," Tony pointed out.

"Wait until we get word from the chief." Bishop looked up from his computer with a slight frown. "What?"

"Now, see, that isn't supposed to happen. You're a touch telepath, not an open telepath."

"And your face is an open book, never

mind that overly casual tone. What's up?"

Tony straddled a chair and faced Bishop across the makeshift conference table in their hotel room. "Nothing good. I just got a tip from a pal back East. He's a journalist. A friend of his is covering the story in North Carolina."

Bishop didn't have to ask which story. "And?"

"The news of a serial kidnapper is about to break."

"Shit."

"It gets worse, boss."

"What else?"

"Samantha Burke."

After a moment, Bishop leaned back in his chair and sighed. "Luke didn't mention her when he reported in yesterday."

"Probably not so surprising."

"No. Not so much."

"Well, what he should have told you is that it seems the sheriff there got all nasty and suspicious of her, so she voluntarily put herself under house arrest in his jail to prove she wasn't a kidnapper."

"Thus alerting the media to the fact that another kidnapping was expected."

"Yep. And confirming that prediction when Detective Graham was taken earlier today." Tony frowned. "So Samantha knew the guy would hit again, and there in Golden. He's been on the move all these months, and now he's staying put? Why?"

Bishop shook his head, frowning.

Tony eyed him, then said, "My pal says the bit about a carnival psychic and her apparently accurate prediction is too good to pass up. It's only a matter of time before images of Zarina in her turban appear on the six o'clock news."

"Naturally. Aside from being colorful, there's also the tempting evidence that future events can be predicted. A lot of people want to believe that."

"Speaking of which, have Luke and Jay confided in the sheriff?"

Shaking his head again, Bishop replied, "They felt he wouldn't be open to the idea of psychic investigators."

"So what happens if Luke's able to connect to the victim? It's not exactly something that would go unnoticed."

"They'll have to wing it. Tell the sheriff only as much as he seems able to accept. He may be more open to it as time goes on. Samantha's prediction of another kidnapping may have at least set the stage."

"Looking for the positive?"

"What choice do I have?"

A little surprised, Tony said, "I seem to

recall that the last time Samantha entered the picture, you were a lot more concerned with the credibility issue."

"She's not connected with the unit," Bishop pointed out.

"She wasn't then. Or is there something I don't know about that?"

"There were . . . possibilities then. That she might join the unit."

"Why didn't she? I mean, it's not as if we have too many seers on the payroll — and if I remember correctly, she's an exceptionally powerful one."

Bishop nodded, but said, "We hadn't built much of a reputation or success record at that point. And we had enemies who would have been quite pleased if the SCU had failed in any sense of the word. The unit was too new then to take the risk of accepting a carnival mystic."

"One mention of a carnival seer on the six o'clock news and we'd be finished?"

"Something like that."

"And now?"

"And now . . . the situation may have changed, at least as far as the unit's concerned. Maybe we could stand up to that purple turban now. But it may be a moot point where Samantha is concerned."

"Because she's bitter?"

Bishop shrugged. "It could have been better handled."

"What about her and Luke?"

"What about them?"

"Hey, remember who you're talking to, boss? I may not read minds very well, but I'm dandy at picking up emotional vibes — and there were plenty between those two."

"You'd have to ask them about that."

Wryly, Tony said, "The only thing that comforts me about a response like that one is the knowledge that you probably guard my secrets as well as you do everyone else's."

Bishop smiled faintly. "We still have work to do here, Tony."

"So I should shut up and get to it?"

"If you don't mind."

"Not at all," Tony said politely, getting to his feet. Then he paused. "We just wait and see what happens in North Carolina, then?"

"It's Luke's case. He and Jaylene are calling the shots, and neither of them has asked for help."

"Do you expect them to?"

"No. Not unless . . ."

"Unless?"

"Unless things get a lot worse."

"You have something specific in mind?"

"No."

Tony sighed as he turned away. "You're a lousy liar, boss." But he didn't ask Bishop to explain what he knew or didn't know. Because it would have been useless, and because Tony wasn't at all sure he wanted to know what the worst might be.

Samantha was aware of being in a vision, as she was always aware, but this one was different. Try as she might, she couldn't turn her head and look around the room in which Lindsay Graham was held captive. It was as though she were a camera fixed on Lindsay's seated, hooded self, on the spotlight illumination that cast everything around the captive woman into deep shadow.

Sam could hear his voice, hear Lindsay's. Hear, somewhere, a faucet dripping. The hum of the fluorescent lights. And she knew what Lindsay was thinking, feeling.

Which was new and more than a little unsettling.

So was the deep cold she felt, a chill so intense it was as if she'd been dropped into a freezer. The sensation was so powerful and her response so visceral that she wondered how Lindsay and her captor couldn't

136

hear her teeth chattering.

"If I'm going to die," Lindsay was saying steadily, "then why not get it over with?"

"I don't have the ransom yet, of course. The good sheriff could demand to see proof of you alive before he pays up."

Samantha knew that Lindsay was thinking about the investigators' conclusion that this wasn't about money, and she felt immensely relieved when the detective didn't mention that.

Instead, Lindsay said, "Okay, then why do I have to die? Why did any of your victims have to die? The ransom was always paid. I certainly can't identify you, and if a cop can't it's not likely any of the others could have."

"Yes, I know."

"You just like killing, is that it?"

"Ah, Lindsay, you just don't get it. I don't kill —"

Samantha opened her eyes with a gasp, so disoriented that for a long moment she had no idea what had happened. Then she realized she was looking at Lindsay's cruiser, the driver's door open, from a distance of several feet. And from ground level.

"What the hell?" she murmured huskily.

"Take it easy," Lucas said. "Don't try to

move for a minute."

Ignoring that advice, Samantha turned her head to look up at him, realizing only then that she was sitting on the pavement and that he, kneeling half behind her, was supporting her. Baffled, she looked down to see that he was holding both her hands, his palms covering hers.

"How did I get out of the car?" It was the only specific thing she could think of to ask.

"I pulled you out."

"How long was I —"

"Forty-two minutes," he told her.

"What?" She realized she was stiff, cold. "It can't have been that long."

"It was."

She frowned down at their hands, vaguely aware that her thoughts were scattered, that she wasn't quite back yet. "Why are you holding my hands like that?"

He released one of her hands, and she found herself staring at a ragged white line across her palm. "What the hell is that?"

"It's called frostnip," he said, covering her hand again with his own warm one. "The first stage of frostbite."

"What?" Was that the only word she knew? "It must be eighty-five degrees out here."

"Nearly ninety," Sheriff Metcalf said.

Samantha jerked her head around in the other direction to see the sheriff and Jaylene standing nearby. He had his arms folded across his chest and looked both skeptical and suspicious. Jaylene was, as usual, serene.

"Hi," Samantha said. "Almost ninety?"

He nodded.

"Then how the hell do I have the beginning of frostbite?"

"You don't know?" he demanded sardonically.

"I'm cold, but —"

"You were holding the steering wheel," Lucas said. "The frostnip is exactly where it would have been if the wheel had been frozen."

She looked back up at him, then swore under her breath and struggled to sit upright without his help. He let her go without protest but remained kneeling where he was as she twisted around so she could see all three of them.

Flexing her fingers, she realized that the white streaks across her palms were numb.

"Tuck your hands under your arms," Lucas advised. "You have to warm the area."

Samantha badly wanted to get up off the

ground and stand on her own two feet but had a feeling that if she tried that too soon, she'd only find herself leaning heavily on Lucas for support. So she crossed her arms over her breasts and tucked her hands underneath to help warm them.

"It doesn't make sense," she told him, trying to gather her scattered thoughts. "It wasn't cold there. Lindsay wasn't cold. So why would I —"

"Lindsay?" Metcalf took a step toward her, then brought himself up short.

Perfectly aware that while he was eager to hear about Lindsay he was unlikely to believe what Samantha told him, she said, "She's okay, at least for now. Tied to a chair and wearing some kind of hood over her head, but okay. She was even talking to him. Trying to find a weakness she could use."

"Sounds like her," Metcalf said, again almost involuntarily.

"Did you see or hear anything helpful?" Jaylene asked.

"I don't think so. There was a kind of spotlight over the chair so the rest of the room was in shadow. I never saw him, and his voice was so . . . bland . . . I doubt I'd recognize it if he spoke to me right now."

"Did you get a sense of the place?" Lucas asked.

Samantha tried hard to concentrate, to remember. "Not really. The hum of the lights, a faucet dripping, the sort of deadened echo you get in an underground room with a lot of hard surfaces."

"Underground?"

"I think so. It felt that way."

"You didn't see any windows?"

"No. Nothing reflective. Just that light shining down on her, and the rest of the room in shadows."

"What else?"

"She was asking him why he killed his victims when they couldn't identify him. He started to answer her, saying she didn't understand, that he didn't kill — something. But I never heard the end of what he was saying, I guess because you pulled me out."

His tone more one of explanation than of excuse, Lucas said, "You were white as a sheet and shivering, and you had a death grip on that steering wheel. It didn't look like a normal vision to me."

Metcalf snorted. "Normal vision?"

Samantha ignored him, saying to Lucas, "It didn't feel like a normal one. I couldn't seem to move, to look anywhere else but at Lindsay. That's never happened before."

Lucas nodded, but instead of commenting got to his feet and helped her up. "We still need a place to start. If you didn't see or hear anything helpful —"

Remembering, Samantha said, "He told Lindsay he didn't have any connection to this town, that it was one reason he felt safe in sticking around. But he has to be living somewhere. And there must be a place he kept Callahan and where he has Lindsay now. If I had to guess, I'd say you're looking for at least two different places. Where he lives, and where he keeps them."

"Somewhere private," Lucas said. "Where he can hold his victims without too much fear of discovery."

Jaylene said, "Sounds like a place to start."

Still looking at Lucas, Samantha said, "That's what you asked for. And it's all I can do. I don't see any reason for me to return to the sheriff's department. So, if you wouldn't mind dropping me back at the carnival before you get started with your search, I'd appreciate it."

Metcalf said, "To get ready for tonight's show, I suppose."

"That is how I make my living."

"Cheating people. Lying to them."

Samantha sighed. "Sheriff, I'm trying

hard to make allowances for someone who's ignorant of what he's talking about and worried half out of his mind because someone he cares about is missing. But right now, I'm cold, I'm tired, my hands are beginning to hurt, and I really don't give a shit what you think. So why don't you concentrate on doing your job and finding Lindsay and just leave me the hell alone."

Metcalf turned on his heel and stalked back toward his cruiser.

"Way to get local law enforcement on your side," Jaylene murmured.

"I don't care if he's on my side."

Lucas was eyeing her thoughtfully. "You usually don't go out of your way to antagonize them, though."

"Usually? There's no usually, Luke, at least not that you know. It's been more than three years since you were any part of my life. Things change. People change. Now, *if* you wouldn't mind, I'd like to get back to the carnival."

"You should see a doctor about your hands."

"Ellis is still an LPN, and I'll see her."

Jaylene said, "I guess one of us can collect your stuff back at the station and drop it off at your motel first chance we get."

"That'll be fine."

Silently, Lucas gestured toward his rental, and all three went to the car. Samantha got in the back and was silent, staring out the window, all the way to the fairgrounds. Once there, she merely said, "Thanks for the ride," and got out before either of them could say anything.

Watching the other woman walk away, Jaylene said, "I think I should be the one to gather up Sam's stuff."

"You think you'll pick up something?"

"I think she's acting strangely. And I think you think the same thing."

"Maybe. She's right, though — it's been years. Maybe neither one of us knows Samantha at all now."

"And maybe there's something specific she doesn't want us to know."

Lucas frowned. "Her whole attitude seemed to change once she had that vision. You think she saw something she didn't tell us about?"

"I think I want to touch her belongings and see if I can pick up anything. And I think we've got some long, hard hours ahead of us trying to find Lindsay."

"Yeah." With an effort, Lucas pushed Samantha out of his mind and turned the car back toward town.

Leo spotted Samantha and met her halfway up the mostly deserted midway. "Hey."

"Hey. Did the sheriff arrest anybody, or was Jay able to stop him?"

"Well, between us we managed to convince him he was wasting valuable time here."

"That must have been fun."

"The high point of my day." Leo studied her and said more seriously, "My guess is that your day was even worse."

"I'll have to tell you about it sometime. At the moment, though, I need to see Ellis. Is she around?"

"Yeah, in her caravan. You sick?"

Samantha showed him her palms. "Just a bit dented."

"How the hell'd you do that?"

"Long story. Leo, I want to open my booth tonight."

Both his bushy eyebrows lifted. "You sure? I mean, we've had tons of interest, even with your poster not out on the marquee, but —"

"Put it out, please. My hours tonight will be from seven until. I'll see as many as I can."

"And when the reporters show up asking to speak to you?"

Her smile was wry. "Tell 'em to buy a ticket like everybody else."

"I'll love the publicity," he said frankly, "but are you sure, Sam? What's good for the carnival isn't necessarily good for you, we both know that."

"I'll be fine."

"You look tired already," he pointed out. "After three or four hours of readings, you'll be half dead."

"As long as I'm half alive." Samantha shrugged. "Don't worry about me, Leo. Just pass the word that my booth will be open tonight, please. I'll see you later."

"Hey, try to take a nap or something before tonight, will you?"

"I will," Samantha lied. She continued on past Leo, heading for the line of RVs parked off to one side of the midway and colorful collection of booths, rides, and tents. She knocked on the door of one RV whose protective awning was hung with multiple wind chimes and whirligigs and, when she received a response, went inside.

"How was the voluntary jail time?" Ellis Langford was at least sixty-five but looked twenty years younger, an improbable red-head with a still–head-turning figure. And she dressed to turn heads.

"Bearable," Samantha replied with a shrug.

"Even with Luke Jordan there?"

"Him being there didn't change a thing."

"Don't tell me what you think I want to hear, Sam, tell me the truth."

Samantha grimaced. "Okay, then. It was hell. That's the truth. Half the time I wanted to scream and throw things at him, and the other half . . ."

"You wanted to find the nearest bed?"

Without replying to that, Samantha thrust out her hands, palms up. "I'm told this is frostnip. What should I do about it?"

Ellis studied her hands, brows rising. "Is the feeling coming back?"

"A bit. Tingling. Sort of an ache."

Ellis went into the kitchen area of her RV and filled a large pot with warm water. Then she returned to the living area and instructed Samantha to sit down and immerse her hands in the water.

Sitting obediently with warm water up to her wrists, Samantha said, "How long do I have to do this?"

"Do you have somewhere else to be?"

"Not immediately. But I want to get my booth ready to open."

Ellis sat down across from Samantha

and picked up her knitting. What she was knitting looked rather like a tulip-shaped vase. Samantha didn't ask what it was supposed to be; Ellis was famous for presenting friends with odd knitted things, and Sam already had quite a collection of tea cozies, caps, paperback dustcovers, and various other colorful accessories.

"So you'll be reading tonight?"

"I thought I would."

Needles clicking, her hazel eyes fixed on Samantha, Ellis said, "You think he's coming back, don't you?"

"Maybe you should be the one doing the readings."

"No, I don't have your gift for reading strangers. I read people I know. And I know you. Why do you think he'll come back here, Sam?"

"Because he likes carnivals well enough to have been here at least twice; much as I love this place, one visit usually satisfies anybody over the age of twelve." With a shrug, she added, "And because he doesn't know about me yet."

"I don't suppose you've mentioned that to Luke."

"It didn't come up."

Ellis shook her head slightly. "Sam, we've had reporters nosing around here the last couple of days. Leo took down your posters, but even so a few photographers got pictures. What if this maniac sees you on the six o'clock news? He'll definitely know about you then."

"I don't think he watches the news. I think he watches Luke."

"Willing to bet your life on that?"

Samantha shrugged again. "The life of a cop I happen to like can be measured now in hours. If Lindsay isn't found by late tomorrow afternoon, she'll be found dead. The other cops are doing their thing. Luke is doing his, or trying to. The only thing I can do is what I can do. Open my booth and do readings, and hope he shows up."

"For a reading? Would he be that reckless?"

"Depends. He might be curious, the way most people are. If I'm for real. If I can sense what he's up to."

"And if you can?"

"Then I'll do my damnedest not to let him know I know while I memorize his face and try to gather all the information I can from him."

"Dangerous."

"Not if I keep my wits about me."

"Even if. And do you really believe he'd

leave someone he kidnapped alone while he visits a carnival?"

"Yes." With a frown, Samantha added, "I don't know why I believe that, but I do. If Luke hadn't pulled me out of that car, I might have seen more, heard more, picked up something to tell me who the bastard is."

Reading between the lines — something she was good at — Ellis said, "Ah. So the frostnip is from the steering wheel?"

"Yeah."

"And since Luke pulled you out of the car —"

"I won't pick up anything by touching it a second time, at least not for a while. Somebody explained it to me once. Something about tapping into and releasing electromagnetic energy. It's like static. Touch something metallic once, and you get shocked; touch it again right away and you don't, because the energy's already been discharged. You have to walk around on the carpet in your socks and let the static build up again." She frowned. "Or something like that."

"You don't really care how it works, do you?"

"Not so much. It is what it is."

"Mmm. But you did pick up enough to

believe the kidnapper likes carnivals."

Samantha looked down at her hands, absently moving them in the water. "I think he likes games. And right now, we're the only other game in Golden."

"The other one being Catch Me if You Can?"

"I don't think it's even that. I think it's I'm Smarter than You Are."

"Than who is?"

"Luke."

"I hope you told him that, at least."

"I did. He wasn't happy."

"I can imagine. Word is, this kidnapper has more than a dozen victims to his credit, all but one of them dead. If it's all just been a game . . ."

"Nightmarish, yeah."

"Certainly not easy to live with. Even if it was beyond your control."

Samantha frowned and lifted her hands out of the water. "The water's cooling. And my hands are tingling and itching like crazy."

Ellis put her knitting aside and went to refill the pot with fresh warm water, saying, "Once more, and then you should be okay. Your hands'll probably tingle and itch for a while, though."

Sighing, Samantha plunged her hands

back into warm water. "You don't seem surprised that I got frostnipped by a vision," she commented.

"I've seen enough over the years to know that your visions are pretty damned real. So, no, not very surprised. But what was cold in the vision? Where she's being kept?"

"No. She wasn't cold at all. But almost the instant the vision snapped into focus, I was freezing."

"Why, do you think?"

"I don't know."

"The universe trying to tell you something, maybe?"

"Well, he's not holding her at the North Pole, I know that much."

"Stop being so literal-minded."

"I'm always literal-minded, you know that. It comes from a lack of imagination."

"You do *not* lack imagination. You just have a practical streak about a yard wide, that's all."

Samantha shrugged. "Whatever."

"Think about it, Sam. If she wasn't in a cold place, then what caused the frostnip? When you think of that sort of bone-deep cold, what else do you think of?"

"I don't know. Something empty. Bottomless. Something dark." She paused, then added reluctantly, "Death. It felt like death."

Lucas would have been the first to admit that what they were doing was searching for a very fine needle in a huge haystack, but that didn't stop him from trying to find it.

Her.

All afternoon, as they sifted through property records and rental agreements supplied by local realtors, he tried to reach out mentally and emotionally, to connect with Lindsay.

Nothing.

"I knew she had a lot of self-control," he told Jaylene as the late afternoon grew gloomy and thunder rumbled in the mountains all around them. "She's the type who won't want to show any fear at all. Which means that as long as she's hiding it from him, she's also hiding it from me."

Jaylene, knowing what was on his mind without any need of psychic ability, said, "There's no way we could have known she'd be taken, Luke."

"Still. If we'd told Wyatt and Lindsay about our abilities — mine, at least — then maybe she'd be trying to reach out to me instead of damping down the fear."

"Maybe. And maybe not. Chances are they'd never have believed us anyway. Wyatt's still convinced Sam makes a living conning people."

"The badge makes a difference. You know that." His mouth twisted. "Credibility."

"I say it was the right call at the time."

"We'll never know, will we?"

"Look, we're making some progress here." Jaylene tapped the legal pad on the table in front of her. "The list of likely properties is fairly long, but at least it's manageable. The question is, can we cover them all before tomorrow afternoon? And how do we persuade Wyatt that having his people storm these places is not the best way to go?"

"He won't do anything to further endanger Lindsay."

"No, I won't," Metcalf said as he came into the room. He looked a bit haggard, but calm. "What is it you don't want me to do?"

"Storm these places," Lucas replied readily. "They need to be checked out, one at a time, but quietly, Wyatt. If we get lucky and find him, we can't forget he has a hostage he could use to hold us off for a long time. We have to be careful, approach

154

every area with all possible caution so he isn't alerted. That means we can't send your deputies searching on their own unless you're very, very sure they know what they're doing and will follow their orders to the letter."

The sheriff considered, then said, "I have, maybe, half a dozen people I'm absolutely sure of. They have the training and experience to do this right, and none of them will panic or jump the gun. They'll follow orders."

"We've got a lengthy list of possibilities," Lucas told him. "All of them remote properties with plenty of privacy."

"Because Zarina says that's where he'll be."

"Because common sense says she's right. He might have taken advantage of abandoned property somewhere, but it would be risking someone showing up and discovering him, and I don't believe he'd do that. If he doesn't have a connection to Golden — and right now, that's all we've got to narrow the search — then chances are good that he leased, rented, or purchased property sometime before Mitchell Callahan was kidnapped and since the victim just before him, two months ago in Georgia."

Jaylene murmured, "Unless he's been planning this a lot longer than we know and got the property anything up to a couple of years ago."

"Oh, hell, don't even suggest that," Lucas said, so immediately that it was obvious he'd been thinking along similar lines. "We have to go with the most likely possibility, and the most likely is that he got the property fairly recently, over the summer."

"We move a lot of property in the summer," Metcalf noted.

"Which is why the list isn't a short one."

Jaylene checked her watch, then listened to yet another rumble of thunder. "It won't be easy if the weather's against us, but I say we get started whether it storms or not. We don't have much daylight left either way — but I don't think we should wait for dawn."

The sheriff had brought in a large county map, which Lucas unrolled on the conference table, and all three bent over it. Within forty-five minutes, they had all the properties on their list marked in red on the map.

"All over Clayton County," Metcalf said with a sigh. "And some of these places are remote as hell. Even with all the luck we can muster, we'll be hard-pressed to check out every location by five o'clock to-morrow."

"Then we'd better get to it," Jaylene suggested. "Wyatt, if you want to call in the deputies you trust to help, Luke and I will start dividing up the list. Three teams, I think?"

He nodded and left the conference room.

Jaylene watched her partner as he frowned down at the map. "Getting anything?"

His eyes moved restlessly from red mark to red mark, and half under his breath he murmured, "Come on, Lindsay, talk to me."

The words were no sooner out of his mouth than Jaylene saw him go pale and suck in a sudden breath, his eyes taking on a curiously flat shine. It was something with which she was familiar, but it never failed to send a little chill down her spine.

"Luke?"

Still gazing at the map, he said slowly, "It's gone now. But for just an instant I think I connected. It was like . . . she felt a jolt of absolute, wordless terror."

"Where?" Jaylene asked.

"Here." He indicated a handsbreadth

area in the western part of the county. "Somewhere here."

The area covered at least twenty square miles of the roughest terrain in the county and held nearly a dozen of their red marks.

"Okay," Jaylene said. "That's where you and I start looking."

6

"I just want to know if he's going to ask me to the homecoming dance." Her voice was so nervous it wobbled, but it was determined as well, and her blue eyes were fixed on Samantha's face with desperate intensity.

Samantha tried to remember what it felt like to be sixteen and so desperate about so many things, but even so she knew she had nothing in common with this pretty teenage girl or her ordinary life. There had been no homecoming dance for Samantha, no high-school rituals or worries about the right dress or who the football team's star quarterback would ask out on Friday night.

At sixteen, Samantha's worries had included putting in long hours to earn enough money so she didn't starve, preferably without selling her body or soul in the process.

But she felt no resentment toward this girl, and her voice — lower and more formal than her usual speaking voice but with no fake accent — remained calm and soothing. "Then that is what I will tell you.

Concentrate on this boy, close your eyes, and picture his face. And when you are sure you have his image in your mind, give me your hand."

She had been using her crystal ball earlier in the evening, but for some reason tonight it had bothered her eyes to stare into it, so she had abandoned that prop for the less dramatic but more direct and often more accurate palm reading.

The teenager sat with eyes closed and pretty face screwed into fierce concentration for a moment, then opened her eyes and thrust out her right hand.

Samantha held it gently in both of hers, bending forward over it to seemingly peer intently at the lines crisscrossing the palm. She traced the lifeline with a light finger, more for effect than because she was "reading" the actual line.

She knew a bit more about palmistry than the average person — but only a bit more.

Her own eyes half closed, she was seeing something far different from the girl's hand. "I see the boy in your mind," she murmured. "He is wearing a uniform. Baseball, not football. He is a pitcher."

The girl gasped audibly.

Samantha tilted her head to one side,

and added, "He will ask you out, Megan, but not to the homecoming dance. Another boy will ask you to the homecoming dance."

"Oh, no!"

"You will not be disappointed, I promise you. This is the boy you are meant to be with at this time in your life."

"When?" Megan whispered. "When will he ask me?"

Samantha knew the exact day but also knew how to make her revelation sound more mysterious and dramatic. "On the next full moon," she said. She glanced up in time to see a baffled look cross the girl's face and was tempted to dryly advise her to look at a calendar. Or to look up at the sky, since the late-afternoon storms had passed and a bright nearly full moon shone hugely.

Samantha couldn't remember if it was a harvest moon or a hunter's moon, though the latter struck her as either an apt coincidence or a deliberate sense of timing by the kidnapper.

"Oh, Madam Zarina, thank you!"

As Samantha released the girl's hand, she couldn't help but add, "Choose the blue dress. Not the green one."

Again, Megan gasped, but before she

could say anything, Ellis appeared from the draperies behind Samantha and swept the girl out of the booth.

Samantha rubbed her temples briefly and drew a breath, trying to keep focused. Then Ellis returned, alone.

"What, am I done?" Samantha demanded.

"Are you kidding? You've got at least a dozen people waiting in line, and Leo says another dozen tickets have been sold so far tonight."

"Well, then?"

"I told them you were taking a ten-minute break. Word's spreading about your accuracy tonight, so nobody's complaining." Ellis vanished behind the draperies again, then returned with a big mug. "I've brought you some tea."

She had known Ellis too long to waste time arguing, so Samantha merely accepted the tea and sipped it. "Sweet. I'm not in shock, you know."

"No, but you need fuel and I know damned well you won't eat anything until you're done tonight. You've been at this two hours nonstop, and it doesn't take another psychic to feel your energy draining away."

"I'm a little tired. It'll pass."

Sitting down in the client chair, Ellis said, "Judging by the reactions — yours as well as theirs — I'm guessing you've been getting hits all night. Psychic hits, I mean. Yes?"

"Yeah. It's sort of weird, really. Not full-blown visions, just these flashes of images. And knowledge. I've never been so . . . on . . . before."

"Why, do you think?"

"Dunno. That weird vision earlier today might have changed something. Maybe left me more plugged in than usual, for however long it lasts."

"You're not doing any cold reading at all?"

Samantha shook her head. It was something she had done in the past and would undoubtedly do in the future — and it was the sort of thing that made cops like Sheriff Metcalf suspicious. Because a really good "seer" could read the body language and "tells" — physical tics and gestures, usually unconscious — of her clients, weaving a subtle pattern of guesswork and half-truths into something that appeared to be genuine psychic ability.

Or magic.

She wasn't particularly proud of that but, as Ellis had noted, Samantha had a highly practical nature and she did what she had to do in order to make her way in the world. The sign outside her booth clearly stated that she read *for entertainment purposes only,* and she weighed her clients carefully before offering them anything more than a show, wary of those who were too desperate or too gullible.

Usually they were like young Megan, anxious to know about their love lives, or whether a promotion at work was forth-coming, or where they could find the strongbox full of cash supposedly buried somewhere in the backyard by Great-Uncle George.

But sometimes . . . sometimes their faces were pale and beaded with desperate sweat, and their eyes were glazed, and their voices were so strained it was like listening to an animal in pain. Those were the ones Samantha did her best to recognize early, before already-intense emotions got out of control.

Half a lifetime of experience helped; she had more than once given a deliberately vague reading in order to avoid either up-setting or encouraging a client in a fragile mental state.

"Then everything you've told the clients tonight has been the truth?" Ellis demanded.

"Pretty much. It's been harmless, mostly. Though I did see a couple of things I didn't think they could handle, so I kept them to myself."

"Tragedies?"

"Yeah. I saw one lady die in a car accident about six months from now — and knew there was nothing I could tell her to change the outcome." She shivered and took another swallow of the hot, sweet tea. "You want to tell them to go hug their kids or make peace with their mothers, or make that list of the ten things they want to do before they die and damned well do them now. But you know — *I* know — they'd only fall apart if they believed me at all, and that would just make the rest of their lives miserable. So I don't tell them. I just look at them . . . and hear the clock ticking off the time they have left. Jesus, it's creepy knowing stuff like that."

"I guess it would be. Do you believe in fate, Sam? You've never said."

"I believe some things have to happen just the way they happen. So, yeah, I guess I do. Up to a point."

"Free will?"

Samantha smiled wryly. "That is the point. I wouldn't like to think my every move and decision had been mapped out

165

before I was born. But I do believe the universe puts us in a position to make decisions and choices that will determine the next fork in the path. Change your decision — and you find yourself on a different path."

"Is that why we're here in Golden right now?"

Samantha drank more of the tea, frowning.

"Or you could just tell me to mind my own business."

"It is your business. You're here too."

Ellis smiled faintly. "So . . . are we here because of your path, or Luke's?"

With a slight grimace, Samantha replied, "Six of one and half a dozen of the other."

"So you're both on the same path?"

"No. Our paths just . . . intersected. The way they did once before. And I'd really like to be able to move on this time without feeling like I've . . . dropped acid and been half eaten by a lion."

Both Ellis's brows shot up. "Lovely imagery. Dropped acid? That's more my generation than yours."

Samantha frowned. "Maybe I picked it up from you. But, anyway, the gist stands. When it was over, I felt like I'd been out of my mind and got mauled because of it. By something with teeth and claws."

"I wouldn't have thought Luke was that ferocious."

"You weren't close to him."

"Were you?"

After a moment of silence, Samantha drained her mug and handed it back to Ellis. "I think my break is over. If you'll please tell the next client he or she can come in, I'll let you go off and check on the concessions." Ellis oversaw food and snacks at the carnival as well as serving as their nurse.

She got up without protest, saying merely, "You can avoid the question when I ask, Sam, but you'd better be honest with yourself. Especially now. Because I've got a hunch it would have taken a pretty strong reason for you to deliberately cross paths with Luke again. Like maybe . . . a life-and-death reason? And when a moment like that comes, the decisions are pure instinct, straight from the gut and the heart."

"Lovely imagery," Samantha muttered.

Ellis smiled. "The gist stands." She turned toward the front doorway of the booth, adding, "Your turban's crooked."

Swearing under her breath, Samantha reached up to straighten the hated thing. Her fingers lingered on the old, fragile purple silk and skimmed over the glittering rhinestones, and she sighed.

Credibility. Or the lack thereof.

Luke and the rest of the Special Crimes Unit had the respected might of the federal government behind them, and even if the long history of the FBI had at times been somewhat checkered, respect for the men and women who served had certainly survived.

Behind Samantha was the Carnival After Dark, loud and colorful and intended as pure fun. Games and rides and sideshows. Like hers.

Like her.

But what had been her choices in the beginning? Precious few. One, really. One choice. One decision. Invent Zarina, with all her seductive mysticism and drama — or starve.

She'd been fifteen the first time she put on the turban. She had begun hanging around the Carnival After Dark when it passed close to New Orleans, where her hitchhiking had taken her. Offering to tell people's fortunes on street corners had done little except get her arrested once or twice even in the Big Easy, and she'd thought a carnival might need or at least want a fortune-teller.

Leo had agreed — once she'd told him somewhat pugnaciously that his mother had been an opera singer, his father a doctor, and that the carnival's knife-thrower had a drinking problem, would nick his assistant's ear at that night's show, and was going to kill somebody if his knives weren't taken away from him.

All correct, at least up to her prediction of that evening's show; after that, he fired the knife-thrower.

And Samantha had joined the Carnival After Dark. She had, over the years, honed and refined her "act." Draping herself in swaths of colorful fabric, and clinking fake gold jewelry, applying heavy makeup to look older — and borrowing a turban Leo's mother had worn on some of the finest stages of Europe.

Samantha hadn't set out to become a carnival mystic. She wasn't at all sure why she hadn't, somewhere along the way, opted out and chosen to do something else with her life, especially once she'd gained confidence and had a little savings and the fear of starvation had left her. Because it had been easier, she supposed, to drift along day after day, year after year, being with people she liked and doing work that demanded little of her. Isolated and insulated in her own little traveling bit of the world.

At least until Luke had come along.

Looking down at her hands folded atop the satin-draped table, she heard the swish of sound as Ellis brought the next client in and then disappeared silently through the curtain behind Samantha.

Beginning her usual spiel, Samantha said, "Tell Madam Zarina what it is you wish to know about —" She had been about to add "tonight" but didn't bother when a ring dropped onto the table near her hands.

"I heard it helps if you touch things." The woman's voice was even, controlled. "So I brought that. Would you touch it, please?"

Samantha looked up slowly, knowing at once that this was one of the desperate ones. She had lost something, someone. She needed answers, and needed them badly.

A brown-eyed blonde of about thirty, she was pretty and casually dressed. And she was haunted. Her face was drawn, her hands writhed together in her lap, and her posture was so tense she practically trembled from the strain of holding herself still. She wanted to *do* something, was driven to take action, any action. This action.

Samantha looked at the ring. A birthstone, she thought. Opal. Plain band with the stone inset, small size. A child's?

She returned her gaze to the woman and said, "Some lost things can never be found."

The woman's mouth quivered, then steadied. "Will you try? Please?"

All Samantha's instincts told her to refuse, to make some excuse, refund this woman's money, and stop this now. But she found herself reaching out, picking up the ring.

The darkness swept over her immediately, and the cold, and she was choking, drowning.

Samantha was never sure afterward if it was the instinct for self-preservation or just the utter certainty of how the vision would end — and how she would end if she remained caught up in it — but whichever it was caused her to drop the ring. And just as suddenly as she'd been drawn into the vision, she was yanked out of it.

She stared at the ring lying on the table, then looked at her palm, where a circular white line now lay across the fading red line that was all that was left of the earlier frostnip.

"Shit." She lifted her gaze to the woman and found her pale, her eyes both shocked and eager.

"You saw something. What did you see?"

"Who are you?"

"Don't you know? Can't you —"

"*Who are you?*"

"I'm — Caitlin. Caitlin Graham. Lindsay's sister."

Despite the clear skies and bright moon, Lucas and Jaylene were having a frustratingly slow and difficult time of it. Not to mention exhausting. And judging by the intermittent radio and cell contact with the other two teams, they weren't the only ones; the terrain in these isolated spots was so rough it was as though they had been swallowed up by some more-primitive time, the strained roar of their vehicles' engines alien. When they could use vehicles, that was.

Sometimes, it was literally hacking their way through clinging, thorny underbrush.

Jaylene held the flashlight to illuminate the map spread out on the hood of their vehicle, and Lucas crossed off the second property on their list.

"At this rate," he said, "we don't have a hope in hell of covering all these places by tomorrow afternoon."

"Not much of a hope, no." Deputy Glen Champion, who Metcalf had assigned to go along with the federal agents because he was not only trustworthy but had grown up tramping all over these mountains, shook his head. "This is some of the roughest terrain in the state, and most of the places are like this one was — inaccessible by anything but a heavy-duty all-terrain vehicle, on horseback, or on foot."

They had borrowed a four-wheel-drive ATV from the sheriff's department motor pool, but even it had found the narrow, rutted dirt roads a challenge, especially after the late-afternoon storm and its torrential rain.

Jaylene said, "Just getting from one spot to the next takes time. Look at the next place — am I wrong, or is it at least five miles away?"

"Five miles of a winding dirt road," Champion confirmed.

"Shit," Lucas muttered.

Jaylene glanced at the deputy, then asked her partner, "Any hunches?"

"No." Lucas was still frowning, and even in the moonlight she could tell his face was beginning to take on that drawn, exhausted look it always acquired as they got deeper and deeper into a case.

She knew better than to comment on it. "Then we move on to the next place on our list."

Champion drove, again more experienced with this type of road than either of the agents. But even with his skill, it still required nearly an hour to travel the five miles.

He parked the ATV seemingly in the middle of the road and the middle of nowhere and cut off the engine. "It's about a hundred yards farther along, just past the top of that next rise."

The area was so heavily wooded that the trees literally pressed in on them from both sides of the road, and since the leaves hadn't yet begun to drop, even the bright moonlight did little to illuminate the road ahead.

It was also very quiet.

Jaylene checked her detail list with the aid of a pencil flashlight, and said, "Okay, this property hasn't had a house on it in about fifty years. Thirty acres of mostly mountainous pastureland and a big barn is all that's left. Says here the barn's still in good shape, and it was sold to an out-of-state developer about a month ago."

"Does the developer have a name?" Lucas asked.

"Not yet. It's a holding company.

Quantico's checking all this, but it'll be tomorrow at the earliest before we know any more than we do now."

They got out of the ATV, moving quietly, and kept their voices low for the same reason that Champion had turned off the police radio a good ten minutes back: because sound carried oddly up here, smothered by underbrush or trees in one spot and bouncing around madly in another.

"We'll stay together until we get the building in sight," Lucas said. "Then split up to search the area."

Jaylene checked her watch and said, "It's almost ten. As much as we'll all hate the lost time, we should definitely stick with the plan and meet back at the station for food and caffeine at midnight. Otherwise, we'll never be able to keep this up all night."

"That is the plan." Not saying whether he agreed with it — or whether he intended to have more than his customary coffee at the break — Lucas concentrated on moving as silently as possible, his gaze probing the dark road ahead of them. "The good news is, we'll be able to move faster once dawn breaks tomorrow."

"And the bad news?" Champion murmured.

"You said it yourself. Not much hope of

getting through every property on our list. So we'll have to find her before we do that."

"Maybe we'll get lucky, and she'll be here or the next place we check," the deputy offered.

"I never had much faith in luck," Lucas said. "Unless I make it myself. And I like shortcuts."

"I'm game for anything you suggest," Champion said promptly. "Lindsay's a friend as well as a fellow cop." He paused, then added less certainly, "I guess you've already talked to Miss Burke."

Jaylene thought he was one of the very few around here who would refer to Samantha with so much respect, but she left it to Lucas to reply.

"That's why we're searching these properties, Deputy."

Jaylene heard the note of frustration in her partner's voice but, again, remained silent. She had picked up absolutely nothing from Samantha's belongings at the station but was nevertheless aware of much the same uneasiness he felt.

If they had not been so desperately pressed for time, she had little doubt that Lucas would be at the Carnival After Dark, doing his best to get at whatever it was that Samantha was keeping to herself.

As it was, they simply had no time for anything but the concerted search for Lindsay.

"We should be able to see the building as soon as we top this rise," Champion breathed.

He was right. As they emerged from the dense forest surrounding them, the top of the rise showed them a moonlit clearing just ahead, with a dark, hulking building at its center.

This was the third property they had checked, so their responses as a team were becoming more certain; with barely a gesture wasted between them, they split up and moved cautiously across the clearing to the barn.

After the long journey to get here, it took no more than ten minutes for them to reach the barn — and see, from the two big doors that were open and half off their hinges, that no one was being held in this derelict place.

Still, they were all cops and all thorough, so they turned on their big flashlights and began to search the interior.

"Moldy hay," Jaylene said, her voice normal now. "Rusted farm equipment. And" — she stiffened but managed not to cry out when something skittered across her foot — "and rats."

"Okay?" Lucas asked her.

"Oh, yeah. I just hate rats, is all." She continued searching the old barn.

"Judging by all this junk, the building hasn't been used for anything but storage in decades," Champion said, his flashlight directed to one wall holding a hanging collection of rather lethal-looking farm implements.

"Hold on a second." Lucas had stopped near one corner, where an old stump — years dead, but still in the ground the barn had been built around — sprouted a rusted hatchet.

Champion said, "Probably used that to slaughter livestock at one time. Chickens, at least. For Sunday dinner."

"I doubt a farmer left this," Lucas said. "Take a look." When the other two joined him, he indicated the folded piece of paper wedged in between the edge of the hatchet and the stump.

While Jaylene held her flashlight steady, Lucas produced a small tool kit and used a pair of tweezers to carefully extract the note and then unfold it on the stump. And they could all see what was block-printed on the paper.

BETTER LUCK NEXT TIME, LUKE.

Samantha wanted nothing more than to fall into bed and sleep for about twelve hours, but instead she found herself waiting in the conference room of the sheriff's department for the search teams to return to the station for a scheduled midnight break.

Nobody had offered her so much as a cup of coffee, but one deputy kept sticking his head in the doorway, clearly keeping an eye on her so she didn't disturb the stacks of folders on the other end of the table or steal a pencil or something.

She thought about that as she sat and stared at the walls. It wasn't a lot of fun being an outcast.

Of course, carnies were, by definition, outcasts of a sort, since they traveled from town to town, never putting down roots and seldom building relationships outside their own close-knit groups. But since her Carnival After Dark friends were the only family Samantha had ever really known, she had never felt an outcast among them or as one of them.

Being psychic was something entirely different.

Viewed as a fraud at best and a freak at worst, Samantha had become accustomed, over the years, to scorn and disbelief. She had become accustomed to aggressive "Tell me what I'm thinking, I dare you!" in-her-face confrontations with bullies, and "routine" questioning from cops whenever there was a problem anywhere near her.

She had become accustomed to the needy, desperate people who visited her booth, with their hungry eyes and pleas for help, for the knowledge they craved. She had even become accustomed to the occasional attractive man being interested in her until, ironically, he discovered that her "act" was at least partly genuine and she was in fact psychic.

She had become accustomed. But she had never learned to like it. Any of it.

"They tell me you've been here more than an hour." Lucas came into the room, carrying two cups. He sat down on the other side of the conference table and pushed one across to her, adding, "Tea rather than coffee, right? With sugar. Sorry, there was no lemon I could find."

Samantha thought he looked very tired and more than a little grim, and even the simmering anger she felt toward him couldn't stop her from appreciating the courtesy.

He was most always courteous, Luke. Damn him.

"Thanks." She sipped the hot tea. "I gather you guys have had no luck."

He shook his head. "No luck finding Lindsay so far. But the bastard apparently guessed where we'd look. He left a note. For me."

"What did it say?"

"Better luck next time."

Samantha winced.

"He's been more than a step ahead all along," Lucas continued. "You were obviously right about this being some kind of twisted game or contest in his mind."

"You couldn't have known that."

"I should have figured it out, and long before now."

Samantha shook her head. "I don't think he wanted you to before now. I think he was busy figuring you out, learning to understand how your mind worked, how you search for lost people."

Lucas frowned. "Are you saying he knows I'm psychic?"

From behind him in the doorway, Sheriff Metcalf said, "What? You're *what?*"

"Shit." Lucas couldn't help giving Samantha a look, but she was shaking her head.

"No, I didn't ambush you. He popped into that doorway like a jack-in-the-box as you were speaking. I didn't know he was out in the hall, honestly."

Metcalf came into the room and moved around the table so he could see Luke's face. "You're psychic? *Psychic?*"

"Something like that."

"You're a federal agent."

"Yes, I am. And my psychic ability is just another tool to help me do my job, like my training, my weapon, and my proficiency with numbers and patterns."

"No patterns here," Samantha murmured, hoping to turn the focus of the discussion from the paranormal to the scientific.

"That's been one of the problems," Lucas admitted. "Nothing to latch on to, either logically or — intuitively."

"Except that now you know he's matching his wits against yours."

Lucas nodded. "Now I know. Which means I'm playing catch-up. If you're right, he knows a hell of a lot more about me than I know about him."

Metcalf sat down at the table, still looking both stunned and distinctly unhappy. "No wonder you were on her side," he muttered.

"I was on her side because I know she's genuine. Not because I'm psychic too, but because I've seen her in action." Lucas turned his head and stared at the sheriff. "We can argue about this, Wyatt, or we can concentrate on finding Lindsay. Which will it be?"

"Goddammit, you know I want to find her."

"Then I suggest we put our energy and abilities into doing that, and discuss the plausibility of the paranormal later."

Metcalf nodded, however ungraciously.

Returning his gaze to Samantha, Lucas said, "I'm guessing you're here because you picked up something during a reading tonight."

"More like had something thrown at me," she said. "Guess who showed up unexpectedly at my booth? Caitlin Graham. Lindsay's sister."

"I didn't know she had a sister."

"Not local; she lives in Asheville." Shifting her gaze to the sheriff, she added coolly, "And heard about her sister's kidnapping, by the way, on the six o'clock news."

Metcalf looked stricken. "Oh, God, I should have called her."

Relenting somewhat, Samantha said,

"Find Lindsay, and I'm sure all will be forgiven. Caitlin's staying at the same motel I am for the duration. She wanted to come here and wait, but I told her it'd be hard enough for one of us to run the media gauntlet outside."

"How did you manage?" Metcalf asked, curiosity overcoming hostility.

"Jedi mind control."

He blinked.

Lucas said dryly, "She's kidding. How *did* you get past them, Sam?"

"I had Leo create a distraction. He's good at that."

"I remember," Lucas murmured.

"Yeah. Well, anyway, he drew them away from the front door, and I slipped in. Hopefully unseen. Despite the news frenzy, I don't think the kidnapper has taken me seriously so far, and I'd just as soon keep it that way as long as possible."

"Why?" the sheriff demanded.

It was Lucas who answered. "So you can continue to be our ace in the hole."

Samantha nodded. "If he's been watching you as long as I think he has, I'm betting he's at least wondered if your ability to find people is paranormal. If he's good enough at research, I also think he may know a lot more about the SCU than

Bishop would be at all comfortable with."

"Great," Lucas said.

"Wait a minute," Metcalf said. "You mean *all* of you, the *whole* unit, are —"

"Wyatt, please." Lucas was frowning at Samantha. "If you're right about all this, then he might just decide to grab a psychic of his own. To keep the playing field level."

Samantha's smile was grim. "The thought had occurred to me."

7

Once she realized she was alone, Lindsay began working on the tape binding her wrists. To her surprise, the tape started to give way almost immediately, and it probably took her no more than twenty minutes or so to free her hands.

She immediately reached up to pull the bag off her head, only to be confronted by total darkness.

At least, she hoped it was darkness.

He had ordered her to get out of the chair and lie on the floor, commands Lindsay had no choice but to obey, and had continued to talk to her casually for several more minutes. Then he had simply fallen silent.

Try as she might, Lindsay hadn't heard anything else. She hadn't heard a sound to indicate that he might have gone away. But, gradually, she had become convinced that he had indeed left her alone.

Now, lying on a cool, hard floor and groping in the darkness to free her ankles from more duct tape, she strained to listen just in case he returned. But she heard only her own breathing, shallow and ragged in the silence. It took longer to get the tape off her ankles, but she judged no more than half an hour or so had passed when the tape finally gave way and she was completely free.

That happy illusion lasted only as long as it took for Lindsay to slowly and carefully explore the space around her. Cool, smooth floor; cool, smooth walls; and a cool, smooth ceiling about a foot above her head when she was standing.

The entire space, she realized, was no more than about eight feet square.

Baffled, Lindsay felt her way around, searching for an opening, a knob, a seam — something. She found only one thing, a small opening that felt like the end of a pipe in one corner of the ceiling. She pulled at it hard, hoping to dislodge it, but it might as well have been frozen in cement.

She thought at first that the pipe might be providing air for the space enclosing her, but she could detect no air coming from it at all. She felt the first real chill of fear then, but shoved it aside determinedly and explored the walls, ceiling, and floors one more time.

Nothing. No opening other than the pipe.

No handle or knob. No crack she could wedge something into — even if she had something to wedge into a crack. Nothing.

Lindsay rapped her knuckles against one of the walls, and realized something.

"Glass," she murmured.

The word was barely out of her mouth when there was a sudden loud sound, and a blinding light came on directly overhead.

For a moment, Lindsay could only blink as her eyes adjusted to the light after being in darkness for so long. When she finally could see, what she saw didn't make sense.

Not at first.

It was the sheriff who said, "Some of the media out there could have seen you, we all know that. If you're a potential catch for this bastard, aren't you taking a chance by coming here and at least appearing to involve yourself even more in the investigation?"

"Maybe." Samantha shrugged.

"Wyatt's right." Lucas gazed at her steadily. "What the kidnapper has seen so far is explainable without unduly linking you to us in any formal sense; you were under suspicion and remained here only long enough to be cleared. But if you're seen with any of us, or seen coming here now that you're clearly not a suspect . . ." He frowned. "Maybe the Carnival After Dark should move on."

"And turn away throngs of the curious, eager to spend money at our games and attractions? If we did that, the sheriff here would lose all faith in his own judgment."

Metcalf scowled but remained silent.

"Sam, don't be stubborn," Lucas said.

With another shrug, she said, "Maybe you'd better hear why I came tonight. Caitlin Graham surprised me by dropping a ring on my table. She told me afterward that it was one Lindsay had worn when they were kids. She wanted me to touch it, to find out if I could pick up anything. I didn't know who she was, so I picked it up."

"And?"

Samantha held up her right hand, palm out. The once-white ring was now, like the line across her palm, a reddish mark, but it was quite visible. "So cold it burned," she said.

"What did you see?" Lucas asked.

"It's not what I saw, it's what I felt." She glanced at Metcalf, then returned her gaze to Lucas. "The places you're searching. Are any of them near water?"

"Streams and creeks," Lucas said without having to refer to a map. "One

189

small lake, I think."

"Simpson Pond," the sheriff confirmed.

Samantha nodded. "You might want to put those places at the top of your list."

"Why?" Metcalf demanded. "Because you *felt* water when you touched a ring?"

She looked at him steadily but didn't answer.

Quietly, Lucas said, "Sam."

"He is not going to want to hear this," she said, her gaze still on the sheriff but the statement clearly aimed at Lucas.

"If it will help us find Lindsay, he'll have to hear it."

"All right." But Samantha returned her gaze to Lucas when she said, "What I felt was Lindsay choking. Drowning."

"Lindsay swims like a fish," Metcalf said tightly.

"She was drowning. It hasn't happened yet, but she's running out of time. I can almost hear the clock ticking."

"Do you really expect us to run this investigation based on some *vision* you had because your turban was too tight or you breathed in too much incense?"

Samantha got to her feet. "Run your investigation any way you want, Sheriff. I'm just telling you what I saw." She was expressionless, her voice calm. Still looking at Lucas, she added, "If I'm right, whatever happens to put her in that water terrifies her."

He half nodded. "Thanks."

"Good luck." She left the conference room.

Metcalf said, "What I can't figure out is whether you two are enemies — or something else. It seems to tip back and forth every time you meet."

"I'll let you know when I figure it out." Lucas drained his cup and rose. "In the meantime, I want another look at that map before we go back out."

"Simpson Pond?" The sheriff shook his head. "Not much more than a wide place in a stream dammed up by a beaver. And the so-called *property* on your list is an old log cabin so remote even the hunters don't like using it."

"If I were a kidnapper holding a victim I needed to keep safely immobile and silent for another fourteen hours or so, remote is just what I'd want."

"I can't believe you're listening to that nut."

Evenly, Lucas said, "It's twelve-thirty. The ransom is due to be delivered tomorrow afternoon at five. Sixteen and a half hours, Wyatt. I say Sam is reliable, and the direction she's indicating makes sense given our kidnapper's M.O. So unless you have a better idea, I plan to continue searching these remote properties — with those on or near water moving to the top of the list."

Metcalf shook his head, the stubborn jut of his jaw mitigated only by the worry and sick dread in his eyes. "I don't have a better idea, goddammit."

"Neither do I. And we didn't need Sam to point out that Lindsay's running out of time."

"I know. I know." Metcalf climbed to his feet, weariness in every line of his body. "So, you're really psychic?"

"I really am."

With the vague understanding that *psychic* covered a wide range of possibilities, the sheriff said, "What kind of psychic are you? What do you do? Look into crystal balls like Zarina? See the future?"

"I find people who are lost. I feel their fear."

Metcalf blinked. "She was warning you? That's why she said —"

"Yeah. That's why."

"Shit," the sheriff said.

At first, Lindsay thought it was odd that

the kidnapper had left her watch on her wrist and untouched. But then, as the minutes ticked away into hours, she began to understand his purpose.

Scaring the shit out of her.

Part of his game.

That dawned on her at about nine o'clock on Friday morning, after she'd made her umpteenth failed attempt to kick a hole through the clear walls surrounding her and into the featureless darkness beyond. The several steel bands wrapping and reinforcing the thick sheets of apparently shatterproof glass provided all the strength necessary to resist her best attempts to break through.

Worse, she had a strong suspicion that she was running out of air. That was when she'd looked at her watch.

Nine o'clock.

Nine o'clock on Friday morning.

He always wanted the ransom delivered by five o'clock on Friday afternoon. And they were positive — almost positive — that he never killed his victims until the ransom had been safely delivered. So she had eight hours, probably.

Eight hours to find a way out of this sealed fish tank.

Eight hours to live.

Assuming he hadn't miscalculated how much air she needed to survive that long.

"Shit," she muttered. "Shit, shit, *shit*." Swearing usually made her feel better. It didn't this time.

She sat cross-legged on the floor of her tank and studied it, trying to remain calm and rational enough to think clearly, trying to find a weakness. She had thrown her entire weight against various points and corners, only to end up bruised, winded, exhausted, and strongly reminded of a bird flinging itself against the bars of its cage.

Think, Lindsay.

Wyatt's face swam into her mind, and she fiercely shoved it away. She couldn't think about him now. She couldn't think of mistakes or regrets or anything except figuring out a way to come out of this alive.

There would be time for everything else later.

There had to be.

Lindsay tried to concentrate, to study her prison. Then she heard an unfamiliar little sound.

Dripping.

She got to her feet and went to the corner where the pipe protruded through the heavy glass. The pipe that had, until now, been perfectly dry. Now it was dripping water. Not much, and not fast, just water steadily dripping.

She looked around at the cage.

At the tank.

Glass walls. Glass ceiling. Some kind of metal floor. All beautifully sealed. Waterproof.

It wasn't about running out of air, she realized.

As she watched, the dripping water became a trickle.

"Jesus," she whispered.

Most of them had taken another short break around noon, but nobody wanted to waste any time. They had managed to check out less than two-thirds of the properties on their list, and no one on any of the search teams was under any illusions that they'd be able to reach all the remaining properties in time.

Everybody was past tired, nerves on edge both because of the circumstances and all the caffeine. And the terrain wasn't helping; the search was physically demanding, even grueling, and exhaustion was creeping into all of them.

By three, Wyatt Metcalf had left the search parties in order to go to his bank and get the ransom money. His instructions were to deliver the ransom alone. Those were always the instructions.

Lucas had advised the sheriff to wear a wire or to hide a tracking device in the small bag that was to hold the money, but he'd also been forced to admit that on every previous occasion when they were involved early enough to take such measures, either the kidnapper had found a way to remove or electronically short-circuit the device or else had simply left the money unclaimed.

And his victim dead.

Metcalf wasn't willing to take any chances, not with Lindsay's life. He intended to follow his instructions to the letter. He had refused to be wired, to be accompanied, or to be watched in any way by law-enforcement personnel.

"Hard to be a cop and a lover," Jaylene murmured when the sheriff reported to them via the spotty radio communication that he was going for the money and would deliver it sans any wire or tracking device.

"He's not thinking like a cop," Lucas said, sounding tired.

"Could you?"

Without replying to that, her partner bent once more over the map spread out on the hood of their ATV and frowned.

"Six more properties on our list. And two of them on or near some kind of water."

Champion joined him in examining the map and shook his head. "If we're still putting the places with water at the top of our list —"

"We are," Lucas told him.

"Well, okay, then there's no way we can cover both those places by five o'clock. There's just no way. Not only are they miles apart, but this one" — he jabbed a finger at the map — "doesn't have *any* kind of a road leading to it now. It'll take us at least an hour and a half from here, and that's assuming the summer rains didn't wash the hills and gullies as badly as they usually do. It'd put us there at about four-thirty, if we're really lucky, and five if the area is as bad as I'm afraid it is. And that's not counting the time it'll take to search what's left of the buildings around that old mine shaft."

"What about the other place?" Jaylene asked.

Champion chewed on his lower lip as he stared at the map and considered. "The other place is the hunter's cabin at Simpson Pond. It's remote, but there's a halfway decent service road running partway, where the old train tracks used to be.

From here . . . less than an hour, probably. But that's in a different direction, so even if we're lucky as hell we won't be able to check out both places. Not before five. Not even before six, if you want my opinion."

"So we can only check out one of them." Jaylene was watching her partner. "One of two places only slightly more likely than the other four on our list. Should we flip a coin? Or do you have something to give us better odds?"

Lucas looked at her for a moment, grim, then drew a deep breath, bowed his head, and closed his eyes.

Champion eyed the federal agent uncertainly, reached up to touch his hat as though instinctively feeling he ought to remove it, then whispered to Jaylene, "Is he praying?"

"Not exactly." She kept her voice low but didn't whisper. "He's . . . concentrating."

"Oh. Okay." Champion clasped his hands behind him in a parade-rest stance and maintained a respectful silence.

Lucas tuned out his awareness of that silence and the curious stare that went with it. He tuned out the familiar presence of his partner. He tuned out the sounds of the forest all around them. And he focused on one small, bright point of light in his own mind.

The technique didn't always work, but it was the most successful meditation exercise he'd been able to develop in his years with the SCU. He was in a sense trying to narrow his own psychic abilities, or at least aim them at the smallest possible target. Concentrate on one thing, only one, and direct all his energies there.

Focus on that small, bright point of light, clear everything else out of his mind, and then picture the face of the missing person. Picture Lindsay.

The situation was unusual in that he had spent time with Lindsay before she was taken. So he knew more than merely what she looked like. He knew the sound of her voice, knew the way she moved, the way she thought. He knew the way she took her coffee and her favorite blend of pizza toppings, and he knew the man she loved.

He pushed all that into the bright, white light, seeing nothing but the light and Lindsay.

Lindsay . . .

The water was up to her ankles when Lindsay admitted to herself that stuffing her sock into the pipe wasn't even slowing it down. There was a lot of pressure in that pipe; every time she got the material wedged in there, it was forced back out, accompanied by a gush of water.

The water was up to her knees when she made a final attempt to kick out the glass, knowing that as the water got deeper in her tank she would be unable to use her full weight in an assault on the glass.

All she got for her trouble was soaking clothes when she slipped and fell in the attempt.

She was trying to stay angry, and at first it hadn't been hard to do that. To yell and swear at the top of her lungs and damn the animal who had done this to her. To scream until her throat was raw, just on the off chance that he'd done the more common criminal thing and screwed up somewhere, somehow, picked the wrong place or made somebody curious enough to check this place out.

Whatever and wherever this place was.

It wasn't hard, at first, for Lindsay to grimly make attempt after attempt to alter or delay her fate, staying focused on *doing* something.

She was no helpless maiden, dammit, to be rescued from the dragon. She'd taken down a few dragons in her time and intended to live long enough to take down a few more.

She had things to do, and not just with dragons. She wanted to see the Grand Canyon, Hawaii, and the Great Pyramid. She wanted to learn to ski. She wanted to have kids. She hadn't realized that until now, but she was sure now, absolutely sure, that she wanted kids. Maybe with Wyatt, if she could knock some sense into his stubborn head. Or maybe with some prince she hadn't met yet.

Prince. *Yeah, right.*

Still, she didn't doubt they were searching for her. A lot of good cops and a couple of good FBI agents. They were searching for her, and Luke and Jaylene were part of that hotshot elite unit that was supposed to be so good at stuff like this, so the odds were at least even that they'd find her.

Maybe better than even.

And maybe they had psychic help to improve the odds even more. At least — they might have if Samantha was as genuine as she seemed, as genuine as Luke seemed to believe she was. Odd, though, that she'd been right about there being another kidnapping but wrong about the victim.

Always assuming she'd told them the truth, of course.

Lindsay spent a good ten minutes thinking about that and finally decided that Sam had no reason to hate her enough to lie about it if she *had* seen Lindsay in that vision. So she must have gotten it wrong somehow.

But Luke and Jaylene, they were specialists at this sort of thing. They knew what they were doing.

Sure they do. And they followed this guy for a year and a half without catching him!

"They didn't know he was playing a game," she heard herself mutter defensively, her own voice a welcome sound over the rushing sound of the water pouring into her tank.

But if they're so good at this . . . shouldn't they have known?

"Different places, always on the move — they couldn't catch up to him. But now they can. Now he's here, staying put. And they're here."

And making great progress here before you were taken, weren't they?

Lindsay grimaced at her own sardonic thought but also welcomed it. Because it kept her angry.

What were they *doing* out there all this

time, all these hours? Sitting on their god-damned hands? They couldn't find the signs that somebody had built himself a fucking *fish tank* big enough to hold people? How could he get the stuff he needed without somebody realizing?

Huh?

How was that even possible? It wasn't like everybody needed huge sheets of shatterproof glass and bands of tempered steel for the little sunroom they were building out back, for Christ's sake!

Golden was a small town, people talked, they talked about *everything*, especially the business of their neighbors, and strangers were *always* noticed, so how had this son of a bitch managed this shit?

And where was Wyatt, goddammit? He was supposed to be here. He was supposed to find her, because he was a good cop and that's what good cops did.

Wyatt, goddamn you, why haven't you found me? You should be able to find me. . . .

The anger lasted until the water reached her waist. She looked at her watch, some clear, calm part of her mind calculating, and realized that the tank would be full before five o'clock. At least half an hour before.

She'd be dead before the ransom was paid.

Dead before anyone could find her.

The bastard was cheating.

He had never intended to give Luke a chance to win this round.

When Lucas sucked in a sudden, painful breath, Champion nearly jumped out of his skin.

"Wha— Is he okay?"

"That's not the question," Jaylene said, her eyes fixed on her partner. "Is Lindsay okay?"

"No," Lucas murmured. His eyes were still closed, his head bowed. All the color had drained from his face, and the tension in his lean body was obvious.

"What's happening, Luke? What's happening to Lindsay?"

"Afraid. She's afraid. She's . . . terrified. She doesn't want to die."

"Where is she?"

"Water . . . getting deeper . . ."

"Show me." Jaylene's voice was quiet but also commanding. "Which way, Luke? Where is Lindsay?"

He was utterly still for a moment, then startled Champion again by turning suddenly toward the west. "This way.

She's . . . this way."

Before Jaylene could look at the map or ask, Champion said, "The mine shaft. That's west of here. The way he's pointing. Should we —"

"Yes, we should. Now."

By the time Champion gathered up the map, Jaylene had guided Lucas into the passenger seat and climbed in back. The deputy got behind the wheel as before, admitting silently that he was a little creeped out by this.

"She doesn't have much time," Lucas murmured. "She's afraid. She's so afraid."

Champion glanced at the federal agent and swore under his breath, more than a little creeped out now. Lucas gazed straight ahead, his face still ghostly pale and now beaded with sweat, and his eyes were peculiarly . . . fixed. As though he were looking at something far, far away.

Champion lost no time in heading west toward the old gold mine.

"How does he know?" he demanded.

Jaylene replied, "She's afraid and he feels it. Luke? How sure are you?"

"She's this way. This direction. It's cold. It's cold and wet . . . and she's alone."

"Glen, are either of the other search teams closer than we are to the mine?"

"I don't think so. And radio reception up here is spotty as hell. But we can try."

"I'll use the radio. You drive." She half climbed far enough forward between the front bucket seats to reach the radio and began trying to contact the other teams.

"Hurry," Lucas said.

"You're that sure? You have to be sure, Luke. If I can reach someone and pull one or both of the other teams away from their planned areas —"

"She's there. She's alone. The bastard left her alone." His voice was strange, thin. Haunted.

Champion swallowed a sudden sour taste in his mouth, for the first time feeling real dread.

Jaylene kept trying to raise the other teams, but by the time Champion judged them to be nearly halfway to the mine she had pretty much given up hope. No radio contact at all, and with absolutely no signal their cell phones were worse than useless. "It's us," she told Champion. "If Lindsay's there, we're the only hope she's got."

"You're sure she's up there?"

"Luke is sure. And when he's like this, he's never been wrong."

"Sit back and fasten your seat belt," Champion ordered, shifting the ATV into a lower gear to climb the almost vertical slope before them.

Jaylene half obeyed, sitting back a little and hanging on to the front seats as the vehicle bounded through ruts deep enough to engulf most other cars or trucks.

"Hurry," Lucas repeated. He coughed, seemed to gasp for air.

"Goddammit," Jaylene said grimly.

"Jesus, is he there with Lindsay?" Champion demanded, pushing the ATV to its straining limits.

"He feels what she feels," Jaylene repeated. "Hurry."

Lucas gasped again. Breathed shallowly.

Champion was glad the ATV was making so much noise, its engine laboring and tires clawing like a cat for traction, because what was happening in the passenger seat was literally making his skin crawl.

It was as if Lindsay was there. Sitting there, in the leather seat. Drowning. Every faint gasp sounded like somebody drowning, and Champion knew it was Lindsay. He felt it was her, so strongly that he was afraid to turn his head and look, because he was absolutely sure she'd be there.

Drowning.

What he didn't know was just how *con-*

nected the federal agent was, never mind how he was doing this. The point was that he was doing it, that he was somehow tied to Lindsay, so what would happen if she did drown?

Champion didn't ask.

Jaylene pulled herself forward and held on to keep herself steady in the jolting vehicle as she peered at her partner. "Luke?"

He coughed, muttered, "Dark."

"Oh, shit. Glen, how far?"

"At least fifteen minutes," he replied, fighting the wheel and the ATV's tendency to buck.

"Luke —"

"No. No, god*dammit* . . ."

Champion sneaked a quick glance at Lucas and realized immediately that whatever thread had connected him to Lindsay had been snapped. He looked dazed, shaking his head as though to clear dizziness.

"Luke?"

Thickly, he said, "The bastard left her alone. He left her *alone*. All those hours."

Jaylene didn't say another word. And neither did Lucas. He sat there in the bucking, straining vehicle beside Deputy Champion, his pale face and haunted eyes telling anybody who cared to look what they would find when they reached the old gold mine.

Even so, when they broke into the cinder-block building that had once served as the storehouse for the mine, Champion wasn't prepared for what they found.

To his dying day, he'd never forget the sight of Lindsay Graham suspended in a water-filled tank, garishly lighted from above, her open, sightless eyes accusing them all.

8

Monday, October 1

Detective Lindsay Graham was buried on a gray and misty afternoon, laid to rest in the family plot beside her parents. They, too, had died before their time, though in their case it had been the fault of a drunk driver and an icy highway. They hadn't been carried to their graves in a flag-draped coffin by uniformed police officers, hadn't been saluted by dozens of other cops, many of them openly weeping, while bagpipes played plaintively.

Their deaths hadn't been front-page news in even the Golden local, far less several regional newspapers, and no news crews had pestered what family survived them for comments.

Lindsay died far more famous — or infamous — than she had ever been in life, a fact that undoubtedly would have roused little in her except cynical amusement. Because in the end, famous or not, Lindsay was lowered alone into the ground just as her parents had been.

Hugging the neatly triangled flag that had been presented to her, Caitlin stood at the graveside long after most of the others had gone, thinking about that. About her sister. For whatever reason, they hadn't been especially close, but they had liked and respected each other, Caitlin thought.

Too late now to wish there had been more.

Wyatt Metcalf stepped up beside her. "I'll drive you back to the motel," he offered.

There would be no traditional gathering after the funeral, not for Lindsay. She hadn't liked the practice of covered dishes and hushed voices, of parked cars lining the long country driveways and funeral wreaths on the homes of the bereaved.

"Bury the dead and get on with living," she had said more than once, perhaps with a cop's hard-won understanding. Or an orphan's. And quite suddenly, Caitlin wished desperately that she knew what in Lindsay's life had taught her that.

But it was too late now to ask.

Too late to ask what she had thought of the latest blockbuster movie, or novel, or whether popcorn was still her favorite snack. Too late to apologize for missed birthdays and unreturned phone calls, or commiserate about the often difficult life of a single career woman, or ask if Wyatt Metcalf had been the one for Lindsay.

Just too goddamned late.

Realizing at last that the sheriff was waiting, Caitlin said, "No, thanks. It's close enough to walk. Everything's close enough to walk here, really."

A bit awkward with her, as he had been all along, Metcalf said, "If there's anything I can do —"

"No. Thanks. I won't be staying long, probably. I have to pack away her stuff, close up the apartment, deal with all the legal crap. However long that takes."

"We'll get him, Caitlin. I promise you, we'll get the bastard."

Caitlin knew the sheriff would be surprised if she told him the truth, that she didn't care if they ever caught the monster who had taken her sister's life. It wouldn't, after all, bring Lindsay back. And, besides . . .

He didn't seem real, that monster. From what she'd been told, there was a curious lack of emotion there, a lack of anything human. No hate driving him, no insane voices directing him to murder.

Just taking people for money and then

killing them when he no longer had a use for them.

"Good," she said, realizing the silence had lengthened yet again. "Good. I'm glad you'll get him. You go do that now." She didn't realize until a tinge of color crept up into his rather haggard pallor how dismissive she sounded. She toyed briefly with the idea of explaining, but it just seemed too much trouble. And she didn't care what he thought anyway.

"Caitlin —"

"I'll be fine." She thought the meaningless phrase should be tattooed on her forehead by now. "Thank you."

He hesitated, then went away.

Caitlin didn't turn to watch him go. She was vaguely aware of others trickling away. Aware that the solemn men from the funeral home were off to the side, patient and unmoving, along with the men ready to finish the physical task of burying her sister.

The coffin still hung, suspended, above its vault, waiting to be lowered. The scent of the flowers was thick in the misty air, a sweet, rather sickly odor that was especially unpleasant mixed with the faint, underlying smell of freshly turned earth.

"You have to leave her now."

Caitlin looked across the dully gleaming

bronze-colored casket to see Samantha Burke. She was completely different from the Madam Zarina of the fortune-teller's booth; without the turban, the colorful shawls and wraps and clinking gold jewelry, and most of all without the heavy makeup, she looked decades younger and rather ordinary.

Or not.

There was something in those unusually dark eyes that was far from ordinary, Caitlin thought. Something direct and honest and unnervingly discerning, as if she could truly see beyond the boundaries of what most people accepted as reality.

Caitlin remembered how Lindsay's ring had seemingly burned a neat circle into Samantha's palm, and wondered what it was like to see and feel things other people couldn't even imagine.

"You have to leave her," Samantha repeated. She hunched her shoulders a bit inside the oversize black jacket and thrust her hands into its pockets, as though chilled by the miserable weather. Or by something else.

For the first time in this endless day, Caitlin didn't respond with platitudes. Instead, she simply asked, "Why?"

"Because it's time to go. Time to get

past this moment." Samantha's voice was utterly matter-of-fact.

"Because Lindsay would want me to?" Caitlin asked dryly.

"No. Because it's what we do. It's how we cope. We dress them in their Sunday best and put them inside satin-lined boxes designed to keep them dry and safe from the worms, like the concrete vaults we put the boxes in. And then we have a headstone or marker engraved, and lay turf over the spot, and at least for a while we come regularly to visit and bring flowers and talk to them as though they can hear us."

Caitlin was conscious of the mortuary people shifting in uneasiness or disapproval, but they naturally said nothing. For herself, Samantha's bracing words sounded like the first real thing anyone had said to her in days.

"I won't even do that," she said. "Visit, I mean. As soon as I've packed away her stuff, I have to go home."

"And get on with your life." Samantha nodded. "The dead have their own path, and we have ours."

Curious, Caitlin said, "So you believe there's something after?"

"Of course there is." Samantha was still matter-of-fact.

"Do you *know* there is?"

"Yes."

"Heaven and hell?"

"That would be all nice and simple, wouldn't it? Be good and go to heaven; be bad and go to hell. Black and white. Rules to live by, to keep everybody civilized. But life isn't simple, so I don't know why we expect death to be. What there is . . . is continued existence. Complex, multilayered, and unique to every individual. Just like life is. That much I am sure of."

Perhaps not surprisingly, Caitlin found that more comforting than all the sermons preached at her since childhood Sunday school.

"It's cold and wet out here," Samantha said. "And those guys over there need to finish their work. I don't think we need to be here for that. Why don't we go get a cup of coffee or something?"

Caitlin returned her gaze to her sister's casket for a moment, then walked around the grave and joined Samantha. "Coffee sounds good," she said as they headed toward the road.

She didn't look back.

Leo Tedesco stood well back from the cemetery, but he had a clear view never-

216

theless. He watched the short graveside service, too far away to hear what was said and not particularly sorry about that; death depressed him. Violent death upset him.

Lindsay Graham's murder made him sick to his stomach.

Samantha hadn't wanted company, so he had followed at a distance without her knowledge and watched. Watched her keep herself apart from the service as she stood back among the graves yards away from where Lindsay was being laid to rest. Watched as she had deliberately kept herself out of Wyatt Metcalf's line of sight.

The two federal agents, Leo realized, were perfectly aware of her presence, but neither approached her either during the service or afterward, and they left without speaking to her.

He found it hard to forgive them for that.

He watched her talking to Lindsay's sister and watched them leave together.

It wasn't like Samantha, Leo thought, to meddle. Inside her booth, Madam Zarina offered advice and answers to troubled questions, but outside it Samantha minded her own business and scrupulously avoided the business of others. It had been a hard lesson learned, but she had learned it well.

So what was she up to now?

The Carnival After Dark was scheduled to leave Golden in exactly one week — always assuming, of course, that Sheriff Metcalf didn't run them out of town sooner. Their schedule was set, with stops planned for several towns in the Southeast as they worked their way back down to Florida and their winter home.

So far, Samantha hadn't asked Leo to alter those plans, but he was uneasily afraid she might. He didn't have to be psychic himself to know she was bothered by this serial kidnapper, that she felt somehow compelled to involve herself in the situation. He even thought he knew why.

Luke.

In the fifteen years he had known her, Leo had only once seen Samantha lose her native hardheaded practicality, and the pain of that experience had changed her forever. Something in her had been destroyed, he thought. Not wantonly or even deliberately, but destroyed nevertheless.

That saddened Leo. It also made him angry.

"Stand out here much longer and you're going to be real conspicuous. Not exactly the best thing to be in Golden right now."

Leo started and turned his head to stare at the man who had seemingly appeared out of nowhere. "How long have you been here?" he demanded.

"Since before the service."

"Why?" Leo answered his own question. "You're watching Sam, aren't you?"

"Don't you think I should be?"

Leo chewed on his bottom lip. "I don't know. She won't like it, I know that."

"I don't give a shit what she likes."

"Then why aren't you following her now?"

"I don't have to follow her. She's with Caitlin Graham, having coffee at that little dive just down the road. What passes for a dive in this town, anyway. The coffee might poison her, but nothing else is going to happen in there."

Leo shook his head, worried. "She's out in the open, exposed. Used to, she could go anywhere off carnival grounds and not be recognized. But the newspapers have been running pictures of her without the Zarina getup. Everybody knows what Samantha Burke looks like now. I mean, she might as well have a giant bull's-eye painted on her back. Have you seen the newspapers? Seen what they're reporting on TV?"

"Yeah."

"The town of Golden may not have made up its collective mind about Sam, but the media sure as hell has. They just love the idea of a genuine psychic. And it's only a matter of time before the state and regional attention goes national. One slow news day, and I'll be fielding calls from CNN."

"They have no proof she's genuine; the sheriff's department refused to confirm that she was ever under suspicion, much less that she predicted Detective Graham's kidnapping — or any kidnapping — and was under voluntary observation to clear her name when it occurred."

"Have you been watching the same thing as I have on TV?" Leo demanded. "Reading the same newspapers? They don't need any proof or confirmation to speculate, and they're speculating like crazy."

"It's good for the carnival."

"In the short run, you bet it is. Plenty of publicity, and droves of the curious buying tickets. I'm not so sure about the long run, though. Or about the effect this is going to have on Sam. She's already working too many long hours and hardly sleeping. You know as well as I do she can't keep that up for long, living on caffeine, her nerves, and the late show."

"You are from a different generation."

Leo frowned. "What? Oh — the late-show reference?"

"Well, it does date you a bit. In this age of twenty-four-seven entertainment, there's no such thing as *late,* let alone a late show. No national anthem and snowy TV screen to lull us to sleep in the wee small hours."

"You obviously remember what it was like."

"Hearsay. An older cousin used to tell us scary stories. He got them from something called *Shock Theater* — his local version of the late show, I believe. Ghosties and ghoulies and things that went bump in the night."

Leo was aware of a little chill he couldn't really explain. His frown deepened. "Do we really need to discuss popular culture right now?"

"One of us does."

"Would you please be serious?"

"I," the visitor said calmly, "am as serious as a heart attack."

Despite his question, Leo hadn't needed the reminder. "Then tell me what you're going to do about this," he demanded.

"I'll do what I get paid to do."

"Which is?"

"For now, wait."

"Wait? What the hell for?"

"Believe it or not, for a sign."

Leo blinked. "A sign?"

"Yeah. I'm told I'll know it when I see it. And I shouldn't allow it to distract me. Nothing so far has looked like a sign, at least not to me. So . . . I wait."

"People are dying, or hadn't you noticed?" Leo met the other man's gaze and had to fight the impulse to take a step back. There were, he decided, men you just didn't want to push. And this was one of them. He really needed to remember that. "I'm just saying," he added hastily.

"Yeah, well, tell somebody who doesn't know. I do."

"Right. Sure." Leo hesitated, then said tentatively, "Any idea when this sign is going to show itself?"

"Not really, no."

"You sound a little . . ."

"Wouldn't you?"

Leo thought about it, and nodded. "Yeah. Guess I would. Frustrated and feeling sort of . . . useless."

"Thank you so much for putting it into words."

Deciding to quit while he was still in one piece, Leo cleared his throat and asked, "Are you coming back to the carnival?"

"Not just yet."

Venturing one last comment, Leo said, "I thought you said you didn't have to follow Sam."

"Didn't say I wouldn't keep an eye on her."

"She was afraid."

Without looking up from the autopsy report he was studying, Lucas said evenly, "Of course she was afraid."

"You say you felt that."

Lucas remained silent.

"Well, didn't you?"

"Let it go, Wyatt."

The sheriff moved restlessly in his chair. "I just . . . I need to know. What she went through."

"No. You don't."

"I *have* to, don't you understand that?"

"You shouldn't even be here today. Go home. Take time to grieve."

"I can't go home. What am I going to do at home? Stare at the walls? Finish the half-eaten bag of popcorn she left at my place nearly a week ago? Go to bed so I can smell her on my sheets?"

Lucas wasn't surprised by the other man's raw emotion, nor that the sheriff would allow that to escape in here, behind the closed door of the conference room and before a relative stranger. Grief would find its outlet, one way or another, and many men could tell strangers what they couldn't tell those closest to them. It was something Lucas had seen before.

But that didn't make it one bit easier to hear.

"I slept on the couch last night, or tried to," Metcalf went on roughly. "Like every night since we found her. The bed . . . I could wash the sheets, but I don't want to do that. Don't want to . . . lose that. We weren't public, she didn't think that would be a good idea, so whatever I have of her is like that, like the sheets. Private." He shook his head, then blinked at Lucas as if seeing him for the first time. "But you knew that, didn't you? That we were lovers?"

"Yeah, I knew."

"Because you're psychic."

Lucas smiled wryly. "No. Because you're a lousy actor, Wyatt. I think most people knew, if the truth were told."

"Think Caitlin knows?"

"Since she doesn't live here, perhaps not."

With a grimace, the sheriff said, "She'll know once she's cleared out Lindsay's apartment. I left stuff there."

"I doubt she'll say anything."

"I don't care about that. I just don't want her to think it was . . . was something casual. Because it wasn't."

Lucas hesitated, then leaned back in his chair and said, "If it helps you to tell her that, then tell her. But I'd give it some time, Wyatt. Let some of the numbness wear off first."

"Mine or hers?"

"Either. Both. Just give it some time."

"From what she said today, I got the impression she isn't planning to stick around for long."

"That was the numbness talking. Once it starts to wear off, she'll most likely want to find out who killed her sister. Some just stay and wait; some try to get involved in the investigation; but virtually all of them want that closure. They need it. Before they can move on."

Wyatt frowned briefly. "I forgot. You've seen a lot of this sort of thing, haven't you? Death. Grief."

"Yeah."

"How do you get through it? How do you keep doing it?"

Lucas had heard the questions before, and answered Wyatt as he had answered others.

"I get through it by focusing on what I can affect, what I can possibly control. Finding someone who's lost or taken, if that's at all possible. If it isn't, if I'm too late, then I try to find what's left, the body. And if I can, I try to find the killer. Put him behind bars, in a cage where he belongs. That's what I can do. That's all I can do, to help the living and the dead."

The sheriff's face seemed to quiver for an instant, and he said, "Just tell me one thing. Why Lindsay? Why did the bastard take her?"

"You know why. To make it personal. To give the victim a very familiar face. And as a taunt, a challenge. She was taken virtually from beneath our noses while we were watching someone else."

"Someone your Madam Zarina told us to watch."

Lucas shook his head. "Wyatt, don't go there. I know you want to blame someone, but don't blame Sam. She may have her faults, but when it comes to her visions she's the most truthful person I've ever known. I'm absolutely positive that she saw what she told us she saw."

"And even *gifted* psychics make mistakes, huh?"

"Yes, they do." Lucas frowned and, almost to himself, said, "Though Sam's visions were always highly reliable. So maybe the question is — why did she see a different victim?"

Unwillingly, Wyatt said, "Maybe Carrie Vaughn is next on this bastard's hit parade. Maybe Zarina just skipped one."

"She saw Thursday's newspaper, said it was exactly the same as in the photograph you were sent."

"Then she lied."

"No. She'd never lie about something like that."

"Are you sure? Can you be?"

"Wyatt —"

"You're a cop and can't smell a setup? She comes in *voluntarily* for questioning. *Warns* us there's going to be another kidnapping and says she'll stay here to prove her innocence. But the supposed victim we're so busy watching is safe and sound while one of our own is snatched, all because little miss *innocent* made a mistake."

"She didn't kidnap or kill Lindsay, Wyatt. You know she didn't."

"Maybe not with her own hands, but who's to say we're only dealing with one kidnapper here? If your so-called profile was more accurate, you would have found him by now. So? What if you guys got it wrong all the way around? Suppose, just suppose, that Samantha Burke had help, Luke. A partner. Or, at the very least, a friend she's covering for. Suppose one of her carnie pals is behind all this?"

"You've checked them out," Lucas reminded him.

"For past criminal records, sure. But you and I both know there are criminals who never get caught. And it'd be a nice little racket, wouldn't it? A traveling carnival, never in one place for very long. Kidnap a local and make a few bucks, then move on to the next little town."

Lucas shook his head. "No. We've tracked this bastard for eighteen months, and the carnival was never in the towns where victims disappeared. I would have known."

Wyatt got to his feet and leaned over the table, hands braced, as he stared at Lucas. "You sat right here in this room and heard her say that all along their route they had *heard* about the kidnappings."

"Kidnappings make the news. So what?"

"So maybe the carnival was a lot closer to those kidnapped victims than you knew. Not in the same towns, but maybe nearby. Within driving distance. Near their regular yearly route, a path they know very well.

228

Maybe even well enough to target victims along the way. Victims whose habits and haunts they had ample time to observe."

Lucas returned the sheriff's stare, saying merely, "You're wrong."

"Am I?" Wyatt straightened. "Let's find out. I'm going to go put my people on checking out the yearly schedule of the Carnival After Dark. I want to know about every town they visited, every fairground and parking lot where they set up shop. I want to know where they were in relation to every kidnapping you've been tracking. I'm going to find out exactly where they've been every day of the last eighteen months."

Lucas didn't try to stop him.

He was, after all, a man who understood obsession.

"Do you like having your abilities?" Caitlin Graham asked as she sipped her coffee.

Samantha wrapped both cold hands around her own mug of hot tea and smiled wryly. "That's a loaded question. Sometimes. Sometimes not."

"Not when you see bad things?"

"Bad, unsettling, frightening. It can feel like I'm trapped in a horror movie, only without the popcorn — or the ability to get up and leave the theater."

"You don't have any control?"

With a shrug, Samantha said, "Again, it depends. At a time like this, with emotions running so high, the visions tend to be very . . . intense."

"As in, so cold they burn your hands?"

"That was a first. I usually just come out of them so tired I want to sleep for a few days."

"But you saw Lindsay. When she was being held."

Samantha nodded. She knew Caitlin needed to talk about this, so she did, matter-of-factly. "Like most good cops, she was working the problem. Trying to find an angle, a weakness she could use to her advantage."

Caitlin chewed her bottom lip, then said, "You're so sure there's something after death. Is it because you've — you've contacted somebody from the other side?"

Without commenting on the terminology, Samantha merely said, "I'm not a medium."

"Oh. So — you don't do that?"

"No. Technically, I'm what they call a seer. In carnival language, I see what is and what will be."

Caitlin smiled slightly at the other woman's deliberately theatrical tone. "Just like on the sign outside your booth."

"Exactly. As I understand it, my primary ability is precognition, seeing the future. When I'm seeing the present but something going on beyond my own sight or hearing, that's a kind of clairvoyance. But unlike most clairvoyants, who tend to pick up information all around them, randomly, what I see is very focused, tuned in to a specific event."

"Like seeing Lindsay."

Samantha nodded again. "It's a secondary ability, much less common to me. I've also been told that I'm a 'touch seer' rather than an 'open seer.' The difference, I gather, is that I have to touch an object to pick up anything."

"Always?"

Samantha thought of her dream, but nodded and said firmly, "Always. Happily, though, I don't go through life picking up visions every time I pick up a can of tuna or a hairbrush."

Very intent, Caitlin asked, "Then what triggers the visions? Why one object and not another, I mean."

Samantha sipped her cooling tea, giving herself a moment, then said slowly,

"People with more scientific knowledge than I have said it's all a matter of energy. Emotions and actions have energy. The more intense the feelings or events, or the longer they last, the more likely they are to . . . leave some of their energy on an area or an object. Sort of imprinting a memory on it. Since my brain is apparently hard-wired to tune in to that kind of energy, when I touch the right thing, I do."

"That doesn't really explain Lindsay's ring. She hadn't worn it for years, and she never came close to drowning as a child."

"If it was easy to explain, it wouldn't seem like magic, now, would it?" Samantha smiled, but also shrugged. "Maybe every individual has his or her own energy signature, as unique as a fingerprint. I've heard that; maybe it's true. They leave their own energy on an object, I touch the object, and — sometimes — my brain homes in on that energy signature. Picks up what's happening or will happen with that person, especially if strong emotions are involved."

"So you picked up her future when you touched her ring because . . . because she wore it so much in her past. Her childhood."

"Maybe. I don't really know, Caitlin. I generally don't think about it a whole lot.

It's just something I can do. I can also juggle, I'm a fair shot — at least at pop-up targets — and I'm the carnival champ at poker."

Caitlin smiled, but said, "Less-troublesome abilities, I imagine."

"You've never beaten Leo at poker. He can be mean."

Her smile remained, but Caitlin's eyes were serious. "If I asked you to do something for me, would you?"

"I'd have to hear what it was first," Samantha replied warily.

"I want you to touch something."

Not very surprised, and still wary, Samantha lifted her brows and waited.

"I had to go to Lindsay's apartment. To . . . pick out what she'd wear today."

Samantha nodded, still waiting.

"I knew she'd been seeing Wyatt Metcalf, so I expected to find some of his things there. And I did see a few things I assume are his. But I also found this." She reached into her purse and produced a small object wrapped in a handkerchief. Placing it on the table between them, she unfolded the clean white cotton. "There really isn't room anywhere on it for a fingerprint, but I picked it up with my handkerchief anyway. It isn't — wasn't Lindsay's."

Lying in the center was a small piece of costume jewelry, a charm or pendant meant to be worn on a chain. A novelty probably intended for Halloween, it was a small black spider in the center of a silvery web.

Staring down at it, Samantha heard herself ask, "How do you know it didn't belong to Lindsay?"

"Because she was terrified of spiders." Caitlin grimaced. "Dumb for a cop, she said, but she'd been that way since we were kids. The last time we talked, she told me she had her apartment exterminated once a month just to make damned sure none of them got in. It was a real phobia, believe me."

"Still," Samantha said, "this isn't a real spider."

"Doesn't matter. Lindsay couldn't bear even a picture of one, and she would never — *ever* — own a piece of jewelry with a spider on it."

"Could have been a gift."

"She wouldn't have kept it. Samantha, I'm absolutely positive this didn't belong to Lindsay."

"Where did you find it?"

"On her nightstand, of all places. She *really* wouldn't have had anything like this near her bed. That would have totally freaked her out. When she was just a toddler, a spider got into her crib. Our mom was downstairs, and it took her a few minutes to get up there; Lindsay always said it was the longest few minutes of her life and that she could remember every second vividly, how she was so terrified she couldn't even move. The spider wasn't poisonous or anything, but she's had nightmares about it ever since."

"So you think . . . somebody put this in her apartment?"

"Lindsay wouldn't have touched it, I know that much."

"If the sheriff gave it to her —"

Caitlin was shaking her head. "From what I gather, they'd been lovers for months and worked together much longer than that. He's not the sort of man to consider something like this a joke, especially since he'd know what she was genuinely afraid of. Lindsay would have told him. Hell, it was practically the first thing she told anybody she met, especially socially. 'Hi, I'm Lindsay and I hate spiders with a vengeance.' Didn't she tell you?"

"As a matter of fact, she did," Samantha admitted slowly. "When I was staying at the sheriff's department, she came down and had coffee with me a couple of times. Sort of jokingly asked if I could look into the future and promise she wouldn't —"

"Wouldn't be bitten by a spider and die," Caitlin finished steadily. "When we were kids, Lindsay was afraid of two things, and only two things: spiders and water over her head. She overcame her fear of water by learning to swim. In fact, she was on a champion swim team in college. But she was never able to conquer her fear of spiders."

To herself, Samantha murmured, "Spiders would have been impractical, maybe impossible. No control there. Just seeing them would have caused her to panic. Not the slow, dawning realization he wanted. The gradual buildup of fear. So he had to use water."

Grim, Caitlin said, "When they told me he'd drowned her, all I thought at first was how horrible it was for her to die that way. The way she'd once feared she would. And what a coincidence that he'd pick that. When I found this on her nightstand . . . It wasn't a coincidence at all, was it? He didn't just want to kill her, he wanted to scare her."

"You're assuming he put this in her apartment."

"Aren't you?"

Samantha nodded slowly. "The question is, did he do it before or after he took her?"

"Had to be after," Caitlin said immediately. "Or at least after she left home that morning. I wasn't kidding when I said she wouldn't have something like this near her. If she'd seen it, it wouldn't have been left there. A pair of kitchen tongs and a paper bag, probably."

"If that's the case," Samantha said, "then this wasn't left for Lindsay to find. It was left for someone else."

"Me? Knowing I'd clean out the apartment?"

"I don't think so. He sent the ransom note to Metcalf. I'm willing to bet he expected the sheriff to be the one to check out her apartment. In fact, I bet he did, right after she disappeared. But she didn't disappear from home, so it wasn't a crime scene and wasn't sealed — and he was extremely upset. Probably just charged in and looked around quickly. He must have missed this."

"I don't get it," Caitlin said. "Why try to alert the sheriff — her lover — to the fact that he wanted to scare her?"

Samantha drew a breath and rubbed her hands together briefly, then reached out for the pendant. "Let's find out," she said.

9

When Lucas reported the conversation with Wyatt and the sheriff's suspicions of Samantha and the carnival, Jaylene thoughtfully asked, "Think he might be right?"

"No. I don't believe there's any conspiracy here, not to commit the crimes and not to hide them. One man. One kidnapper. And he's a loner. An observer. He'd never be a part of any average group, let alone a carnival."

"So you and Bishop still agree on the profile."

"The basics, yeah. That our kidnapper is an older man, thirty-five to forty-five, and probably lacks a criminal record. He's careful, compulsive, highly organized, and goal-oriented. Likely to be single, though he may be divorced or widowed. He could be gainfully employed but is just as likely to be independently wealthy through some inheritance — even before the ransoms he's been paid so far."

"You didn't agree with the boss even in the beginning, though, about the reason why this guy kills his victims. Bishop was by the book: the psychological probability is that a kidnapper kills his victim to avoid identification."

Lucas frowned and, almost as an aside, said, "Odd, that. He so seldom goes by the book in profiling."

"Well, it looks like you were right to suspect another motive. The kidnapper still may be killing them to avoid identification, but it looks a bit less likely now. And Sam *was* right about broken minds not really working the way we expect them to."

"Yeah." But Lucas was still frowning.

"You're worried about her."

He shrugged that off, not entirely convincingly. "Sam can take care of herself."

"Doesn't stop you worrying."

"I'm just thinking we might have missed something very important."

"What?"

"As unlikely as his theory is, Wyatt may be right about one thing. The kidnapper may well be connected to the carnival or the route they took."

Jaylene waited, brows raised.

"It's just a feeling I got while he was talking, laying out this carnival conspiracy he can't get out of his head."

"It's not going to be pleasant," she murmured.

Lucas nodded with a grimace. "If we can't find a more legitimate target for him to focus on, he's going to waste time and energy, and shine a very unwelcome and hostile spotlight on the carnival."

"And on Sam."

"Yeah. No telling whether the town will remain simply curious or become unfriendly once they see where their sheriff's suspicions lie. Especially now that a cop has died, and a female cop at that."

"You could see it in the faces of all her fellow cops at Lindsay's funeral. They're taking it hard. And they want someone to blame just like Wyatt does."

"I know." Lucas shook his head. "Still, when it comes to that sort of thing, as long as it stops short of violence, Leo can take care of the carnival and, like I said, Sam can take care of herself. That's not what worries me."

"Then what? If the kidnapper isn't involved with the carnival, how could he be connected with it?"

"Ever since Sam dropped her bombshell about this guy playing his little game with me, we've considered the possibility if not probability that the kidnapper could have been observing us while we followed along behind him these last months."

"Makes sense, if Sam is right and he sees this as some twisted competition with you. The note we found in that old barn certainly seems to point in that direction. That was a very personal taunt, directed at you by name."

"Yeah. But what if he hasn't just been watching me, you, the investigation? Sam thinks he's a natural profiler, that he's done his research on me and on the SCU. If that's true —"

"If that's true," Jaylene finished, "then he might know about your past relationship with Sam."

"It was in the newspapers, some of it," Lucas said. "The case, the carnival. Sam. Just the local papers, but still. Everything's available now, stored digitally or on the Internet, ready for anybody to look it up. Somebody who knows how could find those stories easily, read between the lines and learn . . . quite a bit."

"Then we have to assume he knows all about Sam."

Slowly, Lucas said, "And about the carnival. About their seasonal route, just as Wyatt suggested. Jaylene . . . I think we'd better compare that route to the series of kidnappings ourselves. We can find any correlation faster than Wyatt and his people will be able to; we have more background info on all the other kidnappings."

"Okay, but . . . are you thinking the kidnapper *made* Sam part of his game? Somehow controlled her appearance here, her involvement? How? How could he have done that?"

"It's not impossible, if you look at it from another angle. He could have done what Wyatt's doing now. Researched the carnival's route, maybe even followed them from town to town last season or even earlier. You said yourself, we don't *know* he hasn't been planning all this for much longer than the eighteen months he's been active. He could have begun setting all this up — setting us up — two or more years ago."

"You really believe that's possible?"

Lucas said, "It hit me while Wyatt was talking. I know every member of the carnival, and none of them is the person we're after. I'm positive of that. But if the kidnappings do coincide with the nearby presence of the carnival for eighteen months, all across the East and Southeast, that *can't* be a coincidence. What isn't coincidence is planned."

"By the kidnapper."

"Part of the game somehow. Or the setup for the game. Getting all his chess pieces on the board. Arranging everything to his liking. Playing God. We have no way of knowing how many goddamned sets of puppet strings he's pulled."

"That would be . . . diabolical, Luke. To involve the carnival, Sam, to pull you in. To spend all that time planning and kidnapping and killing all those other victims, all of it designed to get you here, now, under these circumstances. It's elaborate as hell. *Complicated* doesn't begin to describe it." She paused and stared at him. "Something like this doesn't just happen, we both know that. There's always a catalyst. A trigger. If he went to all this trouble, then something set him off."

"Yes."

"Something personal. He's out to prove to you that he's better. Smarter, stronger, faster — whatever. Just like Sam said. But not because of any media attention focused on you. Not because he just happened to notice how good you were and decided to test your abilities. He's doing this because, somewhere in your past, in his past, you stepped on his toes."

Lucas nodded. "If we're right about all this, I know him. So part of the game will be figuring out how I know him. And what, if anything, I did to him to put him on this path."

"Sam was right about something else, you know. No matter what, you didn't create this monster."

"Maybe not, but I seem to have created the game, however inadvertently. Inspired it, at least. And so far, more than a dozen people have died."

Jaylene knew better than to offer either logic or platitudes, so she merely said, "Sam said she was certain you couldn't win the game without her."

"Yeah."

"And if this guy has been investigating you, tracking you, and does know about you and Sam, then you're probably right about there being nothing coincidental in her presence here. However he did it, he must have deliberately included her in the game, somehow maneuvered her here. And while your psychic abilities haven't been publicized since you joined the unit, hers are posted outside the carnival on a marquee every night."

Lucas nodded slowly. "The thought had occurred."

"Do you think that's what Sam's been hiding from us? The fact that she knows the kidnapper is fully aware of who and what she is?"

"Another thing I think we'd better find out. Because in the wrong hands, Sam could be an unbeatable advantage."

"And in the right hands?"

"An unbeatable advantage."

Getting to her feet as he got to his, Jaylene said, "Am I wrong, or isn't the queen the most powerful piece on the board in chess?"

"You're not wrong."

"Um. Have you told Bishop yet? About Samantha being here? Being involved?"

"He knew, more or less. The news reports."

"Did he say anything about this chess game?"

"Yeah," Lucas replied rather grimly. "He told me not to lose."

As soon as Samantha picked up the small silver medallion, it started.

The black curtain swept over her, the blackness thick as tar, the silence absolute. For an instant, she felt she was being physically carried somewhere, all in a rush; she even briefly felt the sensation of wind, of pressure, against her body.

Then stillness and the chilling awareness

of a nothingness so vast it was almost beyond comprehension. Limbo. She was suspended, weightless and even formless, in a void somewhere beyond this world and before the next.

As always, all she could do was wait for the glimpse into whatever she was meant to see. Wait while her brain tuned in the right frequency and the sounds and images began playing before her mind's eye like some strange movie.

Flickering images at first. Passing so fast they were a blur. Echoing sounds and voices. Everything distorted until, finally, it snapped into place.

It wasn't at all what she had expected.

She found herself looking down on a scene that seemed ordinary enough. A little family. Father, mother, two small children, a boy and girl. They were gathered around the dinner table, apparently for their evening meal.

Samantha tried to concentrate on what they were talking about, but there was a kind of pressure in her ears, as though she were going up in an express elevator or a plane, and all she could hear now was a distant, muffled roaring. She tried to shift position so she could see their faces, but no matter how hard she concentrated she couldn't seem to stop hovering above them.

The scene dimmed before she could begin trying to memorize details, and she found herself once again in the dark, dark emptiness.

It was getting colder.

And it seemed an eternity before another scene brightened and steadied before her. This time, only the little girl was there, or *a* little girl, maybe a different one, huddled in a corner of some unidentifiable room, cradling one of her arms with the other in a protective posture that struck Samantha as jarringly familiar.

It's broken. Her arm. Why doesn't she tell someone? Why is she afraid?

In a blink there was another scene, a woman sitting on a bed in a neat bedroom, her hands folded in her lap, feet together on the floor, the posture oddly stiff. And across from her was —

Cold. Dead. Cold. Dead.

That's what she's thinking. Feeling.

Waves of the woman's fear pushed Samantha away, carried her swiftly to the next scene. A little boy in his bed, visibly shaking, his eyes huge with terror as he stared at the window. And outside, lightning, the rolling boom of thunder, rain pounding.

It'll get me. Get me . . . get me . . .

Another scene, and this time Samantha didn't see another person, just spiders, hundreds of them scurrying toward her across a wood floor, and she tried to back away, looking down, seeing her feet, except they weren't her feet at all —

And then she was in a dark, stinking forest, nearly smothered by the stench of the damp rot all around her, trying to get away from all the snakes that were slithering toward her, grabbing for a limb to try to beat them back, surprised to see a man's hand instead of her own —

Once again, before she could note further details, that scene was gone, this time replaced by a dizzying stream of them, like a slide show revved up to high speed. She thought she was in some of the images, strangers in others, but all of them were filled with terror.

She couldn't take in one image before the next one flashed by. And the confusion of dozens of conversations all going at once nearly deafened her.

Fear pushed at her, washed over her, waves and waves of it battering her, cold and wet and black. She could feel pressure building up, outside and inside, steadily increasing until it was painful, until she knew it was dangerous, until she was almost numbed by the force of it.

And then, abruptly, she was back in the absolute silence, the cold, dark emptiness so lonely that —

What are you afraid of, Samantha?

She opened her eyes with a start and a gasp, her ears dimly registering the thud of the pendant falling onto the table. Her open hand was burning, and she stared at it, at the white imprint of a spider and its ghostly web overlaying the much fainter line and circle that already marked her palm.

"Sam . . . Sam, you're bleeding."

She looked across the table at Caitlin's white, shocked face and felt a tickling beneath her nose. Reaching up with her left hand, she felt wetness, and when she held the hand out saw that it was smeared with scarlet.

Samantha stared at both her hands, one marked with icy fire and the other with her own blood.

"Sam?"

"What are *you* afraid of," she whispered to herself.

"Me? Heights. But it isn't really a phobia." Caitlin grabbed a handful of paper napkins from the dispenser on the table and handed them across the table. "Sam, the blood —"

Absently accepting the offering and holding the slightly rough paper to her nose, Samantha murmured, "Thank you."

"What the hell did you see?"

"How long was I out?"

"About twenty minutes. I was getting worried. In case you don't know, it's very spooky watching you do that. You go as still as a statue and as pale as one made of marble. Except this time you started shivering toward the end. What did you see?"

Slowly, Samantha said, "Maybe what he wanted me to."

"Who? The kidnapper? But you said he probably left the pendant for Sheriff Metcalf to find."

"I did say that, didn't I?" Samantha looked at the other woman. "Know anything about chess?"

"Not much, no. How about you?"

"I know pawns are sacrificed. And I know that a very good chess player is able to think several moves ahead of his opponent."

Baffled, Caitlin said, "So?"

"So I think this guy might just be several moves ahead. Ahead of the cops. Ahead of Luke. Ahead of me. And no matter which way you look at it, that's not good."

It was later that afternoon when Lucas stood in a storage room of the sheriff's department garage, studying the large glass-and-steel tank where Lindsay Graham had died.

The old mine was so inaccessible, it had been impractical to transport CSI officers up and down the mountain the numerous times that would have been necessary for a thorough investigation of the tank. Though trucking it down the mountain had required an entire day and half the department working on the transport. There had literally been no better way, since the heavy forest made any kind of airlift impossible.

Not that having the tank had helped them, as far as Lucas could tell. No useful forensic evidence to speak of had been recovered. Only Lindsay's prints had been found inside the tank, and none whatsoever had been found on the outside.

A few hairs had been found in the tank, at least two of them black, so not Lindsay's. Lucas had sent the lot to Quantico for analysis, along with a request to Bishop to do what he could to hurry things up.

The kidnapper had apparently left the

area before the afternoon rains that had washed away any track. Either that, Lucas thought savagely, or he had sprouted wings and flown his ass out of there, leaving no trace behind.

Dramatic, but hardly likely.

Lucas circled the tank slowly, studying it, trying to get a feel for the man who had built it.

They'd had no luck in finding where the glass and steel had been purchased or when, but it was clear the painstaking work had taken time and concentration. There was no way this had been constructed after Lindsay was taken. In fact, experts consulted offered their opinion that the tank could have required a week or more to build, depending on the skill of the builder.

And then there was the careful piping that had connected this tank to the old mine's water supply, an old reservoir replenished by rainwater in the years since the mine had closed. The simple but lethally efficient clock timer that had opened the valve to flood the tank at the appointed time.

Lucas had never seen anything like it. Never even heard of anything like it.

"Almost like those campy old superhero TV shows, isn't it?"

He turned quickly, disturbed that she had managed to approach without his knowledge.

Stepping into the room, Samantha said, "Glen Champion let me in, and Jaylene told me you were down here. The rest of them studiously avoided me."

"You know cops," he said.

"Yeah. They can't logically blame me — not yet anyway — but they don't like me."

"What do you mean, not yet?"

"Come on, Luke. I don't have to be told that Metcalf is moving heaven and earth to try to find some connection between these kidnappings and the carnival."

"Will he find one?"

Instead of answering that, Samantha turned her gaze to the tank and moved closer. "Weird, isn't it? And a lot like those old TV shows. Remember? The colorful villain would capture our heroes and tie them to some absurd Rube Goldberg contraption designed to kill them — but not until next week's episode. I always wondered why, once he got his hands on them, he didn't just shoot them."

She looked at Lucas steadily. "Why didn't he just shoot them?"

He glanced at the tank briefly. "There

was a timer. If we had gotten there soon enough . . ."

Again, Samantha asked, "Why didn't he just shoot them?"

"Because it's part of the goddamned game. If I'm fast enough, nobody dies. Is that what you want to hear?"

Samantha didn't back down in the face of his ferocity. She didn't even flinch. In the same level, calm voice, she said, "But why is it part of the game? Don't you see? He's deflecting the responsibility, Luke. Certainly with this, with Lindsay. Maybe with all of them. It's not his fault because he didn't kill them, not really, not with his own hands. It's the fault of the police, the investigators, because if they'd done their jobs, no one would have died."

"You're making a giant assumption just because we found one timer."

"That's not why I'm making it. It's what I heard him begin to tell Lindsay. That *he* doesn't kill. He never kills, not with his own hands, not directly. Partly to deflect responsibility. But for another reason too. Kill somebody quickly and all you have is a dead body. There's little suspense, little chance for fear to build until it becomes terror. But show somebody how you mean to kill them a few minutes or a few hours from that moment, and then walk away . . ."

Lucas was silent, frowning.

"The other victim from Golden, Mitchell Callahan. He was decapitated, wasn't he? I heard there was something strange about that, something the ME was surprised by."

Slowly, Lucas said, "He appeared to have been killed by a very sharp blade, in a single stroke. Maybe by a machete or sword."

"Or maybe," Samantha offered, "by a guillotine?"

Lucas's first reaction was disbelief, followed immediately by anger that he hadn't seen it before now. "A guillotine."

"It's obvious the kidnapper knows how to build. Easy enough to build a guillotine. Set on a timer, the way this . . . machine was. With the victim — with Callahan probably fastened in, looking up. Seeing the blade hanging over him. Knowing it would drop. Maybe he could even hear the timer ticking away the minutes he had left."

"Fear," Lucas said. "Bait for me."

"Maybe. Maybe he's creating the fear to lure you. And maybe . . . to punish you."

Lucas wasn't very surprised, but said,

"So you've reached that conclusion too, huh? That I know this bastard, crossed paths with him somewhere?"

"It makes sense. To go to all this trouble, build this sort of . . . of murder machine isn't something a man would do just to win a game. Even a crazy man. Unless the game was personal. It has to be personal, and that makes it more likely than ever that he's done his homework on you. He must know how you're able to find abduction victims, that you feel what they feel. Right up until the moment of death, you suffer along with them."

After a moment, Lucas shook his head. "In the last year and a half, we've arrived on the scene early enough for me to feel anything at all in less than half the cases. If he wants me to suffer —"

"He's doing a damned good job. You might not feel the fear and pain of the victim when you get there too late, but in that case you probably suffer even more. And anyone who's ever worked with you or watched you work knows it."

Lucas fought a sudden impulse to reach out to her, saying only, "*Suffer* is a relative term."

"Not with you it isn't." Her smile was small and fleeting.

"Why did you come here today, Sam?" he asked, changing the subject. Or not.

"I left something with Jay," she replied readily. "A pendant Caitlin Graham found on Lindsay's nightstand. We both believe it was put there the day she was taken."

"Why do you believe that?"

Samantha pulled her right hand from the pocket of her jacket and held it toward him, palm out. "I'm on a roll."

The room where he worked was small and, he liked to think, cozy. The place was remote enough that nobody bothered him, and since no neighbors were close by, his comings and goings were pretty much his own business.

Which is how he liked it.

He bent forward over the table, moving carefully. He wore gloves as he cut words and letters from the Golden local newspaper, from the inside pages no human hand would have touched. A fresh sheet of white paper lay nearby, and glue.

He had to chuckle. It was hokey, of course, as well as completely unnecessary to use newsprint. But the effect, he knew, would be much greater than an ordinary computer-generated, ink-jet-printed note could command.

Besides, it was amusing. To think of their reaction. To picture Luke's face.

Time to up the ante.

He wondered if the agent had caught up yet. Maybe. Maybe he'd figured out at least part of it. Maybe he was beginning to understand the game.

In any case, the clock was moving faster now. There was no longer time for the leisurely trip up and down the East and Southeast, no longer time to allow a lull between the moves of the game.

It was a risk he had taken, confining the end of the game to one place, a small town. There were drawbacks. But advantages as well, and he felt those outweighed the drawbacks.

It was almost over now.

Almost.

Just a few more moves.

He wondered, vaguely, what he'd do when this was over. But it was a fleeting question quickly pushed aside, and he bent once more over his work.

Just a few more moves . . .

"None of that makes any sense," Lucas said finally.

"You're the profiler," Samantha responded.

"Do you expect me to profile a vision?"

"Why not? If a forensic psychologist can develop a psychological autopsy on a dead person, then why can't you deconstruct a vision?"

Jaylene, sitting at one end of the conference table and eyeing them as they sat across from each other, intervened to say mildly, "Off the top of my head, sounds like the vision was about fear."

"Felt like it was too," Samantha said. She sipped her tea and grimaced, murmuring, "I'm going to be up all night."

"Are you reading tonight?" Lucas asked.

"The carnival is open, I'm reading."

"You're tired. Go to bed early, get some sleep."

"I'm fine." She looked at her marked palm, where the imprint of the spider pendant remained, adding, "Dented a bit more, but fine."

"It's dangerous, Sam. You're a target."

"Not until Wednesday or Thursday."

Scowling, he said, "You're the one who warned me not to assume with this bastard. We can't assume he'll play by his own rules, remember? There's nothing to say he won't take someone today or tomorrow."

"Doesn't matter." She looked at him

steadily. "All I can do is read. Play what's in front of me. If I'm one of his pawns, then sooner or later he'll show up to make his move."

Jaylene said, "What if you're his queen?"

For the first time, Samantha looked slightly disconcerted. "Chess isn't my game. I don't know enough about it to —"

Lucas said, "The most powerful piece on the board. The queen is the most powerful piece on the board."

She lifted her brows. "I doubt I'm that."

"He went to a lot of trouble to get you here," Lucas told her. "There's something Jay found out a bit earlier about that circus that got into the next town on your schedule ahead of you. Seems the owner was paid — what he thought was an incentive from someone in the town — to cancel their scheduled two weeks off and go to work instead. It was an offer he couldn't refuse." Lucas paused. "The first maneuver to alter the schedule of the Carnival After Dark. Now you explain how Golden was chosen as an alternate town."

"I told you. I had a dream."

"A vision. What was it, Sam?"

She shook her head slowly, silent.

"We need to know, dammit."

"All you need to know is that the dream

brought us here. I suggested to Leo that Golden would be the perfect alternative. He agreed. We came here."

Jaylene frowned and said to Lucas, "So that wasn't something he controlled."

His gaze still locked with Samantha's, Lucas shook his head. "Nothing was left to chance. Nothing. Sam and the carnival are here because he wanted them to be. Aren't you, Sam?"

From the doorway, triumphantly, Wyatt Metcalf announced, "He got paid. Leo Tedesco was paid ten thousand dollars to bring his carnival to Golden."

Samantha glanced at the sheriff without changing expression, then returned her gaze to Lucas. "Sorry, I thought I mentioned that," she said calmly. "We're also here because Leo was paid what was termed a cash advance to set up in Golden. Bundle of cash and a registered letter, posted from here in town. Supposedly from an anonymous donor who wanted the carnival here for his kids. I'm sure the sheriff has a copy of the letter, or will soon."

Grim, Lucas said, "And none of that alerted you that something shady might be going on?"

"Matter of fact, it did. But, hey, ten

grand. I play what's in front of me, remember?" She looked at the sheriff again, this time steadily. "It's not the first time something similar has happened, though the amount was . . . unusual. And before you start trying to figure out how to arrest Leo for the money, bear in mind that he'd already reported it in last quarter's income records *as* a cash advance. To the IRS. And sent a copy of the letter to document it. If he'd wanted to hide it, your people never would have found a trace of the money."

The dawning realization on Wyatt's face showed that he hadn't considered that, and his frustration was so obvious that Samantha actually felt a twinge of sympathy.

"Sorry," she said to him. "But as I keep trying to tell you, Leo and the carnival have nothing to do with this kidnapper and his schemes."

"I notice you didn't include yourself in that," Wyatt snapped.

"I seem to be in a different position. For whatever reason, the kidnapper appears to want me here."

Lucas said, "You could have made a different choice. Leo could have pocketed the money or reported it, and the carnival could have chosen another town."

"Yeah, well. There was that dream."

"Why the hell didn't you mention the money before now?"

"She wouldn't have mentioned it now if my people hadn't found it," Wyatt reminded him.

Staring at Samantha, Lucas said, "Well?"

With a shrug, she said coolly, "I had to give the sheriff something suspicious to find, didn't I?"

"Bullshit," Wyatt muttered.

"It kept you occupied and out of my hair, for a few hours at least," she informed him politely.

Lucas had a hunch it was more the former than the latter but didn't question her.

Wyatt sat down at the opposite end of the table from Jaylene, still scowling. To Lucas, he said, "We're two-thirds of the way through your list of kidnappings for the last eighteen months."

"And?" Lucas knew the answer already, but asked anyway.

"And . . . in about half the cases, the Carnival After Dark was sited within fifty miles of the kidnapping."

"Half."

"Yeah."

"What about the other half?"

"They were farther away, obviously." Wyatt met those steady blue eyes and grimaced. "A lot farther, in some cases. Nearly two hundred miles away, on average."

Samantha asked, "So will you please leave Leo and the rest alone now?"

"Including yourself this time?"

"No. As I believe I've told you before, I never expect impossible things."

"Smartest thing I've ever heard you say."

Lucas sighed. "Enough. Wyatt, stop wasting time on the carnival. And, Sam, if you don't tell me about that dream —"

But she was shaking her head. "Sorry. I saw a *Welcome to Golden* sign and knew I was supposed to be here. That's all you get, Luke. That's all that matters."

"Maybe," Jaylene said, "that's all we need." She was watching Lucas steadily. "For now."

He shook his head, but said, "That pendant. Wyatt, you don't recall seeing it when you checked out Lindsay's apartment after she was taken?"

"It wasn't there."

"Maybe you missed it."

Wyatt shook his head. "I didn't miss it. It wasn't there, trust me on that. I knew

Lindsay was terrified of spiders, so I damned well would have noticed that thing on her nightstand."

To Samantha, Lucas said, "Is Caitlin back at the motel?"

"Yeah. We both thought it would be wise for her to wait for your okay before she started going through Lindsay's apartment. Because if he was there . . ."

"He might have left some evidence. If we're lucky. Wyatt, we'll need to canvass the building as well as search the apartment. You were there early afternoon on Thursday and didn't see the pendant; Caitlin found it on Sunday morning. Maybe somebody in the building noticed a stranger during that time."

"If we're lucky?" Wyatt shook his head. "Worth a shot, I guess."

Samantha looked at the clock on the wall and rose. "In the meantime, I have to go get ready to open my booth." She started around the table toward the door.

Before Lucas could protest, Wyatt said, "Conning people as usual, huh, Zarina?"

On any other day, at any other time, Samantha probably would have let the jibe pass without protest. But she was tired, her hand hurt, there was a lingering, unpleasant feeling that her head was stuffed

265

with cotton, and she had just about reached the end of her patience with Wyatt Metcalf.

"What the hell is your problem?" she demanded, rounding on him. But before anyone could speak, she added, "On second thought, why don't I find out for myself?"

That was all the warning she gave before reaching out and grasping his shoulder. Hard.

10

"Sam —"

Lucas knew the instant Samantha touched the sheriff that she'd been yanked into a vision. What surprised him was how frozen Wyatt seemed to be, his gaze fixed on her face while his own was both pale and somewhat defiant.

"She is wide open," Lucas muttered, watching them. "It wasn't like this before."

"We all mature in our abilities," Jaylene reminded him. "It's been three years, so maybe a lot has changed."

"Maybe. But for her to do this . . . Dammit, I warned Wyatt to get off her case."

"He seems the type that needs to learn a lesson the hard way," Jaylene suggested wryly. "Maybe it had to happen, sooner or later."

Lucas half agreed with her, but then he realized that Samantha's nose was bleeding. Swearing under his breath, he went quickly around the table to her, digging for his handkerchief and saying to Jaylene, "Not if this is the price."

"I've never seen —"

"I have." He grasped Samantha's wrist and firmly pulled her hand from Wyatt's shoulder. "Sam?"

"Hmm?" She blinked and looked up at him, frowning, and accepted the handkerchief he gave her as if it were something alien. "What's this?"

"Your nose is bleeding."

"Not again. Shit." She pressed the handkerchief to her nose and looked at Wyatt, adding, "I'm sorry. That was an invasion of privacy, and unforgivable."

"You said it, not me," he muttered. But he was watching her intently, frowning, and no one had to ask what he was thinking and wondering.

"I'm also sorry about your friend," she told him matter-of-factly. "But we both know the seer who told him he was going to die didn't force him to kill himself."

He paled and went very still once again. "I don't know what you're talking about."

Samantha knew all too well that most people disliked having their secrets dragged out into the open, and it went against her nature to expose Wyatt's when there were others present. But the other two people in the room were also psychic, and as much as she hated doing it,

Samantha felt that they all needed to know why Wyatt Metcalf so hated and distrusted "fortune-tellers."

"You were very young," she said, holding her voice level. "Maybe twelve or so. You weren't here in Golden — it was on a coast somewhere, at the ocean. You and some friends went to a carnival, and on a dare you all had your fortunes told by the seer."

"She was no seer. She —"

Samantha kept talking, ignoring the interruption. "She let all of you remain in her booth while she told your fortunes, one by one. Most of what she told each of you was vague and positive, not surprisingly. No reputable psychic would ever deliberately tell a client — especially a young one — that something tragic would happen to them, particularly if they could do nothing to avert that fate. But your friend, your best friend, was troubled. He'd been troubled a long time, and you knew it. He'd even talked about killing himself."

"He didn't — I didn't believe —"

"Of course you didn't believe him. Who believes in suicide at twelve except someone who wants to die? But the seer believed him. She knew he was serious, and she took a chance. With all of you listening, she warned him that he would die if he didn't change his life. And that dying would solve nothing, help nothing, and only hurt those he left behind." Samantha paused, adding quietly, "She was trying to help."

"No," Wyatt said. "If she hadn't said that, hadn't put it into his head —"

"It was already in his head. Already his fate. And you know it was. If you want to go on blaming her, then at least be honest with yourself. She wasn't trying to con anybody or deceive anybody, and she certainly intended no harm. She did the best she could for a stranger."

Wyatt stared up at her for a long moment, then pushed back his chair, got up, and left the conference room.

"I just keep making friends, don't I?" Samantha murmured, refolding the handkerchief and pressing it to her still-bleeding nose.

Realizing he was still holding her wrist, Lucas let her go, saying, "Nobody likes their secrets dragged out into the light."

"Yeah. But at least we know he has a reason for his distrust and dislike — not to say hatred. I really was hoping it wasn't just blind prejudice."

She sounded tired, and Lucas heard himself say roughly, "Dammit, will you go back to the motel and get some rest?"

"Maybe I'll take a nap before tonight." She looked at the clock and grimaced. "Or maybe not. Damned makeup takes forever if I want to do it right and not scare the clients."

"Sam —"

"I'll be fine, Luke."

"Will you?" He grasped the hand holding the handkerchief and drew it back so they could all see the scarlet blood. "Will you?"

She looked at the handkerchief, then up at him, saying only, "Has it stopped?"

She had the darkest eyes he'd ever known, unfathomable eyes. He wondered just how much she had not told them. He also wondered why he was so hesitant to press her in order to find out.

And it was Jaylene who answered her finally, saying, "Looks like it. Sam, I don't have to be a doctor to guess that nosebleeds triggered by a vision aren't a good sign." She considered, adding, "If you'll forgive the pun."

Samantha waited until Lucas released her hand, then refolded the handkerchief again and dabbed at her nose to wipe away the last of the blood. "I'll be fine," she repeated.

Lucas moved away far enough to rest a hip on the conference table, and said, "It's happened before, hasn't it? Earlier today?"

"Yeah, so?"

"Jaylene's right, Sam. It is a sign." He tried to control his voice but knew it emerged harshly. "A sign that you're pushing yourself too hard. The last psychic I saw have regular nosebleeds ended up in a coma."

After a moment, Samantha said, "Twice in one day isn't regular. It's . . . an aberration."

"Jesus, Samantha —"

"I'll get this laundered and back to you. Good luck in searching Lindsay's place. Hope you find something. See you later, Jay."

"Bye, Sam."

Lucas remained where he was for several moments, then said to his partner, "I've never met anybody so goddamned stubborn in my life."

"Look in the mirror."

He turned his head to frown at her, but said only, "She needs to be watched, especially tonight while she's reading. Whatever this bastard's *rules* are, I'm willing to bet they don't include sticking to the timetable we've come to expect."

"No, that would probably be too predictable of him. So you really do believe Sam's at risk?"

"He knows about her. He maneuvered her here. That means she's important to him or his game."

Jaylene nodded. "Agreed. But, Luke, other than Glen Champion — who's already pulled a couple of double shifts in the last few days — there's nobody in this department who would willingly guard Sam. And you know as well as I do that unwilling cops can be more dangerous than no cops."

"I'll do it."

Jaylene didn't ask him how he planned to watch Samantha twenty-four hours a day. Instead, she said, "We'll get going on canvassing Lindsay's building and searching the apartment. I'll call Caitlin Graham and tell her. As a matter of fact, I think I'll ask Wyatt to assign a couple of deputies to keep an eye on her."

"Think she might be a target?"

"If he was watching to see who found the pendant, he knows she's here. Better to be safe."

"Yeah."

"The pendant's on its way to Quantico; maybe they can come up with something useful. In the meantime, we have the photos here, if you want to take another look at it."

"You didn't get anything at all from it?"

"No. Maybe because Sam already had." She shook her head. "I really don't like to think about this guy being so far ahead of the game that he *knew* Sam would get her hands on that pendant."

"Neither do I."

"Think he's psychic?"

Lucas frowned. "No. Everything we have so far suggests that he's maneuvering people, maybe influencing or even creating events, but nothing says he's anticipating them in any paranormal sense."

"Then how did he know Sam would touch the pendant?"

"Logically. We've agreed he knows about her. That means he knew or could strongly suspect that she'd get involved in the investigation."

"Especially with you here," Jaylene murmured.

Lucas ignored that. "Logically, he could assume that sooner or later Sam would be asked to touch any object or evidence we found."

"Umm. Now tell me how he managed to imprint all that energy, all that fear, on the pendant."

"I don't know. Unless . . ."

"Unless?"

"Unless he carried it from the beginning. Unless it was a kind of . . . silent witness to everything he did. All the terror he created. All the pain and suffering. All the death. Nothing Sam described sounded like one of the kidnappings or murders, but maybe she got a glimpse into his soul. Maybe that's what she saw. Images of terror and death."

"Christ. No wonder she got a nosebleed. It's a miracle she didn't have a heart attack."

"Yeah." Lucas straightened and glanced toward the door, his thoughts clearly elsewhere, and his absent voice reflected that when he said, "Call me if the canvass or search of Lindsay's apartment turns up anything."

"You don't expect it to."

"I think the only thing he left there was what he wanted us to find. The pendant."

"So who makes the next move?"

"I do." He walked out of the room.

Gazing after him, Jaylene murmured, "Wrong chessboard, though. Then again . . . maybe not."

Caitlin didn't protest when two deputies from the sheriff's department knocked on the door to her room and announced that they'd be close by, should she need anything. She was somewhat relieved, in fact, since the occasional media person — apologizing profusely for "intruding" — persisted in knocking on her door.

She watched from the window as the cops turned away another one not ten minutes after they arrived, and shook her head as the disappointed young woman took her little cassette recorder and returned to her car.

It made Caitlin feel more than a little queasy. What did they expect from her? A sound bite about grief? How it felt to have a sister murdered? A dramatic direct appeal from her to the killer to give himself up?

Jesus.

She moved away from the window and sat on the bed for a moment staring at the muted news on TV, then rose again, restless but barred from moving very far in any direction. Small motel rooms provided little space and even less interest, she'd decided.

Room with a bed, low dresser with the TV atop one end and a big mirror above the other. Nightstands. A round table with two chairs near the window, so-called reading chair on the other side of the bed near the bathroom. Tiled bathroom, with just enough counter space for the little coffeemaker and maybe a small case of toiletries.

Caitlin knew every corner. She knew one of the chairs at the table sat unevenly on its legs. She knew the right-hand nightstand had a drawer that stuck. Ironically, she thought, the drawer containing the Bible.

She knew the shower nozzle was frozen in position so that it couldn't be adjusted, that the water stream was just enough underpressured to be an irritant. She knew the towels were rough. She knew the bed sagged.

It was edging into evening on the day of her only sister's funeral, and Caitlin was alone in a fairly shabby motel room she knew too well in a town she hardly knew at all.

Why had Lindsay chosen this little town in which to live? Because being a cop in a small town was simpler? Because it was easier to be a cop when you recognized most of the faces you saw in the course of your day, when you knew the people you worked to serve and protect?

"I wish I'd asked you, Lindsay," Caitlin

heard herself murmur. "I wish I'd asked you."

She jumped as the TV suddenly switched channels and came unmuted, the dry dialogue of an old movie filling the silence of the room. Frowning, she got the remote from the nightstand and hit the previous channel and mute buttons.

Silence fell as the TV returned to the earlier settings.

Caitlin sat back down on the bed, sighing. The news was depressing, so an old movie might just as well —

The TV began cycling through its channels, pausing on each one only a few seconds before going on. The mute function again turned itself off, and the volume rose slightly. An old movie. A sitcom from the seventies. A biography on a long-dead film legend. A science program on dinosaurs. Music videos.

Unnerved, Caitlin quickly reached for the remote and this time turned the set off.

Silence.

But before she could put the remote down again, the set came back on and, again, cycled steadily through its channels.

Caitlin turned it off again, and this time went over to fumble behind the dresser and pull the plug.

As she straightened in the silent room, the lamp on her nightstand flickered, dimmed, then went out. Seconds later, it came back on.

"A problem with the power," Caitlin said aloud, hearing the relief in her voice. "That's all it is —"

The phone on the opposite nightstand offered an odd, abbreviated ring. Long moments passed. It rang again, and again the sound was shortened, wrong.

Caitlin chewed on her bottom lip, watching the instrument as one would watch a coiled rattlesnake. When it rang again, she went slowly over and sat on the edge of the bed. Drew a deep breath. And picked up the receiver.

"Hello?"

Silence greeted her. But not an empty silence. Instead, there was a low hiss, the faint crackle of static, and an almost inaudible hum that made Caitlin's teeth ache.

She hung up quickly and stared at the phone. Weird. But just . . . weird. Uncommon, but not unexplainable. There had been storms recently, and the phone lines were probably old and wonky in a little town like this anyway —

The phone rang again, this time one

long, continuous ring.

She stood it as long as she could, then picked up the receiver again. "Hello? Who the hell is —"

"Cait."

It was almost inaudible, but clear for all of that.

And it was her dead sister's voice.

"Lindsay?"

"Tell Sam . . . to be careful. He knows. He . . ."

"Lindsay?"

But the voice had faded away. Caitlin sat listening to the weird, hissing silence for a long time before she finally replaced the receiver with a shaking hand.

Despite Samantha's words to her earlier today, Caitlin had never believed there was anything beyond death.

Until now.

As soon as the shaken client backed out of the booth, Lucas emerged from the curtains behind Samantha to say, "You were too blunt, telling him he wasn't going to get that promotion."

"He won't get it." Samantha rubbed her temples. "And stop backseat reading, will you?"

"You wouldn't have been so blunt if he

hadn't been a journalist, that's all I'm saying."

"I thought journalists were supposed to be hot after the truth."

"In a perfect world. These days, it's mostly being hot after a good story and hang the truth."

"You've gotten more cynical." She eyed him as he came around her to check the curtained front entrance of the booth. "I can't imagine why," she added dryly.

He turned to look at her, saying only, "Nobody waiting at the moment, so it looks like you'll get at least a short break."

"I had a break an hour ago when Ellis brought tea," she reminded him. "Luke, I don't need a watchdog."

"The hell you don't."

"I don't, whatever you think. And, besides, it's distracting to have your cell phone ring from behind me when I'm trying to concentrate."

"I forgot to set it on vibrate, sorry. Jay was just reporting in on the canvass and search. It'll take at least another day to talk to everyone in Lindsay's building, but so far no joy — and they didn't turn up anything useful in her apartment."

"Big surprise."

He sighed. "Well, we had to try."

Samantha watched him steadily, forcing herself to stop rubbing her temples before he commented on it. "You think the kidnapper will take someone else soon?"

"I think he'll make some kind of a move. He has to know that the longer he's active here in Golden, the more time it gives us to find him." Lucas shrugged. "It'll take time to check out every property in the area, but it can be done. The town's small enough that we can probably talk to every household individually, not just the remote ones."

"And he's bright enough to know that. He can't afford to stay here for much longer. So he has to move faster, force your hand."

"I would, in his place." He studied her, then said, "I never could get used to talking to you as Zarina. It's not so much the shawls and turban as it is the makeup. You do a very skillful job of aging yourself."

"A true glimpse into the future." She smiled wryly. "It takes less makeup now than it used to, of course."

"Without the makeup you still look like a teenager."

"I wasn't a teenager even when I was one. You know that."

"I never knew it all, though, did I?"

Samantha wasn't at all sure she wanted to drift into this territory with Lucas, but the strange and unsettling day seemed to have done something to the guards she normally kept raised solidly between them. Her head throbbed, and she reached up again to briefly rub her temples, hearing herself say, "You didn't ask. I didn't think you needed to know."

He took a step toward her and leaned his hands on the back of the client's chair. "Would you have told me, if I'd asked?"

"I don't know. Maybe not. We were sort of busy, if you recall. There wasn't a lot of time to dredge up the past."

"Maybe that's what we should have done. Taken the time to do."

More than a little surprised, she said, "You were obsessed with the investigation, remember?"

"Missing kids do that to me."

Again, Samantha was surprised, this time by the defensive tone in his voice. "I wasn't criticizing. Just stating a fact. Your focus was on the investigation, as it should have been. The timing for anything else was, to say the least, lousy."

"So I'm forgiven?"

"For what happened during the investigation, there's nothing to forgive. I'm a big girl, I knew what I was doing. For what happened after . . . Well, let's just say I learned my lesson."

"Meaning?"

Samantha was saved from replying when a new client appeared hesitantly in the curtained doorway. Lucas was forced to retreat to the area behind Samantha, and he was clearly not pleased by the interruption.

As for Samantha, she had to mentally prepare herself yet again to read, even as she was automatically beginning her spiel for at least the tenth time that evening.

"What may Madam Zarina see for you on this night?"

The teenage girl sat down in the client's chair, still looking hesitant, and said, "I'm not here for a reading. Well, not really. I mean, I have this" — she placed her ticket on the satin-covered table — "but I didn't pay for it. He paid for it."

Everything in Samantha went still, and she was conscious that, behind her, Luke had frozen as well. Relaxing her voice into its normal tones, she asked, "Who paid for it?"

The girl blinked in surprise at the change, but answered readily, "That guy. I don't know him. Actually, I couldn't see his face very well, because he was standing in the shadows near the sharpshooting booth."

Because she couldn't help it, Samantha said, "You're a little old to need to be warned not to speak to strangers. Particularly strange men."

"Yeah, I thought about that," she confessed. "After. But, anyway, there were people all around, and he didn't come near me. He just pointed to the edge of the counter there at the booth, and I saw a folded twenty and this ticket. He said the twenty was mine if I'd come tell you that he was sorry he missed his appointment."

"His appointment."

"Yeah. He said to tell you he was sorry about that, and he was sure he'd see you later." She smiled brightly. "He seemed awfully sorry about it."

"Yes," Samantha murmured. "I'll just bet he was."

Jaylene said, "We've checked the phone lines, Caitlin. The phone company says they're working fine. There's nothing wrong with them."

Sitting down on the edge of her bed, Caitlin said, "I'm not surprised. Or very reassured." She eyed the other woman uncertainly. "Sam told me that if anything happened, I should call you. She said you'd understand."

Jaylene sat down at one of the chairs at the table and smiled faintly. "I do understand, believe me. And if it helps, what you experienced is fairly common, one of the most common events in the annals of the paranormal."

"It is? But I'm not psychic."

"No, but you shared a blood connection with Lindsay; the bond between sisters is usually one of the strongest, no matter how emotionally distant that may seem during adulthood. There are many documented cases of recently deceased persons appearing or speaking to relations. Since you were her sister, it makes sense that if she tried to reach out, you would be the one best able to hear her."

"Through the goddamned *telephone?*"

Jaylene said, "It does seem weirdly prosaic, doesn't it? But, again, it isn't terribly uncommon. Our best guess is that, like so much about psychic ability, it has to do with electromagnetic fields. Spiritual energy appears to be based on that, so it follows that the need to communicate could be directed through the natural conduits of power and phone lines. Energy manipulating energy."

"So she couldn't just talk to me, she needed to use . . . a device?"

Jaylene hesitated, then said carefully, "I've been told by mediums that there's a transition time between death and the next phase of existence. During that time, it requires an exceptionally powerful or determined personality to communicate at all to a nonpsychic. It's fairly difficult for them to communicate even to psychics. The fact that Lindsay was able to reach you is remarkable enough. That she was actually able to speak to you . . ."

"Have you ever talked to the dead?" Caitlin demanded.

"No."

"Well, it's creepy, let me tell you." Caitlin shivered unconsciously, then frowned. "What about what she said? The warning to Samantha?"

"I'll certainly pass it on. My partner is with her now, so she should be safe enough." It was Jaylene's turn to frown. " 'He knows.' Knows about what?"

"Beats me. But it must be important, or Lindsay wouldn't have worked so hard to get through to me." She eyed the unplugged TV uneasily. "At least, I think that was her, scanning through the channels. It didn't hit me at the time, but when we

287

were kids she used to drive me crazy turning the channels constantly. So do you think that was her?"

"Probably. Televisions seem more easily affected by spiritual energy, or so I'm told. Something about the literal transmission of energy through the air around us."

Caitlin was more interested in results than in methods, at least at the moment. "Do you think . . . she'll try to get in touch again?"

"I honestly don't know, Caitlin. If it's important enough to her, then maybe. Try, at least. Though it may take a while to re-focus her energy." Jaylene studied her for a moment, adding, "If you'd rather not be alone, then I'm sure we can arrange something."

"No. No, that's okay. If Lindsay wants to communicate, I want to hear what she has to say. I didn't listen enough when she was alive, so I'm damned well going to listen now."

"She wouldn't want to scare you, Caitlin."

"She would if that's what it took to get my attention. She was very single-minded, my sister."

"In that case, you may be hearing from her again."

Dryly, Caitlin said, "Anything you want me to ask her?"

"Well, I would suggest you ask if she knows who killed her, but we've tried before and that question never seems to get us anywhere."

Briefly distracted, Caitlin said, "I wonder why?"

"Our boss says it's the universe reminding us that nothing is ever as simple as we think it should be. He's probably right. He usually is."

"Mmm. Do you think I *will* be able to communicate with her? Or just . . . receive?"

"No idea."

"Will I mess up anything by trying?"

Jaylene smiled and shrugged. "There aren't any rules, Caitlin. Or not many, at any rate. Do whatever feels best to you at the time."

"Easy for you to say."

"Unfortunately, it is." Jaylene got to her feet, still smiling. "I'll call Luke and let him and Sam know about the warning. In the meantime, the two deputies will be outside keeping an eye on this place. If you need anything, or you feel too uneasy to be alone, let them know."

"I will. Thanks, Jaylene." Caitlin sat

there for a long time after the other woman had gone, until it occurred to her that she was waiting — and that this room was going to get very quiet and very boring if she just sat here for hours.

What she needed to do, she decided, was what she would usually do this time of the evening. Call the nearest Chinese take-out place and order her dinner to be delivered and settle in for the night.

Reaching for the phone book in the nightstand drawer, she murmured, "I'm ready when you are, Lindsay."

And she could have sworn the lamp beside her flickered. Just a bit.

Samantha unlocked her motel-room door and came in, saying, "There are two deputies out there keeping an eye on this place; why do you have to be here too?"

"Because they aren't watching you, they're watching Caitlin."

"And because they wouldn't get out of their car to help me if I was on fire?" Samantha waved away his response before he could offer it, adding, "Never mind." She was almost too tired to care. About anything.

"Sam, you heard what that kid told you."

"I heard a lot of things tonight, most of

them inside my own head. I'm tired of listening."

"Sam —"

"I'm going to take a long, hot shower. Do us both a favor and don't be here when I get out."

His jaw firmed. "I'm not going anywhere."

Samantha heard a little laugh escape her. "Fine. Just don't say I didn't warn you." She got a nightgown from one of the dresser drawers and went into the bathroom, closing the door behind her. All her toiletries were there, as well as her robe, and she lost no time in stripping off and stepping behind the shower curtain into the tub.

It was after eleven, the usual time she tended to return from the carnival when she was working. And usually, after the hot shower, she ended up lying in bed staring at the TV or reading far into the night. She was a voracious reader, partly due to a stubborn determination to be well-educated despite her lack of formal schooling, and partly out of simple interest.

Letting the hot water stream over her chilled skin, Samantha tried her best to get warm even though she knew the cold came from inside, where no amount of hot water could touch it. It came from that limbo where the visions took her, where even the wispiest bit of precognitive or clairvoyant knowledge came from, a place she had tapped into far too many times today.

She hadn't been lying to Luke. She had heard too much today, and it had left her feeling raw and, for one of the few times in her life, unsure of herself.

So the kidnapper was watching her.

She had expected that, sooner or later, but still . . .

What was her next move?

She stood under the hot water for a long, long time before finally, reluctantly, getting out and drying off. She towel-dried her hair but didn't do anything more than finger-comb it, put on her nightgown and wrapped herself in the thick terry robe.

As promised, Luke was there when she came out. He was sitting in the so-called reading chair, his feet propped up on the bed, the television tuned, low, to the news.

His holstered gun was on the table near his hand.

That indication of her own vulnerability made Samantha feel even more raw, and she heard herself say tensely, "Don't you have someplace else to be? I mean, isn't there an investigation in full swing right now?"

"It's been a long day for everyone," he reminded her, oddly quiet. "We'll start fresh in the morning."

A little voice in her head warned her that it *had* been a long day and that decisions made when she was this tired had always, always backfired on her, but Samantha ignored it. No more voices. Not tonight.

"I hated you for a long time," she told Lucas.

He got to his feet slowly. "I'm sorry."

"Oh, don't be sorry. Hating you was better than hurting. I wasn't going to let you hurt me, no matter what. That's why I laughed when you said you hadn't meant to hurt me. You didn't. I didn't let you."

He took a step toward her. "Sam —"

"Don't you dare tell me you're sorry again. Don't you *dare*."

He took another step toward her, then swore under his breath and yanked her into his arms.

When she could, Samantha murmured, "Took you long enough. Here we are, right back where we left off. In a cheap motel room."

"It wasn't cheap," Lucas said, and pulled her with him down onto the bed.

Samantha had believed she'd forgotten how it felt, his body against hers, his mouth seducing her. That she had forgotten how well they fit together, how his skin burned beneath her touch, how her own body responded to his with a fierce pleasure she had never known before or since.

She had believed she had forgotten.

She hadn't.

Part of her wanted to hold back, to save something of herself, but she had never been able to do that with Luke. And he was just as unrestrained, his mouth eager on hers, hungry on her body, his hands shaking as they touched her. Even his voice, when he murmured her name, sounded rough, urgent, as potent to her senses as any caress.

Two wary, prickly, guarded people forged a connection in the only way they would allow themselves, flesh to flesh and soul to soul. And even as she lost herself in the pleasure of it, Samantha was conscious of an almost wordless hope.

That, this time, it would be enough.

11

Tuesday, October 2

It was probably around two in the morning when a quiet storm began to rumble outside. Lucas lay in the lamplit room and listened to it, just as he had listened earlier to Samantha's soft breathing.

She slept with the boneless tranquillity of an exhausted child, held close to his side, her dark head pillowed on his shoulder. She fit him perfectly and always had, something that had once made him feel a wordless unease.

He wondered now why he had felt that way. And why he no longer did. Had he changed so much in three years? Or had it been then, as Samantha had said herself, simply a case of lousy timing?

Not that the timing now could possibly be better.

No one had to tell Lucas that he was not the easiest of personalities, or that he tended to keep others at a distance at the best of times, a trait that was magnified many times over when he was in the middle of an investigation. He was driven, obsessive, often single-minded to the point that he unintentionally shut out those around him. But that was the work, not his personal life.

Is there a difference?

Of course there was. He could separate the two.

Can you?

What had Sam said to him? That he had taken the easy way out, letting Bishop clean up behind him as he moved on and told himself it was for the best? Was that what he'd done?

Could he have been that arrogant? That cruel?

"You should sleep," she murmured.

She had always had that facility, he remembered, able to shift in an instant from deep sleep to full wakefulness. Like a cat, she was more likely to nap for short periods than to sleep heavily through the night, no matter how tired she was.

"I will," he said.

Samantha pushed herself up on an elbow to look at him, solemn. "Your gun's under the pillow, and you have one hand on it. Not exactly relaxed enough for sleep."

After a moment, he slid his hand out

from under the pillow and lifted it to cup her cheek. As quiet as she had been, he said, "Christ, Sam, can't you see that you're in danger? The bastard is watching you."

"He's been watching you for months. And don't say you can take care of yourself. We both know I can take care of myself too."

"It isn't a matter of being able to take care of yourself. Lindsay could take care of herself, and she's dead."

"Okay, granted. But there's a patrol car with two deputies in it parked out front. The door's locked, and you've wedged a chair under the handle. And besides all that, if he was watching earlier, and he knows anything at all about you, about us, then he knows you're here with me, he knows you're armed, and he knows you're ready for him."

"Tonight."

"Yes, and after that little message of his, he isn't really likely to make another move tonight, is he? One of the objects of the game appears to be catching us off guard, so warning us ahead of time wouldn't be terribly smart."

"Yeah, I know," he admitted reluctantly.

Half consciously, she rubbed her cheek

against his hand. "Then I think we're safe enough for tonight."

Lucas felt his mouth twist. "From him, I guess."

"But not from each other?"

He had to laugh, albeit wryly. "You have a unique way of cutting through all the bullshit, Sam."

"Life's too short for bullshit." Her smile was also a little wry. "Especially with a killer running around playing dangerous games. Luke . . . you don't have to tell me that neither one of us thought this through."

"Just like last time."

"Not quite."

"What's different, Sam? We're in the middle of an investigation, there's a deadly criminal on the loose, the media are swarming all over you and the carnival —"

"The difference," Samantha said, "is all a matter of expectation. I don't expect happy endings anymore, Luke. So you don't have to worry about that."

"Don't I?"

"No. When the investigation is over, you'll move on to your next case and I'll move on with the carnival. We'll continue with our separate jobs and our separate lives. Which is as it should be."

Her calm fatalism bothered Lucas, and he didn't stop to wonder why. "Says who?"

She smiled, dark eyes very steady. "Says me. I see what will be, remember? The future. And my future doesn't have you in it."

"You're sure of that."

"Positive."

"So I should just relax and enjoy the present, huh?"

"Well, this present. Tonight. Maybe a few more nights, if we can steal them." Her shoulders moved in a slight shrug. "That won't be so hard, will it? We were good together in bed. That hasn't changed."

"It wasn't all we were, Sam."

"It's enough for now."

Lucas might have argued, but her lips were on his, warm and hungry, and his body remembered hers too well and too eagerly to allow for clear thought. Or any thought at all.

She was right. They were good in bed. Very good.

The inn where Jaylene and Lucas were staying was across town from the motel nearer the fairgrounds and, unlike the motel, didn't have a manager who rented at least a few of his rooms by the hour. So it was a quieter place, back off the highway and far enough away from the nearest Wal-Mart to be out of the heavier traffic patterns.

Though they had been here only a week, Jaylene was as comfortable in her room as she was in her own home. One of her most useful traits, Bishop had noted: she was a nester. So she was completely unpacked, her laptop set up on the small desk near her bed, and she had even stopped by a local florist to get a small vase of flowers to make the generic room-without-a-view brighter.

If she had to live much of her life on the road, Jaylene intended to be comfortable.

It was late, so she was already wearing her flannel kitty pajamas, but Jaylene was also a night owl and still up working on her laptop when the storm began — and her cell phone rang.

She checked the caller I.D. and then answered, "You're up late. Or are you still in another time zone?"

"No, we finished up in Santa Fe," Bishop said. He paused, then added, "I tried Luke earlier but got his voice mail."

"He was in Samantha's booth most of the evening. Probably turned his phone off or set it on vibrate after I interrupted a reading with a call."

"I just got the earlier report. Was there any luck in getting an I.D. of the man who passed on his little message through the teenager?"

"No. She didn't get a good look at him and, besides, isn't what you'd call a dependable witness. I think her comment was that he was 'old . . . like about thirty.' "

"Ouch."

"Uh-huh. Anyway, there was no way to contain that crowd soon enough, not out there. Luke called in some deputies to question all the ticket-sellers and people running the other booths before the carnival closed up shop for the night, but they were busy as hell for a Monday, and nobody remembered seeing anything useful."

"And Caitlin Graham?"

"Just what I reported. Possibly a message from Lindsay warning Sam to be careful because *he knows*. *He* is, presumably, the kidnapper. *What* he knows is still a mystery, at least to me. And all this is assuming the message is genuine, of course."

"You have your doubts?"

"About Caitlin's honesty, no. She definitely experienced something paranormal. I could still feel the energy in the room when I got there. But she also admitted that the phone connection — my second bad pun of the day — was iffy and she may have misheard. No way to know for sure, unless Lindsay gets back in touch." She paused, adding, "We could use a medium."

"Don't really have one available."

"Hollis?"

"No. Tied up on another case." He paused, then asked, "How is Luke holding up?"

"You know Luke. The longer this goes on, the more tightly wound he'll get. Finding out he's a personal target of a serial killer's twisted games didn't exactly make his day. Losing Lindsay was horrible, and he felt that on every level."

"And Samantha?"

"How is she, or how is Luke handling her presence here?"

"Both."

"She's quieter, more guarded. Maybe even secretive. Really pushing herself physically and emotionally to read every night, I think because of something she hasn't told us about so far. And she's had at least two nosebleeds that I know of, both after touching something or someone and getting a vision."

"Was there violence in the visions?"

"The first one, yeah, violent terror, according to what she told us. Second one, not so much. There was a suicide, but I don't think she actually saw that."

"Is she having headaches? Sensitivity to light and sound?"

"Dunno for sure. Sam's not one to give away much."

"Opinion?"

Jaylene considered briefly. "If I had to guess, I'd say she was having headaches. I know damned well she's tired as hell and not planning on taking a vacation anytime soon. Luke's worried about her, that's plain enough."

"How are they getting along?"

"Been able to work together, more or less. He's defended her to the sheriff. More or less. He believes what she's told us but also believes she's holding something back, and that hint of mistrust has been fairly obvious. If I see it, she sees it. They've been prickly as hell with each other, at least until tonight. I don't know, maybe they'll settle some things now that they have a little time alone together."

Bishop was silent for a long moment, then said, "You're all convinced this killer is still in Golden?"

She noted that he didn't even pay lip

service to the "kidnapper" definition; to Bishop, a killer was a killer, period.

"We have no way of knowing for certain if the message Sam was given by the teenager was from the kidnapper or just some journalist yanking her chain. Could have been the latter; they want a story and she hasn't been real forthcoming from their point of view. She didn't get anything from the ticket he sent or the twenty he gave the girl, and neither did I. Only the girl's prints, naturally."

"Answer the question, Jay."

She didn't hesitate. "He's still here. For whatever reason, Golden's his endgame."

"Then he'll be abducting someone else."

"I don't find sure things very often, but I'd call that one."

"Testing Luke — or hurting him?"

"Either. Both."

"Which means the killer could be moving closer to Luke. Watch your back, Jaylene."

"I keep my weapon handy, believe me." She chuckled. "But I'm not feeling all that vulnerable, if you want the truth. I spotted your watchdog earlier tonight."

Sounding a little amused himself, Bishop said, "He must be slipping."

"Well, I'll let you tell him that. I gather

we weren't supposed to know he was here?"

"Just a precaution. Does Luke know?"

"He hasn't mentioned it. I just noticed myself a few hours ago."

"Do me a favor and don't tell him unless he asks."

"Keeping secrets from my partner? He will not be happy when he finds out."

"Just tell him I asked, and let me deal with the fallout."

"Gladly. In the meantime, as I'm sure you're aware, the local police aren't all that inclined to keep an eye on Samantha for her own safety. And if Luke plans to stick close from now on, he may have to hand-cuff her."

"Depends on how things are going in that motel room," Bishop murmured.

Severely, Jaylene said, "I just meant that if he intends to be her watchdog for the rest of this case, then the only way the cops in the Clayton County Sheriff's Department are going to accept her presence is if she's handcuffed to his wrist and at least nominally under arrest."

"He can fake it if he needs to."

"You know, for someone who holds a position of legal authority as high as yours, you sure do like to throw away the rule book sometimes."

"Knowing the rules is one thing. Following them blindly all the time is something else again." Bishop sighed, his humor fading. "If it came to that, arresting Samantha would probably accomplish nothing more than brightening the media spotlight on the investigation."

"Yeah, but if she's always with Luke, that's going to happen anyway. A fed with a carnival seer as a sidekick? Or however they choose to define the relationship. And given the high moral standards of the media, *sidekick* is probably the kindest word they'd use."

"I wonder if Luke's considered that."

"I don't wonder. He hasn't. He gets tunnel vision, you know that. It's what makes him so good."

"And so difficult to work with."

"Have you heard me complain?"

"No, thankfully." Bishop sighed. "You two will just have to deal with Samantha's presence as best you can. In the meantime, I meant what I said about watching your back. If this killer wants to test Luke, he's likely to turn his sights on those closest to him. That means you."

"And Sam."

"And Samantha, yes. What bothers me

about that message she was given is that there's no good reason for the killer to alert them he was watching. Unless . . ."

"Unless?"

"Unless it was sleight of hand. And if so, if Sam's the diversion . . ."

"Then where's the trick," Jaylene finished.

It was after five and still very dark outside when Samantha stirred and raised herself up slightly. Lucas lay on his stomach beside her, one arm thrown across her and his face half buried in the pillows. He was deeply asleep, totally relaxed in a way he never was while awake.

Samantha watched him for a long time in the lamplight, just studying his face. What he did aged him; he looked older than the thirty-five she knew him to be. At the same time, his was a face that the years would be kind to, and he would always, she thought, be a handsome man.

Of course, he'd also always be a pain in the ass.

She couldn't help smiling at the wry realization, and as she did, the lamp beside the bed flickered several times. She waited, watching it, and within a minute it flickered again.

Samantha slid out from under his arm and from the bed. She didn't take particular pains to be quiet; once Luke was asleep, it required either a very loud noise or the sense of danger to awaken him.

And no matter what doubts he might harbor when he was awake, Luke's subconscious knew she posed no danger to him.

She was counting on that.

Dressing quickly in warm clothing, Samantha went to the door and removed the chair wedged underneath the knob. She turned to the window by the door and peeked out. The patrol car set to watch the motel — Caitlin Graham, actually — was parked at the far end, closer to Caitlin's room, and Samantha could just make out the deputies inside. As she watched, one got out of the car and walked around, yawning and stretching in an obvious effort to stay awake. The one on the passenger side looked as though he had already nodded off.

Samantha waited until the deputy returned to the car and was facing away from her again, then picked up her key and slipped silently from the room. It took only seconds to vanish around the corner and out of sight of the deputies.

She waited there for a minute or so for

her eyes to adjust to the darkness, then got her bearings and moved away from the motel and toward a little side street nearby. Within fifty yards, she crossed the street and stood in the shadow of an old building that had started out life as something better than the storage space it was now.

"Good morning."

She didn't jump in surprise, but Samantha's voice was a bit tense when she said, "We need to discuss these little pre-dawn meetings. What if your subtle signal with the light alerted the deputies or woke up Luke?"

"The deputies were all but snoring and not even facing in the direction of your room. As for Luke, once he sleeps, he sleeps like the dead, we both know that. I was counting on you to put him to sleep."

"Quentin, I swear —"

"I wasn't insulting you. Would I do that? I only meant . . . Well, never mind." Hastily, he added, "I gather he isn't suspicious?"

"He's plenty suspicious. He knows damned well there's something I'm not telling him."

"Well, now, that surprises me. You being such a good actress and all."

Samantha shifted a bit to take better advantage of what little light was available to her, and peered up at him. "Are you *trying* to make me mad this morning?"

"Take it easy. Jesus, you're as prickly as Luke is. Fine pair you make." Quentin shook his head.

"That," she said, "remains to be seen. I can't stay away long; is there anything I need to know?"

"Yeah. The boss says we're running out of time."

"And they pay him the big bucks to state the obvious?"

Quentin's white teeth flashed in a grin. "You are not going to let him off the hook, are you?"

"Not if I can help it, no."

He smothered a laugh. "Well, I'm not saying he doesn't deserve to be given a hard time in this particular case, but later would probably be better. He's serious, Sam. We've reached a critical point, and if we can't get past it successfully, then this bastard will get away from us here."

"And if he does?"

"You know what happens if he does. You saw it. And what you saw is . . . unacceptable. We stop him here. Whatever the cost."

"Easy for your boss to say. He's not in the line of fire."

Quiet now, Quentin said, "Yes, he is. We all are."

After a moment, Samantha nodded. "Yeah. I know. Doesn't really make it easier, though."

"No. It never does."

"Look . . ." She hesitated, then finished, "I don't know how much I can control from this point on. How much I can change. It's already gotten off-track."

"You mean you and Luke?"

"That didn't happen. It didn't happen because I wasn't here. And I don't know what it'll change. Maybe the wrong things. Maybe too much."

Musingly, Quentin said, "I've got to hand it to Bishop; he said you'd be wavering about now."

She stiffened. "I am not wavering."

"It wasn't an insult," he said in an absent tone. "He said to remind you that when we all agreed to take the first step and try to change what you saw, we were committed. If we stop before the job's done, we could make everything far worse."

"Worse than losing Lindsay?"

"There was nothing you could do about that."

"No?" Samantha let out a brief sigh. "I don't know anymore. She shouldn't have died, Quentin. That's not what I saw."

"You weren't sure what you saw when all this started, not about that. About most of the victims. You saw the devices, the . . . brutal efficiency of an assembly-line killer. And you saw him operating far beyond Golden once he finished up what he meant to do here. No matter what, we can't allow that to happen."

"I know. I wouldn't be here if I didn't agree with that goal. But the balance started to shift somehow with Lindsay; I picked up that handkerchief at the carnival and *saw* another victim killed on the day Lindsay died. So why didn't it happen? Why was it Lindsay instead?"

"Maybe because you warned the intended victim."

She hadn't really considered that, but even as she did, Samantha was shaking her head. "I warned Mitchell Callahan, and he still died. No, it's not that simple. It's something else. It feels like something else."

"What does it feel like?"

Frustrated, Samantha snapped, "If I knew that —"

"Okay, okay," Quentin soothed. "Look,

all we can do — is all we can do. Maybe you'll figure out what feels wrong as time goes on. Maybe you won't. Either way, it doesn't change the game plan."

Samantha offered a last objection. "I don't like being dishonest with Luke."

"You're not lying to him, just . . . omitting some things."

"And you're splitting hairs."

Quentin sighed. "Do you want to stop the killer?"

"Dammit, of course I do."

"Then play the cards in front of you, the way you've done since you came to Golden. You don't have a choice, Sam. None of us has a choice now."

Samantha drew a breath and nodded. "Yeah. Okay. If I'm right, we should be getting another message from the kidnapper, but this one written. A taunt, probably connected to another abduction. It'll be Luke's first real chance to try and get inside his head."

"An opportunity we need."

"I know."

Frankly, Quentin asked, "Can you do what needs to be done now that you and Luke are lovers?"

"I'll have to, won't I?"

It was Quentin's turn to nod, but he

added even more seriously, "The boss also said to tell you to take it easy and rest when you can. Nosebleeds are never a good sign, not for psychics. You burn out now, and we've lost our rudder."

Wryly, she said, "Yeah, well, just tell the captain to keep a steady hand on the wheel, okay? Because the rudder can't hold to the course without it."

Reflectively, he said, "We're getting deep into metaphor here. Never thought of Bishop as a captain. But . . ."

"It's too early for word games," she said. "You guys stick close, that's all I'm asking."

"Will do."

Samantha lifted a hand in farewell, then moved quickly back across the street and to the motel. She was able to slip back into her room without any sign that the deputies out front had seen her, and as she closed the door behind her she saw with relief that Lucas was still sleeping deeply.

She wedged the chair back under the doorknob and took off her jacket and shoes but didn't bother to undress; it was after six and would be light soon, so she knew she wouldn't be able to get back to sleep.

Instead, she got one of the books off her

dresser and sat in the reading chair, stretching out her legs and gently resting her feet on the bed. She sat there gazing at Luke's sleeping face for a long time, then stirred and opened her book.

Softly, she murmured, "You aren't in my future, Luke. Unless I put you there."

Jaylene was still yawning over coffee when Lucas and Samantha arrived, and she knew with one glance that there had been some disagreement.

The observation was confirmed when Samantha said with faint irritation, "Just how long do you think the sheriff will suffer my presence here? Morning, Jay."

Lucas said, "If he wants to argue about it, I'll argue. Whether he likes it or not, we need you. Hey, Jaylene."

"Coffee's fresh," she informed them.

Samantha said, "I should be at the carnival. I have things to do."

"Sam, do we have to keep arguing about this?" He handed her a cup but didn't let go until she met his gaze. "I want you here. I need you here."

She hesitated, then nodded. "Okay, fine."

It might not have been gracious acceptance, but at least it was acceptance, and

Lucas was visibly relieved.

Jaylene knew why. Samantha could be rather slippery when she didn't want to be somewhere.

They sat down at the conference table with their coffee, but Lucas barely had time to ask Jaylene if anything new had come in from Quantico — and she barely had time to reply in the negative — when Deputy Champion knocked on the open door.

"Hey," he said. "I thought the sheriff might be in here."

"Haven't seen him." Lucas looked at the younger man, his brows rising. "Something new?"

Champion sighed and hesitated, then said apologetically, "Sheriff said to take anything to him first, but — hell, it's got your name on it."

"What's got my name on it?"

"This." The deputy produced a small manila envelope, which he slid across the table to Lucas. "It was mixed in with the regular mail, so God knows how many people have handled it. I figured anything useful would be inside anyway."

Lucas was staring down at the envelope. "What tipped you off?" he asked.

"No stamp, let alone a postmark."

Champion shrugged, hesitated, then turned and left the conference room.

"Luke?" Jaylene was leaning toward him. "What is it?"

"Addressed to me here at the station. Neatly typed. And Champion was right — no stamp. It had to be hand-delivered." He left the table long enough to don latex gloves, saying, "We all know there won't be prints on it, but might as well follow protocol."

Making an observation, Jaylene said, "The flap is fastened but not sealed. And no licked stamp. He's taking no chance of leaving a bit of his DNA, is he?"

"He knows better," Samantha said.

Luke nodded in agreement. The two women watched as he carefully opened the fastened but not sealed envelope and drew out a single page that had been folded only once. He unfolded it on the table, and they could all see it.

"Goddammit," he muttered. "The bastard's just having fun. Why use newsprint when he has a virtually untraceable ink-jet printer?"

"For the effect," Samantha murmured. "Imagining our faces. And for the hands-on precision of cutting and pasting the letters and words."

Lucas nodded again in absent agreement, even as he bent forward over the note. It looked crude, the words made up of different-size newsprint, but it was brief and to the point.

THERE IS ONLY ONE RULE, LUKE.
GUESS WHAT IT IS.
I HAVE HIM.
IF YOU DON'T FIND HIM IN TIME
HE DIES.
HAVE A NICE DAY.

"Him?" Lucas looked at the women, frowning. "He's already taken someone? Who?"

There was a long silence, and then Samantha said very quietly, "Maybe we'd better look for the sheriff."

Wyatt Metcalf felt a little groggy and wondered what the hell he'd had to drink before going to bed. He didn't remember much, just the overwhelming urge to get drunk so he could sleep.

Apparently, he'd been successful, because he felt like he'd been sleeping for a hundred years.

He yawned and tried to shift a bit, realizing only then that he couldn't move. His eyelids felt as if they'd been lined with sandpaper, and it took three tries to force them to scrape across his undoubtedly bloodshot eyes and open.

Everything was blurry at first. He blinked painfully until his eyes finally teared a bit so he could see.

What he saw didn't make sense at first. It didn't make sense because it defied belief. Sturdy wood. A rope — no, a cable. And a heavy, gleaming blade of steel.

A guillotine?

Now, what in the world —

He turned his head a little, watching the light glint off that sharp, sharp blade. The blade that was poised to drop.

He didn't really get it until he tried again to move, then craned his head to see as much as he could. What he saw, finally, made sense.

Terrifying sense.

"Oh, shit," he whispered.

12

"Did you know it would be Metcalf?" Lucas demanded, nearly two hours later as they gathered once more in the conference room.

Samantha shook her head. "If I'd known that, I would have told you."

"What did you know?" His voice was flat, hard.

"I knew there'd be another abduction. But you knew that; it was hardly something I had to tell you."

"What else?"

"Again, what you know yourself. The object of this twisted little game is for the good guys to find the victim before his time runs out." Suddenly thoughtful, she said, "Except that in this case he didn't set a time limit, did he? No ransom demand."

"So how long do I have?"

She looked at him, brows lifting. "I'm supposed to know that?"

"Do you?"

Samantha glanced at the silent Jaylene, then looked back at Lucas and said with deliberation, "Is it with all your women,

Luke, or just me? I mean, since this is the second time with us, I have to wonder."

His frown deepened. "What're you talking about?"

"I got close once before. Too close, apparently. And just like now, you spent the morning after grilling me about what I knew or didn't know." She paused, then added coolly, "It hurt a lot, last time. This time it's just pissing me off."

"Sam —"

"I don't have to be here, Luke. I don't have to be involved in this investigation. In fact, I'm sure it would be a lot safer and certainly less troublesome if I went back to the carnival, packed up, and asked Leo to leave a few days early. If I went back to minding my own business. I'm here because I was under the impression that I could help. So why on earth would I lie to you about any of this?"

"*Because* of last time," he snapped.

Jaylene, watching and listening calmly, was highly aware of the precious minutes ticking past. But she was even more aware of the vital need for these two to come to some understanding; at odds with each other, she thought, both were at least somewhat hamstrung. So she watched, and listened, and said nothing.

"Oh, I see." Samantha shook her head with a bitter little smile. "It's revenge I'm after. Is that it? Do you really believe I'd stand by and allow innocent people to die just because you walked out on me three years ago? Because if that's the case, Luke, then you never knew me at all."

"I never —" He stopped, then said evenly, "No, that isn't what I believe. What I believe is that you're holding back on us, Sam. The vision that brought you here —"

"Wouldn't help you find Metcalf or the killer even if I told you every single detail. And as I've already said, I don't intend to share any further details of that vision with you. I have my own reasons for that. You just have to believe — trust — that the reasons I have are good ones."

She held his gaze steadily. "You didn't trust me before. Maybe that's why everything went to hell, or maybe that had nothing to do with it. Either way, this time is a bit different. So you have to decide, Luke. Now. Either you trust me, or you don't. If you do, I'm willing to do whatever I can to help you in this investigation. If you don't, I leave. Now."

"I don't like ultimatums, Sam."

"Call it whatever you like. But make up your mind. Because I'm not going through this little song and dance with you, not again."

Before Lucas could reply, Deputy Champion came into the room, his young face haunted. "Nothing," he reported without waiting to be asked. "No sign of the sheriff anywhere. You guys were at his apartment; did you —"

It was Jaylene who said, "No sign of a struggle or a break-in, though your forensics unit is still out there. His car was in its normal spot. Looks like the bed was slept in."

Lucas turned away from Samantha with a somewhat jerky motion, and said, "Maybe not. He'd been sleeping on the couch, according to what he told me."

Jaylene pursed her lips thoughtfully. "His weapon was on the coffee table, so that fits. And there were a hell of a lot of beer bottles in the kitchen garbage can; I'd say he drank a lot last night."

"He's been drinking every night," Lucas said briefly.

Samantha moved to the opposite side of the conference table from him and sat down, mildly offering her opinion. "I wouldn't have said he was the type to drink until he passed out. So maybe he had help."

Somewhat fiercely, Champion said, "The only way anybody could have taken the sheriff was if he was out cold. Otherwise, he would have fought. And kicked ass. Even if he couldn't get to his gun, he's a black belt, for Christ's sake."

Lucas and Jaylene exchanged glances, and he said, "Which makes some kind of drug even more likely. Wyatt's not a small man, and handling a deadweight isn't easy — but it's a hell of a lot easier than struggling with a big man who knows how to use his muscle."

"Maybe the kidnapper had a gun," Samantha suggested.

"Maybe," Lucas agreed. "Probably. Question is, did he use it to control Wyatt?"

The young deputy was impatient. "The CSU will test all the bottles they found at the sheriff's place," he said. "But even if we find out he was drugged, so what? So what if we know this bastard has a gun? It doesn't help us find the sheriff. Why aren't we out looking for him?"

Quietly, Jaylene said, "The chief deputy is calling in everybody even as we speak, Glen. Every car will be out searching for the sheriff, and every other deputy and detective will be out as well. But . . . "

"But," Lucas finished, "as yet we have no good way of narrowing down the area that has to be searched. This is a big county, remember? With too damned many inaccessible or remote places."

"Then why aren't you doing your thing?" Champion demanded.

"We've sent the original of the note off to Quantico —"

"Not the FBI thing," Champion said, even more impatiently. "The other thing. Your thing. Why can't you feel where he is?"

"It isn't that simple," Lucas said after a moment.

"Why not?"

In the same deliberate tone she had used earlier in a much more private conversation, Samantha said, "Because he has to open himself up in order to do that. And right now, he's closed down tight as a drum."

Lucas turned his head to look at her, an expression almost of shock passing briefly over his features. Without another word, he walked out of the room.

Champion looked bewildered. "Did we make him mad? Where's he going?"

Soothingly, Jaylene said, "Probably just out to check with the chief deputy. Don't worry, Glen; we're going to do everything in our power to find your sheriff."

"Well, let's find him before it's too late, huh?" Champion's tone was a bit uneven suddenly; it was obvious he remembered only too well the sight of Lindsay Graham floating lifelessly in her watery tomb.

"We'll do our best," Jaylene told him. "And you can be a big help. We'll have to recheck those inaccessible locations on the list, and especially check out the ones we didn't get to when we were looking for Lindsay. Form up armed search teams like before, each with at least one member who really knows the terrain."

The deputy nodded and, given a task to accomplish, hurried from the room.

When he was gone, Jaylene looked at Samantha with rising brows. "Do you know what you're doing?"

Half under her breath, Samantha muttered, "Christ, I hope so."

Jaylene nodded, a hunch confirmed. "So it is deliberate, the way you're needling Luke. And has little if anything to do with the last time you two tangled, I'm guessing. Something to do with the vision that brought you here to Golden?"

Samantha frowned down at the table, silent. Her hesitation was obvious; just as obvious was the decision she reached, and her continued silence.

Undaunted, Jaylene said, "It's a dangerous tactic, Sam, pushing him."

"I know."

"He has to do this his own way."

"No. Not this time. This time he has to do it my way."

Wyatt Metcalf was new to terror. Personal terror, anyway. He hadn't honestly felt anything close to terror until Lindsay was taken. Now, as angry and ashamed as it made him, he knew he was terrified for himself. Not that he didn't have reason.

There was a fucking guillotine suspended above his head.

And he was almost completely immobile, strapped down to a table so that all he could do was just barely lift his head. That small movement was just enough for him to see how securely he was strapped in place. It was also just enough to show him that this guillotine was designed a bit differently from those he had seen in pictures.

The table he lay on supported his entire length; no basket was placed below to catch his severed head. Instead, the table bore a deep groove just beneath his neck, where the heavy steel blade would finally come to rest — between his body and his neatly severed head.

The head probably wouldn't even move, except maybe to roll gently to the side.

Jesus.

He tried very hard not to think about that. Or about the rusty-looking stains all along that groove that looked to him like dried blood. Which made it fairly obvious that the kidnapper hadn't tested his little contraption by using heads of cabbage.

Probably on Mitchell Callahan.

Instead of dwelling on that, being a cop, Wyatt tried to get the lay of this place. What little he could see from his position was mostly darkness. Two floodlights — or spotlights — were focused on him and this death machine, which made it pretty difficult to see beyond the glare surrounding him.

"Hey!" he shouted suddenly. "Where are you, you bastard?"

There was no response, and the faint echo told him only that the room was mostly hard surfaces without much if any furniture or carpeting to deaden sound. So he was likely in a basement or cellar or, hell, even a warehouse somewhere. He did have the sense of vastness all around him, lots of space.

But that could have been his imagination, he supposed. Or simply the darkness.

He felt very alone.

And he wondered, suddenly, if this was what Lindsay had gone through. Had she freed herself from the duct-tape bindings — which they had discovered partially cut, presumably so that she *could* free herself within some given time — only to slowly realize that the glass-and-steel cage in which she was imprisoned would cause her death?

Had she known from the very beginning, or had the bastard toyed with her, allowing her to believe that she might escape the tank? Had she been in the darkness, or in a blinding spotlight as he was? Had the water begun to slowly drip from the pipe, or had it gushed?

With a tremendous effort, Wyatt pushed the useless, haunting questions away.

Lindsay was gone. He couldn't bring her back.

And he was going to join her in death unless he got himself out of this. Or . . . unless Luke really could do what he claimed.

"I find people who are lost. I feel their fear."

Wyatt thought about that, keeping his

head turned and his gaze directed beyond the spotlight and into darkness; it was better than looking up at the damned blade hanging over him.

Could that quiet, intense, steely-eyed federal agent really feel someone else's emotions, their fear?

His first reaction was a deep embarrassment that another man might feel the sick terror crawling inside him, might know that about him.

Wyatt didn't want to believe that Luke — or anyone — could do that. Everything in him shied away from the mere possibility. But . . . he had to admit that Samantha Burke had been right when she'd told them Lindsay would drown. She had warned Glen Champion about his defective clothes dryer, which very well could have caused a fire. And as hard as he'd tried, Wyatt hadn't been able to connect the carnival seer in any viable way to this kidnapping murderer and his schemes.

And Champion had described to him, in halting, wondering tones, what Luke had done. How he'd been able to find Lindsay, and how eerie and shocking had been his apparent mental or emotional connection with her in the final tormented minutes of her life.

If he was genuine . . . If Samantha was genuine . . .

If psychic ability was possible, was real . . .

Staring into the darkness, facing his own probable death, Wyatt Metcalf wished he had more time. Because if the world did indeed hold such possibilities, then it was far more interesting than he had believed.

Abruptly, he saw a light flicker on, illuminating the face of a digital clock. It was placed in such a way that it was not only visible to him but was almost inescapable. And it wasn't, he realized immediately, showing the time.

It was counting down.

He had less than eight hours to live.

He turned his head back so that he was staring up at that gleaming blade. He focused on it. And grimly began working his hands in an effort to loosen the straps tying him down.

"Why does he have to do this your way?"

Samantha looked across the table at Jaylene. "We both know that Luke's biggest flaw at a time like this is his tendency to shut everybody out. Everybody. His concentration is so fixed, so absolute, that he can barely relate to anything or anyone except the victim he's trying to find."

"He relates to you."

With a wry smile, Samantha said, "Not really, except on a very basic level. If this were his usual type of case, by the end he'd see me only as a warm body in a bed."

"You mean, last time . . ."

"Yeah, pretty much. He was so shut in himself, so focused on the job in those last days, he barely spoke to me. You remember that much."

Jaylene nodded, reluctant. "I remember. But we were all focused on the job, on finding that child."

"Of course we were. But for Luke . . . it's like his own ability to focus consumes everything else in him. I know you called it tunnel vision then, I guess trying to warn me."

"For all the good it did."

"Yeah, I suppose I could have been more understanding. But it's not easy to find yourself falling for a man who doesn't even seem to see you half the time. Most of the time, by the end."

"Sam, his focus — that flaw — is also his strength."

"Is it?" Samantha shook her head. "I'm no psychologist, but it seems to me that mental focus and concentration that intense can do a dandy job of holding emotion at bay, or even shutting it down entirely. The very emotion Luke needs to feel."

"Maybe," Jaylene said slowly.

"Haven't you ever wondered, Jay, why he almost always has trouble sensing a victim until he's worked himself to the point of exhaustion?" Samantha asked. "Until he's skipped too many meals and too much sleep and tapped so many of his reserves that there's almost nothing left? It's only when he's literally too tired to think that he finally allows himself to feel. His emotions — and theirs."

"When his guards come crashing down," Jaylene murmured, thoughtful.

"Exactly."

"But when the guards do come down, and he feels what they feel, the sheer strength of their terror virtually incapacitates him. He can barely move or speak."

"And maybe that's one reason he resists feeling that for so long. But if he *could* open himself up sooner, before a victim's fear has grown so intense and before his own exhaustion was so overwhelming, then maybe he could function. Maybe he could even function with some semblance of normality."

"Maybe."

Samantha looked toward the open doorway as though expecting someone to appear, but added, "It isn't a conscious thing — it can't be. No matter what it costs him, he wants to find these victims so desperately that he'd do anything he could. Consciously. Even incapacitate himself, if that's what it took. So it has to be something buried deep, a barrier of some kind. A wall created at some point in his life when it was necessary to protect a part of him."

"You're talking about some kind of injury or trauma."

"Probably. A lot of our strengths come from some hurt." Samantha frowned again. "You don't know what it is? What might have happened to him?"

Jaylene replied, "No — and I've been his partner for nearly four years. I probably know him as well as anybody, and I know almost nothing of his background. From the point that Bishop found him working as a private consultant on criminal abduction cases five years ago until now, yes. Before that, nothing. Don't even know where he was born or where he went to school. Hell, I don't even know if he's a born psychic. How about you?"

"No. It all happened so fast before.

There was so much intensity. The investigation, the media blitz, us. Then the tension of knowing his mind was someplace else even when his body was lying beside mine in bed. We couldn't talk, not then.

"And then it all just stopped, the way those strangely vivid, aberrant periods in our lives tend to end. The investigation was over. And so were we. I . . . woke up in an empty bed. With Bishop waiting outside the motel to tell me why I couldn't be a member of his Special Crimes Unit. That purple turban. Credibility."

Jaylene hesitated only an instant. "I had no idea it ended quite that abruptly."

Samantha hunched her shoulders more than shrugged. "Bishop said he'd sent you two off on another case, that it was vital you leave immediately and he hadn't given you a choice in the matter. I imagine that was true. Also true that he felt moving Luke on to the next case as soon as possible would be best for him, after the way he blamed himself for that child's death. And . . . I suppose leaving so abruptly gave Luke a good-enough excuse not to wake me even long enough to say good-bye."

With a wince, Jaylene said, "I almost wish you hadn't told me that."

Seriously, Samantha said, "Don't let your

respect for him be affected by what happened between us. Thinking about it now, I don't think he had much control over how he reacted to me — or how he left me. I think it's all tangled up with that barrier inside him, that refusal to let himself feel until he has absolutely no other choice."

"Those sorts of psychological barriers," Jaylene said, "tend to be real monsters, Sam. The kind that claw us up inside."

"Yeah. I know."

"But it's what you're looking for in Luke. What you're digging for."

Her jaw firmed. "What I have to dig for. What I have to find."

Jaylene studied her for a long moment in silence, then said, "I wish you felt you could tell me what this is all about. I get the feeling it's pretty lonely where you are right now."

"At least you see that. To Luke, I'm being stubborn at best and wantonly obstructive at worst."

"But you understand why that's his reaction. Did you understand that three years ago?"

"No."

"So when he started giving you the third degree the morning after you'd first slept together . . ."

Samantha replied frankly, "It hurt, like I said."

"I think it hurts a little now too. Even though you know where it's coming from this time."

"Knowing something intellectually is one thing." Samantha's smile twisted. "Feelings are something else again. Anyway, I'm not asking him to love me, I just need him to trust me."

"Do you trust him?"

"Yes," Samantha answered instantly.

"Even though he walked out on you last time? How is that possible?"

Slowly, Samantha replied, "I've trusted him from the moment we met. What I trust is that he won't lie to me and that he'd be there if I needed him."

Jaylene shook her head. "Then you're a better woman than I am. The last time I was dumped, it wasn't nearly as public as what you went through — and I very nearly got a buddy in the IRS to audit him for the previous ten years."

Samantha smiled, but said, "You wouldn't have done that."

"Maybe not. But maybe I would have, if more than my pride had been hurt."

Refusing to admit anything of her own feelings, Samantha merely said, "As your

Bishop is so fond of saying, some things have to happen just the way they happen."

"*Is* fond of saying?"

Samantha lifted her eyebrows inquiringly. "Has he stopped saying it?"

"No," Jaylene replied after a moment.

"Didn't think so. I got the impression it was practically his mantra."

Jaylene eyed her. "Umm. Listen, getting back to the subject of you needling Luke, I gather your plan is to force him to break through whatever that barrier is and find out what's on the other side."

"Something like that."

"Yeah, well, my advice is to be careful. We build walls for reasons, and the reasons tend to be painful. Force somebody to deal with that pain before they're ready to, and you risk a mental breakdown. Force a *psychic* to deal with buried traumas, with all the extra electromagnetic energy in our brains, and you risk a literal short circuit that can put them — him — beyond anyone's reach. For good."

"I know," Samantha said.

Bishop had told her.

She found him in the storage room of the sheriff's department garage where the glass-and-steel tank was being kept. He was alone and in one hand held a copy of the taunting note the kidnapper had sent him that morning. His gaze moved from the note to the tank and back again.

Samantha came only a step into the room, and asked quietly, "What are they telling you? The note, the tank?"

"That he's a sick bastard," Lucas replied without turning to face her.

"Besides that."

His gaze went to the tank once more, and he said in a distant tone, "We found several hairs inside the tank, at least a few of them not Lindsay's. I just checked with Quantico, and DNA tests confirmed they belonged to a victim killed in this part of the country some months ago. A woman of Asian descent. Drowned."

"I doubt he missed those hairs."

"So do I. We — I — was meant to find them."

Samantha glanced at the tank, then back at his profile. "What does that tell you?"

"That he used this tank before. Maybe here, or maybe he has some means of transport; there was certainly no evidence it was constructed up at that old mine. Wherever he used it, when his victim was dead, he removed her and left her where she was found — along a creek bed more than fifty miles from here."

"So . . . chances are Metcalf isn't being threatened with drowning."

"No. I haven't checked to be sure, but memory says at least three of the previous victims, counting the woman, were drowned. Lindsay makes four. I don't know if he had this tank all along or built it at some point in order to better control his victims."

"And to terrify them."

"Yes. And that."

"But now you have it. So maybe he's lost — or given up — one of his murder machines. What does he have left?"

His jaw tightening, Lucas said, "Mitchell Callahan wasn't the only victim to be decapitated. Two others were as well."

"So he has a guillotine."

"It looks that way."

"What else?"

"Three were exsanguinated. A very sharp knife to one or both jugular veins."

"I suppose one could build a machine to do that."

"Yeah, probably."

"By my count we've covered nine or ten of the victims. What about the others?"

"Three were asphyxiated. Not manually."

Samantha had spent too much time considering this not to have a suggestion. "The easiest way to smother someone, slowly, over a period of time, and inflicting the maximum amount of terror . . . would be to bury them alive."

"I know."

"So a box somewhere, a coffin, buried in the ground. Reusable."

"Probably more than one," Lucas said, still remote. "It's the easiest to recreate. Just a wooden box and a hole in the ground, nothing fancy. And no timer required. Just cover the box with dirt, bury it. Let the air run out. Put in a canister of oxygen if you want to extend the available air a bit."

"That leaves two or three victims. How did they die?"

"I don't know. In those cases, the remains were left out in the elements long enough to leave us very little; no cause of death could be determined with any certainty. They might have been asphyxiated or exsanguinated or drowned. We don't know."

Samantha frowned slightly at that distant tone, but all she said was, "So you know he has at least three machines — or methods — of killing remotely still available to him. That's assuming, of course, that he doesn't resort to quicker, up-close-and-personal methods, like a gun or a knife."

Lucas nodded. "Which, if we're correct, means that right now Wyatt Metcalf is either staring up at a guillotine, trying to claw his way out of a box in the ground, or trying not to get his throat cut."

"Where is he, Luke?"

"I don't know."

"Because you can't feel him."

He was silent.

"What about this kidnapper, this murderer? Can't you feel him? I mean, he certainly seems to have crawled inside *your* head over the last year and a half."

Lucas swung around to face her, his face tense. "You don't have to tell me that I've failed at every turn," he said, far less remote now.

"That's not what I'm trying to tell you."

"Oh — right. I'm closed up. 'Tight as a drum,' I think you said."

"That's what I said. Want to deny it?"

"Samantha, I'm investigating an abduction. A series of them. I'm doing my job. Either help me, or else get the hell out of my way."

Samantha allowed a long moment to

pass, then said simply, "Okay, Luke." She turned around and left the storage room, and the garage.

He didn't follow her.

She wasn't crazy about walking through the sheriff's department unescorted. None of the cops had said anything to her directly that was openly hostile, but she could feel the stares and the simmering anger. The few who believed she might actually be psychic were angry because she couldn't instantly tell them where their sheriff was, and the majority were convinced she was somehow to blame for all of this. They didn't know how, but she was a handy target.

Samantha didn't really blame them for that reaction; she had seen it before, time and time again; being someone who could always be classed under the heading of "different," she had learned through bitter experience that people were seldom rational when bad things started happening in their lives.

But understanding that didn't make it any more comfortable to walk through a building knowing stares and muttered comments lay in your wake. It was only a matter of time, she knew, until the hostility became open. Unless, of course, she proved herself. Unless she helped find their sheriff.

Samantha thought about that as she worked her way through the building and back upstairs. In the vision that had brought her here, she didn't think this had happened, the sheriff being taken. So the question was, why had it happened this time, with her in the . . . game?

And what could she do about it?

She paused at the conference-room door only long enough to speak to Jaylene. "I'm headed back to the carnival."

Surprised, the other woman said, "Alone?"

"Looks like. I'd stay if I thought I could help, but the only thing I seem to be doing around here is making all the cops even more tense."

"Most of them won't be here much longer," Jaylene pointed out. "Search teams. We still have that list of remote places to check and double-check."

"Still."

"There's media camped outside. Even more than before, with news of the sheriff's abduction out."

"I know." Samantha hesitated, then said, "I may stop and have a word with them. Luke and I might have been spotted this morning, coming in together, even though it was early. If it comes to that, he could have been seen at the carnival last night, hanging around my booth."

"And you think you can head off speculation?" Jaylene was skeptical. "Sort of doubt it, Sam."

"I'm just a bit curious to find out what's in their suspicious little minds — before the next edition of the newspaper hits the streets, or the six o'clock news on TV."

"Throwing gasoline on a fire."

"Maybe. Or maybe water."

"Luke won't like it."

"He's so pissed at me right now he won't notice. Unless somebody points it out."

The two women gazed at each other for a long moment, and then Samantha smiled and retreated.

Staring after her, Jaylene murmured, "So I need to trust you too, huh, Sam? I wonder if I do? I wonder if I even agree that shaking up Luke might be the best thing for him and the case." She got up, adding under her breath, "Shake nitro, and it blows up in your face. Something to keep in mind."

Then she went in search of Luke.

13

Caitlin had considered leaving her small motel room several times that morning, especially when one of the "local" channels she was almost watching broke the news of Sheriff Metcalf's disappearance and probable abduction. But the most she had done was drive to the nearby café to have coffee and one of their huge cinnamon buns while her room was being cleaned.

The two deputies still watching her — or quite likely a new pair on the day shift — kept within her sight but didn't go into the café, and she had to wonder how upset they were over having watchdog duty when they undoubtedly wanted to be in on the hunt for their sheriff.

She could sympathize, at least with having to sit around and basically do nothing. It was not fun.

She returned to her room, which now smelled strongly of antiseptic, and resigned herself to a boring day. Dumb soaps on TV, or movies so old they could only be scheduled in the morning dead zone, or news or weather — those seemed to be her main choices for entertainment.

"I need to go to a bookstore," Caitlin said aloud. "God knows how long it'll take the cops to let me back into the apartment so I can do what I have to do there. If I'm going to be stuck here for much longer —"

The television abruptly went out.

Caitlin sat there frozen for what seemed like minutes, then said tentatively, "Lindsay?"

The surprise she felt in that moment, oddly enough, had less to do with the possibility that her dead sister was trying to communicate with her than it did the timing. For some reason, she had it in her head that the spirits were abroad in the wee hours of the night or at least after dark, not in the middle of the morning.

Which assumption, she thought, might not be so far off, as the minutes passed and nothing else happened.

"Lindsay?" she repeated, beginning to feel foolish. And beginning to wonder how soon she could get her only line to entertainment repaired.

Quite abruptly, the lights went out. And since Caitlin had drawn the heavy drapes over the single wide window, the darkness was complete.

"What the hell?" she muttered. She got

up out of the chair, hesitated, and took a step toward the nightstand and the dark lamp.

Something touched her shoulder.

Caitlin whirled around, trying to see — and seeing nothing. "Lindsay? Dammit, Lindsay, you got my attention, you don't have to scare the shit out of me!"

She stood there in the darkness, half mad and half scared, and wondered suddenly if she had imagined that touch. Surely she had. Surely.

Because there was nothing after death, *nothing,* and wishing there was didn't make it so. Lindsay couldn't be trying to communicate with her, because Lindsay was dead, dead and gone, with all the rest only a figment of her guilty and grieving imagination —

She heard a faint scratching sound that made the hair stand up on the back of her neck.

Long seconds passed, only the soft scratching disturbing the silence.

Then, abruptly, the lights came back on. With a click, the TV also came back on. The very normal sound of human voices filled the silence.

Caitlin stood frozen, blinking for a moment in the sudden light before her gaze focused on the nightstand. Even without moving closer, she could see that the notepad lying there had something written on it.

Before the lights went out, it had been blank.

She drew a breath and went over to the nightstand, picking up the notepad with shaking hands.

HELP THEM, CAIT
HELP THEM FIND WYATT
YOU KNOW MORE THAN YOU THINK

"Miss Burke, is it true you helped the police locate the body of Detective Lindsay Graham?"

"No, it is not true," Samantha answered the reporter calmly. "Solid police work located Detective Graham."

"Not in time to save her life," somebody muttered.

"The killer meant her to die. That's what killers do. It's obviously a mistake to think of this . . . person . . . as anything other than a cold-blooded murderer." Again, Samantha was calm, her tone even. She stood on the top step of the front entrance of the sheriff's department and looked at the small herd of media eager to hear whatever she had to say.

No TV media, thank goodness. She wondered how long her luck on that would hold out, how much time she had before she found herself starring in the six o'clock news. It had only been avoided this far because the "local" TV stations were nearly a hundred miles away in Asheville, and they'd had a few major crimes of their own on which to concentrate in the past few weeks. They had sent a reporter to cover the murders and kept fairly up to date on the facts of the investigation, but so far hadn't ventured into speculation about the carnival or Golden's visiting seer.

Heavy local coverage that *did* speculate in the print media was bad enough, but Samantha was prepared for that. If the regional television stations started paying real attention to the story, then it would be only a matter of time before everything hit the national spotlight — and the fan.

She was gambling that wouldn't happen, even knowing that with every abduction and murder they were moving closer to a much larger and very unwelcome spotlight.

"Are you helping the police now, Miss Burke?" the first reporter asked. She had her little cassette recorder held high, and avid green eyes fixed on Samantha.

Aware of the door behind her opening, Samantha said deliberately, "That appears to be a question open to discussion, at the moment."

"*How* could you help?" another reporter demanded, rather aggressively. "Look into your crystal ball?"

Samantha opened her mouth to reply just as Luke grasped her arm and turned her toward the door, saying to the reporters, "Miss Burke has nothing more to say. And you'll be updated on the facts of the investigation when the sheriff's department has information to share with you."

A barrage of questions were yelled after them, but Lucas merely pulled Samantha into the building and around a corner to be out of sight of the reporters before demanding, "What the *hell* did you think you were doing?"

He was pissed. And it showed.

Samantha eyed him for a moment, then held up her right hand to display the palm. If anything, the marks burned there by a steering wheel, a ring, and a spider-and-web pendant were even clearer than they had been before.

"Pity you stopped me," she said mildly. "I was just about to show them this."

"Why?" Lucas demanded.

She shrugged. "Well, the killer's already watching me; I just thought it was time to give him some idea of what I can do."

"Are you out of your mind? Jesus, Sam, why not just paint a bull's-eye on your back?"

"And why not rattle the son of a bitch if we can? Why not make him wonder if maybe, just maybe, he's not quite as in control of this little game of his as he thinks he is? Everything's been going exactly as he planned so far, so maybe it's time we changed that. I don't know if there's an equivalent in chess to a wild card, but that's me. And I say it's time we let him know the rules just went right out the window."

Lucas was about to say something in response to that — what, he wasn't sure — when he realized, abruptly and belatedly, where they were. In the doorway of the bull pen.

He looked away from Samantha to find that every cop in the place was staring at them with open interest. And even though he felt some embarrassment over losing control, and more than a little anger at the moment, he also noticed that a few faces that had shown open hostility toward

Samantha now appeared at least as thoughtful as they were unfriendly.

"When are the search parties going out?" he asked the chief deputy, whose desk was nearest the door.

Vance Keeter looked down at the clipboard in his hand as if it would answer, then said quickly, "Ten minutes, and everybody should be ready to go."

"Good," Lucas snapped, and headed down the hallway to the conference room, pulling Samantha along with him.

She allowed herself to be towed, a little amused and more than a little interested in this definitely less-controlled side of Lucas. Not that he needed to know that. So the moment they were in the conference room, she jerked her arm away.

"*Do* you mind?"

Jaylene, bent over a map spread out on the table, looked up at them in mild surprise, then sat down in the chair behind her. "Hey, Sam. Thought you were leaving."

She was good, Samantha thought admiringly, even as she was saying, "I got hauled back in here — *and* got scolded like a kid in front of the entire sheriff's department. Which I don't at all appreciate, by the way."

"You're damned lucky I didn't arrest you on the spot," Lucas retorted. "I can make an obstruction charge stick, Sam, and you'd better keep it in mind."

"You might make it stick as far as court, but you'll play hell proving it," Samantha snapped right back. "I'm not an employee of the sheriff's department *or* the federal government, which means I'm free to speak my mind to the press if I so desire. And I have done nothing, absolutely nothing, that a rational person would define as obstructing this investigation."

"You had no business saying *anything* to the press about the investigation."

"I didn't tell them anything they didn't already know."

"That's beside the point, Sam."

"No, that's entirely the point. All I did was finally stop a minute and answer a few of their questions about me. Me, personally. Which is totally my business. And will probably increase my business, now that I think about it."

Lucas refused to wander from the point. "About you? What the hell did you tell them?"

"I told them that sometimes I have visions when I touch things and that the killer left an object in Lindsay's apartment, which I touched. And which told me that this killer is a soulless bastard who feeds on fear."

"Jesus Christ." Lucas was beyond grim.

"Like I said — I want him to know what I can do."

"What makes you think he doesn't already know what you can do?"

Samantha merely said, "If that's the case, no harm done, right?"

"No harm done? God, you're making me crazy."

"Good." She took a step toward him and, in the same fierce tone, demanded, "Where's Wyatt?"

"How the hell should I know?" He was just as fierce, torn between anger at her irresponsibility in talking to the press and surprise that she would do something so reckless, and hardly knew what he was saying.

"You know where he is," she snapped. "Think about it. *Feel* it. Where is he? Where's Wyatt?"

"Goddammit, how should I —"

Six hours left. Six fucking hours . . .

Lucas went very still, instinctively trying to listen to that whisper in his head.

. . . no way to get loose . . . goddamn guillotine . . .

"It's the guillotine," he murmured. "Wyatt's strapped into a guillotine."

"Where?" Samantha snapped, her tone still fiercely insistent.

"He doesn't know."

"What does he feel? What's around him?"

"Space. Darkness. Maybe a basement."

"Some part of him felt it when he was being moved, even if he was out cold. What did he feel? Where is he?"

"He doesn't know."

"*Listen. Feel.* Remember what he can't."

"Water. Running water. A stream."

"What else? Was it dark when he was moved?"

"Yes."

"Was it near dawn? Did he hear birds?"

"Birds. A rooster."

"Dirt roads, or paved?"

"Paved — only for a few minutes. Then dirt. A very rough dirt road. A long time 'til it stopped."

Watching in complete fascination even as she took quick notes, Jaylene almost held her breath. After four years of working with him, she had believed she was as good as anyone could be at directing and focusing Lucas's abilities, but she acknowledged silently, now, that Samantha's method was masterly. At least this time.

The question was, what would it do to Luke?

"Which direction was he moving in?" Samantha demanded.

"He doesn't —"

"He *knows*. Somewhere inside him, he knows. He has an internal compass, we all do. Find it. Which direction?"

After a long moment, Lucas said, "Northwest. Always northwest."

"Northwest from his home?"

"Yes."

Less than six hours . . . oh, Jesus . . .

Abruptly, Lucas was back, that wispy tendril of contact snapped. He blinked at Samantha, then sat down, hardly aware that Jaylene had positioned a chair for him.

"Less than six hours," he said slowly. "Wyatt has less than six hours left. There's a clock counting down. He can see it." He was a little pale.

So was Samantha. But as she joined them at the table, her voice was perfectly calm, even cool. "That wasn't so hard, was it?"

Jaylene half expected an explosion from Lucas, but he was staring at Sam, curiously intent.

"That's why you've been needling me all

morning," he said.

She didn't deny it, saying merely, "You shut down on me once before. Think I'm going to let that happen again? I'd rather you were pissed and snapping at me than looking right through me. Besides, if there's a hope of finding the sheriff alive, you're it."

"You said I couldn't win without you."

"And maybe this is why. Because I *can* piss you off. A dubious talent, but mine own." With a shrug, she added briskly, "Anyway, now we have a slightly narrower area to search. And we know how much time is left on the clock."

Jaylene was once more bent over the map spread out on the conference table. She pinpointed the sheriff's house, then drew a straight line out from it to the northwest. "How far do I take this? To the Tennessee line?"

Looking away from Samantha at last, Lucas got to his feet and joined his partner. "Yeah. For now. We may have to extend it, but that covers a lot of area."

Pursing her lips thoughtfully, Jaylene said, "And if we start with, say, twenty miles on either side of the line . . ." She marked the arbitrary boundaries on the map.

They both stared down at what was a considerable search area, its only saving grace the fact that it contained at least half of the small red flags marking specific areas already on their search list.

"Could be worse," she murmured.

Before Lucas could respond, Samantha spoke up to say, "There was a stream. That should narrow it down a bit more."

"And roosters along the way," Jaylene said. "That takes it well out of town, at least from what I've seen. And the fact that he was on a rough dirt road most of the time means we'll be away from all the main roads in the area."

Glen Champion appeared in the doorway, clipboard in hand. "All the search teams are ready," he said. "But I wanted to check with you before we finalize assignments."

"Good," Lucas said, gesturing him closer. "We want to concentrate on this area."

The deputy didn't question it, just bent over the map, studying it with a frown. "There are at least eight places on our list out in that general area. I've got five search teams ready to go — six if you guys want to join in again."

Immediately, Jaylene said, "Luke, why

don't you and Sam go with Glen, and I'll join one of the other teams."

"I'm not a cop," Samantha said, not so much protest as simple statement of fact.

"We can deputize you," Glen said, rather uncertainly.

Her smile was faint. "I don't think that would go over very well with the other officers."

"I'll take official responsibility for Sam going along," Lucas said. Then, to Jaylene, he said, "Think you might pick up something?"

"I don't know, but we might as well spread our assets as far as possible. Sam can clearly keep you focused if you manage to make contact, and I may be more help elsewhere." She eyed Glen. "Though I'd prefer to be on a team most likely to accept a request for a change in direction if I *do* happen to pick up something."

He looked at his clipboard, saying, "Then I'd suggest you go with John Prescott's group. His grandmother had the sight, and he's been pretty vocal in support of Miss Burke."

"He has?" Samantha said in mild surprise.

"Not all of us think you're a witch," Glen said frankly.

She winced. "I'm glad."

Lucas smiled slightly. "Then, if you don't mind, Glen, Sam and I will go with you."

"S'fine by me. How do you want to divvy up the search area? I mean, which location do you want to search?"

From the doorway, Caitlin Graham said in a voice holding more doubt than certainty, "Maybe I can help with that."

Less than six hours.

Wyatt could feel himself begin to sweat. This place, wherever it was, held a damp chill, yet sweat beaded on his forehead and temples and ran down into his hair.

He tried not to look at the clock, but it was placed in such a way that he almost had to.

Five and a half hours now.

Five and a half fucking hours left.

Those red seconds counting inexorably down. Fifty-nine, fifty-eight, fifty-seven . . . And then, when it reached zero, to see another minute gone, the next minute counting down with relentless detachment: fifty-nine, fifty-eight, fifty-seven . . .

"It's my fucking life!" he wanted to shout. He knew it was irrational, to see the clock as something alive and watching him, mea-

suring his time left so cavalierly, but he could hardly help how he felt.

Desperation, that's what he felt. A deep, gnawing terror.

He wondered, suddenly, if he should stop trying to damp down that sick dread, holding it all inside. Should he just let it out, let it go? Scream out his fear, and to hell with his stupid pride? Because if Luke *could* really sense fear . . .

Wyatt gritted his teeth and muttered a curse under his breath. He couldn't do it. Not deliberately. It went against his very nature to give in to fear. If he gave in to fear, then the bastard doing this to him would win.

He stared up at the gleaming guillotine, and once more went to work trying to loosen the straps binding his raw wrists.

"I can't be sure about it," Caitlin said. "I mean, even assuming that note really was from Lindsay, the fact that this is the only area on the map that seemed familiar to me probably doesn't mean anything. Really." She had uneasily offered the same disclaimer twice since they had left the station.

"We were going to search this general area anyway," Lucas told her. "And your hunches are probably as good or better than any of ours."

"But I never lived around here. It's just that Lindsay was more apt to send a card with a note jotted inside, or write a letter, than she was to call. And she talked about the place, the countryside. She mentioned hiking somewhere around Six Point Creek, and it was an unusual enough name that I remembered it. That's all."

"Maybe that's what she was counting on you to remember," Samantha said.

"Then why didn't she just write *Wyatt's at Six Point Creek?*"

"They never do," Lucas murmured.

"Maybe the universe won't let them," Samantha suggested. "Too much help from beyond would make things too easy for us."

"And why the hell *can't* they be easy?" Caitlin demanded.

Samantha smiled. "You'd have to ask the universe. All I know is that my visions tend to complicate rather than simplify my life. After a while, you sort of get used to that."

Sticking determinedly with the normal rather than paranormal, Glen said, "We know there's an old mill on the creek that hasn't been used in donkey's years, but last time I was hiking up here it looked in pretty good condition. There's a big cellar cut into the granite back away from the creek, where the people who used to live in the area kept most of their food. Sort of communal storage. Not that there were many who tried to make a go of things way up here."

"In any case," Lucas said, "all those qualities could make it a prime spot for someone needing a remote location, privacy, and a virtually soundproofed, enclosed space in which to hold someone, even though it wasn't on our list. So we search it."

"A deputy, a fed, and two civilians," Samantha said rather dryly. "Wouldn't the press love this."

"With any luck at all, they won't know about it," Lucas said. "They were told in no uncertain terms to remain back at the sheriff's department, and two deputies made sure they did while the rest of us left. We don't need reporters tagging along on a search, especially in this kind of country."

"It is wild," Glen agreed, hanging on to the ATV's wheel as the vehicle bounded across a washed-out section of the dirt road they were following. "Don't forget that fugitives — federal fugitives — have successfully hidden out up here for years on end."

"And don't think our killer didn't have that in mind when he picked Golden," Luke said. "This is the perfect area for him, with plenty of remote land, many with old settlements, abandoned cabins and barns, even a few defunct mines. Lots of hiding places we'll have to work hard even to get to. He planned well, all right. And he has no doubt that he'll accomplish everything he sets out to."

From the backseat beside Samantha, Caitlin said, "What's he accomplishing, beyond killing people?"

"In his mind, he's winning the game," Luke told her. "Every victim we weren't able to save just proved to him that he's smarter than we are."

"Sick bastard," she muttered.

Samantha said, "Broken minds. I do wonder what broke his. I mean, if he wasn't born this way. Luke, did you draw any other conclusions from that note he sent you this morning?"

"He feels in complete control of the situation, you were right about that," Lucas replied. "His confidence borders on cockiness, even a sort of giddiness. It's as if . . . as if he's reaching the end of a long path and he feels he can begin to relax. That bit about there being only one rule, and then the line *Guess what it is* is almost playful."

Samantha was silent for a moment, then said, "Why did he take the sheriff?"

"To up the ante, maybe."

"Snatching a law-enforcement officer from beneath everyone's nose?" Samantha frowned. "But he did that with Lindsay. Would he repeat himself? I mean, now that you know it's a game, a competition. Would he?"

Lucas turned in his seat to look at her. "No. He wouldn't."

"Okay. Then why the sheriff? If he isn't repeating himself, then he must have another reason. Something personal, maybe?"

"I don't know."

With wonderful politeness, Samantha said, "This is the point where you tap into your other senses."

"Needling me again won't work, Sam."

"Think so?"

In some surprise, Caitlin said, "You're psychic too?"

"He is sometimes," Samantha told her. "When he lets himself be. Control issues. You know how it is."

"Cut it out, Samantha."

"That means he's getting pissed at me.

He only uses my whole name when I've irritated him."

Ignoring that, Lucas looked at his watch and said, "Less than four hours left now. Glen, is there a shorter way?"

"Only if you're a bird. Those of us on the ground have to take this lousy dirt road that leads to an old logging road that's even worse. It'll take us another hour, easy."

Caitlin said desperately, "But what if I'm wrong? You had decided to search another spot, hadn't you, before I showed up? Something already on your list?"

Still twisted around in his seat in order to see her, Lucas said, "I hadn't made up my mind, Caitlin. But, as I said, your hunch is probably as good as anyone else's, and this mill on the creek sounds a likely place."

"And," Samantha said in that same spuriously polite tone, "following your hunch rather than one of his own sort of absolves Luke of responsibility, you know?"

Instantly, Lucas said, "You know goddamned well that isn't true. If I didn't believe we could find Wyatt up here, I wouldn't have come. If we don't find him, it certainly won't be Caitlin's fault."

"No, of course not. So whose fault will it

be, Luke? Who gets the blame if Wyatt Metcalf dies because we couldn't find him in time?"

"Me. I get the blame. Is that what you want to hear?"

"No, I want to hear you feeling what he feels, right now, this minute."

"Don't you think I'm trying?"

"As a matter of fact, I don't."

"You're wrong."

"No, I'm not, because you're still closed up. Think I can't feel that, Luke? Lie to yourself if you want, but you can't lie to me, not about this."

Caitlin, following the quick, back-and-forth conversation warily, half expected the two to come to blows. She'd never heard either of them sound so fierce, but she barely knew Lucas and wasn't sure how unusual it was for him. It was Samantha's pitiless determination that surprised her; she would never have expected such force from the slight, watchful, quiet woman she'd thought she knew.

Seemingly transformed by anger, Samantha was leaning as far forward as her seat belt would allow, one hand gripping the shoulder strap and the other braced on the seat. Her face was tense, her heavy-lidded eyes narrowed and normally full lips thinned, and every word bit with sharp teeth when she repeated, "Not about this."

"You're not a telepath, Sam," Lucas retorted.

"I don't have to be. Think I can't read you, Luke? That I couldn't always read you, all the way down to your bones, to your soul? Think again."

"Sam —"

Abruptly, in a soft voice that was nevertheless audible over the straining engine of the ATV, Samantha said, "I even know about Bryan, Luke."

By sheer chance Caitlin's gaze happened to be on Lucas when Samantha spoke, and she wanted to look away from what she saw. Shock, and then a flash of pain, intense, raw, draining the color from his face. He looked like a man who had just been knifed in the gut.

"How could you —"

"*Feel*," Samantha snapped, her voice intense again. "Damn you, open up and *feel*."

Clearly unhappy, Glen Champion said, "Hey, you guys — is this really the time? I mean —"

"You just drive," Samantha ordered, never taking her eyes off Lucas. "Feel, Luke. Reach out. Open up. Wyatt Metcalf is going to die if you can't connect with him. Do you really think the kidnapper is going to leave his victim in a place you're likely to search? No, not this time, not again. He meant you to find Lindsay, meant her to die before you could get there, but he won't take a chance you might find Metcalf in time, so he's hidden him from you, very deliberately."

"I don't —"

"Where is he, Luke? He won't be anywhere on the map, on that list you've drawn up. He won't be anywhere you expect. And when time's run out and Metcalf is dead, you'll get another taunting message telling you *exactly* where you can find the body. Do you want that? Do you?"

"Stop."

Glen jammed his foot on the brake, instinctively obeying the harsh order.

Softly now, Samantha repeated, "Where is he, Luke?"

"North," Lucas replied slowly.

"At the old mill?"

"No. North."

"This road is pretty much a straight shot northwest," Glen said, bewildered. "There isn't another, at least not for miles."

"North," Lucas said again.

Caitlin thought he looked almost hypnotized, not quite there with them but somewhere else. At the same time, his gaze was fixed on Samantha, and there was certainly awareness of her in his eyes.

"How far?" she asked him.

"A mile, maybe."

"Glen? How long will it take us to cover a mile in this terrain?" She never took her eyes off Lucas.

"Christ, I don't — experienced hikers in good shape and with the right equipment could do it in an hour or thereabouts. But I don't know about you guys. North from here is straight up the fucking mountain."

"We'll just have to do the best we can," Samantha said briefly. "Let's go."

Caitlin was more than a little surprised to find herself out of the vehicle and going along, climbing up a steep slope with the help of the deputy while Lucas and Samantha led the way. Nobody had told her specifically to go or stay, Caitlin just went, her fascinated gaze fixed whenever possible on the couple ahead.

No longer staring at each other, they were nonetheless connected, holding hands whenever possible but connected in a less tangible and possibly stronger way as Samantha determinedly kept him focused. From time to time Caitlin could hear her calm yet curiously relentless voice, asking the same question again and again.

"What does he feel, Luke?"

Caitlin heard the question asked over and over, but only once did she hear the response. His voice low, haunted, Lucas said, "Terror. He's afraid. He knows he's going to die."

Caitlin shivered and grasped a sapling with one hand, grimly pulling herself up the steep, rocky slope.

14

It was getting cold. Wyatt didn't know if that was because his surroundings were actually growing colder, or if it was sheer, icy terror.

There was certainly that. He was far, far beyond the point of being able to dampen or ignore it.

His wrists were raw, his body sore from his attempts to free himself from the guillotine, and he was just as securely fastened as he had been hours ago.

Too many hours ago.

There was only half an hour left. Twenty-nine minutes and thirty-odd seconds to go.

Jesus.

It wasn't enough time. Not enough time to reconcile himself to death. Not enough time to make peace with himself, to think about all the guilts and regrets of his life. Not enough time for what-might-have-beens or what-ifs. It was over.

Just . . . over.

And there wasn't a single goddamned thing he could do about it.

With that realization, that certainty,

Wyatt accepted what was going to happen to him. For the first time, he relaxed, his body going boneless, and his mind was curiously quiet, almost at peace. He heard his own voice speaking aloud and was a little amused by the conversational tone of it.

"Always wondered how I'd face death. Now I know. Not with a bang or a whimper, but just . . . resignation." He sighed. "I'm sorry, Lindsay. You'd probably be disappointed in me, wouldn't you? I bet you were never resigned. I bet you fought with your last breath, didn't you, baby? I know you didn't want to die. I know you didn't want to leave me."

"They're coming."

Wyatt blinked and stared up at the blade suspended over him. He could have sworn he'd heard her voice, though whether in his head or out loud he couldn't have said. "I guess a dying man hears what he wants to hear."

"Idiot. They're coming. Just a few more minutes."

He frowned slightly, and said, "I don't think my own imagination would call me an idiot. Although —"

"Just hold on."

"Lindsay? Is that you?"

Silence.

"Didn't think so. I don't believe in ghosts. Don't think I even believe in heaven, though it would be nice to believe you were waiting for me somewhere beyond this life."

"Don't be maudlin."

Wyatt found himself grinning. "Now, that sounds like my Lindsay. Come to keep me company in my final moments, baby?"

"You aren't going to die. Not now."

Deciding he was probably just quietly hysterical rather than being as calm as he'd thought, Wyatt said, "Twenty minutes left on the clock, babe. And I don't hear the cavalry."

He didn't hear her voice again either, though he did try to listen for it. And hoped for it. Because there were, he thought, worse things to take into death than the voice of the woman he loved.

When Lucas stopped suddenly, it caught Caitlin off guard. She leaned against an oak tree, trying to get her ragged breathing under control, and stared at the two just a couple of yards ahead of her. Her legs felt like rubber, there was a stitch in her side, and she couldn't remember ever being this weary.

They had finally reached the top of the

ridge they had spent more than two hours climbing and from this position could see across a fairly level clearing to where the mountain again began rising steeply upward.

Caitlin stared up at that vast, looming shape and knew without a shadow of a doubt that she couldn't go on. Not up that . . . thing. She was just about to gather the breath to tell the others, when she heard Samantha speak.

"Luke? What is it?" She sounded remarkably calm and not the least bit breathless.

"He's not afraid anymore."

Samantha frowned up at him. "But you can still feel him?"

"Yeah. But he's calm. Not afraid anymore."

Glen looked at his watch and said desperately, "We've got less than fifteen minutes. Where is he?"

Lucas turned his head and looked briefly at the deputy, frowning, then began moving forward again, faster. "Over there. The mine."

"There's a mine up here?" Glen sounded surprised, but then followed that question with a disgusted, "Oh, Christ, I forgot all about the old mine on Six Point Creek. It closed down when my grandfather was a kid."

Caitlin, somehow finding the strength to hurry along with the others, was about to ask where the creek was when she nearly fell into it. Swearing under her breath, she followed the others as they jumped from rock to rock to cross the twenty-foot-wide, fairly shallow stream.

The entrance to the mine lay nearly hidden behind what looked like a thicket of honeysuckle, and all Caitlin could think was that it had to be really, really dark in there.

Glen paused long enough to shrug out of the backpack he'd grabbed from the ATV, and quickly handed out big police flashlights. He started to draw his weapon, but Lucas spoke, his voice certain.

"Nobody's here except Wyatt. At least . . ."

Hesitating with a hand on his gun, Glen said, "At least what? Has he booby-trapped the place?"

Lucas seemed to be listening, and after a brief moment, he turned on his flashlight and shoved the tangle of vines aside to enter the mine. "No. No trap. Let's go."

The mine shaft was fairly clear of debris and angled slightly upward into the mountain, with plenty of room for them all to move freely. They traveled probably sixty or eighty feet in a straight line, and then the shaft turned sharply to the right — and widened considerably into a sort of cavern.

They saw the light then, bright and harsh and focused on the deadly, eerie guillotine and its captive.

Both Glen and Lucas, cops acting on instinct, rushed forward. Caitlin leaned a hand against the damp wall, feeling decidedly weak with relief — because that gleaming blade was still suspended above Wyatt. Still, she didn't think she breathed normally until she was certain that Glen held the cable so that the blade remained securely up while Lucas was unfastening the straps holding the sheriff prisoner.

She looked to the side then and saw that Samantha also had paused for a moment. There was just enough light for her to see the other woman lift a shaking hand briefly to her face, and then Samantha was moving forward and speaking calmly.

"Can I help?"

Lucas was easing up the wooden block pinning Wyatt's neck to the table, and said, "Got it, I think. Wyatt —"

The sheriff lost no time in sitting up, removing himself from harm's way. He slid to the edge of the table so that he was sitting on it. He was pale and haggard, but there was also a peculiar peace in his face. "The cavalry did come," he said, only a slight quiver in his voice. "How about that."

Then he turned his head, and they all followed his gaze to watch the nearby clock's digital readout counting relentlessly down. Nobody said a word as the last two minutes on the timer ran out — and Glen found himself suddenly supporting the weight of the heavy steel blade as a soft click announced the release of the cable. He carefully eased the blade down until it rested in the stained groove of the table.

"Shit," Wyatt said in a wondering voice. "I thought I was a dead man."

"You almost were," Lucas said. He went to study the clock, which was actually attached to a metal rod hanging downward from the lighting. "And the bastard really wanted you to know it, didn't he?"

"I'll never look at a clock the same way again." Wyatt frowned slightly as first Samantha and then Caitlin entered the circle of bright light. "Hey. Where the hell are we, anyway?"

"The old Six Point Creek mine," Glen told him, sounding considerably relieved.

"And if you'll all excuse me, I need to get out of here so I can radio the other search teams. Assuming I can get a signal out here, that is." He hurried away.

Still eyeing the women, Wyatt said, "What are you two doing here?"

Lucas immediately said, "If it hadn't been for them, we would never have found you in time."

"Yeah? Did Lindsay talk to one of you?"

They all looked at him in surprise, and it was Caitlin who said somewhat hesitantly, "She talked to me. Sort of. Left me a note."

"Which pointed us in this direction," Samantha said. "After that, it was Luke connecting to you that got us here."

Wyatt flinched slightly, and said to Lucas in a wry tone, "I won't talk about it if you won't."

"Done," Lucas said immediately.

Samantha said, "Did Lindsay talk to you, Sheriff?"

Surprising them all again, Wyatt replied firmly, "You know, I think she did. Could have been my imagination, of course, but I'm pretty sure it wasn't. She told me you were coming."

Samantha wanted to ask him if that was why he'd stopped being afraid, but didn't.

Whatever Wyatt Metcalf had experienced here in this dark and lonely mine with a clock counting down and a steel blade set to end his life was his own business.

Instead, she said, "It'll be dark by the time we get back down to the truck. Luke, I know you want to examine this place —"

"That can wait," he responded. "We'll send a couple of deputies to keep an eye on things tonight, then come back first thing in the morning with the CSU team. Not that I expect them to find anything useful. Wyatt, I don't suppose you saw the bastard?"

"Didn't even hear him. As far as I could tell, when I woke up this place was deserted. Except for me."

"He's being very careful," Samantha noted. "He talked to Lindsay. Talked to most of the other victims, didn't he?"

"We can't know for sure," Lucas told her. "Only the first victim survived to tell us."

"Can't legally know for sure, but you know, don't you?"

He looked at her for a moment, then said, "Yeah, I'm pretty sure he talked to all of them, at least up to a point."

"Then left them to die alone."

Lucas nodded.

Samantha eyed the sheriff and said slowly, "I wonder why you were different? Maybe . . . because you would have recognized him? Even his voice?"

"It's certainly a possibility," Lucas said. "A change in M.O. at this late stage has to mean something."

"Can we talk about it after we get off this mountain?" Wyatt requested. "I feel the need for fresh air — and maybe a nice, hot shower. And a cup of coffee. And a big steak."

No one was about to argue with him. They left the cavern exactly as it was, bright lights blazing, and used their flashlights to illuminate the way back to the mouth of the mine. When they reached it, they found Glen about to enter. He had made contact with one of the other search teams, so the word was being passed that Sheriff Metcalf had been found alive and was safe.

"They'll meet us back at the station," he said.

"Good enough," Wyatt replied. "I say we get the hell out of Dodge. I've had more than enough of this place."

From his vantage point near the sheriff's department, he saw the search teams begin to return and instantly knew something was wrong. Some of the cops were smiling, and all looked far less upset than they would have been had their search been fruitless or their sheriff's body been found.

He checked his watch and swore under his breath, then settled down to wait.

It was nearly an hour later when the last search team returned. In the harsh lights of the sheriff's department parking lot, he saw them get out of the hulking ATV, with media shouting questions and flashbulbs popping. And he saw the sheriff, who had obviously taken the time to shower and change after his ordeal.

Wyatt Metcalf was alive.

Alive.

The search team that had found the sheriff disappeared rather quickly into the building without stopping to answer questions, as did Metcalf — after making a stale joke about the reports of his death being greatly exaggerated.

Watching, teeth gritted unconsciously, he knew all he needed to know. On this move, at least, they had won.

Luke.

Caitlin Graham.

And Samantha Burke.

He discounted the deputy automatically,

knowing there was no threat from him. But the others . . .

What was the Graham woman's part in all this? It bothered him that he didn't know, that he hadn't expected her to turn up here in Golden. That he hadn't even known Lindsay Graham had a sister.

It was what came of changing his plans, he knew that much, though at the time he hadn't seen another choice.

He hadn't intended to take Lindsay Graham, and from almost the moment he had, things had felt . . . wrong. He had the uneasy idea that from the instant he had decided not to take Carrie Vaughn — principally because it had both irritated and surprised him that the carnival "seer" had figured out who his target was and had warned the woman, following that surprise by managing to somehow convince the sheriff to watch her — that his mastery over events had slipped, if only a bit.

He really hadn't expected the sheriff to listen to Samantha, whatever she told him. Metcalf was a hard-nosed cop who had no patience with carnival seers; everything in his past and professional record said as much. Just as Samantha Burke's past involvement with the police indicated both her lack of credibility in the eyes of law-enforcement officials and her reluctance to involve herself in anything outside her carnival world.

She had been an active participant in an investigation only once, three years before, and the disastrous ending of that — both the investigation and her turbulent, short-lived relationship with Luke Jordan — had sent her fleeing back to the safety of the Carnival After Dark.

She had seemed a handy tool, not because he believed that she could see the future but because of the personal turmoil she would undoubtedly cause Luke, and the media storm she was likely to attract to the investigation. So he had lured her here, intent on using her in that way. To keep Luke off balance and draw his attention away from his job.

It was, he had decided, a necessary step to take once the game settled here in Golden. He no longer had the advantage of moving constantly, forcing Luke to follow after him. So he needed Samantha's presence to keep his opponent just that little bit distracted and unfocused.

To tip the odds more in his own favor.

But her behavior had been unexpected from the beginning. And rather than distract Luke, or rattle him with the unexpected presence of a discarded lover, she seemed rather to have insinuated herself both into the investigation — and back into Luke's bed.

And instead of being the distraction he had planned her to be, it appeared that she was actually helping Luke.

He didn't understand that. He understood how pain and fear could — for want of a better phrase — call out to anyone with the right makeup to be able to hear: the simple electromagnetic energy of emotions and thoughts alive in the very air around him made perfect sense to him. It was an ability he understood, not so much paranormal as it was a sharply enhanced extension of otherwise normal senses.

He even understood, because he had made it his business to, how and why Luke's ability was a difficult one for the man to control at all, far less master. And why it drained him physically, exhausted him.

It's what he had wanted, a man driven past his limits and emptied of everything but the memories of the pain and suffering of the victims he had not found in time, and the unbearable knowledge that he had failed.

A broken man.

A man who understood, at last, why he had been judged and was being punished.

Instead, the man he had watched enter the sheriff's department after a successful search and rescue of Wyatt Metcalf had not seemed at all exhausted, and certainly wasn't broken.

For a long time after the small search team had disappeared from view, he remained where he was, still. Even the media had dispersed by the time he reached into his inner coat pocket and drew out a plastic Baggie containing an envelope. Inside the envelope was the note he had written to Luke, telling him where he could find the sheriff's body.

He took the envelope out of the bag and methodically, viciously, tore it into small pieces.

"Think you've won, Luke?" he muttered. "Wait. Just wait."

"I've put in a request for an agent to talk to the first kidnapping victim," Lucas said. "But I don't expect to get much if anything beyond her original statement. She told us what she knew and then pretty much asked us to leave her alone. Understandably, she's kept a low profile in the last year and a half, and I very much doubt she'd be willing to come down here to talk to us."

"Not with him here," Samantha murmured. "And who could blame her."

Lucas nodded but didn't look at her, and Caitlin wondered at the other woman's twisted smile. They had an odd relationship, those two, she decided. So solidly a team during the search for Wyatt, they were now, she thought, separated by much more than the length of the conference table.

"I don't know if she can tell us anything we don't already know," Lucas went on. "But she is the only one he released unharmed."

"And I'm the only one he's lost — so far," Wyatt said. He frowned and looked at Samantha. "You really think the fact that he didn't talk to me might mean something?" He was making a determined effort to at least pretend that he'd emerged from his ordeal unscathed, and everyone around him was playing along — for which he was grateful.

She shrugged. "Just struck me, is all. He's picked Golden as his last stand, apparently, and he clearly knows the area. That means he had to spend some time here before now. If he didn't talk to you, then maybe it's because he was afraid you might recognize his voice."

"But he left me for dead."

"Yeah, but even with all his confidence, he had to know there was at least a chance you'd be found in time. And if we know anything about him, it's that he's careful."

"I've lived here all my life," Wyatt told her, "and I've met a lot of people. Talked to a lot. Residents, tourists, people just passing through. If we can't narrow it down more than that, there isn't a chance in hell I'll be able to figure out who he is."

Lucas said, "It's a point to keep in mind, but with, as you say, no way to narrow it down, not very helpful at the moment. What baffles me is how he's managing to get in and out of these remote places, machinery or parts to build it in tow, without leaving much if any evidence."

"Maybe he has wings," Wyatt grunted, just about half serious.

Jaylene spoke up to offer, "Or a hell of an ATV. And something that big and rugged gets noticed, even in these mountains."

"I didn't see any tracks near the mouth of the mine," Lucas told her. "Maybe we'll find something tomorrow morning, but if it's the same as at every other crime scene . . ." He shook his head, adding, "And why weren't mines on our search list? Especially after Lindsay was found at one."

Wyatt shrugged. "Because none of them are marked on any of our maps, probably. Haven't been for decades. Virtually all the old mines in this county have been closed for so long that most of us have forgotten about them.

"Thing is, people have been digging in these mountains for generations. Gold, emeralds, whatever else there is or was. Lot of defunct mines up there that companies shut down when the veins petered out. And that's not even counting amateur efforts or natural caverns. Plus old cellars and other shelters hacked out of the granite during the last century or two and left abandoned. A big part of this county is federal land now, but it wasn't always."

"In other words," Lucas said grimly, "we've got a wilderness full of countless places where he could hold a hostage."

Wyatt lifted his brows slightly. "I take it you expect him to grab somebody else?"

"Until we've got our hands on him, it's a given."

The sheriff sighed. "Great. Well, what you said pretty much sums it up. Hell of a lot of land and not many ways of narrowing down the list of places to search.

We might be able to find out who owns various remote parcels, but there's nothing to say he's even tied to them in any legal sense. From what we've seen so far, it looks like he's just taking advantage of places nobody's made use of in so many years most of us have forgotten there was anything useful there."

"Which," Caitlin said, "is another point in favor of what Sam said. That he's been here long enough to know the area very, very well."

Wyatt frowned very slightly as he looked at her. "Not that I'm complaining, but are you sure you want to stay involved in all this?"

A bit self-conscious, she shrugged. "Might as well. I mean, if it's okay with you. I don't know that I can help, but it sure beats hours alone in that motel room."

Jaylene spoke up again to say, "Ask me, we can use all the help we can get. But I vote we start fresh tomorrow morning. It's been a very long day."

"I'll second that," Wyatt said. "Not that I plan to go home tonight, but the couch in my office is very comfortable, and it won't be the first time I've slept there."

None of the others probed for his reasons, simply accepting that a man who had faced his own death a few hours previously might not want to return to an empty apartment and spend the night alone. Better here, with people about and the pulse of life going on all night.

After a quick glance at her partner, Jaylene said to Caitlin, "I'll take you back to the motel. Maybe we can stop on the way and have dinner somewhere."

Caitlin nodded, but said to Lucas, "Am I still being guarded?"

He nodded immediately. "I think you should be, Caitlin. If he's been watching, he knows you're involved now."

Unnerved, she said, "You think he's been watching us? You mean — today?"

"I'd be surprised if he wasn't somewhere nearby when the search teams returned. He'd have wanted firsthand confirmation of just how successful this move was."

"But, still, why would he target me?" she demanded.

Samantha said, "I'm betting you're an unknown factor to him, and that's got to make him uneasy. He'd expect the cops and feds to be involved in a search, and he already knows about me, but you? Not only a civilian, but the grieving sister of a previous victim, so what are you doing with a search team?"

"He has to wonder," Lucas agreed. "And with a mind as twisted as his, wondering about anything could make him even more dangerous. So I think we're better safe than sorry, don't you?"

Caitlin sighed. "Yeah. Yeah, thanks."

"If you'd rather stay somewhere else —"

She shook her head, getting to her feet as Jaylene rose. "No, the motel is fine. Hell, maybe Lindsay will be in touch again." She eyed Wyatt, then smiled. "Or maybe she used all her ectoplasm or whatever to help save your sorry ass."

Soberly, Wyatt said, "I'll do my best to make it mean something."

"I was kidding. Lindsay was too smart and too stubborn to waste her time, believe me." Without waiting for a response, Caitlin lifted a hand in farewell and left the room with Jaylene.

To Lucas, Wyatt said, "Do you seriously believe she could be in danger?"

"I seriously do. Bringing you out of one of his killing machines alive just upped the stakes; I don't expect him to wait long before he makes another move. If we openly keep watch on Caitlin, at least we serve notice that we know he's still out there, and still a danger."

Wyatt didn't question that, just nodded and said, "I'll go reassign the watchdogs. And I'm going to send one of my people for takeout. That steak I mentioned earlier. You two want anything?"

"I need to get back to the carnival," Samantha said.

Lucas looked at her briefly, then said to the sheriff, "We'll get something on the way. But thanks."

"Okay. See you in the morning." Wyatt paused in the doorway to frown back at them. "Did I say thank you, by the way?"

"In your own way," Samantha murmured.

He grinned at her for the first time, and said firmly, "Thanks for getting to me in time. Both of you."

"Don't mention it," Lucas said.

When they were alone in the room, Samantha didn't wait for the silence to lengthen, as she suspected it would.

"Shall we talk about this, or is it your plan to give me the silent treatment for the duration?"

"There's nothing to talk about, Sam."

"Sorry, but that's not good enough. Not this time."

He turned in his chair to look at her, the length of the table a more-than-symbolic space between them. "It's been a long day and we're both tired. I hope you aren't planning on reading at the carnival tonight."

Deliberately, she said, "If I have a choice between reading strangers or being in that motel room for the next twelve hours or so with your anger between us, I'll take the carnival."

"I'm not angry."

"No, you're furious. I got too close again, this time emotionally. Tell me about Bryan, Luke."

He got to his feet, face closed. "We should stop on the way and get something to eat. You haven't eaten in hours."

"Neither have you." Samantha rose to her feet as well, conscious of weariness and a distant pain she didn't want to acknowledge. She followed Lucas from the room, and not even several rather awkward attempts from some of the deputies to thank her as they passed through the building could rouse more than a fleeting smile.

She had known there would be a steep price demanded of her for this. Bishop had tried to warn her.

"He's been obsessed too long, Samantha, and he won't thank you for trying to dig that out of him."

Understatement, Samantha thought now. By the time this was over, Luke might well hate her.

For all her determination, she didn't know how to deal with that possibility. She couldn't stop pushing him, not for long; that had been the plan from the beginning. No matter what it did to her, to them, she was convinced it was the only way to get at the inner pain driving Luke.

And that was the only way to save him.

The cell phone in the pocket of his vest vibrated a summons, and Galen answered it without taking the binoculars from his eyes.

"Yeah."

"What's happening?" Bishop asked.

"Not a whole hell of a lot, at the moment. They stopped at a steak place for supper, and now they're at the carnival. In Sam's booth. She must still be getting ready; there's a line forming, but Ellis hasn't let anybody in yet."

"I just tried to call Quentin and couldn't reach him. Where is he?"

"Playing Daniel Boone. He managed to take a look at the mine before the deputies Luke assigned to watch the place got there. Now he's trying to backtrack and find out which way the bastard got his little toy in there." Galen shifted position slightly, adding, "Probably not surprising you couldn't raise him on the cell; wild country up there."

"And dark, with only a quarter moon. What does Quentin think he can find?"

"You'd have to ask him. All he told me was that his spider sense was tingling." Once Galen would have used that phrase sardonically, but he had been a member of the team too long not to have learned that — comic-book terminology notwithstanding — the enhanced senses of some of the SCU members were both accurate and often surprisingly prescient.

"If you hear from him, keep me advised. And especially if you don't hear from him. I don't want any of you alone or out of touch for too long."

"Copy that. He should be reporting in any time now."

"How's Luke holding up?"

"Judging by what I could see, Sam was able to make him mad enough so that he'd find Sheriff Metcalf. They're both looking a little ragged, though. Hard to say whether her plan is working as well as she'd hoped, but whatever else it's doing, it's obviously a strain on them."

"And she's reading tonight?"

"Looks like. Whatever's going on between her and Luke, I think she believes this killer is a regular visitor to the carnival. And maybe she's right. He does like games."

Bishop was silent for a moment, then said, "You're still keeping an eye on Jaylene whenever she's alone?"

"Of course. Right now, she's with Caitlin Graham, so deputies are watching them both. As soon as Quentin gets back, he'll take over here and I'll make sure Jay's covered." He paused as his binoculars swept the carnival grounds slowly, then returned to Madam Zarina's booth.

"She spotted you, you know."

"Who, Jay?" Galen chuckled. "I must be slipping."

"That's what I told her."

"She's not mad at having a watchdog, is she?"

"No. She knows anyone close to Luke is a possible target. This killer has abducted two police officers; I doubt he'd hesitate to grab a federal agent."

"No, he has balls enough for just about anything, if you ask me. And right about now, I'm betting he's pissed as hell."

"I'll take that bet," Bishop said. "Question is, what's his next move?"

15

The reporter, eyes shifting uneasily, backed out of Samantha's booth, muttering, "That's okay, I think I got my money's worth."

Lucas immediately came out from the curtained-off area in back, took one look at Samantha, and handed her his handkerchief. As Ellis stepped into the booth, brows lifted, he said to her, "That's enough. Tell them she's done for the night."

Holding the handkerchief to her sluggishly bleeding nose, Samantha said, "Bastard beats his wife."

Ellis shook her head. "Maybe you can alert the sheriff."

"He's an out-of-towner, dammit."

Shaking her head once again, Ellis went back outside to offer rain checks to those still waiting to see Madam Zarina.

"Sam —"

Heading off whatever he'd been about to say, Samantha said, "It's only when I sense violence of some kind that this happens."

"Maybe, but it's something new for you, Sam, something unusual. And that makes it a danger sign." He didn't sound particularly worried about it, merely matter-of-fact.

Samantha yanked off the turban and set it on the table before her, her gaze fixed on his face. "Okay, so fix it so I don't have to keep doing this. Find him."

"Oh, for Christ's sake, don't you think we've been trying?" Despite his words, his voice was still calm, his face expressionless.

"The cops, yes. The feds, yes. You? Well, you've been looking at maps and lists and autopsy reports and compiling profiles. You even climbed half a mountain today. But you weren't trying to find him, you were running behind him trying to find his victims. The way you've been doing for the past year and a half."

"Don't do this, Sam."

"Why not?" She refolded the handkerchief and dabbed at the last of the blood, looking away from him at last to watch what she was doing. "You're going to despise me by the time this is done anyway, so I might as well get everything I have to say said and out into the open."

"This is not the time or the place —"

"This is the only place we have, Luke, and time's running out. Or hadn't you noticed? You won one today, remember? You beat the bastard. And we both know he is *not* going to be gracious in defeat. He'll be on to the next move, probably already. Selecting his next victim, if he or she wasn't already chosen long before now. Getting one of his remaining killing machines all polished up and ready."

Lucas drew a breath and said steadily, "It's nearly ten. Why don't you get changed and take off the makeup, and we'll get out of here."

"You can find him, you know."

"Sam, please."

"He feeds on fear, Luke. If what I saw when I touched that pendant is true, he's been feeding on fear for a long, long time. It's all inside him. You can feel that. All you have to do is tap in."

"I'll wait for you outside." He left the booth.

Samantha gazed after him for a long moment, then got to her feet and went into the curtained-off area in back. She changed out of her Madam Zarina getup and creamed away all the makeup, thinking as she studied her face in the mirror that there was less and less difference, these days, between the aged face of Madam Zarina and her own.

Moving more slowly than was usual for

her, she neatly put away her makeup and other supplies, finished clearing up the space, and then went outside the booth to join Luke.

Looking at the bright, noisy carnival all around them, she said absently, "I wonder if he's here? Watching us. I wonder what it is about this place that fascinates him."

"You," Lucas said.

Before she could respond to that, Leo appeared, to say worriedly, "Sam, Ellis told me about the nosebleed. Are you all right?"

"I'm fine. Just a little tired."

"I'm taking her back to the motel," Lucas said.

"Try to get her to sleep late, will you?" Leo asked. "And, Sam, no reading tomorrow night. In fact, no carnival. I've already posted the notice that we'll be closed tomorrow night."

"No need to on my account."

Leo shook his head. "On everybody's account. You haven't been around much, so you haven't realized that everybody is on edge and anxious. There's just too much going on around here. I've even been asked by a few to pull up stakes in Golden and move on."

Samantha didn't look at Lucas. "We're

only supposed to stay here until next Monday."

"Yeah. And we will — unless you change your mind about that."

"We'll see," she said.

"Just let me know." Leo sighed. "In the meantime, it'll do everybody good to have a night off. Matter of fact, I think most of them want to go into town, stay at the motel. I can't make out whether it's nerves or just the usual occasional need to sleep somewhere other than the caravans."

Lucas took Samantha's hand, rather surprising her, and said to Leo, "Keep an eye on your people. I don't think this killer would target any of you, but I can't be sure. So watch your backs."

"We will, Luke. Thanks."

As he led her back toward the parking area and his rental car, Samantha said quietly, "Leo's still grateful that you stood behind the carnival three years ago. When that garbage about gypsies stealing children hit the papers, a lot of ugly things started happening. If you hadn't convinced the local police to provide some security for us and gone on the record as saying no one in the carnival was involved, God knows where it would have ended."

"I was doing my job."

"You did more than your job, and we both know it."

Lucas silently unlocked the rental car and opened the passenger door for her.

She got in, once again conscious of weariness. And she wondered, as he came around the car and slid behind the wheel, if her plan was going to work. She wasn't sure, not anymore. Yes, Luke had been able to find the sheriff today, in time and against all odds, but she had the sense now that his walls were even higher and thicker than they had been before.

She had gotten too close and he had shut down. Maybe for good.

As they left the fairgrounds, he said, "I need to stop by my room and pick up a few things."

"You don't have to stay with me tonight."

"I'm not going to argue about this, Sam. I'm staying. For the duration."

"If I have to have a watchdog, I'm sure Jaylene wouldn't mind a roommate."

"Stop pushing, Sam."

"I'm not pushing, I'm trying to give you an out."

"I don't want an out."

"Right, you just want to punish me with the silent treatment."

"I'm not trying to —" He shook his head. "Christ, you make me crazy."

"It doesn't show. Very little shows, really, most of the time. On your face. There's intensity inside, force, but you keep it damped down almost always, out of sight. Is that the way you were raised, to show no emotion, no feeling? Is that part of it?"

Lucas didn't answer. In fact, he didn't say a word for the remainder of the trip to his motel and then back to hers. Samantha remained silent as well, and once they were inside the room she left him locking the door and went to take her usual shower.

She didn't linger, this time, under the hot water; it failed to either relax her or even begin to warm the chill deep inside her. She got out and dried off, put on her nightgown and robe. She toweled her hair, then used the wall hair dryer to completely dry it because she felt so cold.

When she came out of the bathroom and into the bedroom, she found Lucas on his feet but frowning at the television, and when she followed his gaze she could see why.

The exterior of the sheriff's department — and their arrival with Wyatt Metcalf.

The anchorwoman was briskly introducing the reporter on the scene, and then he was on-screen with the sheriff's department behind him. His voice held that urgent if muted excitement that was so common in television journalism, as he quickly brought viewers up to speed on the investigation and then detailed today's search and rescue of the sheriff of Clayton County.

". . . and a source close to the investigation claims that deputies and federal agents were aided in their search for the sheriff by an avowed psychic. The woman's name is Samantha Burke, though she uses the name Madam Zarina when she tells fortunes in a carnival currently set up here in Golden. My source claims that she has apparently involved herself before in police investigations."

Amazing, Samantha thought, how "involved herself" could sound so suspicious.

"Tom, have the police or federal agents confirmed that Miss Burke helped them to locate Sheriff Metcalf?"

"No, Darcell, officials refused to comment. However, my source is certain that she played a major role in recovering the sheriff alive, and locals are talking of little else. Earlier today, Miss Burke herself made a brief statement on the steps of the sheriff's department, claiming that the person who abducted and murdered Detective Lindsay Graham last week had left an object in the detective's apartment, which Miss Burke says triggered a vision. She did not share details of the supposed vision, but stated that she was certain the same person had abducted Sheriff Metcalf. She appeared willing to say more, but one of the federal agents involved in the investigation cut the statement short and pulled her into the building."

Samantha sank down on the edge of the bed and murmured, "Shit."

The anchorwoman, with only the faintest note of disbelief in her voice, said, "Kidnapping, murder, and mysticism in Golden; we'll look forward to further reports, Tom."

Lucas used the remote to turn off the TV and then dropped it onto the bed. He walked over to the window and pulled the curtains slightly to one side, gazing out.

Samantha knew a delaying tactic when she saw one, and wondered if he was actually too angry to speak. Part of her wanted to say something that might defuse the situation, but she knew she couldn't do that. Not now.

Deliberately offhand, she said, "I just

can't get the hang of talking to reporters, can I?"

"Is that all you have to say?" His voice was very quiet.

She wanted to tell him the truth, that she had gambled her little press conference would only make the local papers and that it had been designed as much to anger him as anything else, another of her tactics intended to push through his walls.

But she was just too tired to get into all that, so she merely said, "Well . . . I can say I didn't expect a TV reporter to quote me on the eleven o'clock news, naive as that sounds. There wasn't a TV camera there, so . . . I can even say I made a mistake talking to the press at all. But what difference would any of it make, Luke? I became part of the story, and they were not going to let me pass unnoticed."

"Just like before." His words dropped into the quiet room like icicles.

"So it's my fault, what happened before? It's my fault that a reporter lied and claimed I knew who had abducted that child, that I'd seen it in a vision, and the kidnapper panicked and killed her?"

"I never said that."

"You never had to. Oh, you blamed yourself for not finding her quickly

408

enough, but we both know if I hadn't been involved, that reporter would never have made his claim, would never even have speculated there was anything paranormal in the investigation. And maybe, just maybe, that little girl would have lived long enough for you to find her alive."

Samantha had known that in pushing and prodding Luke she was likely to open her old wounds as well as his, but she hadn't expected the strength of the pain.

Lucas turned but remained at the window. His face was hard, expressionless. "It wasn't your fault," he said.

"Once more with feeling."

"What do you want from me, Sam? I never believed it was your fault. What I did believe, what I came to understand, was that Bishop was right about the issue of credibility. Because any unscrupulous reporter would find it a lot easier and a lot safer to fabricate something as coming from the mouth of a carnival mystic than from a federal agent."

"I won't apologize for who and what I am."

"Have I asked you to?"

"Sometimes it feels that way."

He shook his head. "Even though you haven't told me everything, I know enough to understand that you didn't have many choices fifteen years ago. Life in a carnival over life on the streets? No question you made the better choice."

Samantha waited for a moment, then said, "You aren't going to ask, are you?"

"Ask what?"

"Ask what happened to leave me, at the age of fifteen, with just those two choices." She kept her voice steady.

He hesitated visibly, then shook his head once. "This isn't the time to get into —"

"Like I said, we're running out of time. I honestly don't expect much more, not for us. You aren't in my future, remember? And if all we have is now, then I'd just as soon get all the skeletons out of their closets where we can both see them. Just in case we ever do meet again. Or just in case we never meet again."

"Sam, you don't have to do this."

"You don't want me to do this," she said, knowing only as she spoke that it was the literal truth. "Because it'll make it harder for you to walk away if I do."

He frowned slightly but didn't protest that statement.

She turned a bit on the bed in order to face him more fully and clasped her cold hands together in her lap. "Have a seat.

This may take awhile."

Lucas came away from the window and did sit down on the other side of the bed, but said, "It's late. You're tired, I'm tired, and we have another long day tomorrow. We have a killer to hunt down, Sam."

"I know. Remember what I said that first day? You can't beat him without me."

"Because you can piss me off?" he asked.

She drew a breath, too tense to be able to see any humor now. "Because I make you listen to things you don't want to hear. You refuse to let yourself feel pain or fear until you have absolutely no other choice. So I'm not giving you a choice."

"Sam —"

Ignoring the beginning of protest, she said steadily, "I was six when I became psychic. It happened the first time he threw me against a wall."

Jaylene watched the same news report and grimaced as she turned off the TV in her room. She wasn't surprised when her cell phone rang a summons just minutes later.

She checked the caller I.D., then answered with, "You saw the news report, huh?"

"Yes," Bishop said.

"Uh-huh. And just how long have you been close by?"

"Long enough."

Jaylene sighed. "I had a hunch there was more going on than you were willing to say. I mean, I know you sometimes send in a watchdog or two without alerting the primary agents, even someone working undercover, but you don't often turn up personally when another team member is leading an investigation."

"This killer has more than a dozen notches on his belt, Jay, and he's shown no signs of even slowing down. Or of conveniently wanting to be caught. He has to be stopped, and here."

"No argument. But why the cloak and dagger? Why not just tell us you're involved?"

"Because the killer's focus is on Luke — and I'm too recognizable to the media."

Jaylene knew that the latter, at least, was quite true; he had a memorable face and presence, did Bishop, and it was only very rarely possible for him to work undercover.

"You think if you showed up publicly, the killer would shift his focus?"

"No. I think he'd leave Golden and try to take his game elsewhere. He knows about us, Jay. About the SCU. And if any other team members showed up publicly, he'd very likely come to the conclusion that we had a decided edge in his game. A psychic edge."

Thoughtful, Jaylene said, "And yet he lured Sam here. Think he doesn't believe she's genuine?"

"My guess is exactly that. Her involvement in the investigation three years ago was more or less a public fiasco, at least from the media's reporting of it; anyone reading those reports would probably decide she was a phony."

"So he wanted her here as a . . . distraction . . . for Luke?"

"Why not? Even if that angle didn't work, chances were good the media would grab on to Samantha as a good story and at the very least add to the tension. Among the investigators and the townspeople."

"Making it even harder for Luke to concentrate." Jaylene frowned. "Yeah, but if this guy really is matching wits with Luke, why work so hard to turn the game to his own advantage? I mean, why not a level playing field?"

Bishop said, "A nicely sane, competitive mind would want that, yes. But a sociopath? He just wants to win, and never mind fair play. He wants to prove, in his own mind, that he's better than Luke. Smarter, stronger. Manipulating people and events is just another way he's doing that."

"So we were being naive in even trying to figure out his rules."

"I'd call it an exercise in futility."

"Guess you're right. Sam said something about broken minds not working the way we'd expect them to."

"She's right about that. The only thing we can know for sure," Bishop said, "is that he has a personal grudge against Luke."

"I assume you're checking on that?"

"We've already gone back through his cases in the last five years, and nothing looks promising in the way of a lead. Harder to find out about his cases before he joined up, but we're working on that." Bishop paused, then added, "I don't know if Luke could remember anything helpful, but it wouldn't hurt to steer him in that direction."

"He doesn't talk about his past, you know that."

"Doesn't talk about it with a vengeance, yeah. But I'm hoping Samantha has had some effect."

"Oh, she's having an effect. I'm just not

sure, when all's said and done, what that effect will be." It was Jaylene's turn to pause, and then she said, "Straight out, boss — did you get in touch with Sam, or did she get in touch with you?"

Bishop sighed and murmured, "It really is hell trying to keep information away from psychics."

"That isn't an answer."

"She got in touch with me."

"It's that vision she had in the beginning, isn't it? The one that made her decide to take the bait and come to Golden."

"Yes. That's all I can tell you, Jaylene. And more than Luke needs to know right now. He also doesn't need to know that Galen is keeping an eye on you whenever you're alone or that I'm anywhere near Golden."

"More secrets from my partner?" She sighed.

"I wouldn't ask if I didn't believe it was important."

"Yeah, you don't need to remind me of that."

"No," Bishop said. "I didn't think I did."

Lucas had expected something bad. Samantha was too intelligent to have bailed out of any kind of normal family life, even at an age when hormones and youthful stupidity tended to rule far too many decisions and actions.

So he had expected bad. He hadn't expected this.

Those dark, dark eyes never left his face, and her voice was steady, almost indifferent, as if the telling meant nothing to her. But he could see the tension in the hands knotted together in her lap, and he could see the pain in her pallor.

See it. But not feel it, not feel her pain.

Only his own.

"He was my stepfather," she said. "My real father was killed in a car accident when I was still a baby. My mother was the type of woman who had to have a man around, had to feel she belonged to someone, so there was a succession of *uncles* while I was a toddler. Then she met him. And married him. And I don't suppose she knew in the beginning that he liked to drink, and that drinking made him mean. But she found out. We both found out."

"Sam —"

"I don't remember what set him off that day. I don't even remember being thrown against the wall, not really. I just remember waking up in the hospital and hearing my mother anxiously telling the doctor that I was clumsy and kept falling down the stairs. Then she put her hand on my arm, patting it, and I . . . saw what had happened to me. Through her memories. I saw myself flung against the wall like a rag doll."

"A head injury," Lucas murmured.

Samantha nodded. "Severe concussion. Kept me in the hospital for more than two weeks. And I still have horrendous headaches sometimes, lasting for hours. So bad they literally blind me."

"You should have told me that sooner, Sam. Those nosebleeds —"

"Seem to be related to visions of violence. The headaches just come, suddenly, out of nowhere. I've never been able to pinpoint a specific cause." She shrugged. "All part of the psychic package, apparently."

Lucas muttered a curse under his breath but didn't say anything else. There wasn't much he could say; the SCU had learned long ago that moderate-to-severe headaches *did* seem to be the norm for a large percentage of psychics.

Samantha said, "I didn't understand, of course, what it all meant. I didn't understand about being psychic. All I knew was that I was different. And I came to know that being different made me a target of his rages."

She paused, then added, "I learned to stay out of his way as much as possible, but as the years passed, he got worse. The rages got more violent, and he always wanted a target. He beat up my mother from time to time, but something about me seemed almost to . . . draw his anger."

Roughly, Lucas said, "You know damned well it wasn't you, wasn't in any way your fault. He was a sick son of a bitch, and he hurt you because he could."

Samantha shook her head. "I think he knew, somewhere inside him, just how different I really was. I wasn't something he could understand, the way he understood my mother's need of him. I never tried to argue with him or defy him, but I never gave him the satisfaction of hearing me cry, and that baffled him. I think he was afraid of me."

Lucas felt another twinge of pain as he thought of how she must have looked beneath the brutal blows of a domestic monster, small, slight, defiantly silent. "Maybe. Maybe he was afraid of you. That doesn't make it your fault."

With a shrug, she said, "He was the sort who struck out at anything he feared, and when he drank he got paranoid as well as mean. Like I said, I did my best to stay out of his way. As I got older, it was a bit easier to find somewhere else to be, even if it was only the library or a museum. But, eventually, I'd have to go home, and I'd find him waiting for me."

Lucas didn't ask why none of her teachers or neighbors had noticed the abuse and reported it to the authorities. He knew too well that what bruises and cuts weren't hidden beneath long sleeves and pants would likely go unnoticed. And that most people were hesitant to get involved.

"After that first time when he put me in the hospital, he was more careful, or at least I suppose he was. He seemed to know just how far he could go without inflicting enough damage to send me to a doctor. Usually it was bruises and minor cuts, nothing that wouldn't heal or couldn't be hidden.

"It might have gone on years longer, I guess, since I was stubbornly determined to finish school despite him. I even had dreams of winning a scholarship and going on to college. But then, not long before my fifteenth birthday, he went too far and broke a couple of ribs."

Lucas swore under his breath. It hurt him to hear this; he couldn't even imagine how much the reality of it had hurt her.

"I didn't realize at the time; I just knew it wasn't easy to breathe. But the next day at school, a teacher noticed the careful way I was moving and sent me to the school nurse. I tried to tell her I'd just fallen — not to protect him but because I'd seen kids going from bad homes to worse ones in the foster system, and I preferred the devil I knew. But she didn't believe me, not once she had my shirt off and saw all the half-healed cuts and old bruises.

"So after she bound up my ribs, she called my mother and him to come to school. She talked to them in the other room, so I don't know what was said. But when he came back into the room to get me, I could tell by his face that he was angrier than he'd ever been. One of those simmering furies of his that could last for days before he exploded."

When she fell silent, Lucas had to ask. "What happened?"

Samantha replied, "He grabbed my wrist to pull me up from the cot I was sitting on, and even though it had never happened before, his touch triggered a vision."

"What did you see?"

"I saw him kill me," she answered simply.

"Jesus Christ."

For the first time, Samantha seemed to be looking beyond Lucas, her eyes distant, almost unfocused. "I knew he'd do it. I knew he'd beat me to death. Unless I ran away. So I did, that night. I packed everything I could carry in one bag, stole about fifty bucks from my mother's purse, and I left."

She blinked and was suddenly there again, her gaze fixed on his face. "That's when I got my first lesson in changing the future. Because he didn't kill me. What I saw never happened."

Lucas hesitated, then said, "You know it's not that simple. The vision was a warning of what *would* happen if you didn't leave, didn't remove yourself from that situation. It was a possible future."

"I know. And I learned, over the next years, that some things I saw couldn't be changed. I even learned that sometimes my own intervention seemed to bring about the very thing I was trying to avoid, what a vision had shown me." Her smile was twisted. "The future doesn't like to be seen too clearly. That would make things too easy for us."

"Yeah, the universe doesn't like us to get too complacent."

Samantha sighed. "It was like walking a high wire sometimes, especially in those early years. The only talent I had was . . . telling fortunes. Sometimes I'd try to change what I saw, and sometimes I felt almost paralyzed, unable to act at all."

"You were very young," Lucas said.

"Like I said, I wasn't young even when I was." She shook her head, adding more briskly, "I headed south, knowing that the weather would be milder if I had to sleep outside. And I usually did. Told fortunes on street corners for a few bucks. Got busted a couple of times. And finally hooked up with Leo and the Carnival After Dark."

"How long were you on the streets?"

"Six, seven months. Long enough to know I wouldn't be able to have any kind of a life that way. As you said, the carnival was a much better option." She looked at him steadily. "And if you're wondering, I don't want your pity. Lots of people have sad stories; at least mine had a relatively happy outcome."

"Sam —"

"I just wanted to remind you that you aren't the only one who knows something about pain and fear. You aren't, Luke. It was a long, long time before I could sleep through the night. A long time before I stopped expecting him to suddenly show up in my life and hurt me again. And a long time before I learned to trust anyone."

"You trusted me," he said.

"I still do." Without waiting for a response, she got up from the bed and began turning the covers back. "The shower's yours. I'm going to bed. Can't seem to get warm."

Lucas wanted to say something, but he didn't know what. He didn't know how to bridge the distance between them, far too aware that he was responsible for it. He knew what Sam wanted from him, or at least he thought he did — her needling had made that plain.

She wanted him to tell her about Bryan.

But that was a wound that was still raw and untouchable, and Lucas shied away even from thinking about it.

Instead, he gathered what he needed from the bag he had brought from his own motel room and headed for the shower, hoping the hot water would help him to think.

He had no doubt that without her needling and pushing, he would not have found Wyatt in time. She had found a way — however painful — to force him to reach beyond his walls, to lash out in anger, and in so doing to open himself to the fear and pain he'd been designed by nature to intercept.

It disturbed Lucas deeply that his own anger seemed a better key to unlocking his abilities than anything else he had discovered in years of concentrated effort. He had to believe, just from what he knew of psychics and psychic ability, that his was not supposed to work that way.

He should have been able to consciously, calmly, tap his abilities, focus them — and to do so long before he was so drained and exhausted the effort very nearly incapacitated him.

He knew that.

He had known that for a long time.

He even knew why he had been unable to do so, though it was not something he allowed himself to consider very often.

As badly as he wanted to find the victims of the crimes he investigated, as badly as he wanted to find those who were lost and in pain and terror, there was a part of him that dreaded and even feared what it cost him.

He felt what they felt.

And their terror, their doomed agony, pulled him into a hell of torment that was a memory he couldn't bear.

The bedroom was very quiet and semidark when Lucas came out of the bathroom. He checked the door again, just to be sure, then slid his weapon under the pillow beside Samantha's and got in that side of the bed. The lamp on his side was on low, and he left it that way.

He lay beside her for a long time, staring at the ceiling. Then he felt her shiver and, without hesitating, turned toward her and pulled her into his arms.

"Still cold," she murmured, unresisting.

He pulled her a bit closer, frowning, because her skin wasn't cold, it was just this side of feverish. And he had the sudden, unsettling realization that the cold place Samantha tapped into to use her abilities, the place a brutal animal had awakened with violence, was as hauntingly dark and tormenting as anything he had ever experienced.

And, for her, inescapable.

16

Caitlin Graham honestly didn't know why she was still involved in the investigation of kidnappings and murders. Why she wanted to be here, and why they allowed it. She thought of herself as the only civilian in the bunch, despite Samantha's lack of law-enforcement credentials; the other woman clearly understood the procedures involved, as well as possessing an obvious investigative knack.

"The only thing we have that even re-motely resembles a lead," she was saying now, "are those ATV tracks the CSU found up at the mine this morning."

Looking over a printout he'd just re-ceived, Lucas said, "Preliminary report is that the vehicle is likely to be a Hummer, just like we've been driving up there."

Wyatt grunted. "We have four in the motor pool. Other than those of us who have to patrol in the mountains around here, they aren't all that common — though more so than they used to be."

"Impressive TV ads," Caitlin said. "And they're on some high-profile TV shows. So now they're sexy."

The sheriff agreed with a rueful nod.

"Still out of reach of most car owners, though," Lucas noted. "And still pretty rare. I'm getting a list covering owners in every state in which there's been a kidnapping, including this one."

"And then?" Wyatt inquired.

"Hoping a name will jump out at one of us," Lucas replied with a sigh.

"Would he be driving with an out-of-state tag?" Jaylene wondered aloud. "Wouldn't it make him look even more conspicuous?"

"At this time of year?" Wyatt shook his head. "Place is full of tourists, especially in October. They come to hike, look at the leaves, camp. Even with all the publicity lately — or maybe because of it — the numbers I'm seeing are up over last year."

"Lost in a crowd of strangers," Samantha murmured.

"My bet," Lucas said, "is that he only drives the Hummer when he has to. When he's moving around here in town, he'll have something a lot more ordinary and inconspicuous."

"Bound to," Wyatt agreed.

"Look," Jaylene said, "he can't be staying at any of the motels in town, right?"

"Unlikely," Lucas said. "He's a loner; he won't be around other people any more than he has to."

"Okay. And so far, he's been leaving his victims in remote areas, mostly up in the mountains. But he knows we've been searching those places, at least the ones on our list of possibles, which is probably why he hid Wyatt away in a mine that wasn't on any of our maps and that no one remembered."

"Big assumption," Wyatt said. "The mine must have been on *his* list, otherwise he wouldn't have had time to get his guillotine up there."

She nodded, a bit impatiently. "Yeah, but that's not what I'm thinking. He has to be staying somewhere during all this. We've had rangers and cops checking campers and hikers since we got here, obviously with no luck, but he has to know what we're doing."

"He's watching," Samantha said.

Jaylene nodded again. "He's watching. So he won't put himself in a position to be noticed or questioned. And he won't be too far away, not any more often than he has to be. Which means he can't be sitting in a cozy tent off the marked campsites and trails way up in the mountains. He has to be close. Most of the time, he has to be close."

"Pretending to be a member of the media?" Caitlin guessed. "Lost in that crowd of faces?"

Lucas considered, then shook his head. "He's too focused on his game to be able to act a part, and he'd know that. But I wouldn't be surprised if he hadn't tried to talk to a journalist at least once in order to get information. Probably after those periods when he'd been occupied by a kidnapping."

Wyatt lifted his brows. "I can put a few people to questioning the media — if you don't think it might tip our hand in some way."

Lucas didn't have to consider that. "I think we need to get as much information as fast as we can."

Samantha was looking steadily at him. "You feel it too. Time's running out."

He returned her stare, nodding slowly. "You were right — we beat him yesterday. And he is not going to want that hanging over his head for long."

"Another kidnapping so soon?" Wyatt said. "Christ."

"If we're lucky," Lucas said, "he'll act

out of haste, or at least out of anger, make a move before he takes the time to work out all the details. Because that's the only way we're going to catch this bastard — if he slips up."

He had no idea how much those words would come to haunt him.

"What're you, made of iron?" Quentin inquired somewhat irritably as Galen continued to pace from window to window in the living room of the small house rented for the duration. "Get some rest, for Christ's sake. They're all together and watching each other's backs; we need to sleep while we can." He had been trying to follow his own advice, stretched out on a rather lumpy couch.

"Something's wrong," Galen said.

"Yeah, there's a kidnapping murderer on the loose. Got the memo."

Ignoring the characteristic sarcastic humor, Galen merely said, "I thought you were supposed to be precognitive."

"I am."

"And you can't feel that something is about to happen?"

Quentin sat up and eyed the other man. "None of my senses are telling me anything except that I'm tired as hell. Comes of tramping over half a mountain and then spending the night on guard."

"You didn't need to watch Sam; Luke was with her."

"Habit. Besides, I couldn't sleep. Then. I'd like to now, if you don't mind."

Galen moved from a side window to the front one and stood to one side of it as he peered out.

Still watching him, Quentin said, "If we're seen during the day, it could blow our cover. Well, mine, at least. You blended nicely into the carnival these last weeks."

A flicker of amusement showing briefly on his harsh face, Galen said, "Jealous?"

"Didn't you want to run away and join the circus when you were a boy?"

"No. Wanted to run away and join the army. Which I did." He paused, eyes narrowing as he gazed out the window. "As with most fantasies, it turned out that reality wasn't nearly as much fun as what I'd imagined."

Quentin was about to take the opportunity to further explore his taciturn companion's rather mysterious past when fate intervened, in the form of one of the flashes of knowledge with which his ability often gifted him. He went perfectly still, concentrating.

Galen turned his head, eyes still narrowed. "Something?"

"Oh," Quentin said. "Shit."

"What?"

"We need to get to the carnival."

"Why?"

"Games," Quentin said. "He likes games."

"I need to touch it," Samantha said.

"No." Lucas's voice was flat.

They happened to be alone together in the conference room, at least for the moment, but Samantha kept her own voice low and steady. "So far, I haven't touched any of his murder machines. But he built them, Luke. With his own hands and all the hate inside him."

"Which is why you aren't going to touch either the tank or the guillotine," he said.

"They're all we've got. And just because science couldn't find any evidence on them doesn't mean I can't."

"Jaylene tried. Nothing."

"I'm stronger than she is, you know that. And I've already touched this maniac's mind, with the pendant. I can connect with him by touching his machines. I have to try to do that."

"No."

"We have no leads worth pursuing. We're questioning journalists and waiting for a list of Hummer owners on the East Coast you know as well as I do will be hundreds of names long. We're waiting, Luke. Waiting for him to make his next move. We're playing his game, just like he wants. And we can't afford that luxury anymore. You know that."

He was silent.

"One of us has to connect with him." She allowed that statement to hang in the air between them, never taking her eyes off his face.

Lucas almost flinched, but his gaze remained steady. "Then I will."

"Your ability doesn't work the same way. Touching doesn't help you connect. So how're you going to connect, Luke? How are you going to open yourself up enough to feel your way into this monster's mind?"

"I don't know, dammit."

Caitlin came into the room just then, holding the cup of coffee she had gone to get and saying, "One of the journalists is saying he remembers somebody asking a lot of questions. Luke, Wyatt thinks you should hear what he has to say." She stopped suddenly, looking from one to the other of them, and added uncertainly, "Should I leave?"

"No," Lucas said. Then, to Samantha, he repeated flatly, "No." He left the room.

"A man of few words," Caitlin noted, still uncertain.

"And all of them autocratic."

"You don't really mean that. Do you?"

Samantha got to her feet. "Let's just say that this is one time I can't let Luke tell me what to do for my own good."

"Have you ever?" Caitlin set her cup on the table and followed Samantha from the room. "Hey, don't get mad at me. I just —"

"I'm not mad. At least, not at you. Or at Luke, really. He can't help being the way he is; if he could, there wouldn't be a problem."

Caitlin wasn't sure where Samantha was going, or why she was following her, but didn't allow either question to stop her. "I gather this has something to do with you making him so angry yesterday so he was able to find Wyatt?"

"Something," Samantha agreed, turning into a stairwell that took them down to the garage basement of the building. "I don't seem to have the energy to do that again today. So I'm going to try something different."

"Like what?" Caitlin followed her across the currently deserted garage to a room off to one side. When she saw what it contained, she felt a chill. "Sam —"

Samantha looked at her with a small smile, then moved to stand between the glass tank and the guillotine that were placed about four feet apart. "I'm sorry, Caitlin. I shouldn't have let you come down here."

"That tank. Is that where —"

"It's how he killed Lindsay, yes. I'm sorry."

Caitlin looked at it for a moment, thinking only that it seemed so unthreatening, just sitting there on the concrete floor, empty of water and life. And death. Or at least, so it seemed to her. She looked at Samantha. "What're you going to do?"

"I have to touch both of these machines. He built them. I have to try to connect with him."

Remembering the pendant and Samantha's frightening vision-induced pallor and nosebleed, Caitlin said, "Nobody has to tell me this isn't a good idea, Sam."

"I have to try. I have to help them find him, if I can."

"But —"

"I'm running out of time. I have to try." She reached out with both hands, her right one touching the steel blade resting in its stained groove and her left one touching the glass of the tank.

Caitlin knew instantly that whatever well of emotion or experience Samantha had been psychically dragged into was very deep and very dangerous. She actually jerked, a faint sound coming from behind the lips pressed so tightly together, and what little color she could claim drained from her face.

"Oh, shit," Caitlin muttered.

As Lucas listened to the journalist — a newspaper reporter from Golden — talk about the "really nosy guy" who had twice approached him with curious questions during the past week, something began to nag at him.

"He didn't have much of an accent," Jeff Burgess said thoughtfully. "Not from these parts, that's for sure."

"Can you describe him?"

"Well . . . not a young man, but not quite middle-aged. Maybe forty or so. Tall. One of those barrel chests you see on some men, the bull-strong ones. Otherwise very average. Brown hair worn short. Grayish eyes. One thing — he tilted his head just a bit to one side after he asked a question. Funny sort of studied mannerism, I thought. And irritating. Somebody should have told him to quit it years ago."

"What else?"

"Well, would you believe it, he called me 'sport.' I mean, how long since you've heard *anybody* use that? 'Don't mean to bother you, sport, but I was just wondering' . . . whatever. Probably why I remember him so well. Had a funny sort of smile too, like a guy who knew he should be smiling but didn't really want to, you know?"

"Yes," Lucas said. "I know. Mr. Burgess, I'm going to ask you to repeat this to a deputy, if you don't mind, so we'll have a written account."

"Nah, I don't mind." Burgess's eyes were sharp. "So he wasn't just a nosy tourist, huh?"

"When I find out," Lucas returned pleasantly, "I'll let you know."

Burgess snorted but didn't protest as Lucas waved a deputy over to take the statement.

Retreating to the conference room, Lucas was barely aware that both Wyatt and Jaylene were following him, and he was honestly startled when his partner spoke to him.

"Something rang a bell?"

Lucas looked at her, his mind working quickly. "Maybe. The description . . . mannerisms . . . and I imagine he could certainly hold a grudge against me, though he never showed it then."

"Luke, who is it?"

As if he hadn't heard her, he murmured, "I just don't understand how he could be doing this. Not killing, and not this way. He was a *victim*. He suffered, I know he did. He lost — He lost. *I* lost. Maybe that's the crux of the whole thing. I lost her, wasn't able to find her in time, and he blames me. I should have found her, it was my job. It was what I *did*. But I failed, and he suffered for it. So now it's my turn to fail. My turn to suffer."

Jaylene sent Wyatt a somewhat helpless look, then said to her partner, "Luke, who are you talking about?"

His eyes cleared suddenly and he looked at her, saw her. "When Bishop recruited me five years ago, I was working on a missing-persons case out in L.A. A girl, eight years old, never came home from school one day. Meredith Gilbert."

"Did you find her?" Jaylene asked.

"Weeks later, and far too late for her." He shook his head. "Her family went through hell, and very publicly, since her father was a real estate baron out there. Her mother never got over it and killed herself about six months later. Her father . . ."

"What about him?" Wyatt asked intently.

"He'd started out in construction, I'm pretty sure, so he knew how to build. Big man. Tall, barrel-chested. Amazingly powerful physically. And he had a habit of addressing another man as 'sport.'"

"Bingo," Jaylene said. "If he blamed you for not finding his daughter and, by extension, for the suicide of his wife, then he could have been carrying around a hell of a grudge, Luke. Five years to plan, plenty of money to do what he needed to do. Background in construction. Even a solid knowledge of real estate could have helped him plan and set things up here in the East. It even explains his bribe to Leo Tedesco; a man like that *would* think of buying what he needed or wanted."

"I would have sworn he didn't blame me." Lucas shook off the thought, saying to Jaylene, "We need to check it out, find out what happened to Andrew Gilbert after the deaths of his wife and daughter.

And there was an older son, I think — away at school at the time, so I never met him."

"I'll call Quantico and get them on it," she said, turning away.

That was when Lucas realized something else. "Where's Sam? I left her in here."

"Didn't see her go out the front," Wyatt said.

Lucas barely had time to feel the beginnings of a cold knot in the pit of his stomach when Caitlin appeared in the doorway, her face white.

"It's Sam. The basement — hurry."

Samantha barely felt the physical contact of the tank and the guillotine. All she felt . . .

The black curtain swept over her, the darkness as thick as tar, the silence absolute. For an instant, she felt she was being physically carried somewhere, all in a rush; she even briefly felt the sensation of wind, of pressure, against her body, as though she was actually moving.

Then the familiar abrupt stillness and the chilling awareness of a nothingness so vast it was almost beyond comprehension. Limbo. She was suspended, weightless and even formless, in a cold void somewhere beyond this world and before the next.

As always, all she could do was wait, grimly, for the glimpse into whatever she was meant to see. Wait while her brain tuned in the right frequency and the sounds and images began playing before her mind's eye like some strange movie.

But from that point on, nothing happened as it always had.

Instead, scenes from her own past played before the unblinking gaze of her mind's eye. Stark, harsh, unrelenting, and in vivid color.

The beatings. His fists, his belt, once a broom handle. The times he had burned her with his cigarette. The really, really bad times when he had slammed her against walls, thrown her across furniture, tossed her about like a doll, and all the while she could hear the roaring fury of his drunken rage.

And the words, over and over, hateful words.

"Stupid little bitch!"

". . . good for nothing . . ."

". . . ugly . . ."

". . . runt . . ."

". . . pity you were ever born . . ."

Pain blazing along every nerve ending

and the bone-deep aches of afterward when she could barely move. Dragging herself to her room, to huddle beneath the covers and choke back the whimpers she never let him hear.

When she *could* drag herself to bed. When he didn't toss her into the tiny closet and shove a chair under the doorknob, leaving her in there for hours and hours . . .

The remembered terror stirred in Samantha, so cold, so awful, and as it did the scene she saw changed abruptly. She found herself staring at a man she'd never seen before. He was standing at the open door of a hulking ATV and seemed to be looking past her. Then he moved suddenly, reaching for the gun on the vehicle's seat.

He got off at least one shot, the loud report of it hurting Samantha's ears. And then there were other shots, scarlet bloomed abruptly on his chest, bubbled from his lips, and he opened his mouth to gasp —

Blackness swallowed Samantha before she could hear whatever it was he said. It seemed to last forever, or maybe it was only seconds. She didn't know. Didn't really care. Blackness and silence and a chill that followed her up, slowly, so slowly, out of limbo.

"Sam?"

She hurt. She was cold and she hurt. And he, she thought dimly, would not make it better. Maybe could not. Maybe nobody could. . . .

"Sam!"

Conscious then of the weight of her body, conscious of being back, she forced her eyes to open.

"Hey," she whispered. Funny how rusty and unused her voice sounded.

"Christ, you scared the hell out of me," Lucas said.

Vaguely surprised, she said, "I did? How?"

He showed her a bloody handkerchief, and said roughly, "You've been out for nearly an hour."

"Oh. Sorry." Samantha realized then that she was lying on a sofa in the lounge of the sheriff's department. Lucas was sitting on the edge of the sofa, and Caitlin and the sheriff were standing a few feet away.

When she met the other woman's gaze and saw her pallor, Samantha said with more contrition, "I really am sorry, Caitlin. I knew it'd be bad, but I had no idea —"

"Then why the hell did you do it?" Lucas demanded.

She looked back at him and winced. "Not so loud, please. My head is splitting." And she felt incredibly weak, dizzy, and nauseated.

Wyatt said, "Are you sure she shouldn't be in a hospital? I've never seen anybody so pale."

"There's nothing a doctor could do for her, otherwise she'd be under the care of one now," Lucas said, but in a quieter voice. He frowned down at her and held the handkerchief to her nose, adding, "But if this bleeding doesn't stop soon . . ."

Samantha took the cloth from him and held it herself. "It'll stop. Listen, about this killer —"

"We have a name," Wyatt told her. "Somebody Luke remembered from his past. Jaylene's checking county property records now to find out if the bastard was arrogant enough to use his real name, like Luke thinks he did." Clearly, the sheriff could hardly wait to get his hands on the man who had trapped him in a guillotine.

"So," Lucas said to Samantha, "there was no need for you to put yourself through this."

"Maybe not." She refolded the handkerchief and held it to her nose again, feeling very tired. "But when you find him, he'll be standing in the open door of his truck, an ATV. You'll need to be careful. There's a gun on the seat. Don't let him get to it, or he'll get off at least one shot."

Wyatt whistled half under his breath. "Now, that's what I call a useful prediction."

"Not a prediction. Fact."

He nodded. "Okay."

She eyed him, searching for sarcasm, but saw none.

"Hey," he said, understanding the look, "I'm a convert. Funny thing about facing death. It really does open up your mind to possibilities."

"Yes," Samantha said. "I know."

Jaylene came into the room then. "Hey, Sam, glad to see you back with us."

"Glad to be here."

Addressing Lucas, his partner said, "Got him. You were right, he used his real name. Probably figured we'd never go back so far in checking property records. Andrew Gilbert bought some property here two and a half years ago." She looked at the sheriff, brows lifting. "From you."

He blinked. "Say what?"

"You sold a hundred-acre tract of land

that had belonged to your parents. Mostly mountainous land, not good for much, with a little piece of a valley on which sits a small old house and a much larger old barn. About twenty miles outside town. It wasn't included on any of our earlier searches because, even though it's fairly remote, there are other working farms in that valley, neighbors who would have, presumably, noticed someone carting tanks and guillotines and bodies about."

"His home base," Lucas said slowly. "Maybe where he stashes the ATV when he isn't using it — assuming there's a back way into that barn so his neighbors don't see."

Wyatt said wryly, "And I'll bet they think he's just a regular guy but quiet, keeps to himself."

"Bound to," Jaylene agreed.

"For God's sake. Yeah, I remember the guy. Said he was looking for quiet land he could retire to in a few years. Talked about building a log cabin, hunting cabin, like he'd always wanted. Offered a good but not outrageous price, and since I was trying to sell land I didn't need, I took it."

"Which is why he never stuck around to speak to you yesterday," Samantha said. "You might have recognized his voice."

Wyatt hitched at his belt and said, "Goddammit. Let's go."

Samantha began to sit up, but Lucas pressed her back. "You're staying here," he told her.

She hesitated, not because she believed she could help him capture a killer safely but because she still felt uneasy. And because she had a strong hunch that if she tried to get off the couch she'd fall on her ass. "I could stay in the car," she offered.

"You can stay here," Lucas said. "I doubt you could even stand up without help, not right now. Just stay put, Sam. Rest for a while, at least until the bleeding stops. Wait for us to bring the bastard back."

"Dead or alive?" she murmured.

"Whichever way he wants it." He said to Wyatt, "Get everybody ready. We go in in force, and we go in prepared. Everybody wears a vest."

Caitlin said to Wyatt, "I can help with the phones or whatever while you're all gone. I mean, I know the place won't be deserted, but if I can help?"

"You can," Wyatt told her.

When they had gone, Jaylene said, "I'll go call the boss, Luke."

He nodded, and to Samantha's inquiring

look said, "Standard procedure if we're about to go into a probable dangerous situation."

"Ah." She looked after his partner for a moment, then checked the handkerchief before once again pressing it to her nose. "Dammit."

"The price you pay for being reckless," he told her.

She decided not to bother arguing. "Just be careful, okay?"

"We will." He went as far as the doorway, then hesitated and looked back at her. "You *are* all right?"

"I will be. Go do your job."

Samantha waited there for some time, listening to the bustle in the building as the deputies and agents got ready to go out. Eventually, the building quieted, and her nose stopped bleeding. And it was only a bit longer before she tried sitting up.

On the third attempt she managed it, and about ten minutes later made it to the conference room. A desk shoved up against the wall held the room's only phone, and Samantha sat down there to use it.

Maybe Luke was right about being reckless, she thought, fighting the dizziness and nausea. It had never been this bad before, and between that and her pounding head, she was seriously considering returning to the couch in the lounge and napping for a day or three.

Because her part in this, she thought, was over. She was almost positive that she had been able to change the outcome she had originally seen.

In the vision that had brought her to Golden, Andrew Gilbert had not come close to being caught, and he had certainly not been the one to die.

She got through to Quentin on the first attempt, which was rarely possible calling a cell phone in this mountainous area. "Did you hear from Bishop?" she asked immediately.

"Yeah, just now," he replied. "So our killer is a ghost out of Luke's past, huh?" He sounded just a bit distracted.

"Looks like. Where are you guys?"

"Fairgrounds."

"Why?"

"Just a hunch."

"You don't have hunches, Quentin."

"Whoever said that is a rotten liar."

"Quentin."

He sighed. "Okay, okay. I knew something would be going on here, that's all."

She waited a beat, then asked, "What's going on?"

"Well, it's a funny thing," he said thoughtfully. "The place is practically deserted — but all the rides are going."

17

"What do you mean?" Samantha demanded.

"Just what I said. The Ferris wheel, bumper cars — everything but the pony rides. All running. Sort of spooky, actually, in broad daylight and without any music or people."

"Where's Leo?"

"Can't find him."

"What?"

"Don't panic. Couple of the maintenance guys said he went into town this morning. They're currently trying to get the rides stopped."

"They all have switches; what's the problem?"

"Switches are jammed."

Samantha's uneasiness increased. "I don't like this, Quentin."

"No, me either. Spider sense is tingling like mad."

"You think maybe this Gilbert guy knows the cops are on the way? That maybe he's waiting for them?"

"You saw them take him down in a vision, right?"

"Yeah, but —"

"Look, this doesn't necessarily have anything to do with that, you know." When she remained silent, he sighed and said, "Okay, so I don't believe in coincidences either. Assuming they can be reached out there, Bishop will warn the cops to watch their backs. And their fronts. You stay put, Sam. Galen is staying here, and I'm heading over to get you."

"I'm in a police station."

"Yeah, a practically deserted one. Sit tight, and I'll be there in fifteen minutes."

Samantha cradled the receiver and frowned down at the phone, absently rubbing her temples. She kept remembering her vision, and the dying words of Andrew Gilbert that she hadn't been able to hear.

She had an uneasy notion that something would be different if she had heard those words.

Trying to think about that made her head pound even more violently and the sick dizziness increase, however, so she quickly gave it up and began to make her way very cautiously back to the lounge.

Jeez, the place really *was* deserted, she realized, hearing only an occasional ringing phone and muted voices from the bull pen at the front of the building.

Samantha hesitated in the doorway of the lounge for a moment, trying once again to grasp the source of her uneasiness, then gave it up and went to lie down on the couch.

The property Wyatt had sold Andrew Gilbert *was* remote, but it was nowhere near as troublesome to reach as the places they had been investigating the last couple of weeks. In fact, a decent dirt road led from the highway practically to the front door of the small, old farmhouse.

Not that the cops took that route all the way. Instead, they stopped all their vehicles more than a mile and a half from the house and approached on foot, spreading out to cautiously surround the house and barn.

It was a chilly day, and smoke rising from the house's chimney indicated someone was home.

Wyatt, crouched near Lucas as they sheltered behind a granite outcropping and peered down at the house and barn about fifty yards away, said quietly, "That old house has no heat except for the fireplace, not unless he had something more modern installed."

Lucas nodded, but said, "I want to stay put for a few minutes and watch. Glen" —

he looked over his shoulder to see the young deputy nearby — "can you work your way around and find out if that barn has a back entrance? And see if it looks like an ATV's been moving in and out recently?"

"You've got it."

"Is your boss's warning bothering you?" Wyatt asked.

All the radios had been silenced, but they had thankfully discovered that their cells worked at least intermittently up here, and Lucas had taken the call from Bishop about half an hour before.

"I take any warning seriously," Lucas replied, not adding that what bothered him most was Bishop's brief confession that at least two other agents had been working in the background for the past couple of weeks. Not that Lucas objected to their presence — though he wasn't the first SCU agent to wish his boss wasn't quite so secretive about some things.

What made him uneasy was the nagging certainty that other things also had been going on all around him without his awareness. Maybe too many things.

He had never been able to develop the enhanced senses that other SCU members called their "spider sense," because, according to Bishop, his concentration shut out rather than focused on external stimuli. And for the first time, Lucas began to seriously question whether Samantha was right in pushing him to tap into his own emotions in order to use his abilities more effectively.

To reach outside himself, let his guards down — no matter how vulnerable and out-of-control it made him feel.

"Look," Wyatt breathed suddenly.

Down below, a man emerged from the old house and started across the half acre or so to the barn. Halfway there, he stopped and pulled a ringing cell phone off its clip on his belt.

Lucas frowned and murmured, "Why do I get the feeling this is not good?"

Binoculars pressed to his eyes, Wyatt said, "He looks pleased. Now he's . . . upset, looks like."

Even without binoculars, Lucas could see Andrew Gilbert looking around warily, and he hoped silently that all the deputies were well hidden and quiet.

"Somebody's warning him," Lucas realized.

"Who?" Wyatt demanded.

"I don't know."

"You said he was working alone."

Lucas barely hesitated. "I still think so. He wouldn't trust a partner. Not him."

Gilbert hurried toward the barn, still talking into his phone, then returned it to his belt as he opened the walk-in door and disappeared into the building.

Lucas glanced at his watch and quickly told Wyatt, "Pass the word to the other group leaders that we'll move in two minutes, at three twenty-two exactly. In the pattern discussed."

Wyatt grabbed his cell phone.

Glen appeared then to quickly report to Lucas, "There is a rear entrance to the barn, and it's well hidden from neighbors. Takes an old cattle trail up into the mountains. And it's been used a lot recently. I passed Jaylene on the way, and her group is moving to increase coverage on that side of the barn. She said to tell you he won't get past them."

"Good enough," Lucas said. "Especially with two of the sharpshooters with her. Glen, you're with us. We're going in the front — and we're not declaring ourselves until we're inside."

"Hope there's some cover in there," Wyatt muttered, but not as if the question bothered him too much.

Remembering Samantha's vision, Lucas

hoped that what she had seen was as literal as her visions usually were. He checked his watch, then signaled the others and began moving swiftly but silently down the slope toward the barn.

As he neared the building, Lucas could hear faint sounds from inside and guessed that Gilbert was gassing up his vehicle in order to leave, probably from small gas cans that could have been inconspicuously brought up here. And luckily for those surrounding the barn, a Hummer did not have a small tank.

When they reached the door, Lucas gently turned the old piece of wood being used as a bar and then, without hesitating, pushed the door open and charged inside, his weapon held at the ready.

There was, luckily, cover in the form of numerous hay bales stacked just inside of and to one side of the door, presumably ready to be moved to block the view of anyone looking curiously into the building. Lucas, Wyatt, and Glen tumbled behind the hay bales and took up firing positions, with Lucas shouting, "Freeze, Gilbert! FBI!"

Standing in the open door of his Hummer and turned facing the rear of the vehicle and the cops, Gilbert did freeze.

For just an instant. But then a snarl twisted his lips, and he reached toward his vehicle.

None of the cops hesitated.

Three shots rang out, even as his hand jerked up, the pistol falling from it. He was slammed back against the vehicle's door, his pale shirt and jacket shining wetly with spreading stains of blood.

Lucas came out from behind the hay bales and moved toward him, weapon still ready, and he was only a few feet away when Gilbert coughed, blood sputtering from his mouth, then slid down the open door until he was sitting on the ground.

As Lucas stood over him, Gilbert looked him straight in the eye, and with a strange, fixed grin and last, bloody gasp, muttered, "Checkmate."

Wyatt, joining Lucas in time to hear that, grunted, "At least the bastard knew you beat him."

"Did he?" Instead of triumph or even satisfaction, Lucas merely felt a vague uneasiness. He bent down to get Gilbert's gun and holstered his own, adding, "We need to search here and at the house. All we really have tying him to the kidnappings and murders is circumstantial evidence, and precious little of that."

"We both know he's our guy."

"Yeah. But there has to be evidence tying him to the crimes, and we need to find it."

"How about this?" Glen asked from the rear of the Hummer.

He had opened the hatch to check the cargo area and now stared inside the ATV.

The two other men joined him, and Lucas was barely aware of other cops coming into the barn as he gazed into the cargo area.

Lying on its back in the area that was just large enough to hold it was an obviously hand-built, high-backed wooden chair. It looked fairly ordinary, except for two odd brackets on either side of the high back, almost at the top.

There was a string-tied bundle of canvas wedged beneath the back; when Lucas pulled it out and untied it, two razor-sharp knives were revealed.

After a long moment, Lucas used a corner of the canvas to hold the knife, fitting it neatly into one of the chair's brackets. Pointing inward.

"The victims who were exsanguinated," he murmured. "He tied them in this chair with some restraint to keep their heads from moving forward and positioned the knives to just touch the jugular veins. Sooner or later, the victims' strength would give out, and their heads would fall to one side or the other. Cutting their own throats."

Grimly, Wyatt said, "I'd call this evidence. The goddamned thing still has bloodstains on it."

Lucas turned away, feeling unexpectedly sickened. "I guess this is what happens to a man who has his wife and child stolen from him."

"No," Wyatt said flatly, "it's what happens to a man who was twisted to begin with. Grief doesn't create monsters, Luke, we both know that. Not grief alone, not just that."

He did know, but it didn't make it any easier.

Jaylene hurried up just then, frowning. "Luke, Quentin just called. He's at the sheriff's department. He went there to keep an eye on Sam, the way he and Galen have apparently been doing for some time. But they were distracted by something weird going on at the carnival, and by the time Quentin could get to the sheriff's department . . . Luke, Sam's missing."

Lucas stared at her, everything inside him going cold. "Somebody warned Gilbert," he murmured. "Somebody told him we were coming. Somebody else. Oh, Christ. That's what he meant. I didn't make the last move. He did."

Trying to fight her way out of sleep, Samantha had a fuzzy memory she wasn't sure she trusted. Between the pounding headache, dizziness, and nausea, she had just wanted to lie on the couch in the lounge with her eyes closed for as long as possible. She supposed she had fallen asleep, except for this vague, unsettling memory of not being able to breathe because something was covering her nose and mouth.

Now she felt even more queasy, her head was still pounding, and it was amazingly difficult to pry her eyelids open. It took several tries, and all the while she was wondering irritably what was causing that hissing sound.

At first, she didn't understand what she saw.

Wood?

Wood, over her, no more than eight or ten inches above her face. Now, why on earth —

Then a cold realization crawled into her mind, and she heard her breath catch.

She reached up slowly and pushed against the wood.

Nothing.

It didn't give so much as a fraction of an inch.

Samantha pushed harder, desperation lending her strength, and still the solid wood failed to budge.

She lifted her head as far as she was able and looked down toward her feet. A battery light was placed there, providing just enough illumination for her to see.

To see the canister of oxygen lying beside her and hissing softly as it slowly leaked its contents.

To see the dimensions of the box in which she lay.

To understand that this was her coffin.

Even as cold terror washed over her and panic fought for a foothold in her mind, Samantha remembered her vision, remembered seeing Gilbert say something at the last, something she hadn't been able to hear.

She thought she knew, now, what he had said.

"Checkmate."

Even as the cops took him down, Andrew Gilbert had been sure he had won the game. Because the final move had been his. Somehow, he had done this.

He had buried her alive.

Asphyxiation.

Lucas couldn't stop thinking about it. It had been Gilbert's other preferred method of remote murder. And Samantha had said herself that the easiest way to asphyxiate someone over a period of time would be to bury them alive.

Oh, Christ, Sam . . .

Jaylene and Wyatt were supervising the rapid search of the house and barn, both hoping that something they discovered would point them in the direction of Samantha.

Back at the sheriff's department, Quentin and Galen were attempting to do the same thing, asking questions and trying to find some shred of information, assisted by the deputies who had returned there.

Lucas stood outside the barn, vaguely aware of people rushing all about him with driven efficiency. He stared toward the other end of the valley, blindly, the coldness in the pit of his stomach spreading outward until even his fingers felt frozen.

"Luke."

He didn't want to look at Jaylene's face,

didn't want to hear what he knew his partner was going to tell him.

"Luke —"

Wyatt joined them, his face grim. "One of my junior deputies is missing. Caitlin is saying she saw him heading back toward the lounge where Sam was resting, and says she never saw him after that. He took a cruiser out, but he's not answering his radio."

"He wouldn't have had a partner," Lucas murmured. "He wouldn't have trusted a partner. I'm sure of that."

"Yeah, well, here's the thing," Wyatt said, even more grim. "On a hunch, one of your people just ran the prints we had on file for this deputy, who was calling himself Brady Miller and had absolutely no criminal record under that name. Only that isn't his name. Turns out his name is Brady Gilbert. He's Andrew Gilbert's son."

"Why were his prints on file?" Jaylene asked.

"Petty theft, out in L.A.," Wyatt told her. "Couple years ago. He was barely old enough to avoid the juvenile system and got a slap on the wrist due to Daddy's money. After that, not a peep from him. Until now. I'm guessing Daddy's money also paid for his nice new name and pristine background."

Jaylene looked at her partner. "He would have trusted his son, wouldn't he, Luke? To do what he couldn't?"

"Maybe," Lucas said, feeling even colder. Some part of him had hoped against hope that Sam had merely left the sheriff's department, maybe to return to her motel or the carnival. Had hoped that it had simply not been possible for Gilbert to get his hands on her. And it hadn't.

But . . . he enjoyed killing by remote control.

He would have viewed his son as an extension of himself, particularly if he felt secure in his domination. So that tracked, that made sense.

And with the sheriff's department nearly deserted, how difficult would it have been for a junior deputy to incapacitate an already fragile Samantha, perhaps with chloroform, carry her down to the garage, and drive away with her?

The box had already been prepared and ready for what Gilbert and his son had waited for — the chance to grab Sam. All Gilbert's son had to do was put her in it, cover it over with dirt, and leave.

Leave her alone there. Buried alive.

"I've got an APB out on Brady," Wyatt was saying. "And your boss made it federal as well, on the grounds that he was undoubtedly involved in the kidnappings."

Lucas heard himself ask, "Gilbert's death — is that out yet?"

Wyatt swore and said, "It went over the police radio that we got him. I'm sorry as hell, Luke, but . . . if Brady was still in his cruiser, then he knows."

"And has no reason to stick around," Lucas said. "They would have been prepared to run. Another car, maybe an SUV or ATV, probably already packed. He'd ditch the cruiser immediately and follow his father's plans. He's gone."

Jaylene took her partner's arm and turned him bodily to face her, an action so unexpected that Lucas found himself staring at her, seeing her.

"Which means you have to find Sam," she said flatly.

"Jay, you know I can't just —"

"We're not going to find anything here, Luke. You know that. Quentin and Galen won't find anything helpful back at the sheriff's department. And we're running out of time, Sam's running out of time."

"Goddammit, don't you think I want to find her?"

"I don't know, do you?"

He stared at her, literally feeling whatever color he had left draining from his face.

Jaylene pressed on, her voice insistent. "I don't know what it'll cost you, I really don't. I don't know what this block inside you is. But I know Sam was right in thinking you'll never be able to use your abilities as they were intended to be used until you *get past it*. And if this won't do it, if saving the life of the woman you love isn't enough . . . then you'll spend the rest of your life as a half-functioning psychic who can only tap into your abilities when you're too tired to think. Is that what you really want, Luke? To be half alive? To lose Sam? Is avoiding your own pain really worth that price?"

No.

"No," he said slowly. "It isn't."

"Then open up and reach for Sam," Jaylene said, releasing his arm. "Find her, Luke. Before it's too late for both of you."

Lucas wasn't even sure how to do this with deliberation, not with anger or out of exhaustion but to clearly and consciously tap into his abilities. He had never been able to do that.

But . . .

All he knew was that he needed Samantha and that he was *not* going to lose someone else he loved. He had to find her, had to help her. . . .

And a wave of icy black terror swept over him with such force that it dropped him, literally, to his knees.

Samantha couldn't even pretend that she wasn't terrified. She didn't think she'd ever been so frightened in her life. Even though . . .

Memories of her stepfather and that tiny closet wouldn't leave her alone, tortured her. She heard herself whimpering out loud, like that brutalized, terrified child had whimpered when, finally, late in the night, he had gone away and she could allow her terror to find its voice.

When he was angriest he had left her in there, for hours and hours, sometimes for days, loudly forbidding her mother from so much as talking to her. The house would get quiet, still. Dark. And she felt so utterly alone.

She had dreaded that "punishment" worse than anything else he had inflicted on her. Because she had been convinced that one day he would simply not open the door.

And she would die in there, terrified, hurting, and so alone there weren't even words for the vast emptiness of the feeling.

Now Samantha fought the panic, or tried to, but those memories, those old feelings of helpless terror, kept swamping her. She heard herself sobbing, felt her hands begin to ache as she pounded on the rough wood above her.

A distant, rational part of her mind told her she was using up precious oxygen, that the tank's hissing had grown quieter as it emptied its contents into her coffin, but the panic overrode everything.

Until . . .

Sam.

She went still, trying to choke back a last sob.

Sam, I'm coming.

"Where are you?" she whispered.

Near.

"There isn't much air left," she whispered again, realizing with another jolt of terror that it was becoming difficult to breathe.

Lie quietly, Sam. Close your eyes. I promise you . . . I'll get there in time.

It was one of the hardest things she'd ever had to do in her life, but Samantha managed. She closed her eyes and forced her throbbing hands to lie quietly at her sides.

There was just enough trust left in her to trust that Luke would reach her in time.

Just enough.

There were a dozen willing hands and shovels following him when, after more than an hour, Lucas stopped the Jeep suddenly on the road out of Golden and raced about twenty yards off to one side of the pavement. And he didn't have to tell them where to dig, because the freshly turned earth, in its chillingly gravelike shape, was obvious.

Immediately, the men were frantically digging, driven by their own fears and by the ashen, haunted face of the federal agent who was using his hands to scrape away the dirt filling Samantha's grave.

Other men were ready with pry bars, and the instant wood was uncovered, they were prying up the boards. And a collective gasp sounded when the sight of Samantha's white face and closed eyes greeted their efforts; in that instant, most of them thought she was gone.

But Lucas knew better. On his knees beside the shallow grave, he reached down and grasped her wrists, avoiding the badly bruised flesh of her hands, and pulled her up.

She opened her eyes only then, blinking in the fading light of the day. Then, as he murmured her name, she drew in a deep breath of the clean country air and threw her arms around his neck.

18

"But I don't want to spend the night in the hospital," Samantha said.

"Because, of course," Lucas said, "a few broken bones in your hands are nothing, right?"

She frowned down at the heavily bandaged hands resting in her lap. "You heard the doctor. The bones in the human hand can be fragile and easily broken. But they'll knit. And I'll be fine. So I don't need to spend the night here."

Bishop said, "Feel free to arrest her, Luke."

"She's staying put," Lucas said. "I'll be here all night to make sure she does."

Samantha sighed and abandoned protest. "Well, if I have to be here, it's a good thing they gave me a big room. If Wyatt and Caitlin hadn't left to take Leo back to the carnival, you wouldn't all fit." She eyed the crowd of people around her bed, singling out Bishop to say, "I wondered when you were going to show your face."

"I thought it was time," he responded calmly. "Your being snatched wasn't exactly part of the plan."

Standing on the other side of the bed, Galen said, "And maybe that'll teach you not to be so damned cryptic next time. *Wait for a sign. And don't let it distract you.* Jesus."

"Actually," Bishop said, "the carnival thing didn't figure into it at all. The sign we told you to wait for never happened. It was supposed to be a rather impressive fireworks display: a couple of crates of ammunition burned, we assumed, to distract all of you while Gilbert got away."

Galen blinked, and said to Quentin, "He might have told us that before now."

"He never does," Quentin said.

"If that's what you and Miranda saw," Samantha said, "why didn't it happen?"

"We saw that back in the beginning." He smiled, the expression softening his very handsome but rather dangerous-looking face. "Before you began changing the future you'd seen. Once that happened, anything we'd seen before then became moot."

"Might have told us that too," Galen grumbled.

Lucas, who had been listening silently, spoke up then to say, "Just what was the plan, if nobody minds me asking?"

"Bishop broke one of his rules," Quentin

told him. "That whole some-things-have-to-happen-just-the-way-they-happen thing. I was shocked."

Looking at Samantha, Lucas said, "Your vision."

She nodded and said, "Everything I told you was true, I just didn't tell you all of it. When Leo got the bribe, we both decided to pass, to not come to Golden. We didn't know what was going on, but whatever it was didn't look legit. Then, that night, after we'd made the decision to continue on, I had a dream. Only it wasn't a normal dream, it was a vision. And I knew, without a shadow of a doubt, that I had seen what would happen if I didn't go to Golden."

"That was when she called me," Bishop murmured.

Lucas sent him a glance, then returned his gaze to Samantha's face. "Why? What had you seen?"

"Murders." She didn't quite stop herself from shivering. "Murders going on for years, getting more and more vicious. Men, women — children. All of them dying in those horrible machines he'd built, and more like them."

"Why didn't you —" Lucas broke off and dismissed that with a gesture, saying, "Never mind. Go on."

"Whatever had set Gilbert on his path, the murders themselves eventually destroyed whatever humanity was left inside him. He had — or he would — begin killing for the sheer pleasure of it. That's what the vision showed me." She sighed. "I knew when I woke up that there was only a . . . small window of opportunity to stop him. I knew that, without question. He had to be stopped here, in Golden. If he left here free, the killing would go on for years."

"What else?" Lucas asked steadily.

"Might as well tell him," Bishop said when Samantha hesitated. "Not many secrets in a group of psychics."

"Except yours," Galen muttered, mostly under his breath.

She sighed again, and said to Lucas, "In the dream, the vision, I also saw him kill you. He won his little game. And winning didn't stop him."

"She wasn't prepared to let that happen, any of it," Bishop said. "And neither were we. So we decided to intervene, to try to change what she had seen."

Expressionless, Lucas said, "And I was kept out of the loop in order to minimize that interference?"

"You and Jay both. We were reasonably

sure that the fewer people who knew what we were trying to do, and the fewer people actively trying to change what Sam saw, the better. The more control we would have. But . . ."

"But," Samantha continued, "with the first change — the carnival and me arriving in Golden — the future I had seen began to shift. And except for a couple of constants, like my conviction that the only way to save you was to force you to use your abilities a different way, and Gilbert's insane gamesmanship, everything was up for grabs. All I could do was follow the plan and hope like hell we were doing the right thing and not making the situation even worse."

"And all we could do," Bishop added, "was keep watch over all of you as quietly as possible. It was obvious Gilbert had done his homework and knew about the SCU; the last thing we wanted him to know was that you and Jay weren't the only team members here."

"Except that he did know," Jaylene said, her voice dry. She looked at Samantha. "That was what Lindsay's warning was all about. *He knows.* He knew about the watchdogs. Knew he'd have to draw them away in order to get to you. And by then, he really wanted to get to you."

"Was that why the thing with the carnival rides?" Quentin wanted to know. "To draw us away from town?"

"Well, it worked," Jaylene reminded him. "If you two had stayed in that little house you'd rented, you would have had a clear view of the back of the sheriff's department. Brady would have found it a lot harder to get Sam out of the building unseen."

"And he had nothing to lose by trying the distraction," Bishop pointed out. "With Sam apparently safe in the sheriff's department, you two were more likely to be drawn away, if only for an hour or so. All the time he needed."

"What I don't get," Samantha said, "is why Gilbert was killing time out at his little house while his son was stalking me."

Bishop said, "My guess is that they had no idea when an opportunity to grab you would present itself. The grave was readied, and Brady Gilbert had his orders: to keep an eye on things here and take the first chance he saw."

"He didn't warn his father as soon as everybody headed up the mountain?" Jaylene asked.

"He probably didn't realize what had

happened," Bishop responded. "He'd been assigned a routine funeral-escort job, and by the time he returned to the station — after a quick trip out to the fairgrounds to start up every ride and jam the controls — nearly everyone at the station was gone. The sergeant at the desk merely told him another search party was out looking for the killer. He was undoubtedly pleased that his distraction had worked and that he had a chance to grab Samantha.

"It wasn't until he was carrying her down to his cruiser in the garage that he passed the armory and realized it was practically empty. That must have set off bells."

"Any sign of him?" Lucas asked.

"No. The bulletins are out, but I wouldn't be surprised if he was able to go to ground up in the mountains, at least for a while. We will get him, though. Sooner or later. For what it's worth, I have a hunch he put the oxygen canister in with Samantha against his father's orders."

"Because," Samantha said slowly, "killing me slowly wasn't the point, not this time. Killing me — and torturing Luke — was. That's what Gilbert would have wanted."

Bishop nodded. "I also have a hunch that when we've sifted through the evidence found at Gilbert's base and catch up with Brady, we'll find that Brady was used by his father to gather information and to help transport the machinery, but that he had never actually killed or even helped abduct or transport any of the victims. Until Samantha."

"Why didn't you suspect Gilbert?" Lucas asked him. "I assume you've been looking into my past cases ever since Sam got in touch, so —"

"Andrew Gilbert was supposed to be dead," Bishop answered. "He'd done a fine job of faking his own death almost four years ago. A fire at one of his warehouses, a body the right size and sex found wearing his watch and wedding ring. We'll have to contact the authorities out there and have that body exhumed, attempt identification. There will probably be some connection to Andrew Gilbert. He needed a body and would have looked close to home. Probably his first murder."

"Setting his plan in motion even then," Quentin said, shaking his head. "The things people will get up to."

"Speaking of which," Jaylene said, "I'm ready for my supper. Now that all the shouting's over and you guys can all be public, who wants to buy me a steak?"

It was a fairly transparent attempt to get them out of Samantha's room, but Sam appreciated the effort and smiled at the other woman.

Jaylene linked her arms with Quentin and Galen, and said, "Boss, you coming?"

"Meet you at the elevator."

"Good enough. See you tomorrow, Sam."

"Good night."

When they were gone, Bishop said to Samantha, "I meant what I told you earlier."

"Turban and all?"

He smiled. "That turban might come in handy for undercover work someday."

"What about the credibility issue?"

"I think the unit's reputation is strong enough now. You're welcome, Samantha. We could really use another seer, especially one as strong as you are. Give it some serious thought."

"I will."

"We also might be able to help with the headaches and nosebleeds. Meditation techniques, biofeedback. The methods help some of our psychics."

"Something else I'll bear in mind. Thanks, Bishop."

"Good night, you two." He left the room.

Lucas gazed after him for a moment, then sat on the edge of Samantha's bed and looked down at her. "We make a good team," he said.

"Only because I can piss you off," she said, but smiled.

"Join the unit, Sam. I need you."

"But do you want to need me. That's the question."

"I found you today because I needed you. Because I couldn't imagine my life without you in it. And I found you because you were right about my abilities. What the SCU couldn't uncover in five years, you touched in less than two weeks."

"It's only a beginning," she said.

"I know. It's going to take time. For me to deal with the pain I've been carrying around all these years, and for us. We have a lot of things to settle, I think, a lot of things to work through."

Samantha drew a breath, and said, "I'm willing if you are."

He took one of her bandaged hands gently in both of his and said in a very steady voice, "Then I want to tell you about my twin brother, Bryan, and about the man who abducted, tortured, and murdered him when we were twelve years old."

So she sat there in her hospital bed and

listened to the tragedy that had created in him an obsession to find other lost souls — and the psychic abilities to do it. And as he talked slowly, painfully, she saw the beginning of healing.

And knew the rest would come.

Epilogue

Friday, April 5

"Damn," Samantha said.

"You're trying too hard," Lucas said, handing her his handkerchief.

She held the linen to her nose and peered at him in faint amusement. "Like you, I don't know any other way to try. What *is* that, anyway?" With her free hand, she gestured to the twisted bit of metal on the table before her.

"What did you see?"

"Smoke, flames. Heard a crunching sound. Caught a glimpse of a man, I think, moving through the smoke. Looked like he was carrying a gasoline can."

Lucas smiled. "Arson. The police chief who sent us this thought so but hasn't been able to prove it. There was stored gasoline on the property, so finding traces of the fuel wasn't proof of arson."

"Okay. But my vision isn't proof either."

"No, but having his suspicions confirmed is all he wanted. He'll work on the investigation the traditional way and hopefully find the proof he needs."

"You still haven't told me what this thing is."

"An old car was parked in the garage of the building, and the chief suspected the fire started there. This is a piece of it." Lucas picked up the twisted metal and returned it to the evidence bag. "I'll have it returned to him."

Samantha refolded the handkerchief and held it to her nose briefly, then checked the cloth and gave it back to him. "You know, I've been waiting for you to tell me to buy my own handkerchiefs, or at least start carrying tissues, but you never do."

"My husbandly duty."

Samantha started laughing. "Was that in the vows? Because I don't remember it."

"Right after the 'for better or worse' part, I think." He pulled her up from her chair, smiling, and into his arms.

"We're at work," she reminded him.

"We're off the clock," he countered. "Just stopped by to clear this last thing off my desk before we leave. And I'm hoping we get out of here before Bishop finds another case for us."

Entering the room just in time to hear that, Bishop said, "Would I be that cruel?" And when Samantha appeared to consider the matter seriously, he smiled and added, "No, I wouldn't. Besides, we've an unusually light caseload at the moment."

"Is that why Quentin is among the missing?" Samantha wanted to know. "Finally taking his vacation time?"

"Yeah, but it's a busman's holiday," Bishop replied. "A cold case he wants to reopen."

"Sounds tame enough," Lucas commented.

"With Quentin involved?" Bishop shook his head. "The last off-the-clock case he worked got Kendra shot."

"Then let's hope he finds nothing but dusty paperwork," Samantha offered.

"It would be a welcome change. Especially since things are nice and quiet around here."

"Here you are," Miranda told him as she came into the room. "And bite your tongue. All it takes is for one of us to comment on not being busy, and we find the entire unit snowed under with cases."

"Then," her husband said, "I suggest we get out of here ourselves."

"Now, there's an idea." She smiled at the other couple. "I say you two take off and enjoy your honeymoon. We'll still be here when you get back. And you," she added to her husband, "owe me dinner. I was right about that lawyer."

"I'm not arguing." Bishop took his wife's hand and said to the other two, "Have fun. And don't come back a day early."

"We won't," Lucas promised.

Gazing after the other couple, Samantha said musingly, "Bishop and Miranda, Tony and Kendra, Isabel and Rafe, you and me. Is there another unit in the FBI with four married teams?"

"No. But, then, there's no other unit like the SCU, is there?"

"True enough." She smiled up at him. "The carnival seems like a long way away. And a long time ago."

"Do you miss it?"

"No. The life we have . . ." She shook her head a little. "Beyond anything I ever dreamed of having. In case I haven't said thank you —"

Lucas kissed her and said, "You have. And I have. And now we're going to spend a couple of weeks lying on a Florida beach saying all the other things we want to say, and all the things we couldn't say before now — and probably a few things one too many margaritas will make us say."

Samantha started laughing.

"You've never seen me after one too

many margaritas," he warned her solemnly.

"Something I'm looking forward to." She kept her arm around his lean waist as they turned toward the door, adding, "Hey, who knows? I might even tell your fortune."

"No need," Lucas said with a smile. "I know how the story ends."

About the Author

Kay Hooper is the award-winning author of *Sense of Evil, Touching Evil, Whisper of Evil, Once a Thief, Always a Thief,* the Shadows trilogy, and more. She lives in North Carolina, where she is at work on the next installment in the Fear Trilogy.